JOEL AUSTIN

THE LAST ONE OUT

VINCI
BOOKS

By Joel Austin

Frank Sherman Thrillers

Happenstance

Reckoning

Perpetua

Nomad

The Last One Out

Regime Change

A Long Violent History

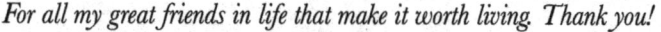

For all my great friends in life that make it worth living. Thank you!

Vinci Books

vinci-books.com

Published by Vinci Books Ltd in 2025

1

A CIP catalogue record for this book is available from the British Library.

Paperback ISBN: 9781036705367

Part I

Kabul, Afghanistan—August 2021

Chapter One

Rotor wash from a loitering Blackhawk helicopter rocketed debris through the open trailer door. Captain Frank Sherman watched amusedly as a West Point lieutenant tried to close the flimsy hatch. The young man was late to the war through no fault of his own, but that didn't stop Sherman from smiling at the officer's misfortune.

By the time Sherman sat down that morning, Afghanistan was two-thirds kindling and one-third matches. At any moment, the whole place would go up in smoke along with decades worth of blood and treasure. The question wasn't of when, but what would survive the inferno.

Circumstances aside, Afghanistan was in Sherman's blood as much as any other place. The country could almost claim the title of home for how many years he'd spent there. All his twenties and most of his thirties passed in places no tourist would dare tread. Hot beds like Iraq, Syria, Somalia, and Mali. The places where soldiers like Sherman deployed often.

"Get that damn door shut," shouted Major Sanders.

The major was Sherman's commanding officer. He was short and wide, with hands that could probably bend rebar. As the lieutenant was discovering, Major Sanders was a no-bullshit, get-it-done, kind of man.

The soldiers sat around what remained of their ragtag command center. Troop drawdowns and the impending American exodus left much of the JSOC base in disarray.

"At least we still have a door," remarked Sherman.

"I could run a war from a damnable cave, if need be," replied Sanders, who still eyed the lieutenant like he might fall over from the wind.

Sherman wanted to make a joke about Sanders being old enough to plan the caveman's first war but thought better of it.

"Alright, enough dawdling." Sanders dropped a folder on the table and said, "We have less than twenty hours to finish this."

The officers grabbed copies and examined the contents.

"More asset extraction, sir?" asked the young lieutenant. He was either on loan from some other department or had connections—Sherman couldn't remember which.

Sanders paused and looked in the young man's direction. "Think of it as repaying a debt. Everyone on that list risked their lives to help their country. Getting them out before the Taliban strings them up from telephone poles is the least we can do."

Chastened, the lieutenant returned to his copy and said no more.

"If you recognize a name, call it out," added Sanders. "Otherwise, it's luck of the draw."

Sherman scanned through the dozens of names, looking for one he knew would eventually make its way through American bureaucracy. It hadn't been on the first iteration, nor the five subsequent lists, but he found the name near the end of this one. Lowest of the low priority.

"We'll take Colonel Khada and family," he said.

Sanders looked up for a moment with a question in his eyes but nodded. "Anyone else?"

No one spoke up and he assigned out names and locations to his men. Each glanced down and memorized the details before leaving to assemble their teams. No questions remained and a quiet concentration filled the room.

"Captain, a word," said Sanders.

Sherman stepped aside.

"Your choice comes with logistical difficulties. Colonel Khada went into hiding last night."

Sherman held up the paper listing an address in Kabul, just down the road from where they sat. "How far out did they go?"

"Near Baghlan."

"I see." Sherman didn't need a map to find Baghlan or know that it sat squarely in front of the Taliban advances in the north. "Did they say why?"

"Credible threat," replied Sanders.

"It must have been bad to hide up there. The Taliban will raise their flag there next week."

"Someone threw a grenade through their kitchen window."

"Shit."

"Apparently, there is an old family connection in town. I didn't get the details, but it will complicate the extraction?"

"How?"

"Political sensitivities," replied Sanders with a shrug. "A jackass in a suit decided we shouldn't interfere, remember?"

"Some things never change," said Sherman as he turned to leave.

"One more thing, Captain," Sanders began, and Sherman knew he wasn't going to like what came next. "We've had a request…"

"I'd rather not," replied Sherman.

"You don't have to take the lieutenant, if that's what you're thinking."

Sherman sighed in relief.

"It's a reporter," said Sanders.

"Can I refuse?"

The major smiled sympathetically, and Sherman knew he didn't have a choice. The reporter was coming along, and he had no say in the matter.

"For what it's worth, they say he's very good at his job," added Sanders.

"I'm good at my job. He's a hindrance."

Stepping outside, July swirled around oppressively. The heat had its own weight that pulled you to the ground. Despite all his deployments in the area, Sherman always found the intensity astonishing.

"Captain Sherman," said a man standing in the building's shade. He was thin and wiry with a streak of gray stubble across his face. Short dark hair rested atop a deeply tanned face and inquisitive brown eyes. He was roughly the same age. "I'm Danny Bashir with Reuters."

Sherman stepped into the shade and shook the man's hand. Common decency, his mother always told him.

"Tell me, Danny, what brings you to Afghanistan?"

"It's the graveyard of empires."

"Ours included?" asked Sherman.

"No, I imagine not, but it's the story of our generation. Hard not to cover it."

"Couldn't you do that from the trailer or Kabul?"

Danny smiled and nodded. "I could, but that's not how I work. Have you read any of my pieces?"

Sherman read the news religiously, especially the international section. Knowledge was power and a headline one morning might translate into a mission the next.

"Jog my memory," he said.

"I wrote a bit for the Times on the Ethiopian war in Tigray. Then one regarding the recent Taliban advances in the southwest."

The African article ran a bell in Sherman's memory. The reporter snuck into rebel territory to get the story.

"I read the Tigray one. How'd you get over the border?"

"In a cardboard box full of donated clothes."

Sherman smiled and laughed at the effort. "Alright."

"What about the Taliban article?"

"I'm gonna lay down a ground rule here, Danny. You can ask about the past but not current missions. Is that clear?"

"Crystal."

"Good, I'll introduce you to the team."

Two men stood nearby, chatting casually like any other office job. They stopped when Sherman approached, trailed by the reporter, who wore light brown body armor and a scuffed-up helmet.

"Sergeant Gournsey and Corporal Lopez, meet Danny Bashir from Reuters," said Sherman as a brief introduction.

"Pleasure to meet you both," said Danny.

Sergeant Gournsey gave a half-hearted smile. The affable Kentuckian stood a good six inches taller than the reporter and could have tossed him in the air like a sack of potatoes. The sergeant had served with Sherman longer than anyone else on the team—anyone alive, at least.

"Who are we picking up today?" asked Lopez, who ignored Danny altogether.

The corporal carried a general disdain for anything unrelated to the mission at hand, which didn't bother Sherman. Lopez could have worn a tinfoil hat and babbled about an alien invasion for all he cared because Lopez had a gift. The Central Valley native could shoot a head of cauliflower from two miles away.

"Colonel Khada and family," answered Sherman.

Both men gave a satisfied smile.

"About time," said Gournsey.

Sherman nodded in agreement. It had taken far too long.

"What are we waiting for?" asked Lopez. "I'll drive."

"He's not in Kabul," answered Sherman.

"Credible threat?" asked Gournsey.

"Why is he running?" asked the reporter, who stood at a polite distance.

"I imagine because he doesn't want to see his daughters raped and his wife beheaded," answered Lopez with a remarkably even tone.

Danny nodded politely. "I understand the likely outcomes. My question is, why now? Did the Taliban find them?"

"Danny," said Sherman, "you're already forgetting my ground rule. No questions about the mission."

"Professional curiosity," replied the reporter.

"Killed the cat," added Lopez.

"Where did they go?" asked Gournsey.

"Baghlan."

"Not ideal," replied the sergeant.

"Wheels up in twenty. Grab your gear," said Sherman.

His men nodded but said nothing. This was their twelfth mission in the last week, and the war's unraveling left little time for rest. Endings required as much energy as beginnings.

Sherman walked off to get his own gear as the reporter followed like a bloodhound sniffing out a story.

"Captain, who is Colonel Khada? Why did he make the list?"

"A patriot," replied Sherman tersely.

"I get that, but he must have done something significant to get a ticket stateside."

Sherman swiveled to face the man. "Bring extra water, a few snacks, and ditch any big-ass camera you plan on bringing. We're traveling light and quick."

Danny held up a pen and notepad. "This is all I need."

By the time Sherman reached the helipad, Gournsey and Lopez were already aboard the Blackhawk. The mercury topped triple digits and Sherman handed his men ice-cold bottles of water he'd pilfered from the officer's quarters.

"Thanks, Cap," said Lopez. "What's the plan?"

Sherman retrieved a map from his pocket and spread it out for his men. He pointed to Baghlan.

"You remember it?" he asked.

Gournsey and Lopez nodded.

"We kicked down some doors there last year," added the sergeant.

"Two years ago, but who's counting," said Sherman. "We can't land near the town without making waves and alerting the Taliban."

"I thought we had a fancy agreement," said Lopez. "We both look the other way while this place falls apart."

9

"Whatever got signed over mint tea in Doha doesn't mean shit up there. Remember, it's their country. We're just passing through."

"Some fucking country," added Gournsey.

"Do you think the Taliban will take over after we leave?" asked Lopez.

"You've seen the Afghan Army in action. Without American air support, they're ruined," said Sherman.

"They have superior numbers, years of training, and a billion-dollar arsenal," interjected Danny, who had just climbed aboard. "Or so we say. Although, it doesn't feel like it."

Sherman sighed. No amount of money ever won a war without the will to fight. It didn't matter how the generals or politicians spun the facts—he knew time was not on their side. American troops would leave in two months or less and the ending would not be pretty.

"I'm checking with the pilots," he said and walked off.

Danny stowed his gear and took a seat next to Gournsey.

"Tell me, sergeant, who is this colonel you're trying to save?"

"He flew helicopters, but I imagine you found that out."

The reporter gave a brief smile. "And that's worth all this?"

"We have a saying in my holler… Blood over Bourbon."

The reporter looked baffled.

"He owes the colonel his life," continued the sergeant.

"Who does?"

"The Cap," answered Gournsey and motioned towards Sherman, who was deep in conversation with the crew.

"What happened?"

"It ain't my story to tell."

"Are any of the stories true? I asked around. Captain Sherman has quite the reputation in certain circles, off the record, of course."

"Like what?"

"I heard he took out a Hind helicopter with a grenade launcher in Syria, killed an ex-Iraqi general with a letter opener, and single-handedly cleared an ISIS cave complex."

Gournsey's grin split wider than the San Andreas fault. "No, none of that shit is true."

The reporter's face fell a little with disappointment as he watched Sherman return to the helicopter.

"Nope," repeated Gournsey and slapped Danny on the back. "It was a spoon, not a letter opener."

Danny's eyes widened as Sherman took his seat.

"I hope the sergeant isn't filling your head with tall tales," said Sherman after noticing the look on the reporter's face.

"Did you really kill a man with a spoon?"

Sherman joined Gournsey and Lopez in a short fit of laughter. "Last time I heard this story, it was a pen."

"I heard fire poker," added Lopez.

"So, it's not true?"

"Just a bunch of smoke," said Sherman, then he motioned for the pilots to take off.

"But I've seen some of your declassified after-action reports. They're not nothing."

Sherman nodded. He had killed a man with a utensil, but it was a butter knife, and the man was a terrorist who blew up schools. He doubted those facts ever made it into a printed report. People just wanted to have their heroes, even if they had to invent them.

"Once we're wheels down, I want you to stick close to Sergeant Gournsey. Do whatever he says. Clear?"

Danny nodded. "Got it."

"Good. Welcome back to Afghanistan. Don't worry, you didn't miss a goddamn thing."

Chapter Two

Heat swirled so thickly in the tiny apartment that Asal Khada felt like she was inside her grandmother's stone oven —the one she used to make naan bread every morning. The thought of calmer times brought out a tear that evaporated while rolling down her cheek.

Esin, her youngest daughter, lay in Asal's lap, lazily swatting away the flies that buzzed around her face. Asal gently stroked her hair, trying not to think about the dangers lurking everywhere. Only the day before, someone had thrown a grenade through their kitchen window. God granted them mercy that day because no one got hurt, but they'd gotten the Taliban's message loud and clear. Death awaited them as traitors of the state and thus God.

Across the room, Asal's husband peered anxiously through the curtains, straining at every flitter of movement and loud sound. She hadn't seen him so nervous since the night before he joined the Afghan Air Force to help the Americans. That night, Zarak Khada paced across their living room so many times, he left a trail across the rugs.

Asal felt a surge of pride then for her husband and the stand he took against the Taliban. It had been difficult and she often stayed up late waiting for him to return or for bad news.

In time, life normalized—if life in a war ever sits on an even keel. They moved into a nice flat in Kabul. Zarak rose through the ranks and soon earned a colonel's salary. They had two beautiful daughters, born into the dawn of a post-Taliban Afghanistan. The girls went to school. They learned and grew and explored. It wasn't a perfect life and Asal longed for more, but it was a good life, and knowing her daughters might find a wider world gave her hope and comfort. The horizon was wide and colorful.

Those colors faded, and the view constricted to nothingness as the Americans began winding down their war. As if the country was a small child that you could simply put down and leave alone. Asal knew better, and so did her husband. Zarak started the asylum application the first day it opened, but hope dwindled with each passing week. News of the Taliban advances made Asal's chest burn, and even her daughters carried a sallow, forlorn look reserved for adults who know the end is near. Seeing them absorb such fear and hate hurt her soul.

Then came the grenade and a hasty drive away from Kabul. Her great aunt offered them the apartment and she would have refused if there was any other option. Zarak called the Americans to tell them what happened, and someone noted their location. Everything, Asal mused, rode on a note that may or may not exist.

"I hear trucks," said Zarak.

Asal gently placed her youngest daughter's head on a pillow and joined her husband at the window.

"Did they stop?" she asked.

"I think so," he replied.

"No one knows we're here. Maybe they'll pass through," she said, but the words had the taste of lies as they left her mouth.

"God willing," he added.

Asal nodded and went back to waiting, which felt more like melting than sitting.

"Wait... I see something," Zarak said.

The constant fear and heat had numbed Asal's nerves, and she didn't move. "What do you see?"

"Taliban," he replied.

Asal rocked her daughters awake and spoke to them in a frayed voice. "Grab your bags, my loves."

"But, Mommy," protested Esin, the youngest.

"Now, my darling. Do it now."

The girls heard the fear in their mother's voice, and quickly gathered their belongings in their backpacks and held close.

Asal sent up another silent prayer, one of a thousand in the last twenty-four hours, and pulled her daughters closer.

"They're asking people on the street," announced Zarak.

"Should we leave?"

Zarak shook his head. "They would see us go."

Their apartment was on the top floor of a two-story building. An exposed walkway ran in front of the doors leading to stairs at either end. Most of the widows had bars preventing robberies and escapes.

Fear sucked the air from Asal's lungs as she prayed for their lives.

Voices echoed down the walkway. Loud commands to open doors. Commotion filled the building as a few residents gathered in the dirt courtyard.

Zarak shut the curtains and they all ducked behind a wooden table, praying the Taliban would think the apartment was vacant.

Loud knocking followed. Fists pounded on doors. Asal wept with her children while her husband's jaw clamped tighter.

Then came the crash of the first door and a fleeting hope of survival slipped through Asal's fingers like water.

Chapter Three

The pilot's voice erupted into Sherman's headset, overpowering the dull roar of the helicopter. His daydream of a tropical beach dissipated like shifting sands and the present moment jittered into focus.

"Captain, command just reported significant Taliban activity in the area. They're concerned about a potential issue if we fly much closer and ordering us to RTB."

Returning to base and the colonel's survival were incompatible ideas. Sherman understood that outcome perfectly.

"How far out are we?" he asked.

The co-pilot glanced down at the map to confirm what Sherman already guessed.

"Ten minutes out."

"Did you confirm that order?" asked Sherman.

The pilots smiled at each other. They'd flown Sherman's team before and both men knew Colonel Khada and what he'd done.

"I'll buy you five minutes and have command reconfirm

Taliban activity, but you'll still be hiking in," answered the pilot.

"I never pass up a good hike."

"No guarantee when we'll be back," added the co-pilot. "You'll be on your own."

"Understood," said Sherman before he switched channels so his team could hear. "We've got a situation."

"Did they beat us here?" asked Gournsey.

"The pilot is confirming an RTB order, which means our infil is longer than expected."

"Wait… does that mean we're still going?" asked Danny.

"We are," said Sherman. "You can head back with the Blackhawk."

The reporter glanced around at the seriousness etched into the three faces surrounding him. "This guy must be worth it."

Sherman said nothing.

"If I go back, I'll miss the story."

"Make some shit up."

"It doesn't work that way."

Sherman shrugged.

The co-pilot waved a finger in the air and the helicopter descended.

"Your choice, but time is running out," said Sherman.

"You're not leaving them much choice," said Danny.

Gournsey flashed a maniacal smile and flung open the door. Wind and dust rushed through the opening as the pilots touched down between two poppy fields.

"Damnit," groaned the reporter as Lopez and Gournsey slipped out, moving towards an old stone wall for cover.

"Story of a generation," said Sherman. "There'll be lots of coverage. Doesn't have to be your war."

When Sherman reached the wall, it did not surprise him to see Danny moving towards them. Fear of missing out was a powerful motivator, and the reporter seemed keen on writing the end to this chapter of American history.

"Zulu One, Echo Nine. We are proceeding on foot to the target location. Over," radioed Sherman.

"Echo Nine, the area is hostile. Repeat, the area is hostile. Over."

"The country's hostile," muttered Gournsey.

"Zulu One, understood. Over."

A moment passed, then Major Sanders cut in, "Echo Nine, confirmed. Good hunting. Out."

Sherman winked at Danny. "Let's find your story."

The dust and emptiness of Bagram Air Base with its Hesco barriers, razor wire, and fast-food restaurants was but a memory. Baghlan sounded similar but sat west of the Hindu Kush Mountains in the terraced green wonderland of ancient homes and even older farms. In the valley, where the water flowed, people grew wheat, rice, barley, and poppies. Even in July, the greens boldly splashed across the otherwise brown landscape.

Sherman loved and hated this part of the country. He loved the stark beauty of the mountains, the orchards of fruit, and the hospitality of the locals. He hated that so many friends had died in ambushes, killed to hold territory in an unwinnable war.

"This is an amazing place," said Danny as they crossed under rows of thorny acacia trees. "Reminds me a bit of Libya."

"Reminds me of Lodi," added Lopez.

"You reported from Libya?" asked Gournsey.

"Yeah, during the Civil War, before things totally went to hell."

"What was your take on the place?"

Danny gave a brief chuckle. "I wrote nearly twenty thousand words on the country, and I still don't understand it."

"And Afghanistan?"

"This was my first assignment. Straight out of college. Thought it would be a few months, maybe a year. Yet here I am."

"Here we all are," said Sherman.

"Our generation's Vietnam."

Sherman shrugged. "Different war altogether."

"It's gonna end the same," added Danny. "They hold together this place with glue and paperclips."

"You're not wrong."

"Can I quote you on that?"

"Not a chance," Sherman answered.

The four soldiers hurried towards the outskirts of Baghlan and the colonel's last known location. The city stretched out below them in a cluttered checkerboard of square brown buildings and brightly colored billboards.

Sherman didn't need a map to know where they were going. They could see the apartment building in the distance, next to a vacant dirt field on one side and a gas station on the other. Even without the clear line of sight, he would have found it. Navigation was one of those inherent skills some people possess, like always knowing the time or sleeping on command. Sherman couldn't do either of those, but he could navigate anywhere in the dead of night and end up exactly where he planned.

Angling down the hill, he aimed to approach the building through the empty field, which contained some old mud walls. Had the Taliban not sped up their advance and had the government put up a proper fight, they could have landed the Blackhawk there and gotten everyone out in a matter of minutes. He would have preferred that but let those what-ifs drop to the wayside and focused on the options in front of them.

"Captain, do you think the American withdrawal is foolhardy?" asked Danny.

"Above my pay grade," he answered, annoyed by the question, which pulled his attention away from the next hundred yards.

"He ain't gonna answer you anymore," whispered Gournsey.

"Why not?"

"He's on point. All he cares about is the next few minutes and us living through it."

"Oh, I didn't mean to…"

"Just keep your voice down and your eyes up," said Gournsey. "They call it the graveyard of empires for a reason."

Minutes slid by in concentrated silence as Sherman maneuvered the team. They passed through a young grove of slender trees and past a toothless farmer who offered them tea. Sherman politely declined but spoke to the man in Pashto for a few minutes. Local intelligence was the best kind.

"What are they saying?" asked Danny.

Gournsey glanced over his shoulder. "The weather, his crops… uh, favorite World Cup team, and if the old man's seen any Taliban."

"And?" asked Danny, his voice edging towards fear.

"The old man is an Italy fan but doesn't think they have a chance."

Sherman returned to the group. "He also said the Taliban are looking for collaborators."

"You speak Pashto?"

Sherman ignored the question. "Sergeant, any thoughts on our approach?"

Gournsey pointed to a battered Toyota that had recently parked by the apartment. "Looks like we're late to the party. Probably not a great idea to roll up in force."

Peering over a mud-brick wall, Sherman saw at least three mujahideen fighters talking with some locals. If four Americans suddenly appeared, it would be a shoot first kind of ending.

Sherman motioned to Lopez, who didn't need any further instruction. The lanky young sniper headed back up the hill towards a spot with better sight lines.

"Post up here and cover our retreat," ordered Sherman. "I'll secure the family. Once I have everyone, we'll move back over the hill to the LZ."

"Where do you want me, Captain?" asked Danny.

"Never over three steps from the sergeant."

The reporter nodded. "Gotcha."

Time slowed for Sherman as he dashed across the open field toward the apartment building. Filled with adrenaline, his mind perceived all the terrible possibilities. All the angles he might catch a bullet. All the places for a cruelly hidden mine. Yet he didn't slow or let up. Those thoughts and threats had not left his reality for years, even when he wasn't downrange.

Loud yells sounded from the front when Sherman arrived. He eased towards the edge to get a better view. The apartment had two stories and resembled an old roadside motel he'd seen as a kid. A big rectangle with the short end facing the empty field. The front doors of those living on the bottom floor opened onto a parking lot of broken asphalt. There was no internal hallway. At either end, stairs led up to a second floor and a concrete walkway with a flimsy metal railing. Sherman was on the short end, peering down the long rows of doors toward three heavily armed fighters.

The men sported thick beards, flowing linen pants, and Cheetah sneakers made by a Pakistani shoe company. The unofficial Taliban uniform.

He keyed the radio. "Three tangos. Armed. Three-One, do you have a visual?"

"Affirmative," replied Lopez. "Three angry Talibs."

The men were arguing with a group of locals and Sherman heard the words traitor and dog used several times.

"Looks like we're at the right place. I'm moving to the second floor. Plug 'em if they follow. Over."

"Copy that. Over," replied Lopez.

Sherman slipped around the corner. He climbed the stairs while cooler heads tried to convince the Taliban to leave.

No one was on the second-floor walkway and Sherman breathed a sigh of relief.

Below, the arguing erupted into shouting and pounding. Time was running out as Sherman made for apartment 206.

"Echo Nine, things are getting hot downstairs," came Lopez's calm voice, which never seemed to change. He didn't bat an eye even under an artillery barrage.

As Sherman reached the door, a loud crack of splintering wood rang out. The curtains in the apartment blocked his view inside. He knocked gently, twice slowly, then three times fast. The agreed-upon signal if the intel file proved accurate.

A deadbolt slid open with a click. The door cracked a

sliver. In the fraction of light, he saw Colonel Khada's face melt with relief.

"Captain, come inside, quickly."

Colonel Khada ushered Sherman inside the hot, stale room.

Against the far wall, three people huddled together. Terror stretched across their faces like dirty smudges that wouldn't come off. He knew the look. Parenting and growing up in a war zone left more than just visible scars.

"I'm Captain Frank Sherman, and I'm here to get all of you out of the country. Are you ready to leave?"

The woman and her two daughters nodded. They staggered to their feet. He wasn't sure how old the girls were, but a sparkle lingered in their eyes despite the fear. Maybe they were even young enough to move beyond the terrible things they'd seen.

"Listen carefully. If you follow my instructions, we'll be fine. First, we head down the stairs. Then cross the dirt field behind the building. Do you all understand?"

All four heads nodded.

"Good. Run towards the mud wall on the far side of the field. My men are there. Don't stop and don't look back, no matter what happens."

More nods and fearful faces.

Sherman smiled. Their bravery gave him solace. As if there was something worthwhile left to do in the country.

"Echo Three-One, are we clear to leave? Over."

"Second floor is clear but hold at the stairs. They are going door-to-door."

Sherman led the family out of the stifling apartment towards the top of the stairs and waited for Lopez.

"Two are searching," radioed Lopez. "One is watching the exit."

Another door splintered apart, and Sherman knew they'd head upstairs next.

"After they kick the next door down, take the one outside. I'll deal with the other. How copy?"

"Waiting to send one."

Sherman smiled at the colonel and his family. "You're going to follow me down and then run across the field."

"We understand," said his wife.

"What's your name?" asked Sherman and extended his hand.

"Asal," she replied and shook. "This is Esin and Dara."

"Nice to meet you all," replied Sherman as calmly as he could.

Lopez's voice crackled into his earpiece. "Here we go."

Another door crashed apart. Sherman moved down the two flights of stairs in great bounding steps. He arrived at the bottom in time to see the head of one fighter disappear in a wet cloud of pink. There and gone in a heartbeat. The suppressed report of Lopez's rifle followed almost instantly.

The family ran as instructed and without hesitation. Sherman stepped over the dead sentry and towards the broken door. Cries of surprise and alarm came from a few residents standing in the parking lot.

Drawn by the noise, two Taliban soldiers turned to exit the apartment they'd broken into. Sherman caught them standing side-by-side. Their guns pointed down, disappointed by their failure to find any traitors.

Sherman's rifle didn't waver.

The time between seeing them and pulling the trigger was a fraction of a second. No hesitation or doubt, just muscle memory and survival instinct.

One, two, three, four cracks in quick succession.

Both men took two bullets to the head in that briefest of encounters. They fell together in a tangled, lifeless heap.

Blood pooled into the doorway, but Sherman didn't need to see the aftermath of his actions. He kept moving.

The locals shouted louder.

"Three down," he radioed. "Coming back to you."

Gournsey was waiting when he arrived. The colonel's family looked small in the sergeant's shadow.

"Did that go to plan?" asked Danny, peeking over the mud wall.

Sherman glanced at the growing crowd around the dead Taliban. "It didn't swing their way, if that's what you're asking. And I don't think the brass will be happy, but I'd say it's going swimmingly."

Gournsey gave a lopsided smile and patted the reporter on the shoulder. "When faced with violence, always act faster than the other guy."

"Take them uphill, I'll secure our egress," ordered Sherman.

"Follow me, folks. We've got a long hike and no in-flight entertainment, but I have free snacks, unlike those damn budget carriers."

Sherman stayed long enough to cover their exit before following. The crowd outside swelled in size and volume. They shouted and pointed towards the field.

"Three-One, how's the crowd looking?"

"Angrier than a junkyard dog. They're making calls as we speak, and I don't think they're ordering pizza."

Sherman understood. Company meant trouble. Trouble meant more Taliban. Experience said a dozen guys in pickup trucks with old Russian machine guns mounted in the back. That was before they started taking over the country. Now it was two dozen guys in Humvees appropriated from the retreating Afghan Army. Getting shot by a taxpayer bullet was as equally likely as an old communist one.

"Zulu-One, Echo-Nine. Contact with Taliban forces at the target location. We are moving towards extract one. Over."

"Echo-Nine, are you currently in contact? Over."

"Negative, but we expect reinforcements. Requesting immediate extract for eight. Over."

"Echo-Nine, the bird is refueling. ETA forty minutes. I repeat, forty minutes. Over."

"Fuck," muttered Sherman, looking at his map.

They were twenty minutes from the landing zone. That left them waiting in the open for twenty more minutes while the Taliban circled their wagons.

"Zulu-One, correction. We are rerouting to secondary extract. Confirm. Over."

"Echo-Nine, confirmed. Out."

Between the drooping boughs of a cedar tree, Sherman caught Gournsey's eye. He flashed two fingers and the sergeant nodded, having heard the back and forth with command.

The dirt trail snaked up the dusty hillside between ancient fields and resolute stone structures older than the American invasion or the Russian invasion. Older even than the British and the First Anglo-Afghan War almost two hundred years earlier. A true graveyard of empires.

The farmer still sipped his tea as they passed.

"*Taliban*," said the man and pointed down towards the city.

Sherman stopped. "*A few*," he replied in Pashto.

"*They'll come through there*," added the farmer and pointed a gnarled finger along the ridgeline above them.

"*On the donkey trail?*" asked Sherman, remembering what he'd seen on the satellite images.

The old man nodded. "*They come and go with poppies.*"

"*Thank you,*" added Sherman and hurried to catch up with Gournsey.

Another hundred yards later, his earpiece hissed to life. "Looks like they figured us out," said Lopez. "We have four Talibs heading up the hill. Over."

"Copy. Fall back and link up. Out."

When Sherman and Lopez caught up with the others, they were resting under the pitiful shade of a small ash tree. The girls panted from the exertion and the heat and the head-to-toe clothing they wore. Asal also looked flushed and overheated. Gournsey had passed out snacks and water like a doting tour guide, which helped a little.

Sherman kneeled next to Asal. "Not to pry, but do they have anything else to wear?"

She glanced at her husband before answering, "We have shorts and t-shirts on underneath."

Surprise stretched across Sherman's face. He'd assumed they were devout based on their clothing, but he quickly realized his mistake. They were devoutly trying to preserve their lives by whatever means. Survival at all costs. That he could understand.

Asal smiled at him. "We're Christian, this is just a show to stay alive."

"Why don't you all lose a layer? Besides, I'm the one who sticks out like a sore thumb around here."

She nodded to the girls, and they stuffed their burkas into their backpacks. Sherman knew they had nothing else in the world besides what existed in their bags. A whole life crammed into hand-me-down Jansports.

"Sergeant," said Sherman. "Get everyone moving again."

Gournsey nodded and his massive shoulders turned to shepherd his newfound flock over the last of the hill and towards the landing zone.

"Corporal, what's our head start?"

Lopez looked back towards the city with unblinking eyes. "Ten minutes, probably less."

Thirty minutes had passed since they'd left the apartment. They were still another fifteen minutes out from the secondary extraction site. The timing was tight—too tight.

"Cap?" asked Lopez, following Sherman's gaze along the ridgeline.

"The farmer said the Taliban would attack from the donkey trail and I agree with him."

Lopez gazed towards the hilltop before pointing at a collapsed mud house five hundred yards further on. "That's my pick for covering our ass."

It was the same spot Sherman mentally picked minutes before. "Agreed, but it's a long sprint to the LZ."

Lopez didn't blink. "Doable."

"Alright, you and I will provide cover while the sergeant gets everyone onboard."

Lopez didn't need help and the corporal's look confirmed as much, but Sherman wasn't about to risk losing a man hours before their war ended.

"Sergeant," yelled Sherman and the massive man nodded. He'd heard everything and didn't question Sherman's decision.

"Zulu One, Echo Nine, we are approaching the LZ. Where is our ride? Over."

Sanders responded, "Echo Nine. Bird is ten minutes

out. Diverted around Taliban activity. How's the weather up there? Over."

The major's comment sounded innocent, but the meaning made Sherman chuckle. Typical answers ranged from beach weather to shit-storm, depending on enemy activity.

"Hot and getting hotter," he replied. "Do we have close air support? Over."

"I've tasked a Reaper to your location. ETA ten minutes. Over."

"Patch them through when they're on station. Over."

"Wilco. Out."

Small splotches of dust floated up from the Khada's footsteps as they traversed across the ridgeline. Their goal was a flat but barren patch of dirt barely wide enough for a Blackhawk to land. There was no shade and the girls sat on great white slabs of rock, slurping down juice boxes Gournsey produced from his backpack.

Lopez and Sherman took up position in the ramshackle structure that might have been a farmer's seasonal hut two or three hundred years before. Across the ridge, everyone else waited and sweated and waited some more. Time came and went in places like Afghanistan.

Brakes squealed in the distance. High-pitched screams of maintenance arriving with the thrum of a small engine. Not the heavy thump of jet turbines. A truck. Maybe two.

Their time was up.

"Contact front," said Lopez.

Sherman turned away from the family and looked across the ridge towards the old donkey trail. Through the twisting branches of an ancient Juniper tree, he saw two battered pickups pock-marked and rusted from years of conflict. Seven or eight men jumped out and scattered into the trees. More men from the city joined them in the shade.

Audible now in the distance was the roar of a helicopter. A great collision was upon them, and Sherman knew the timing could not have been worse.

"Zulu One, Echo Nine. I have enemy fighters three hundred yards northwest of my position. ETA on the Reaper? Over."

"Echo Nine. The drone is five minutes out. Can the extract bird land? Over."

"Affirmative. Out."

Shouts came from the Taliban fighters and one man clambered into the pickup truck with an RPG over his shoulder.

Sherman squeezed Lopez's arm. "Make sure that bird lands safely."

Lopez didn't reply, but the crack of his rifle answered Sherman's call to action. The distant figure spun wildly around and toppled backward, part-way out of the truck. His top half dangled limply toward the ground while his feet somehow remained stuck in the truck bed. Sherman thought he looked like one of those inflatable advertising gimmicks waving in the used car parking lot, but with all the air gone.

By the time Lopez racked another round into his rifle, bullets hissed and snapped overhead. Chunks of mud brick exploded and sent bits skittering across the ground. The clattering of gunfire rippled across the ridge.

Lopez fired again and Sherman knew another life had vanished. There and gone in a millisecond.

In the distance, he watched the Blackhawk swoop and whirl with unimaginable precision, coming to a sudden stop on the tiny patch of hard earth. Gournsey pushed everyone inside and then turned to head towards the battle. The man never turned away from a fight.

"Echo Nine, where do you want me? Over," he radioed.

"Push around our right flank. Over."

"Wilco. Out."

Sherman sat down next to Lopez as a Taliban bullet ricocheted around the old hut.

"Zulu One, Echo Nine. Clear that bird and patch me through to the Reaper pilot. Over."

Sanders answered, "Echo Nine. Patching you through. Out."

"Echo Nine. This is Lima Three. Where do you want me? Over."

Sherman reached into his bag and grabbed an infrared strobe only the drone could see. He placed it in the rubble of the roofless hut.

"Lima Three. Confirm my IR strobe. Over."

"Echo Nine. Strobe confirmed. Over."

"Lima Three. Do you see the trucks northwest of my position? Over."

"Echo Nine. Affirmative. Over."

"Lima Three. Fire at will. Over."

"Echo Nine. Keep your heads down. Incoming. Out."

In the cloudless sky above, a spark of yellow flashed, then came a whoosh of speed, and finally, an earth-shaking explosion. Dirt splashed, bits of metal clanged, and a fire hissed. Men shouted and groaned in the distance.

"Lime Three, good effect on target. Any stragglers? Over."

"Echo Nine. Affirmative on stragglers. Three tangos still moving one hundred yards west of your position. Over."

Lopez swiveled on his belly and shook his head. "No visual."

"Hold here," replied Sherman before he slipped out the back. Trickles of sweat rolled down his back and the heat caught under his tactical vest like an oven.

The Taliban had hidden among a walnut orchard downhill from the hut. Old trees, gnarled by time and climate, drooped to the ground. Sherman skirted left until he found a wide one and stopped.

"Echo One Two," he whispered into the mic, which picked up almost any voice. "What's your position? Over."

Gournsey's voice sounded distant and small yet amplified by their gear. "Coming up behind them. Over."

Sherman shouldered his rifle—a HK416—and watched. Thirty yards away, a dirty green headscarf flapped in the scant breeze. The owner lay just out of view, stomach glued to the ground. Hoarse whispers of panic carried across the orchard.

"Echo Nine. Are you ready? Over."

Sherman took a breath and brought all his focus to the present moment. The heat disappeared, so did the colonel's family and the distant thump of retreating rotor blades. The war melted away. The ending no longer mattered. The whole world shrank. Nothing existed besides the gnarled walnut trees and his rifle.

"Fry 'em," replied Sherman.

A ripping crackle filled the air as Gournsey fired his M249. The long burst of gunfire hissed and sang. Dirt spewed up in volcanic hiccups and wood splintered from broken tree trunks.

The green headscarf bobbed up into view. Sherman saw the man and gray eyes filled with a familiar expression of resignation. Not a young man, but the sun-burned creases on his face made the Taliban look older. Maybe Sherman's age, maybe not.

As the man with the green scarf and gray eyes raised his AK-47 in Gournsey's direction, Sherman squeezed the trigger. He didn't miss. He rarely did. Not from that distance.

When Sherman and Gournsey moved forward, the green headscarf was brown with blood and dirt. Death was no stranger to their world. Both men had seen its face up close so many times—those familiar features, that it seemed commonplace. Like seeing a neighbor out picking up their newspaper in the morning, but with none of the pleasantness.

"Lima Three, Echo Nine. Do you see any other movement? Over."

"Echo Nine. Negative. Area is clear. Over."

"Thanks for the assist. Out."

Gournsey gazed down at the carnage they'd wrought. "What a fucking mess."

"And a waste," added Sherman.

"Shouldn't have chased us."

Sherman nodded. "I shouldn't have blown up the trucks."

"Why? It was the right call."

"True, but now we're walking back."

Part II

Colorado, USA—One year later

Chapter Four

Class wound down and Sherman's students fidgeted attentively, but the weekend loomed large in every mind. Twelve sets of eyes followed his rather crude chalkboard drawing of a firefight he'd survived five years earlier in Syria. None of the students bore any scars, not yet. Newly commissioned officers. A room full of lieutenants that liked to question Sherman's actions all those years before.

"Sir, why didn't you flank to the right?" asked one particular alpha male in a class composed mostly of the type. "It was the best tactical choice."

Sherman didn't answer. Not at first. His mind drifted miles away from Fort Carson and Major Sanders' cruel attempt at forced rest. 'Go and teach a class or two', the major had said. Nothing about the order had gone well. He didn't mind being challenged, but all he got were ill-conceived questions. He agreed with Gournsey... there were many ways to skin a cat, but the students lacked imagination.

"It was the obvious choice," replied Sherman.

The ego-swollen lieutenant looked back with incomprehension.

"Quickness is the essence of war," Sherman continued.

"Captain, I don't see how that applies here."

Sherman rubbed the bridge of his nose. *Almost Saturday*, he thought. Only one more week of this foolishness remained.

"It's a quote from Sun Tzu," said a voice from the back. The young woman was pointing at the chalkboard. "You couldn't flank right because it would have taken too long."

Sherman smiled. At least someone paid attention. "Yes and no. We could have gone right through these buildings, but that was the slower and more obvious choice. With each engagement, you need to respect your enemy. On this mission, we were operating against a hardened group of veterans. Once discovered, the best choice is often speed. We lived through that not by textbook tactics, but from speed and violence. Speed is often more important than handbook tactics."

Pens scribbled notes and Sherman went back to rubbing the bridge of his nose. Classroom teaching didn't suit him. He wasn't built that way.

"Alright, that'll do for today. Next week, we're gonna gear up and see what you've learned."

Grunts of acknowledgement followed. He knew several of his students looking forward to the opportunity of getting the better of Captain Frank Sherman.

Outside, the long light of fall cascaded over the mountains and across the base. Sherman hadn't spent much time in Colorado. A few nights here and there with friends, but mostly passing through save for a rafting trip on the Upper Colorado River.

On the further reaches of the Rockies, great swatches of

yellow spread between green pines. Aspens prepared for their autumn dance. Sherman stood in the sun and soaked up some warmth.

"Rough day, Professor?" asked Gournsey.

The sergeant was also suppressing his rage over forced rest, but Sherman knew his friend could still enjoy the time away.

"I'd say it's a generational thing and kids these days, but I was just like them once."

Gournsey patted him on the shoulder with his meaty paw. "To be honest, I can't imagine you young. You've always been a grumpy old man in my mind."

"You're an asshole."

"But I'm right."

Sherman sighed and let himself laugh over the triviality of taking things personally.

"Did you give them the Syrian example?" asked Gournsey.

"Yup."

"Let me guess," said Gournsey. "A wide right flanking maneuver to gain the high ground followed by close air support."

Sherman nodded. "Wide right. The tactically correct option as they eagerly pointed out."

"Did you mention they'd mined that building in hopes we'd flank right?"

"No, but I'll need your help next week with a field exercise."

The mention of a fight, however fake, perked the sergeant up.

"How far can I take it?"

"Don't break any bones," answered Sherman. "But a little blood will do them good."

Gournsey winked and they started walking back toward their shared base apartment, which had all the charm of a cheap roadside motel.

"A few Delta boys are getting beers in Denver tonight, you in?" asked the sergeant.

Any excuse to take his mind off the classroom sounded good to Sherman.

"Count me in, but I've got dinner with Colonel Khada and his family tomorrow, so don't keep me out too late."

"Old man indeed," teased Gournsey.

Sherman laughed but felt the sting of truth in the sergeant's words. Perhaps he was too old for it all.

The Denver skyline sprang out from the vast flatlands abutting the Rocky Mountains like the remnants of a steel avalanche. Not that the city was out of place, but Sherman always found it odd that a city so connected with the mountains was not actually in the mountains.

They parked in a neighborhood that must have been a contraction or abbreviation, maybe both. New glass buildings mingled with renovated brick lofts and young professionals swarmed over the place. How young? Sherman didn't know, not anymore. Younger than him, but old enough to die in a war.

Gournsey navigated them towards their first stop. The brewery was new, the building old. It felt far too dimly lit for Sherman's tastes and too industrial. They ordered while the other Delta guys filtered inside.

The beer was beer. Neither good nor terrible. Average.

The conversation rocketed between reliving the good old days and their current operations, which no longer came hot and fast. Sherman listened and laughed and drank, but part of his mind drifted. He couldn't say why, but it happened with increasing regularity. Another impact of age.

Bar number two was closer to downtown, and the buildings got older and bigger, with crumbling red bricks held together by steel stars. They were passing a cozy restaurant with warm yellow light spilling onto the sidewalk when Sherman stopped.

"Are you still hungry, Cap?" asked Gournsey.

He wasn't hungry. Despite the customers visible in the window, he hadn't considered the food on the tables. Sherman was too busy staring at a woman sitting at the bar.

"I'll catch up with you later," he said.

"You look like you've seen a ghost."

"Something like that," Sherman replied and stepped inside the restaurant.

The hostess smiled politely, but when Sherman pointed towards the bar, she set the menu back down and nodded. Sitting alone with the dying embers of a bourbon between her hands was Sherman's ghost. Special Agent Megan Landers of the FBI. Her blonde hair was in a ponytail just like Sherman remembered from their last meeting in California.

He wondered, *Was it two years ago or more?*

Sherman took a seat next to her at the bar before she saw him. Agent Landers still wore her work clothes—a dark blazer and pants. Unless she only owned work clothes.

She looked over at him and the smallest hint of a smile leaked out of her otherwise placid expression.

"A little presumptuous of you, Frank."

"Are you waiting for a date?"

"No, but I could have been."

41

"Can I buy you a drink?" he asked.

"Does that mean we're on a date?" she asked with a smile.

"One bourbon does not constitute a date," Sherman replied and motioned to the bartender.

Landers turned his direction and leaned an elbow on the bar to rest her head.

"Tell me, what the hell are you doing in Denver?"

The bartender deposited two glasses and Sherman took a sip, enjoying the sudden glow of whiskey.

"Teaching at Fort Carson."

Landers let out a small chuckle and her smile widened. "So, they finally put you out to pasture."

"For the time being. Downtime was a word used to describe it, along with decompression."

"Is it?" asked Landers.

"More like depressing."

She nodded.

"Enough about me," added Sherman. "Why are you sitting alone at a bar in Denver still dressed for work?"

"Maybe these are my out on the town clothes."

"Do you usually get drinks out with your service pistol?" asked Sherman as he pointed toward her hip where the contour of a Glock was barely visible.

"It's been a long day."

"Are you based here now?"

Landers nodded. "Transferred from L.A. after the incident in Buford."

"Did you ever make a case against the crooked officer who was selling off our old arsenal?" asked Sherman, curious to know the aftermath of his last visit to California.

"As I recall, he ended up with a giant hole in his head. You wouldn't happen to know anything about that?"

Sherman smiled and said nothing. He'd pulled the trigger and sent that traitorous prick back to whatever afterlife he belonged in, but Sherman wasn't about to admit to it. Besides, he reasoned, Landers knew all about the officer's unfortunate ending. He'd taped her business card to the ninth-hole flag as bait.

"Truthfully, that case rankled the real power players in the Bureau. They couldn't send me to Alaska or anything so bold, but I bet they wanted to. Instead, I got reassigned here."

"From what I've seen, here isn't too bad," said Sherman.

"I suppose."

"Not your scene?" he asked.

"They've got me running down bullshit white-collar cases. CEOs stealing from the corporate piggy bank and stuff like that."

The comment reminded Sherman of the alpha lieutenant who didn't care for lectures or expertise.

"Kinda like teaching," he said.

Landers downed the rest of her bourbon and threw some cash on the bar. "Come on, I've got better stuff back at my place."

"Is it a date now?" he asked with a grin.

"I don't think a drink at a friend's apartment constitutes a date."

"We're friends?" he asked.

"You got me shot, so we're either friends or foes."

Sherman smiled and stood up. "Another drink sounds great."

They'd walked a few blocks towards the glass and steel towers of downtown when he asked, "How's your leg doing?"

Landers rubbed it absentmindedly. "Still hurts occasionally when it's cold, and I don't know if you've heard, but Colorado gets fucking cold."

"I'm glad to see you're still walking," he added.

"I probably owe you for that."

"You were doing just fine," Sherman added, but the memory of Landers applying a tourniquet to her shattered leg flooded his mind. "I'm sorry for how that went down. Your partner seemed like a good guy."

Landers stopped walking and sighed. An invisible weight hovered over her, but Sherman could see it. He carried it too. Just like all those who'd served and lost.

"Yeah, he was a good guy," she replied and kept walking.

They reached the front of some angular monstrosity of steel and glass. Landers slapped a plastic keycard on a small box and the shiny chrome doors slid open. As apartment lobbies went, this one was clean and well lit. Soulless, yes, but full of the amenities young professionals liked. Landers did not fit the bill, and to Sherman's understanding, never had been that type of person. An ex-MP, Landers was a driven investigator who didn't give a shit about amenities.

In the elevator, she hit the ninth-floor button and the door closed with a soft thud.

"It's close to my office," she said as if in answer to Sherman's unspoken question of 'why here?'.

"I didn't say anything," he pleaded.

"But you were thinking it."

"You should see what they put me in."

Landers gave him a dismissive look and took off down the hallway. "You don't strike me as a guy who cares about décor."

Sherman smiled. She was a quick and accurate observer of the human species. He'd almost forgotten how good.

The door to her apartment opened and he followed her inside. If the lobby was soulless, her place was devoid of anything. No personal pictures hung on the walls. Only the most basic furniture occupied the space. Nothing fancy. The couch still looked new. The place was clean, but only because there wasn't enough stuff to get dirty. About the only thing stocked was an oak liquor cabinet that glowed with sheens of gold under the cool light.

Landers tossed her jacket on the table and locked up her service pistol in a small safe. A pile of files stood on the table and Sherman tried not to look. Although, his security clearance was probably higher than hers.

"What's your poison?" she asked.

"You pick," he replied and walked outside onto a small balcony.

The sun had set hours before, but a faint glow silhouetted the distant mountains, turning them into dark blue teeth in front of a yawning abyss.

A good view indeed, he thought. *If you ignore the city.*

Landers followed him out a few minutes later with two glasses. She'd changed into yoga pants and an athletic-looking top like she was going for a run or heading to the gym. The booze, however, said otherwise.

They sat on cheap plastic chairs, sipping bourbon, and watching the moon rise. The stars were hard to see through the haze of city lights, but Sherman sensed them above and he longed for the clarity of a desert night.

"Do you like it here?" he asked.

"I'm barely home so it serves its purpose of four walls and a roof."

"And the city?"

Landers shrugged. "It's a city. Nicer than L.A., I suppose, but a city just the same."

He nodded and kept searching for stars.

"Frank, what are you doing here?"

"You invited me."

She rolled her eyes. "Why did you even stop at the restaurant? I didn't exactly treat you well… shit, I outright coerced you into helping me."

"I'm not easily coerced into anything. You had a job to do and I had a string to pull. I don't hold a grudge over that."

Landers took a long sip and sighed. "At least you got to go back to your life and career."

"My war ended last year. Who knows if they'll ever let me out of the classroom."

"Wars come and go. We both know that."

"So do cases," Sherman added. "There's always more crime."

Landers raised her glass. "To wallowing."

"To the next thing," replied Sherman.

Chapter Five

Dawn lingered unseen over the horizon when the alarm went off. Asal Khada rolled over and slapped at the off button. She didn't want to wake up Zarak. He worked late at the airport as a baggage handler—a job she knew he hated, but he said nothing. He kept going for them. He'd always done everything for his family.

As Asal rolled out of bed, something was wrong. She knew it as surely as she'd known anything. She knew it in her bones. But what was wrong? That she couldn't say, not at first.

Maybe her husband would know, so she turned to squeeze his arm to gently wake him up, but there was no arm to squeeze.

He wasn't there.

His side of the bed was empty.

His coat did not hang on the hook.

His shoes did not litter the floor.

Maybe he worked extra late and slept on the couch,

thought Asal. She went to look, and her chest tightened. Zarak had not come home at all.

Looking out the window of their apartment, she did not see his car parked on the still dark street. It wasn't in his usual spot. The one he bickered with their neighbors over whenever they took it.

"Mama," said a voice from behind and Asal grabbed her chest in surprise.

Her youngest daughter stood in her pajamas, clutching a stuffed penguin.

"I'm hungry, Mama."

Asal opened her arms and pulled her daughter close. She took one last look at the empty street and started a kettle for tea and a pot for oatmeal.

Dawn broke and the sun flooded down with long autumn light. Esin, the youngest, was coloring quietly on the couch when her sister, Dara, emerged.

"Mama," she said. "What's for breakfast?"

Asal smiled and pointed at the table with the still warm tea and oatmeal.

Dara ate in silence, her eyes roving around the room. Finally, she turned to her mother and asked, "Where's Papa?"

Asal's heart cracked with worry. It reminded her of the fear they'd felt in Kabul when the Taliban came back. The strangling blanket of unknowns she felt each time Zarak stepped outside or her daughters went to school.

"He must have worked an extra shift," Asal lied. "I guess I got the day wrong."

Dara looked hard at her mother but said nothing. Asal could see the wheels of doubt turning in her daughter's mind. How long would the lie hold? Not long. Not long at all.

Asal cleared away the dishes, still clutching at her worry. She found her phone and called around. The Afghan community in Aurora was small but close-knit. Most of her news and gossip came from such calls.

Fear closed around her heart. Call after call ended with nothing. Empty theories, but no help. An insinuation of infidelity fell flat in her mind. Zarak would never stoop to such lows. She knew that in her bones.

"When's Papa coming home?" asked Dara. Her eyes pleaded for information as if she already knew Asal had no answers.

"I don't know, my love. I don't know."

"Why not?" she retorted, raising her voice like the soon-to-be teenager she was.

"Quieter, my love. I don't want to worry your sister."

"Why are you worried, Mama?"

"I'm not," Asal said and tried to mean it.

"Yes, you are… like back in Kabul."

"I'm sure it's a misunderstanding. He'll be home soon. Now, please help your sister clean up."

Dara scrunched up her face into a ball of disbelief, but she went to help clean up Esin's mess.

Calling the police was an option, but despite her year of relative safety in Colorado, Asal held a deep and abiding distrust of law enforcement. They weren't to be trusted in Kabul and she couldn't shake that feeling in her new home.

Asal hesitated, wondering if she was overreacting. Yet, no matter how she tried to stuff the fear away deep inside, it bubbled up. Something was wrong. It had to be.

Under a magnet from the refugee resettlement agency was a small piece of paper. Asal plucked it out and turned it over in her hands. Once, twice, three times. Then she dialed. As it rang, she mouthed a silent prayer that all they'd escaped over there had not followed them back here.

Chapter Six

With each successive ring of the phone, Sherman's head hurt even more. Trill noise after trill noise. He fumbled around wildly in the unfamiliar room before crawling out of bed in search of the device. He found it in his pants, which were still on the floor, and answered before the call went to voicemail.

"Hello," he said, trying not to sound as hungover as he felt.

"Mr. Sherman. This is Asal Khada."

"Good morning, Asal. Don't worry, I'm still coming tonight. Which reminds me... should I bring anything specific?"

"No, it's not that."

Worry seeped from her words.

"What's wrong?" asked Sherman.

"I don't know, but I'm scared. Zarak never came home from work last night. I don't know where he is."

All the usual places a man might go flashed through Sherman's mind, but Zarak was not that kind of man.

He sat up and tried to focus his mind.

"He's not answering his phone?"

"Zarak doesn't have a cell phone," said Asal.

"Oh," said Sherman with a hint of jealousy. "Did you ask around?"

"Yes, of course. No one has seen him since yesterday."

"Did he get to work?"

"Yes, but nothing after that."

"Did you call the police?" asked Sherman. He knew the answer but asked anyway. He didn't want to step on any toes.

"No, I… I don't trust them. I trust you. Please, Frank, help me find him. I would try but we only have one car and I never learned to drive. And the girls…" she trailed off.

"Asal, of course I'll help. Uh, give me forty-five minutes and I'll be there."

"Thank you," she said with palpable relief.

"No need to thank me. I'm still in his debt."

Sherman hung up and surveyed the wreckage of his night.

"Whose debt are you in?" asked Landers.

She was lying naked across the bed, looking almost chipper. *How?* he thought. She drank the lion's share.

A thin beam of light danced over her leg and small shadows flickered across her scar—the outcome of their last meeting when Landers lost her partner and nearly her life.

"Colonel Zarak Khada," replied Sherman as he hunted for his underwear.

"He must have done something pretty spectacular to earn your loyalty."

Sherman pulled up his pants and nodded. "He saved my life."

"Ah."

"And my team."

"Oh, I see. And you're getting dressed because?"

"He's missing," answered Sherman as he pulled on his shirt.

Landers sat up. "Let me guess. They don't trust the police."

"They didn't have an outstanding track record in Afghanistan."

"No, they didn't," she replied and walked over to her dresser.

Sherman stopped looking for his shoes and watched her cross the room. "What are you doing?"

"Helping you."

"It's not your problem."

Landers laughed. "Someone needs to drive."

Sherman said nothing, but she must have read the question hovering on his lips. Government plates would only make things worse.

"Don't worry, we'll take my personal car."

"Bring your badge," he added.

"I thought we are being inconspicuous."

Sherman finished tying his boots and stood up. "We might need it to visit the morgue."

Leaves and bits of litter tumbled down the street as they arrived. Landers drove fast, which suited her profession. Something about federal agents and speed, which always gave them an aura of impatience.

They'd arrived a few minutes earlier than Sherman's prediction. First impressions said they weren't in a desirable part of town. The cars parked on the street were all twenty-plus years old and most had at least one part attached with duct tape. In comparison, Landers' bland newish American sedan looked like a sparkling Mercedes.

The apartment building looked shabbier than the vehicles. Acceptable sixty years before, the buildings still stood but that was the nicest compliment Sherman could think of to give the three-story hunk of crumbling brickwork. A façade of faded paint, broken screens, and warped roofs.

"I never saw where they resettled," said Sherman.

"It isn't much," replied Landers.

"It never is."

"Which building?" she asked.

Sherman pointed at the middle of three identical brown structures. "Bottom floor. Number 102."

Landers nodded and moved across a patchy lawn that had more dirt than grass.

"So, where are we?" asked Sherman.

The question was rhetorical. Geographically, he knew. Socio-economically, he understood. As for the local context, he hadn't a clue.

"Aurora, just off Colfax."

He nodded.

"A lot of refugees get dumped here. It's about the only thing they can afford once the federal assistance runs out."

"Refugees from where?" asked Sherman.

Landers stopped. "All over," she answered with a smile. "You're thinking like a cop, wondering if a neighbor with a grudge moved in nearby."

"The thought crossed my mind."

"Maybe, or maybe your friend crossed the local gang." She pointed toward a smudge of paint that Sherman couldn't decipher but understood the meaning. When stressed or stretched thin, everything turned tribal. Gangs, cliques, or platoons. They were all different words for small unit cohesion. Sherman understood that.

When they reached the apartment, Sherman rang the doorbell but nothing happened. Disconnected or broken or both. He knocked on the metal security door and waited. Asal appeared a few minutes later.

She smiled at Sherman but frowned when Landers stepped into view.

"It's okay, Asal. She's a friend."

"Of course, I'm sorry. Please come in."

She ushered them inside and hastily closed the door.

The smell hit Sherman first. Was it the spice mix or the cedar incense? He couldn't decide, but whatever the scent, the result was the same. Instantly, he was back in Afghanistan and traversing through an outdoor market trying to win hearts and minds while dodging Taliban bullets.

In another life, Landers served in Iraq, and he could see her eyes glaze over with some distant memory too. Good or bad? Sherman hadn't a clue.

"Can I offer you some tea or something to eat?" asked Asal.

"No, thanks," said Landers.

Sherman shook his head and explored the apartment. It was small. Two bedrooms and one bath. All of it in need of repair. Despite the shortcomings, Asal had created a home with soft spaces, cozy corners, and traditional fabrics.

"Asal, the place is wonderful," said Sherman.

She frowned and sat down in a tiny dining space next to the galley kitchen.

"Frank, I don't know what to do. I've called everyone we know. No one has seen Zarak since he got off work last night."

Sherman pulled up a chair next to her. "Tell me what you know."

"He works at the airport loading bags. He left yesterday at his normal time."

"When?"

"Uh, around noon. He works from 1:00 PM to 1:00 AM."

"How does he get there?" asked Landers, who stood at the edge of the conversation.

Asal looked to Sherman for reassurance, and he nodded.

"He drives to a park and…"

"Park-and-Ride?" added Landers.

"Yes, that. Then he takes the train to the airport."

"Do you know which one?" asked Sherman.

"61st and Pena, I think."

"Okay, go on."

"He worked a normal shift. Our neighbor, Hassan, works there too. He saw Zarak running to catch the train after work, but he didn't see him after that."

"Has this happened before?" asked Landers. Her voice was even and professional. Just another day in the office.

"What do mean?"

"Has he ever come home late or not at all?"

Asal's lips trembled. "No, never. You don't know my husband. He's devoted to his family."

Sherman could tell that Landers harbored doubts over the colonel's familial devotion. Statistics show men cheat in twenty-five percent of marriages. Cops knew things like that, but she didn't say it out loud.

"Believe me," continued Asal. "We've been through so much, I'd know if he was—"

"Cheating on you," finished Landers.

Asal nodded and buried her face in her hands.

"Have you filed a missing person report?" asked Landers.

"We don't trust people like… like you."

Landers smiled softly. "Don't worry, I won't take it personally. A lot of refugees don't trust law enforcement. Have you or your husband had any issues with people in your neighborhood? Maybe someone from back home."

Asal rubbed her hands together as she thought. "Not that I remember. There are some, uh, drugs, but nothing like Kabul. We keep to ourselves. Zarak works and then sleeps. He doesn't have time to do much else."

"Did he mention anything new or out of the ordinary?"

"Nothing—" Asal began saying, but her oldest daughter's voice interrupted.

"The American," said Dara. "He saw someone he'd known during the war."

Asal swiveled as if to scold her child, but her frown softened. "That's right. Zarak mentioned someone he knew from Kabul."

"Someone from my team?" asked Sherman, knowing it wasn't true.

"No. Another American, but that's all he said and even that was in passing."

Landers turned towards Dara. "Do you know where your dad might be?"

Dara looked from Landers to her mother, pleading for permission.

"It's okay," said Asal.

"Daddy told me not to say anything, but sometimes he stops for pie after work. I found a receipt once and he swore me to secrecy."

"Pie?" asked Asal.

Dara looked at the ground as she spoke. "He said that sometimes he wants someone else's baking."

Asal frowned and buried her face again.

Landers and Sherman exchanged a quick glance they both understood. One secret never remained alone.

"Do you know where?" asked Sherman.

"A restaurant off the freeway. He said it was in a truck stop. Daddy always found such things strange. Commits, I think."

"Comet's," corrected Landers.

"Yeah, it was something space-related."

Something about the way Landers said the name caught Sherman's attention. The agent knew the place in a professional capacity. He was sure of it.

"What kind of car does he drive?" asked Sherman.

"An old Hyundai Elantra," answered Asal.

"What color?"

"Black."

A practical car for a practical man. Sherman understood the choice.

Landers looked at him. "Should we start at the Park-and-Ride?"

Sherman nodded. It was the logical choice. If the car was still there, then Zarak didn't make it much past the train. Maybe a mugging or robbery gone wrong.

"We'll look," said Sherman.

Asal gave a tight facsimile of a smile and led them to the door.

They'd barely reached the car when Sherman asked, "What's the deal with this restaurant?"

"So much for my poker face," replied Landers.

Sherman said nothing.

"It's not so much the diner as the truck stop around it.

The place is on our radar as a hub for smuggling, or so I'm told."

"What variety?"

"Drugs, money, guns, and girls. The full criminal smorgasbord."

"And if he hid the pie from Asal, there might be more."

Landers nodded. "Not to condemn the man over a slice of pie, but secrets never lie alone."

"So they say," added Sherman.

"So it is," said Landers.

Chapter Seven

The Park-and-Ride was about half-full when Sherman and Landers arrived. That still left over five hundred cars to search.

"We forgot to ask for the license plate number," said Sherman, realizing the time-consuming scope of his mistake.

Landers dismissed him with a wave of her hand. She angled her phone in his direction. It showed the colonel's photo and DMV details.

"Definitely glad I bumped into you," he said.

"What? Last night wasn't good enough?"

The night had been more than worth it, but things had changed. Sherman knew it. So did Landers.

"You have a good bourbon collection," he said.

"And you have a good scar collection."

"It was a highlight on the recruiting brochure," Sherman added.

Landers laughed. "Right next to see the world, but only the shitty spots."

"Oh, you got the same brochure," joked Sherman.

She shook her head, but the smile remained.

"What now?" he asked. "Park and go on foot?"

"No cop walks," she said and laughed some more. "I'll look left, you check right. Call out if you see the make and model. It's easy to switch plates."

Sherman wasn't a car guy. They were useful for getting from A to B, but he didn't keep up with trends. Telling a 2021 Hyundai from a 2011 or a 2001 was not one of his skills.

They hadn't gone twenty feet when he said something. Landers stopped and turned to look. She immediately kept going.

"Too new," she said.

This pattern repeated itself several times until they passed down the last row.

"Not here," said Sherman.

"Not here," agreed Landers.

"He catches the next train home and makes it to his car, but doesn't make it home," Sherman narrated.

Landers nodded along. "I'll call a friend with Denver PD and see if they have a Zarak Khada in custody or any record of him last night."

She pulled into an empty row and took up three spots.

Sherman waited as she talked with the measured tones of someone who'd seen too many misdeeds to be surprised by one husband who didn't come home. The thought of spending an afternoon seeing if Colonel Khada had shacked up with a mistress was ludicrously strange. He almost laughed out loud. Of all the close calls and near misses, this was what it culminated in. Infidelity or maybe a car crash. *How benign*, thought Sherman.

Landers hung up the phone. "Denver and Aurora PD

have no record of him and nothing from ambulance records."

Not a car crash.

"If I didn't know better, I'd say his slice of pie evolved into the waitress and they ran off to Vegas," he said.

"You don't see that as a possibility?"

"I do, but it lives low on my list."

"What's high on your list?" she asked.

"In my world, when people disappear, they don't come back."

Landers flipped her hair to one side. "Not in one piece."

He nodded. The Special Agent had seen it all and more in Iraq. She knew the outcomes, few of which ended with the colonel alive.

"Let's check the truck stop then," he added.

"You can check the truck stop. I don't want anyone to see me poking around off-duty."

"Why does that matter?"

"I don't want a pissing match over cases or some internal bullshit."

"You think it's under surveillance."

"Officially, no. Unofficially, probably. I don't want to find out I stuck my foot in it by stopping for coffee."

For a truck stop, Comet's looked busier than usual. Cars and semi-trucks filled the great sea of asphalt surrounding the main building. Twenty-plus pumps stood on one side for normal vehicles. The opposite side had larger spaces for diesels. The front and back were parking lots. Sherman saw every imaginable mode of wheeled transportation—RVs, vans, trucks, sports cars, motorcycles, those tricycles with two wheels in the front, and even some electric cars.

Landers parked on the far side of the lot, well away from the hustle and bustle of activity. A large neon sign looked down on them. A giant pink circle with trailing lines of yellow. *The comet*, thought Sherman, although it looked more like an asteroid to him.

"I'll call around the morgues while you're inside. Try not to cause a scene," said Landers.

Sherman offered his hands in mock indignation. "Scouts honor," he replied.

She eyed him warily. "I'm conflicted. Part of me says you made Eagle Scout. Part of me says that's ridiculous. I'm not sure which part to believe."

"Trust your gut," Sherman replied and jumped out of the car before she could protest his non-answer.

Weaving through a warren of trailers and cars was a tactical nightmare. All the angles and potential threats made Sherman's mind whir with activity. At least fifty people milled about the back parking lot. Families changed diapers, truckers went to or woke up from sleep, and at least one guy slept off a heavy night of drinking. A microcosm of the human experience.

The heart of Comet's was a single building the size of a small supermarket. Brightly colored signs wrapped around the façade advertising the amenities inside. The usual suspects of gas, snacks, and restrooms came before a list of different food options. There was a sandwich place, a taco joint, ice cream, and an All-American diner. The latter advertised 'Best Pie in the West,' which Sherman took to mean mediocre. Such hyperbole almost always rang false.

Through the sliding glass doors lay a vast convenience store. Aisles of snacks stretched down the middle and coolers filled with sugar and beer lined the walls. With a practiced sweep of his eyes, Sherman took in everything he needed to know.

The colonel wasn't in line or flipping through bins of beef jerky. A few patrons might have warranted a second look if he was a cop, but he wasn't.

Sherman moved through the main entryway, passing beyond the snacks and restrooms into a dining area. A food court to his right contained sandwiches, tacos, and ice cream. The tables were small but clean and the room had a modern feel.

The colonel was nowhere to be seen. Not munching a breakfast taco or licking a scoop of Pralines 'n Cream.

Turning left, Sherman followed a sign for the Best Pie. He walked down a hallway carpeted in burgundy that proved to be a dirty red on closer inspection. He got the impression the diner came first, some seventy years earlier, and everything else got tacked on recently.

Through a frosted glass door etched with the name Franklin's, Sherman found a bustling restaurant. Cups and dishes clattered while the hum of conversation pulsed through the room. Sizzling bacon and grease reached his nostrils. He suddenly felt the weight of his hangover and an acute awareness that he'd missed breakfast.

The sign by the door said, 'Take a seat, but leave it here'. Sherman did just that at the counter.

A waitress wearing a yellow uniform and white apron spotted him and walked over. She was in her late forties with thick-framed glasses and graying brown hair. Her nametag read Barb.

"You look like a man in need of coffee," she said and flipped over the cup in front of him before he could answer.

"You read me like a book," he replied and gave his best

smile. The kind that used to get him into or out of trouble when he was younger.

"That's my job," Barb replied. "What else can I get you?"

The menu on the counter looked thick, but Sherman already knew what it contained. He'd been to dozens of diners like this one.

"Two egg breakfast with bacon and hashbrowns."

Barb took out a notepad and scribbled.

"You don't look like the scrambled type, am I right?"

Two for two, thought Sherman.

"Over easy will do," he said.

"Toast?"

"I'll let you guess," said Sherman, who enjoyed watching a seasoned professional in action.

"Sourdough," she replied without hesitation.

"You're batting a thousand."

Barb smiled and tucked the pen behind her ear. "Be back soon. Holler if you need anything."

Sherman sipped his coffee and watched the natural flow of things. Families and elderly couples sat in the booths. Truck drivers and workers took up the counter. In the very back, almost cordoned off from the primary space, were a couple of larger tables. He couldn't quite see, but it looked like a group of cops.

No, not cops.

Security guards or the like.

One guy stood up and Sherman recognized the tattoo on his arm. Marine Corps, just like Sherman's father. An ex-jarhead judging by the longer-than-regulation haircut.

Sherman didn't have any ink, not because he disapproved of the idea but because it was an identifying mark, and he wasn't in the business of being identified in his line of work.

If there was a vast criminal enterprise at work, he didn't see it. Maybe some small-time dealing from an overattentive busboy, but nothing egregious. Nor did Sherman see Colonel Khada tucked away in a booth.

"Here you go, sweetie," said Barb and deposited his plate.

"Thanks," Sherman replied and admired the piping hot plate of fried food.

He ate leisurely, watching the customers come and go. Tired families sat down, and the parents melted with relief over endless sodas and impossibly high stacks of pancakes. Truckers chatted about the weather and grumbled over working conditions. The only table not to turn over was the one in the far back with the ex-Marine and security guards.

When Barb came to collect his plate, she gave an odd smile. "Most people don't linger so long. Can I get you something else?"

"My friend said I should try the pie. He's a regular of sorts."

"Oh," said the waitress, sounding both puzzled and proud. "We've got quite a few devotees. Is he an evening or morning pie man?"

"Super early morning or late night, depending on how you look at it. He works at the airport."

Barb snapped her fingers and smiled. "Z," she said. "It's got to be him."

Having never heard the colonel's first name reduced to its starting letter, Sherman couldn't help but raise an eyebrow.

"Is your Z from Afghanistan?" he asked.

Barb tilted her head to one side.

"Huh, you know what, I never asked. I just figured he was Indian."

Sherman guessed it was some variation on the brown guy with a mustache stereotype.

"I missed him on the way to work, thought I might see him on the flip side," said Sherman in a twisted lie.

The leading comment, while sounding innocent, was Sherman's shot in the dark. If the smile worked, he might get a nugget of information.

"He was here alright. Sitting right over there when I got in. But he skipped his usual pie and drank coffee instead."

The colonel, in Sherman's limited experience, was not a coffee guy. Like most Afghans, Zarak favored tea. Usually mint and not caffeinated. Drinking cheap coffee after work struck Sherman as odd. Not the obvious choice of a man going home at the end of a long day.

"I hope that didn't mess up his sleep cycle," added Sherman and forced a laugh to seal his next unspoken question. "I'd be up all night."

Barb nodded along at the thought. "Yeah, not his drink of choice, but he looked pretty alert when he left."

Sherman wanted to ask what time Z left but thought better of it. He'd pressed his luck asking what he did. Genial conversation about a mutual acquaintance is one thing. Specific questions about that person, including the time of his departure, were bound to raise suspicion. If the colonel was in trouble, Sherman certainly didn't want to make things worse by asking stupid questions.

"Maybe I'll join him for the next slice," he added and slid across forty dollars.

"That'll get you a few slices. What do you want?"

"Just a bacon breakfast burrito to go. I'll get the pie next time."

Barb smiled and said, "Sure thing, sweetie."

Sherman glanced around the room to see if anyone's gaze lingered. Nothing noticeable. More truckers at the counter glanced in his direction, but they were a gruff sort and didn't feel out of place.

Barb came back a few minutes later with the burrito and his change.

"All yours," said Sherman, taking only the food from Barb's outstretched hands.

"Thanks, you have a nice day now."

Sherman nodded in his best parody of a man tipping his hat. He stuck with the charm to the end.

When he got back to the car, Landers looked half asleep with the edges of a hangover forming. Which, given her consumption the previous night, was long overdue.

"What took you so damn long? I almost thought something was wrong but I didn't hear any gunfire, so I figured you ate breakfast."

Sherman handed her the burrito.

"At least you didn't come back empty-handed."

"Well worth enduring some overcooked eggs."

"Your friend was here?" asked Landers between bites.

"Early this morning, like usual."

"Confirms he lied to his wife."

"True," said Sherman. "But here's the interesting part. Instead of a nice slice of pie after work and before going home to sleep, Zarak got a cup of coffee."

"And that's odd because… he's a tea drinker?" asked Landers.

"Last time I checked, the unofficial beverage of Afghanistan is still tea."

"Which means he wasn't heading home," added Landers.

"I assume not."

"Then where did he go?"

Sherman shrugged. "Ain't that the question of the hour."

"Did you ask how Zarak was acting? Was he nervous or worried?"

"I'm not a cop," Sherman replied. "I didn't ask more than a friendly conversation allowed, it not being a good idea and all."

"Fair point," admitted Landers. "Speaking of cops. I spotted two surveillance vans in the vicinity."

"Yours?"

"Not sure. I'd have to dig and people around here don't like nosey agents poking around their cases."

"Well," said Sherman. "We've got a couple of problems then. First, where did Colonel Khada go this morning? Second, and related, is how do we see the surveillance footage?"

"I'd need a reason to go snooping on the bureau servers."

The dim light of memory clicked on, and Sherman smiled.

"What if you got a call from a reporter looking into a story about a federal investigation of Comet's truck stop in Denver?"

Landers' eyebrows shot up with surprise. "You know a reporter that would take that kind of professional risk?"

"I know a guy," Sherman answered. "He kind of owes me one."

Landers put down the nearly finished burrito and handed over her business card.

"Have your friend call me at that number. It will make it

into the official record. I can at least ask around and get the summary notes."

"Thanks, I know that puts you out on a short limb."

"Meh," said Landers and waved away his concern. "Compared to the bullshit they have me working, a few answers are nothing."

"And the federal secrecy you're breaking?"

"Then I better not tell you anything," she answered with an almost imperceptible wink.

Chapter Eight

That Danny Bashir answered Sherman's call was a minor miracle. Called ID didn't register his number and hardly anyone knew it. A bit of smoke and mirrors, but a necessary ruse. Army intelligence didn't want anyone to know Sherman existed, let alone call him.

"What?" demanded Danny, sounding like a customer exasperated by scams.

"Danny, this is Captain Frank Sherman. Do you have a few minutes to talk?"

Wheels of thought spun in the following silence.

"Captain, I didn't think I'd hear from you again."

"Because of what you wrote about the war and my team?"

"I never used your name," said Danny.

"The Army knew."

"But the public didn't," Danny protested.

"Look," said Sherman. "I don't give a shit about what you wrote, but it's gonna cost you."

Danny sighed. "How much do I owe you?"

"One call," answered Sherman.

"To who?"

"An FBI agent. I need you to ask about the federal surveillance of Comet's truck stop in Denver. Are you writing this down?"

Papers rustled and Danny said, "Yeah, yeah. I'm writing it down."

"Good."

"What else?"

"Nothing else," said Sherman. "They'll likely say no or whatever standard non-answers the feds give these days."

"Can I ask why?"

"No, you cannot. Do this and we're even for that article, then you can ask questions for the next favor."

Another prolonged pause followed before Danny answered, "Fine. Give me the number, I'll call them tomorrow."

"No. You'll call now."

"It was a good article," Danny added.

"It was a great article," said Sherman. "But quality doesn't top stupidity. You described us and you shouldn't have."

"Fine. This clears my debt," said the reporter.

"Fine."

Sherman ended the call and waited for Landers' phone to ring. He didn't wait long.

She answered the call and put it on speakerphone.

"This is Special Agent Landers."

"Hello, Agent Landers. This is Danny Bashir with Reuters. We're working on an interstate trafficking story and wanted your comments."

"He's good," mouthed Landers to Sherman before answering, "I'm not at liberty to discuss active cases."

"To your knowledge, is the FBI currently surveilling Comet's truck stop in Denver."

"I can neither confirm nor deny such details," she replied in an unbelievably flat tone.

"Thanks for your time, Agent Landers. Have a nice day."

The call didn't last a full minute. Question two's answer was in motion. Now Sherman could focus his energy on finding Colonel Khada.

"I'll log the call," said Landers. "I can also see if the city has any nearby traffic cameras. They don't require a warrant to see the last twenty-four hours of footage."

"Good idea. I'm going to buy some images."

"What?" asked Landers.

Sherman pointed up towards the sky. "Did you know that a commercial imaging satellite crosses over every four hours?"

"How do you know that?"

"Because the spy satellites are hourly," he answered with a grin.

"So many secrets," she muttered before starting the car. "My laptop is at work, I'll drop you off at the Khada's apartment on my way."

"Works for me."

On the drive back, Sherman called Major Sanders to break the news. The major and the colonel were friends going back before Sherman knew the pilot. The old man had overseen the Khada's flight out of Afghanistan. On the last flight, no less. Although Sherman doubted the major knew their current accommodations, he would blow a gasket if he saw the apartment.

"Captain, I hope your students are still breathing."

"I'm not calling to complain, sir. I've got some unsettling news. Colonel Khada is missing."

Forever unphased, Sanders didn't miss a beat. "How can I help?"

"I need all the commercial sat images of my location for the last twelve hours."

"That doesn't come cheap."

"Use the team card," said Sherman.

"Alright, I'll send them over shortly," said Sanders and hung up.

"What's the team card?" asked Landers.

"It's not my Amex," replied Sherman and dialed another number in hopes Landers would forget about her question.

She wouldn't and he knew it, but Sherman's secret slush fund was none of her business. The team used it for various purchases the government wouldn't or couldn't make. Funeral extras for a fallen brother. House repairs for a widow. Surgeries not covered by the VA.

He held up a finger as Landers launched into another question. On the other end, Gournsey answered.

"Let me guess, your walk of shame ended at the nearest coffee shop and now you want a ride," said the sergeant.

"I wish things were so simple."

Upon hearing the tone of his voice, Gournsey dropped all pretext of humor. "What's the situation?"

"Colonel Khada didn't come home last night. Asal is worried sick. No one knows where he went, but we know he was at a diner early this morning."

"What was he doing at the diner?" asked Gournsey.

"Drinking coffee."

"And not heading home," added the sergeant.

"Exactly."

"Do you think he's in trouble? Or causing it?"

"I don't think this starts any other way."

"I can be there in ninety minutes."

"Check with the major first, I bought some satellite images and I need your eyes to find a match in a match factory."

Gournsey grunted in acknowledgement. "What am I looking for?"

"A dark-colored 2002 Hyundai Elantra. It was in the parking lot of Comet's truck stop around one or two this morning. I need to know which way it went, if that's possible."

"Copy that. Dark old sedan. I'll check back in sixty."

Sherman ended the call as they pulled up in front of the Khada's apartment building.

"You have no intention of telling me about the team card, do you?"

"No," answered Sherman as he opened the car door.

She leaned over in his direction. "Fine, keep your secret money a secret." Then she drove off without another word.

The apartment front door opened before Sherman got within knocking distance. Asal stood, framed by the grimy trim, looking smaller than hours before. Worry swept across her face like the wind whipped down the street.

"Did you find him?" she asked.

"Not yet," said Sherman. "But we have a lead."

She stepped back. "Please, come inside."

Tea was already waiting on the table as they sat down. Asal poured two cups and clung to the porcelain with both hands to keep it from shaking.

Not wanting to prolong the suspense, Sherman spoke quickly. "We know Zarak went to work and finished as usual. Then he went to a diner, which was also usual. Turns out he's a regular."

Asal's frown deepened.

"He ate pie, usually," Sherman clarified as if that softened the lie.

"Another woman's cooking," she snapped and then sniffed as if surprised by her own reaction. "Sorry, I'm still angry and sad and…"

"It's okay," said Sherman. "Feel it all. None of those emotions are wrong."

Asal smiled bleakly, "Thanks, but why didn't Zarak come home?"

"I don't know, but he was drinking coffee."

A deep look of confusion consumed Asal. "The only time he drank coffee was before a long mission."

The thought that Colonel Khada might fly again hadn't even crossed Sherman's mind. Zarak had no pilot's license or friends with helicopters, but Sherman didn't know about the pie either. In fact, he knew little about the colonel's life in Colorado.

"Had Zarak talked about flying again?"

"All the time," Asal said with a laugh. "He misses it terribly, but there was nothing he could do. He couldn't get a license here. None of his war experience counted and we can't afford it."

Sherman nodded but said nothing. A fresh idea had taken hold and he didn't like where it led. An ex-combat pilot. A truck stop full of smugglers. He didn't need Landers' help to connect those dots. Maybe Zarak wasn't missing at all.

"Did he mention any other job opportunities?"

Asal shook her head slowly, but not confidently. "Not that I remember. Zarak dreamed of quitting the airport and those endless bags. But they were… just dreams. We'd be homeless if he lost his job."

"And no troubles in the neighborhood, right?"

"Some boys who think they're important, but it's not worse than Kabul."

"That's not saying much. The Taliban threw a grenade through your window."

"I can handle the small indignities and petty crime because my daughters can go to school without fear of retribution because of their gender."

Sherman smiled and finished his tea. "You're an amazing mother. Dara and Esin are lucky to have you."

"Thank you, Mr. Sherman."

"Please, call me Frank."

She nodded and they sat in momentary silence until Sherman's phone rang with a call from Gournsey.

"You find my match?" asked Sherman.

"Yeah, but you're not gonna like it."

Chapter Nine

The sun reached its angular zenith as Sherman stepped outside. He didn't want Asal or the kids to overhear terrible news.

"Alright, what did you find?"

"We got four images. First is from 10:00 PM. That's our baseline. Then three more every four hours."

"Okay."

"The first image has nothing of interest, but the place was busy."

"Okay," said Sherman again, tempering his impatience.

"Our second image from 2:00 AM shows a smattering of cars, including one that matches the colonel's. Luckily for us, infrared tech has improved."

"That fits with what the waitress told me."

"Right, but here's the problem… he didn't leave. The car was still in the same spot at 6:00 AM."

"What? Are you sure?"

"Ninety percent," answered Gournsey. "The 2:00 AM

78

one is a bit of a guess, but by six, there was enough light to see it clearly. Same spot and same make of car."

"What about the last photo? I didn't see his car when I was there at 10:30 this morning."

"No, I imagine not, but it was still there."

"Don't toy with me, Sergeant."

"As of ten this morning, the colonel's car was parked across the street from Comet's, next to a warehouse."

"Still ninety percent sure?" asked Sherman.

"He's got a particular sticker on his window."

"There's no way the colonel sat at that counter for five hours sipping coffee. The waitress made it sound like he wasn't there any longer than usual. Either she is lying, or he left with someone else."

"I compared the images, hunting along the same line. There were two SUVs in the parking lot in the 2:00 AM image that were gone four hours later. It ain't much to go on, but it's all I got."

"Good work. You better pack an overnight bag and hit the road."

"Already packed," replied Gournsey. "What about hardware?"

"Ask around, but don't take anything official, and keep it quiet. I don't want people to think we're kicking down doors on US soil."

"I'll check with the boys from last night. You know me, I'm a model of modicum."

Sherman considered correcting the sergeant and his contortionist vocabulary, but changed his mind and said, "Meet at the colonel's apartment."

"Wilco."

Sherman ended the call and placed the phone in his pocket. He closed his eyes and let the sun's warmth roll across his face. The sergeant was right, he had bad news, but also a speck of hope. On the bad side, Zarak was involved in something. Leaving with another party confirmed that suspicion. The only bright spot, if you could be so bold as to call it that, was that someone moved his car. Maybe that meant the colonel would wash up again. Or not.

Either way, Sherman needed to get eyes on that warehouse sooner rather than later. Which meant he needed a ride.

Before he could call Landers, the sound of scuffed footsteps met his ears. He opened his eyes to the sight of two young men approaching. They didn't walk so much as saunter.

At the edge of his peripheral vision, Asal frantically waved at him inside like a tornado might touch down at any moment.

Trouble, he recognized, but what kind of trouble?

"Taking a nap, *abuelo*," said the kid on the left.

He was in his late teens with tattoos that crept up and across his cheek. Not that Sherman had anything against that, but he recognized the symbol from the news—a gang of sorts, although the context escaped his recollection.

While the kid on the left certainly had South American ancestry, his friend might have been from Kansas. The local boy was plump and shaded pink from the sun. Friends of necessity or convenience.

Sherman didn't move. He stood impassively like a wall and waited to see what kind of trouble had found him. At first glance, it appeared petty and delusional. Kid stuff of puffed-out chests and posturing. But even the most docile of imbeciles could go over the edge and fall into violence.

"You deaf?" said the Midwestern boy.

They came to a stop three paces from Sherman with cocky smiles, reeking of weed and testosterone. The left kid was skinny but wiry. The right kid was all weight and power. Speed and strength, but not in the same body.

"That ink on your neck," said Sherman, looking at the Latino kid. "Did you earn that?"

"*Tu puta madre*," he hissed. "Of course! I earned it by pulping a *pendejo* just like you."

"And your friend, he doesn't look the type, if you know what I mean."

"Fuck you, old man. I'll rearrange your face if you keep mouthing off."

The tattooed kid laughed and leered at Sherman, who made a quick mental decision. Trouble had certainly found him, but it only ran ankle-deep. Part of the tattoo on the kid's neck was backward and not the real thing, like a photocopied twenty-dollar bill.

"Are you guys packing?" he asked, still not moving.

The facsimile gangster reached for his shirt, ready to lift it up in some grand reveal. Sherman used the distraction to step in with his left leg and sent the right slicing towards the kid's knee.

The steel toe of his boot connected to the joint, which gave a dry crack as bone broke and tendons snapped.

While the kid howled in pain, Sherman swung an elbow into the placid nose of the Midwesterner who hadn't moved. The damage was immediate. His nose broke as intended. Blood spurted out, and like most people who experienced such trauma, the kid grabbed his face in reflexive shock.

Sherman swiveled and landed three successive punches into his hapless opponent's stomach, liver, and kidneys. He didn't go all out and left the kid breathing.

The fight ended two paces from where it began,

Reaching down, Sherman pulled up the kid's shirt hoping for a gun he could use but found nothing but a belt.

"That's a shame," he said and kneeled between the two teenagers. Both of whom whimpered in pain. "Alright, boys, if you want to eat solid food again, I suggest you listen to me closely. Are you listening?"

They nodded and whimpered some more.

"Good. Go home and play some video games. Forget about this gangster shit, it's not for you."

They nodded again and he stood up, towering over them.

"If I see you again, and believe me, I'll see you first, you'll go home in a wheelchair with a feeding tube. Do you know what a feeding tube is?"

Another round of nods, this time more emphatic.

"Alright then," said Sherman, then he walked toward the Khada apartment but stopped. His trouble was over, but the deed felt half-done. "One more thing... if you mess with anyone in this building, I'll kill you and then go about butchering everyone you ever loved or fucked. Clear?"

Sherman didn't wait for a verbal response. Fear consumed their entire bodies.

Asal waited for him inside by the window. She'd seen the entire affair and had a faint glimmer of a smile.

"Kids," he said with a shrug.

"They broke into our car. Twice."

"They shouldn't bother you anymore, but just in case, do they live nearby?"

Asal pointed down the street to another rundown apartment complex. "Somewhere over there."

Sherman noted the drab beige bricks and sagging roof,

just in case the boys hadn't fully grasped his warning. Sometimes youth had a way of blurring hard-learned lessons.

"Let's sit down. I've got some news. Nothing bad, though."

Asal made more tea, and they sat around the dining table in the cramped apartment. He relayed the information about Zarak's car and Asal jumped to her feet, almost knocking over her chair.

"Mama," Dara called out. "Are you okay?"

"Yes, my love. Can you see if Mr. Edoh is home?"

Dara looked puzzled but followed her mother's instructions.

"Mr. Edoh drives a taxi. He could take us there."

The idea of two Khada family members embroiled in the evolving mess did not sit well with Sherman. There were too many unknowns and the warning bells buried deep inside his brain had begun to softly toll.

"I'd feel better if you stayed here," he said. "I don't want to unknowingly put you in danger."

"You think he's in danger?"

"You wouldn't have called me if he wasn't."

With a deep, lung-emptying sigh, Asal nodded. "Do you think he's alive?"

"I have no reason to think otherwise," answered Sherman, which was mostly true. If the colonel's car was still there, then maybe they could expect him to return. If not, the car would head for the crusher, along with any hope of finding Zarak.

"Mama, I found Mr. Edoh."

Dara led in a man with graying hair and sleepy eyes. He was in his early sixties and Sherman guessed he hailed from West Africa.

"Mrs. Khada, good morning," he said with the warmth

of post-colonial English. "Young Dara here said you needed help."

"We do, Mr. Edoh. Would you be kind enough to give my friend, Mr. Sherman, a ride this afternoon? I know you're not working, but I would pay for your time."

Mr. Edoh smiled slowly and gave Sherman a studious glance. "Any trouble?" he asked.

"Zarak had some car trouble," she lied. "But I can't get ahold of him because we only have one phone."

"Come along," said Edoh, waving Sherman out of the house and down the street.

"I appreciate the help," Sherman said.

"Of course. Mrs. Khada made me dinner every day for a month when I was ill. Family, that's what I'd call them."

"Glad to hear that."

"Where to, Mr. Sherman?"

"Comet's truck stop off I-70. Do you know it?"

Mr. Edoh nodded, and his gray head shimmered in the sun. "Good pie, but some bad people."

"How bad?"

"Ah, my friend, it is all… relative. Is that the right word?"

"Yeah, that's what I feared. No worse than where you or Zarak grew up."

"Yes, yes, exactly."

Sherman sighed and got into the taxi.

For a relative newcomer to the United States, Mr. Edoh's encyclopedic knowledge of American politics surprised Sherman. After he exhausted Sherman's limited interest in local government, Edoh quizzed him on all the places he'd been or could admit to entering.

When they arrived at the intersection, Sherman pointed

another block up. He didn't want to hop out right in front of the warehouse or the truck stop.

"Are you sure, my friend?"

"Very."

"Okay, well, I wish you luck. Tell Mr. Khada a good hello from me when you see him."

Sherman handed the man forty dollars, which Edoh refused.

"I cannot," said the driver.

"Pay it forward," said Sherman.

"What does that mean?"

"It means take this money and help young Dara with school supplies or extra clothes."

Mr. Edoh's face lit up at the idea. "Pay it front. I like it."

Sherman slipped out of the back seat and the taxi pulled into speeding traffic. This was not a pedestrian-friendly part of town and for good reason. Besides the truck stop sitting below the roaring interstate, there were no other retail businesses in sight. Most of the buildings were ware-houses or industrial sites. One appeared to produce oil drums, another smelled of fresh asphalt. With no reason to stop, the cars sped by the narrow sidewalk with an abandon usually reserved for those escaping hungry lions on the open savannah.

The only other pedestrians congregated around a bus stop comprised of a metal bench and three plexiglass walls. The roof had long since blown away. A young woman in a cleaning service uniform sat on the furthest possible edge, trying her best to avoid the destitute man on the other side. He did not appear conscious.

Using the bus stop as cover, Sherman surveyed the warehouse. The façade didn't give away any information. A sign that once hung above the steel entrance had since vanished. If not for the cars parked on the side, he would have assumed it was abandoned.

The overflow parking from the truck stop made logical sense, but there were so many spots empty at Comet's that such an explanation felt unlikely.

Stepping back from the street, Sherman called Landers.

"Who is this?" she answered.

"Your date," he said.

"Frank, you know your number comes up as unknown."

"Yeah, that's the whole point of the phone."

"So do scammers," she countered.

"Good thing you answered."

"Anyway, I'm plugged into the city feed around the truck stop. There is a camera at the stoplight, but it doesn't cover much beyond the intersection."

"I've got some news on that front."

"Communication, Frank, is the key to a good relationship... and don't read into that statement."

"Noted."

"What have you learned?" she asked.

"Zarak arrived last night, but I expect you saw that."

"I did."

"Well, he didn't leave until sometime between six and ten. At least his car left then."

"What do you mean his car?"

"Someone moved his car across the street between the hours of six and ten this morning,"

"How do you know that? Or that it wasn't him?"

She was thinking like a cop. All skepticism.

"I don't, but my gut tells me he left with someone else around two or three. Another party handled the car bit, lest it look suspicious sitting there all day."

"What..."

"They moved his car across the street. I'm looking at it now."

"You're there?" she asked.

"Nearby."

"Christ alive. Frank, you shouldn't have done that."

Sherman said nothing.

"Well, is he in it?" she asked.

"Empty."

"Don't move, I'm on my way."

"Best if you don't," Sherman added. "I'm gonna grab some lunch at the diner."

Landers sighed deeply and he could visualize her eyes rolling.

"I'll look through the video again. Do you have any other vehicles in mind?"

"Two SUVs. Big ones."

"I take it this came from those commercial satellites you mentioned."

"Correct."

"Okay. Two big SUVs leaving between two and three this morning."

"Correct again," he said.

"And how will I get ahold of you?" she asked.

"I'll call you in an hour."

Landers didn't respond, letting her frustration end the call. Sherman took one last look at the colonel's unoccupied car and crossed the road towards Comet's.

Chapter Ten

Barb wasn't behind the counter as Sherman entered the diner for a second time that day. He took a table by a window looking out across the busy road filled with impatient commuters. Between the rows of traffic, he could just see the colonel's car. Still parked. Still empty.

"What can I get started for you?" asked the waitress.

She was younger than Barb by a decade with tawny hair and a careworn smile but wore a hardened 'I've seen it all' look. The name tag on her uniform read Doris. It occurred to Sherman that the name tags, like the job, might get passed on through the decades.

"Water and a BLT with fries," he answered, again not bothering to look at the menu for an item he knew existed.

"Coming right up."

All around, the sounds of the diner pulsed. Sherman took it all in. The clinking plates and orders being taken. The dishwasher beeps and the hissing of a grill. All of it.

The customer base at lunch resembled the breakfast crowd minus the families. Taking their place were a smattering of workers out for a bite to eat—construction work-ers, mechanics, customer service reps, and a few tech-looking guys with lanyards hanging around their necks. A different group of truck drivers sat at the counter, captivated by Barb's younger replacement.

Behind him, Sherman spotted the same group in the far back room, shielded from most of the restaurant. He hadn't seen a waitress check on them.

When Doris returned with his BLT, Sherman pulled her aside.

"Quite the convention you got back there," he said, motioning over his shoulder towards the back room.

"Oh," replied Doris and her eyes darted hesitantly towards the group. "Just the… uh, regulars," she added and hurried away like Sherman might be contagious.

Sometimes, Sherman found, you needed to poke the bear for no other reason than to find out the species. Was it a black bear that would run away or something larger that would poke back? Perhaps it was a polar bear, who would stalk its prey for miles in dogged pursuit. Either way, it was good to know, and Sherman settled in for a wait.

Sure enough, just when she thought he wasn't looking, Doris slipped into the back room. She wasn't in there long. A few seconds at most. Sherman kept eating his fries, but he knew.

"Can I get you anything else?" she asked when he caught her eye.

"What's your pie recommendation?"

Doris smiled a cheerfully fake expression. "Well, they're all so good, but my favorite is the berry."

"You've convinced me. One slice of berry."

"Any whipped cream or a la mode?"

Sherman didn't agree with either of those options. Pie was pie and should be served as such. "Just the pie," he said.

Doris disappeared and returned a minute later with a large slice of delicious-smelling pie. After taking a bite, Sherman knew why the colonel kept coming back. The sign was accurate. It really was good pie.

Sherman took his time, eating slowly and with joy. There was no rush. Gournsey was in transit and Landers buried in grainy video footage. The only immediate concern was the bear he poked, but even the most aggressive species wouldn't make a move in the restaurant. Especially if it served as the bear's cave.

Doris left the check as he finished and licked the plate. Sherman left an adequate tip considering the excellent service but tempered against her tattling. Although, she probably didn't know better. Just keeping her ears open for anyone asking about the back room. Innocent enough.

While exiting, Sherman glimpsed movement. Catching sight of his pursuer didn't matter. He could hear the guy clomping after him with big boots. The diner door opened again after he left, letting out the sounds within. The boots thumped on the burgundy carpet.

Sherman kept walking, neither fast nor slow. The pace of someone stuffed from lunch and in no hurry to get back to work. He carried on through the convenience store, past the gas pumps, and towards the outer edge of the parking lot. Sherman didn't look back, acting like he hadn't a care in the world.

The boots kept coming. Falling in quick succession as the asphalt ended.

"Hey," yelled a voice.

Sherman turned nonchalantly as if there was someone else nearby and maybe they meant to address them and not him. There wasn't anyone else. They were alone, just like Sherman wanted.

"Can I help you?"

"Yeah," replied the man, whose boots were at least size thirteen and stood an inch taller. He outweighed Sherman by a good forty pounds, although most of that was in his belly, which must have appreciated the pie. Short hair and a tangled beard stressed his wild look.

The bigger bear. They always sent the largest to intimidate, but size still didn't confirm the species.

"You can stay the fuck away from here."

"I beg your pardon," said Sherman. "Why would I need to stay away? I like the pie."

The man straightened up, stretching his frame to look larger. "Because I said so."

"Oh, and who are you?"

The man rolled his shoulders and sneered like the answer was obvious. As intimidation went, it did not impress Sherman. A black bear. Easily pushed around.

Then another man appeared from behind a semi-truck. Part of the same group. Same green shirts and stupid cargo pants tucked into shiny black boots. Only drill sergeants and desk officers shined their boots.

One-on-one, Sherman felt confident. Two-on-one dented that confidence, but it was still possible. He'd take some hits and there'd be pain. Because, unlike the two kids from earlier, these guys knew violence. It hung from them like a cloak.

"I see you brought a friend," said Sherman.

The first guy chuckled and glared at Sherman like he was a dog that needed kicking. "I told you to leave, but you ain't done so yet."

"Yet, I believe is the operative word," Sherman replied.

"Yet implies there's still time," said a third voice, who stepped out from behind a panel van.

Sherman hadn't heard him approach, so the newest arrival had skills, or he was getting old.

"Look, guys, I'm just out for lunch. If I disrespected the waitress or something, tell her I'm sorry."

"Lunch and breakfast," said the third man, who hadn't got the uniform memo. He had the same green shirt but wore jeans and combat boots. Nothing shiny about them. Scuffed and well-worn. Same as Sherman's, right down to the size. He also didn't need an aggressive haircut. Authority exuded from him.

"I like a greasy spoon," Sherman added but could see his ruse was over.

"Luckily for you, there are plenty in this fine metropolis," replied the third man.

He spoke with a southerner's flair for words but without an accent.

Sherman felt the sudden weight of his tactical error. He'd led the first guy towards the edge of the parking lot so no one would witness him sucker punch the guy. Now he was in a corner. Three-to-one fights ended painfully in his experience, unless he had a weapon, which he didn't.

"Time is up, friend," said the third man.

Like the crack of a starting pistol, the other two goons plunged forward, moving their heavy frames with vicious intent. Sherman bounced on his feet, waiting to break the first guy's clavicle. The gap between them vanished. Not bears at all, but wolves.

A trill car horn blared right before the collision and the pain. The two men froze. Sherman stepped back.

Behind them, laying on the horn with her window rolled

down was Agent Landers. Her left hand draped out the window. Her hair stayed down, not the usual ponytail.

"Hey, honey," she shouted with milky sweetness. "Did you go to lunch without me?"

Under a sudden public eye, the men retreated but kept their gaze on Sherman. All the way back they went, glaring at him like angrily fixated spotlights.

Once inside the car, Sherman spotted her service pistol wedged between the seat and console. He knew she had it pointed at them through the door, ready for use.

Landers wasted no time exiting the parking lot with a chirp of the tires.

"I see you made some new friends," she said a few blocks later as they sat at a stoplight.

"Thanks for the save."

"Call the press," she announced. "Frank Sherman admitted he needed help. I'm marking this day in my diary, and no, I don't have a diary."

Sherman smirked through the hazing but knew she was right. He'd been careless, wandering in without a safety net.

"Your friends," continued Landers. "Did you get any names or who they work for?"

"The conversation wasn't so congenial, but one was ex-military. Wore the same boots as me. The other two were paper tigers."

A tilt of Landers' head showed her confusion.

"Like rent-a-cops," he added.

"Interesting, and why did they corner you in the parking lot?"

"I poked the bear, ever so gently, but they recognized me from earlier. Stupid me thought I'd get one or two alone in the parking lot and have a little chat."

"Lucky that I showed up."

Sherman shrugged. "I would have taken them. The first guy had a bad knee and the second hesitated with his first step, but you'd probably be taking me to urgent care, and I would have bled all over your car."

If Landers hadn't known Sherman, she might have shown surprise at this apparent display of ego, but she knew him and accepted it as truth.

"What did you say to them?" she asked.

"Very little. I joked about the guys in the back room. Nothing else."

"Maybe they were expecting someone to show up."

Sherman shook his head. "It didn't feel that way. It was reactive, but they're an organized bunch. I bet they have control over the security cameras or maybe even their own. One guy following me out says cocky, two guys says they're worried, three guys says they're prepared and willing to act."

Landers drummed her fingers on the steering wheel as they went. "That tracks with the phone call I got."

Sherman's eyebrows popped up with interest. "The reporter trick worked?"

"It did. Got a call from the Special Agent in Charge telling me to zip it."

"That's it?"

"He's in charge of Major Crimes in the region. Which means whoever operates that truck stop is part of a serious criminal organization."

"Shit. Colonel, what have you done?" muttered Sherman.

"A task force like that usually deals with the cartels or terrorism."

In Sherman's mind, terrorists were an everyday experience, but what he'd seen didn't fit with ISIS or Boko Haram.

"Domestic terrorism," added Landers as if reading his confusion.

The phrase didn't sit well with him. He knew a lot of guys —old team members who voted one way and looked the part —but they weren't terrorists. Were they patriotic? Yes. Bored? Perhaps. Misguided? Maybe. Terrorists? Not a chance.

"Did this Special Agent in Charge admit to the surveillance?"

"Denied it out of the gate, which means, yes, the place is under constant surveillance."

"And I thought military politics was bad, you all are on another level of disfunction."

"Just the way J. Edgar liked it," Landers added.

Sherman scratched what remained of his beard, which wasn't much more than stubble since leaving Afghanistan.

"We're playing on your turf, and I scrapped my play-book. What's the next move?" he asked.

Landers eased off the freeway and headed toward the Khada apartment.

"First, I have some video footage we can look through, but I'm curious… what would come next in your playbook?"

Sherman gave her a hard, no-nonsense look. "I'd wait until one of those guys left for home, scoop him up on his way, cut him until he talked, then dump him in the woods with a hole through his head."

Landers nodded but showed no signs of shock. After all, she'd seen him operate before.

"Let's start with the video," she said.

"And then?" asked Sherman.

"Dinner, or did you forget?"

Chapter Eleven

Roasted lamb overwhelmed Sherman's senses well before they entered the Khada's apartment. He smelled it as Landers parked her car. The rich aroma carried him back in time and place.

He was younger then. President Bush Jr. had just made his famous Mission Accomplished speech on board an aircraft carrier off the coast of San Diego. While America held its breath over Iraq, the war in Afghanistan kept grinding. Sherman was a lieutenant then and recently adopted into the special forces teams. Hearts and minds was the goal. Nation building said the generals, but all Sherman did was ambush Taliban fighters or anyone old enough to look the part.

In August of that year, Sherman's team rotated into a valley that looked to be carved from stone. The rock walls fell down the steep slopes with such vertiginous speed that it made one motion sick to behold. Where the sides ended, lush green fields of barley and sorghum began. Through the center flowed a small river that raged torrentially during the rainy season.

For Sherman's team, their orders were simple. Win over the villagers who farmed the valley and disrupt the Taliban supply lines coming in from Pakistan.

Neither task, so easy sounding on paper, was possible. They could kill the Taliban, but the men in the village were all Taliban, just not all the time. On some nights, they'd dust off their Soviet-era rifles and shoot Sherman's outpost full of holes. On other nights, they'd hold a feast and invite the Americans.

During one such event, when all the men gathered, Sherman enjoyed roast lamb for the first time. Under a vast black canvas of twinkling stars and intermittent electric lights, the village feasted. All the fighters put down their guns, except for the Americans, whose rifles dangled from slings. People who tried to kill each other that morning, drank tea together and ate. Oh, what a feast it was. That night, Sherman fell in love with Afghan food, perhaps the country too, and strangely, maybe with the war itself.

All those memories came rushing back like that valley river after a week of rain. He smiled wider than he had in months, but it was bittersweet. For when he opened the door, Zarak was not there to greet him. The hole he left was palpable, but Asal didn't let it slow her down. She threw herself into the meal, but Sherman knew it was only a temporary distraction. A momentary reprieve.

The man who filled the room was Sergeant Gournsey. His bulk made even the largest chair appear small and the Khada's furniture was modest.

"About time," he said when Sherman and Landers walked in.

The smell so distracted Sherman that he hardly heard the words.

"Are you going to introduce me?" asked Landers.

Garlic and mint filled Sherman's thoughts that it took a moment to anchor himself in the present.

"Special Agent Megan Landers, meet Sergeant Raylan Gournsey."

Gournsey extended his ham-sized hand to Landers. "Nice to meet you, ma'am."

"Don't ma'am me," she replied, but the thin edge of a smile crept across her face.

"Sorry, ma'am," said Gournsey with his own mischievous grin. "I hope your leg healed up alright."

Landers glanced at Sherman with a troubling question on her lips. "He knows?" she mouthed.

"I told him some particulars about what happened."

Landers returned her gaze to the sergeant. "I imagine you know a lot of skeletons in the closet."

Gournsey gave a lighthearted shrug.

"He's why they're skeletons," added Sherman.

Asal came out of the cramped kitchen to serve them tea. She looked tired but determined.

"You didn't have to make all this," said Sherman. "But it smells divine."

"I was going to make it anyway, maybe Zarak will smell it and come home to us."

Sherman smiled politely and Asal wiped away some tears.

"The lamb won't be ready for a few hours. Please have some tea and dates."

Landers, Gournsey, and Sherman sat down at the one and only table to savor a glass of mint tea.

"Where were you?" asked Gournsey.

"Lunch at the diner," said Sherman.

"More like almost getting his ass kicked in the parking lot, unless you call that lunch," Landers added.

Gournsey started laughing, booming a deep-throated bass. "You poked the bear, didn't you?"

Sherman scratched his ear sheepishly. "I may have."

"What species of bear did you find? Wait, don't tell me, uh… a nice big brown bear with more snarl than teeth."

"Wolves," Sherman replied.

Gournsey's smile soured. "What are wolves doing here?"

"Not sure, but it doesn't bode well."

Leaning forward, Landers whispered, "Can someone explain the fucking metaphor to me? I thought you were poking a bear."

"We're the wolves," Gournsey answered. "The captain is saying he saw one of us today."

"The guy with your boots? I thought you didn't recognize him."

"I didn't," said Sherman. "But I know him just the same."

"That could help us," replied Landers. "It means he's in the system."

"Remember what happened when you searched for my records?"

Landers reflexively reached for her wounded leg. "Vividly."

"Let's watch your video footage," Sherman said, trying to pivot from her painful memories.

After rummaging around her bag, Landers produced a small laptop. "I downloaded this earlier. It starts with Zarak arriving and then runs for another two hours."

Landers hit play and grainy images flowed in stumbling succession with a slow frame rate.

"Here," she said and stopped the video with her outstretched finger pointing to a dark Hyundai Elantra. Even with the poor quality, Sherman recognized Zarak behind the wheel.

"Just after one, as usual," said Sherman.

Landers hit play and let it roll. All eyes remained glued on the pixelated screen.

Forty minutes of traffic passed, and Sherman was on his third cup of mint tea when Gournsey tapped a button.

"There," he said.

Landers and Sherman leaned in and squinted.

"What are we looking at?" she asked.

"The SUV. It turned toward the truck stop five minutes ago and now it's pulling out."

"Gas?" asked Sherman, whose eyes hurt from a long day that began hungover. The camera didn't show the truck stop, so it stood to reason they stopped to refuel.

"Can you go back?" asked the sergeant.

Landers deftly moved the video backward until the SUV turned into Comet's.

"Did you see it?"

"No," replied Landers and Sherman.

"Play it again."

Once more, the smudgy SUV rolled into and out of view.

"Looks like two people in the front," said Landers.

"The back window was half-open," added Sherman. "I didn't see anyone else."

Gournsey nodded. "Now go forward to when it left."

With a few keystrokes, the SUV reappeared, this time,

pulling out of the truck stop. When it turned right, the same window was visible.

"Wow," exclaimed Landers. "You have an expert eye."

Sherman patted his friend on the back and said nothing.

On the screen, for a brief frame, Colonel Khada was visible sitting in the back of the SUV.

Landers scribbled down the license plate and pulled out her phone. She started inputting the number but stopped. Her eyes narrowed.

"You're worried it's flagged," said Sherman.

"I am."

"Can you tell?"

"Not really."

"The major could do it," offered Gournsey.

Sherman nodded and the sergeant stepped away to make the call.

"Did they come down on you that hard last time?" asked Sherman.

"I'd like to keep this posting," answered Landers. "I could end up in Alaska and then my leg would really hurt from the cold."

Sherman understood. She didn't want to lose her career over a case that wasn't even hers, even if the cause was worth it.

"I appreciate your help," he said.

Landers smiled at him but didn't reply as Gournsey returned to the table with a note.

"The major ran the plate. It came back registered to a holding company. MFL Inc."

"Who owns that?" asked Sherman but guessed the answer.

"Unknown," answered Gournsey. "It's all a shell game, but the major is looking into it."

"Is that Zarak?" screeched Asal, who stood behind them, wide-eyed with shock.

Gournsey turned in time to catch the bowl that tumbled from her hands.

"Yes," answered Sherman. "He went to the diner after his shift and got into that SUV about an hour later."

"But... but why?" she stammered.

"We don't know," Sherman replied. He moved the image back a few frames until the driver and front passenger were visible. "Do you recognize them?"

Asal leaned in until her nose almost touched the screen. "No, I don't think so."

"Do you?" asked Landers. She was looking at Sherman.

"No one that I saw at the truck stop."

Dejected and unnerved, Asal moved back into the kitchen. Gournsey followed her with the bowl.

"Can we track them with other traffic cameras?" asked Sherman, unwilling to drop what little steam they'd gathered.

"They're turning toward the freeway. We'll never catch them."

"What's the timestamp?"

"1:55 AM."

"Sergeant," said Sherman, and Gournsey poked his head out of the kitchen. "Do you have those satellite images handy?"

A moment later, they were zooming in and out of Gournsey's phone.

"If they got on the freeway at 1:57 AM," said Gournsey. "Factoring in acceleration, they could have made it about three miles."

"Say five as a buffer," said Sherman.

"Assuming they didn't get off," added Landers.

Gournsey moved five miles east of the center and they stared. The work was painstaking. Nighttime images were normally useless, but these were infrared, which gave them some advantage. Still, the task proved impossible.

"Never mind," said Sherman.

He rubbed his eyes and tried to focus on the problem at hand.

"Scoop 'n shoot?" asked Gournsey.

"Is that what I think it is?" asked Landers.

Sherman nodded. "Our playbook."

"No, not going to happen," she replied and crossed her arms for effect.

"Can your friend at Denver PD run the plates? Maybe they got a speeding ticket or something." Sherman was swinging in the dark, but he kept going.

"I'll try," she said and stepped outside.

Gournsey leaned in and whispered, "Are we going to acknowledge the fact that Zarak went willingly?"

"Define willing," said Sherman.

"Fine, not under obvious duress. No gun to the head or anything like that. The waitress didn't mention any disturbances."

Sherman nodded, then shrugged. "They could have threatened Asal and the girls. He'd do anything for them."

"Maybe he is doing it for them. I can't imagine baggage handlers get paid well."

The possibility intrigued Sherman because he knew the colonel as a man driven to succeed. He wouldn't have been the first person to step over a few gray lines to get ahead.

"Wouldn't he tell her?" asked Sherman.

"Maybe he forgot or didn't think things would take this long. Besides, Asal would have talked him out of anything illegal, so maybe he couldn't tell her."

"Assuming it's illegal," Sherman replied.

"You think a lot of legitimate stuff happens there at two in the morning?"

Sherman said nothing and the sergeant rested his case.

The grin on Landers' face when she slipped inside gave both men a modicum of hope.

"No speeding ticket that night, but that particular SUV received multiple parking tickets at the same location in the last week."

Both soldiers stood in unison.

"Asal, we'll be back for dinner," yelled Sherman.

A hand popped out of the doorway and waved.

"I'll drive," said Landers.

"Shotgun," called Gournsey.

Protesting was useless. Sherman learned that the hard way. The sergeant just didn't fit in most back seats.

Chapter Twelve

The sun lumbered towards the mountains. Afternoon, but not quite evening. Golden leaves of an aspen rustled nearby, but Sherman couldn't hear them. The road of jets and turboprops drowned out what little idyllic nature remained across the street.

They'd parked right in front of the airport, which wasn't possible for most commercial flights, but the address Landers got wasn't Denver International Airport. Instead, they found themselves front and center at a private facility.

"How did they even get a ticket here?" asked Gournsey.

"Construction," replied Landers. "They were re-doing the parking lot or something."

Sherman's experience with flying was mostly military, but the lack of structure amused him. There were no arrival or departure signs. Not bag drops or car rentals. Only four enormous buildings with numbers on them and signs that read CoJet and DeluxeCharter.

"I saw a helipad on the way in," said Gournsey.

The colonel only flew helicopters in the war. Mostly

excess Soviet birds and the rare American leftover. What-ever the Afghans got on the cheap.

"Assuming they took him here," added Landers.

"He doesn't have a lot of other marketable skills," Gournsey suggested.

"Neither do we," said Sherman and both men laughed at the truth.

"What do you think he was transporting?" wondered Landers.

Sherman shrugged. "People, guns, drugs, or money. Pretty much anything you can fit."

"Wouldn't they be tracked?" she asked.

"In theory," answered Sherman as he motioned towards Gournsey.

The sergeant started searching for flight records. Most of them existed within the public record and he dove in. The younger man had a knack for technology that Sherman did not. At least he did not choose to use it often.

"I only see one departure last night, but it doesn't have a flight plan and radar only shows it going across town."

"He could have flown NOE from there," said Sherman.

"NOE?" asked Landers.

"Nap-of-the-earth, or hold on to your pants as we like to say," added Gournsey.

"Below radar," said Landers.

"Yeah."

"If he left from here last night, what was he doing?" she asked.

"Delivery," offered Sherman.

"Or a pick-up," added Gournsey.

"Either way, disappearing like that makes sense only if you're doing something you shouldn't," said Sherman. "Or surprising a bunch of Taliban while they're cooking breakfast."

"They never saw us coming," said Gournsey with a smile.

Landers said nothing because it wasn't worth asking. They'd never give her a proper answer about that mission.

She started the car. "Well, boys, I don't think sitting here is going to help. And from what you're saying, neither will going in search of the helicopter."

Sherman agreed but didn't enjoy sitting still. The colonel's disappearance had turned on his downrange mentality. Over there, sitting still got you killed.

"I only see one option and two means to achieve it," he said.

"I'd prefer we try it my way first," said Landers. She'd seen him operate. They both knew the outcomes.

"Our way might get you in less trouble."

"Professionally, yes. But it's a moral quandary. You don't know anything about those guys at the truck stop."

"I know they wanted a piece of my hide."

"They ain't alone. A lot of folks want to mount your head on the wall," added Gournsey.

Landers frowned. "All bullshit aside, Frank, I'm trying my way first. If that's a problem, then we need to part ways."

"Like I said, I'm following your lead. We'll keep them holstered," Sherman replied, but added a silent 'for now' in his mind. A fact, he knew, Landers fully understood. First-hand experience and all.

Gournsey nodded solemnly like a kid with a pinkie promise when Landers glanced his way.

In the distance, beneath the fancy private jet signs, a black SUV pulled up to the curb. Sherman assumed it was a car service. A Suburban or Tahoe. Whichever GMC was bigger. After all, he wasn't a car guy.

Two people got out—a man in a silk shirt and pants that shimmered in the afternoon light. Not a typical chauffeur uniform, but Sherman had never been chauffeured. Maybe the black suit was out of style. Maybe it came from an app on someone's phone.

Beside the man stood a woman with long blonde hair and pale skin. She wore a dress, but more than a dress—an entire ensemble with a purse and jacket and a belt big enough to make a WWE star jealous. Yet her shoes looked almost sensible. Like someone who was on her feet all day.

"Are you seeing this?" asked Gournsey.

"The life of luxury," Sherman replied.

Landers shifted into reverse but then hesitated. The doors to the private charter building opened and the spectacle grew.

Out tumbled a half-dozen young women dressed like they'd walked straight out of a Las Vegas nightclub. Even with the mildness of fall, they weren't wearing enough clothing to stay warm.

Landers shifted back into park.

Another guy, bald and muscular, followed them out. Security, Sherman assumed. The group gathered by the SUV. Gesturing ensued. Not all of it friendly.

"I don't like where this is going," said Gournsey.

Landers glanced between the unfolding chaos and her phone. She didn't respond but her body stiffened.

The woman with the sensible shoes pointed her finger at one of the young women, who said something.

Then came the slap.

The sensible shoe lady reared back and walloped the poor girl who didn't see it coming. She stumbled back into the bald guy, who then pushed her forward like a bouncy ball between two walls. The woman landed in the arms of shiny pants, who grabbed her by the hair and tossed her forcefully into the SUV.

Chastened by the sudden violence, the other women followed her inside the vehicle. Then they were off like nothing out of the ordinary.

Before Sherman could reply, Landers pulled out after them. Gournsey looked pleased with the possibility of a fight, even more if it was against abusive assholes. Growing up in Kentucky, he'd seen his fair share and Sherman knew the sergeant would gleefully break their bones.

"I thought we were keeping things holstered," said Sherman as Landers weaved through traffic in pursuit.

"How much do you want to bet those girls were trafficked?" she asked, her voice rising. "Tricked and sold like livestock to the highest bidder."

"I wouldn't bet against you," Sherman answered. He'd seen too many terrible things to doubt her.

"Nor should you," she replied and handed him the phone. "I ran the plates of the SUV. Guess who's listed on the registration."

"MFL Inc. Small fucking world," said Sherman.

"The same?" asked Gournsey.

"The same company that took Colonel Khada for a ride this morning," she said.

"Different players, though," said the sergeant. "Those two weren't the ones who picked up Zarak."

"Are we following them all the way?" asked Sherman.

"Yes," grunted Landers.

"And what happens when we get there?"

"I haven't mapped that out yet," she said and eased off

the accelerator as if she'd suddenly realized they'd been following too closely.

"Scoop 'n shoot?" offered Gournsey, only half in jest.

Landers exhaled in measured breaths, and when she spoke again, her tone was all business. "Once they park, we'll do a quick drive-by and then circle around. I'll let you two out if you agree to play by my rules. Understood?"

"Yes, ma'am," answered Gournsey.

"Your rules," said Sherman, although personal experience taught him that Agent Landers had a very flexible grasp of the rules.

They followed the SUV from a respectable distance. From the private airport, it headed west, escaping the tree-lined suburbs and sporadic office parks. Then they headed north towards downtown, with its growing spectacle of high-rises and towers.

The last time Sherman visited Denver, it still had a sleepy Western feel to it. Laid back but not caught up with itself. That vibe, if casual indifference could ever be called such a thing, was gone. For lack of a better word, Sherman thought of Denver as hip. A word that made him shake his head whenever he used it, even if unspoken.

Landers knew how to tail a car. Watching her navigate the complexities of the process made the soldiers smile in appreciation. Current risks aside, bumping into her was the best thing Sherman had done since landing in Colorado.

Somewhere past the giant blue bear that had Gournsey pointing in childhood glee, the SUV turned. It entered a private garage at the base of a glass-clad residential building only someone famous could have designed. The openness and lack of privacy felt anything but homely.

"Frank, you are with me," she said. "Raylan, there's—"

"A bar across the street from the entrance," he cut in. "I'll be staring into pale ale if you need me."

Long shadows fell across the streets and buildings. Sherman glanced up at the partially obscured sun.

"I told Asal we'd be back for dinner."

"I know," said Landers. "One quick pass, just to ground truth the place."

"And a pint," added Gournsey, who took off ahead of them.

"You know if Zarak is involved with this, I... I can't protect him, even though he's your friend."

They started walking towards the building. Landers took Sherman's arm. Another form of camouflage. The happy couple out for a stroll.

"If the colonel is willfully involved in trafficking women, I'd shoot him myself, but that wouldn't be half as bad as what Asal would do."

"She's a strong woman," Landers replied.

"Without a doubt. You couldn't know this, but the Taliban took her sister during the war. She went out one day—an unaccompanied and self-assured woman. Asal never saw her again."

"Oh," said Landers. "Did you know her?"

Sherman shook his head. "I hadn't met the colonel at that point."

"Did they ever find her body?"

"That's the thing. Asal doesn't know what happened. They took her off the street and then poof, she's gone. Maybe they took her to Pakistan or the tribal areas. Maybe she's some jihadi asshole's wife now. Forced into a life of servitude. Maybe she's dead."

Landers could only sigh in response.

"That's why I don't think Zarak is willfully involved.

Asal would sooner him disappear for good than see him involved in kidnapping women."

"Frank, you know an unwilling crime is still a crime."

"I'm just giving you some context if we find him alive."

They turned the corner and walked toward the tower arm in arm, her head on his shoulder, a picture of bliss. One of a dozen meandering down the sidewalk on a lovely autumn afternoon.

"We're not alone," said Sherman.

"Blue Chevy," replied Landers.

She too had spotted the car parked down the street on the opposite side. The driver looked far too comfortable to be coming or going. Chip bags littered the dashboard. The seat tilted back. He wasn't wearing a seatbelt.

"One of yours?"

Landers leaned in closer using Sherman's shoulder to hide her face from the car.

"Yeah. I've seen him around the office."

"There must be more in one of the adjacent buildings."

"Of course," she said.

"Do you want to bug out?" asked Sherman.

"No, I live four blocks from here. If anyone asks, we were out on a date."

"I haven't been on a date for so long, I must have forgotten what they're like."

"Shut up," she said but squeezed his arm tighter.

They passed the garage entrance first. A metal barricade prevented unauthorized users, but Sherman didn't see any security guards. No bald, muscular men or shiny pants. Lots of cameras, yes, but cameras didn't save anyone. The most they provided was evidence after the fact.

The building entrance had no such shortages. Keycards prevented access. Beyond the front doors, a security guard sat behind a lavish wooden desk. Sherman knew that with so many cameras, the front guard was not alone. A building that size would need at least three, maybe up to five.

"Tight security," he said.

"Expensive place. Expensive clothes. Private jets. Must be expensive girls too."

"Basic business math, unless they aren't the only product," said Sherman.

"Let's go. I've seen enough."

Arms still linked, they circled around the block and back to her car. Gournsey showed up a minute later smelling of beer.

"Blue Chevy," he said.

"We saw," said Sherman.

"The bartender told me most of the place gets rented out to rich people who show up a few times a year. That and some corporate suits coming and going."

"They could run the girls out of there," Landers suggested. "Easy access to money."

"Great," said Sherman, looking up at the tower shimmering with evening light. Pink and orange hues reflected across the surface, distorting an unseen horizon.

When Asal opened her door and the tidal wave of aromas swept over them, Sherman let his worries and anger recede away. The cramped apartment vibrated with a tenuous hope and a yearning for time lost. Roast lamb was the center stage, but all his favorites were there.

"Asal, this is amazing," said Gournsey.

"Thank you," said Landers.

"We helped," said Esin, who stood smiling by her older sister.

Asal pulled them in for a hug before turning to her guests. "My mother always said that even in the stormiest of times, the simple kindness of a meal cooked with love is all we need."

"May this storm soon pass," said Sherman.

"Please, sit down," said Asal and motioned towards the dining chairs whose numbers grew with the addition of a neighbor's plastic lawn chairs.

Of all the meals Sherman had eaten, there were few he enjoyed more. Divine food and excellent company always carried the day. If only the shadow of Zarak's disappearance had not flitted around the edges of the conversation. The girls put on brave faces, but Sherman saw their fear and worry. Zarak had always come home... until he hadn't. The cruel truth of that weighed them down.

Asal sat between them and stroked their hair until it was time for bed and all the dessert was gone.

When she returned, the lines of worry stemming from her eyes turned into great canyons of fear. She sat and streams of silent tears tumbled down her cheeks.

Landers hooked an arm around Asal's shoulder and gave some words of solace that Sherman couldn't hear.

Asal straightened up and nodded. She seemed sturdier. Bolstered.

"I forgot to thank you for earlier," she said. "Those were the boys who thought so highly of themselves and so little of others."

"Did you scare some kids off?" asked Landers.

"Something like that," answered Sherman.

"That explains the blood on the sidewalk," said Gournsey, who was still nibbling on a bite of lamb.

Landers shot him an inquisitive look. Not questioning why as she'd seen him operate, but rather looking for details.

"Local trouble," Sherman added. "Nothing to worry about."

Landers hesitated before saying, "Because they're not…"

"Walking," replied Asal. "They crawled off."

Landers shrugged and her eyes darted around. Sherman knew the trafficked girls weighed heavily, far heavier than wannabe gangsters. A fire still crackled inside her. An eagerness for justice. The same he'd seen in California. But this time, he had pulled her into the morass, not the other way around.

Chapter Thirteen

Not even the faintest sliver of dawn stretched over the plains when Sherman awoke. Darkness shrouded the street like wet wool, but Landers sat on the couch bathed in the white light of her phone. They'd all slept in Asal's cramped apartment, bloated and exhausted from dinner.

Sherman and Gournsey stayed on the floor, indifferent to the hardness after years in the field. Landers took the sofa after much protest. She too knew the stiffness of an ill-suited slumber.

"Did you sleep?" he whispered.

She glanced down at his prone form and said, "No less than I usually get."

Sherman nodded and squinted at the clock. It read fifteen minutes past four. Early, even by his standards.

"What's got you hooked?"

"The flight path of the helicopter," she replied.

He got up and took a seat on the couch.

"It ends here," she said and pointed at the map. "But there's nothing nearby. Not even a road."

Sherman looked at the map for a moment and toggled over to a topographic view. The lines and contours spoke to him, conjuring an entire world of elevations and angles from its 2D surface.

"He spotted this missing piece within moments. "Here, he went along this canyon."

"At night?" she asked.

"I've seen him do it before while getting shot at."

"If he did all that to avoid radar, then it must be serious," she added.

"Whatever 'it' is."

Landers zoomed out, revealing the Western half of Colorado. Thousands of square miles of mountains and valleys stretching out to the Utah border to the west and Wyoming or New Mexico, depending on if you turned right or left. Colonel Khada could have gone in any direction from that point.

"How do girls like that get into the country?" he asked.

"Depends," she answered and put down her phone. "Eastern Europeans get tricked into jobs with fake modeling companies. Better life. Fur coats. Fancy cars. You can imagine. Their passports get confiscated until they pay off their debt. Of course, they don't. They're told that if they tell the cops, they'll go to prison. Which is almost worse than death in their part of the world."

"Bait and switch," said Sherman.

Landers nodded. "They use the same trick around the world, but with different bait. Sometimes it's a nanny job or the offer of American citizenship. There are plenty of desperate women in the world that yearn for a better life."

"Huddled masses and all."

She nodded.

"Do they enter legally?"

"Most of the time, yeah. Either a tourist or student visa. By the time they've overstayed, it's too late. They're stuck."

"Those are commercial flights," said Sherman. "Through legal channels. What about the ones smuggled in?"

"The Chinese prefer shipping containers. I've seen how well those work. Great for microwaves, not so good for humans. They die stacked like firewood."

"Anything Colorado-related?"

"Maybe those moving north from the border. That usually happens in a semi... which stops at places like Comet's."

"If the shoe fits," said Sherman.

As they considered the interconnectedness of interstate crime, a phone rang. Sherman made a lunge for his own, hoping it wouldn't wake the girls, but it was silent. Gournsey slapped around half-awake, but it wasn't his either.

They heard Asal answer from her bedroom. The walls were thinner than an Army issue tent. The conversation was brief. It comprised 'Hello,' followed by a pause and then shouting. Moments later, Asal appeared in her doorway wearing a second-hand nightgown.

"Zarak called," she said, almost panting from surprise.

Proof of life, thought Sherman.

"What did he say?" asked Landers.

"منډه کړه," she replied.

"What?" asked Landers, louder than before.

"He told her to run," said Sherman, jumping to his feet.

Gournsey followed. They didn't need an invitation or orders. Colonel Khada's words were enough to send them into action.

"Asal, gather up some clothes and get the girls packed.

You know how this works. One bag each. Nothing more," said Sherman.

"Mama," murmured Dara, who was hugging Esin tightly. They'd just appeared from their room.

Asal ran to them. "It's okay, my loves. Daddy just called. He said we need to stay somewhere else for a few days. Go and pack your bags but be quick."

Dara, who remembered those dark days in Kabul, took her sister's hand and went into the bedroom they shared.

"Anything?" Sherman asked Gournsey who was peeing between a crack in the cheap plastic blinds.

"Nothing obvious. How much of a warning do you think he gave us?"

"I don't want to find out. Where's the hardware?"

Gournsey slid a short black case out from behind the couch where he'd hidden it for the girls' sake. The hulking man stooped with a balanced ease and unclipped the latches. Inside, sandwiched between foam, were two pistols that had probably seen action during the Soviet invasion of Afghanistan. The serial numbers meant nothing in America. Lost guns. Tossed to the wayside and thus untraceable.

Sherman picked up one pistol. An old Makarov 9mm with an eight-round magazine. Scratched and dinged and used. A trophy, just like the one his father secreted back from Vietnam.

He checked the trigger pull and slide. It appeared in working order. But he never knew until he knew. Satisfied, he inserted a loaded magazine and chambered a round.

A few feet away, Landers watched the soldier's precise movements with a look of growing unease.

"Frank," she said. "A word."

They stepped into the kitchen while a flurry of activity unfolded around them.

"We still don't know what's going on. You might be aiding a criminal," she whispered.

"I'm keeping a family safe. I've done it before, and I'll do it again if need be."

She nodded in understanding. "Fine, I get that, but the arsenal?"

"Standard operating procedure," he said with a shrug.

She frowned. "You promised to keep them holstered. Metaphorically, I realize, but now I'd like that to be literally."

He glanced down at the gun and the holster clipped onto his belt. "It stays there until I need it… and I sincerely hope we don't need it."

Landers frowned again and ran her hands through her hair. "I wish I believed you."

"Look, maybe Zarak is overreacting, but I'm not taking any chances."

"Alright, let's get them out of here but I don't like how this is unfolding," she added.

"Noted."

They stepped back into the main room to find the girls sitting nervously on the couch, each clutching a small backpack. *Déjà vu,* thought Sherman. It took his breath away to see their bravery in all the swirling uncertainty.

"Are you ready?" he asked Asal.

She nodded. "Where are we going?"

"That's step two," Sherman answered. "First, we leave." He turned to Gournsey. "I'll go first. Once clear, you follow."

Gournsey nodded, but Landers interjected.

"Take them to my car," she said. "We can convoy from there."

"Alright, you have more room anyway. Move when I tell you. Not before."

With most of the apartment lights turned off, Sherman slipped outside into the crisp autumn darkness. Only a faint glow followed him into the night. The nearest streetlight flickered and buzzed, giving off a scant amount of illumination. He waited in the dark for his senses to adjust, then set off across the mostly dirt lawn toward the cars parked on the street forty feet away.

A few steps further Sherman heard the buzz of an engine. Then came swaying lights. The vehicle turned at the corner and headed toward him. *Not a coincidence*, he thought. With an increased urgency, Sherman ran to the Jeep. He crouched behind the hood. Using the engine block as a ballistic cover if things came to that kind of kinetic outcome.

The oncoming car slowed as it approached and inched toward the curb as if preparing to park. Headlights caught Sherman's silhouette and things transformed.

The engine roared and the vehicle stole into motion. In the pale, flickering light, Sherman saw an SUV speeding forward. His pistol came out of the holster without conscious thought. He crouched lower, bracing himself.

Only the faintest of glints gave it away—a split-second image seen and processed by Sherman's brain in a way few civilians could. He ducked as great flashes of light illuminated the SUV's interior. The crackle of gunfire and breaking glass instantly filled the cool night air. Ten shots, maybe more.

As the SUV passed at speed, Sherman leaned out from behind the front hood and dumped the Makarov's magazine into the passenger's window. The booming echo behind him said Gournsey had done the same.

Tires screeched as the SUV raced down the street and out of the neighborhood, which had seen its share of shootings.

Sherman reloaded and motioned toward the apartment. Gournsey appeared seconds later, shielding the girls behind his wide torso.

"Get going," he ordered Landers, who needed no further prodding.

She'd opened the doors to her sedan. Asal and the girls piled inside. Their eyes shimmered with fear.

"Call me in five," she shouted and whipped the sedan around in a squeal of rubber on pavement.

Gournsey already had the Jeep running and in gear when Sherman hopped inside. Broken glass littered the floor. The driver's side window was gone.

"You whole?" asked the sergeant.

Sherman patted himself down and, finding no blood, answered, "For now."

"Good. Are we chasing?"

"Hell yeah, we're chasing."

The two-door Jeep surged forward as Gournsey flew down the block and around the corner in pursuit.

On paper, the Jeep was no match to race the SUV, which Sherman recognized as an oversized GMC. A Suburban or the like, he still couldn't tell.

Despite the technical shortcomings, Gournsey was a better driver. He hurtled the Jeep around corners with practiced abandon while Sherman called out for oncoming cars or clogged intersections. Luckily for them, there was only one accessible freeway entrance nearby. Sherman guessed the SUV would head for it.

After a couple of minutes of aggressive driving that nearly cost a stray cat its life, Sherman spotted the SUV.

"Up ahead. Right lane."

"Seen," replied Gournsey. "What's the call, Cap?"

Sherman wanted to unravel a long string and see where the shooters went. A failure like that would send them back to base. There would be recriminations and blame, some yelling, and finally, the resolve to try again. Which was fine with Sherman. He understood the mentality. But he wanted information from an individual, not the collective. Therefore, waiting was bad. Immediate action was better.

"Cut them off before the freeway. I want to take one alive."

Gournsey grunted in acknowledgement and mashed the accelerator. The Jeep surged forward and closed the gap. Hundreds of yards melted away. Soon, they were only fifty feet behind the SUV and still unseen as Gournsey didn't have any lights turned on.

With the engine roaring in third gear, the sergeant slipped to one side of the SUV and went in for a PIT maneuver. Where Gournsey picked up the skill remained a mystery, but he used it often.

The SUV driver saw them and panicked. They swerved hard. Trying to use the three-thousand-pound vehicle as a bludgeon against the smaller Jeep.

The GMC made a hard right aiming to smash them into a tree. Sherman braced his right arm against the dashboard, knowing there were no airbags underneath. The Jeep was practically a collector's item.

Using his significant lower body strength, Gournsey stomped on the brakes. The force launched them against their seatbelts but saved them from the SUV's path.

The night was not without the sound of crunching metal. While Gournsey avoided unwanted deceleration, the GMC did not. Having missed them, the SUV driver found a Kentucky Coffee tree instead. The trunk of which sat in the radiator's usual position. Steam hissed from the hood while the car dinged all manner of warning bells.

Sherman bolted out of the Jeep before it came to a complete stop. He ran hard for the SUV a dozen yards away. Reaching it, he wrenched open the driver's door.

Dazed by the crash and airbag deployment, the driver moaned and held his head. Sherman didn't hesitate to inflict more trauma. Using the bottom of the Makarov like a hammer, he swung hard at the driver's temple, generating as much force as he could in the confined space. Slumped by the blow, the man fell forward against the center console like a wet noodle.

The passenger, a young man in his mid-twenties, was in worse shape. His buzz-cut head rested on the deflating airbag. Blood drenched his right shoulder and Sherman knew it came from their exchange of gunfire. His boyish face was pale and sweaty. He wheezed, fast and shallow. The guy needed help and fast. Blood loss and shock were already setting in. A Level One trauma center could have saved his life.

Instead, Sherman raised his pistol and made an extra hole. He didn't think about the action or debate the morality.

Not in the least.

He pulled the trigger and moved on.

Gournsey arrived moments later to cut the seatbelt and help extract the driver. Together, they pulled the unconscious man from behind the wheel. The sergeant kept dragging him towards the Jeep with the ease of someone pulling an empty trash cart.

Sherman jumped inside and rummaged through the SUV, which was almost rental car clean. He pulled a pistol from the dead man's waist and a cell phone from the floor under the brake pedal, which must have fallen during the crash.

Then they were gone.

From crash to escape, less than a minute passed. A few porch lights popped on during that time, but Sherman didn't see anyone gawking. No sirens sounded in the distance. In the length of a Super Bowl commercial, they'd taken two lives. One permanently and the other contingent on his knowledge and cooperation.

They got on the nearest freeway on-ramp and headed west. Sherman found a map in the glove box. He started looking for sparsely populated locations not too far away. Somewhere private and not heavily trafficked. A place they could converse with their captive.

"Don't worry," said Gournsey. "I know a spot."

Chapter Fourteen

The soft but straight shadows of an evergreen danced across the man's bloodied face. He sat propped against the trunk of a pine with hands bound by baling wire. The wire was tight, and his hands were almost white from lack of circulation. Nothing about his current state bothered Sherman, who wasn't one to shy away from the gruesome side of his world.

They'd parked off some dirt road far from anywhere—a veritable black hole in communications. Yet, one ridge over, the Denver skyline rose in the distance. The spot was perfect.

Between the crash and being pistol-whipped in the temple, their prisoner looked like a banana left to bounce around a kid's backpack. Bruised and oozing. Crusts of crimson stuck to his lip.

He wasn't a young man. Late forties or early fifties. Streaks of gray laced through his hair and white dots peppered his stubble.

Sherman sat down on the dry pine needles and opened

the man's wallet. It was a good two inches thick and crammed with all the minutia of life. Credit cards. Five hundred dollars in cash, all in twenties. Receipts to Best Buy. Loyalty cards for many grocery stores and gas stations. Long expired coupons. But most surprising to Sherman was the Denver Police ID card.

He held it up for Gournsey to see.

The sergeant gave a low whistle. "Well, well. Things have certainly swerved towards the convoluted."

"Detective Darrel Bradford," read Sherman.

"I guess he forgot to take his badge this morning."

"What about the piece?" Sherman asked. He pointed at the gun Gournsey removed while loading the detective into the Jeep.

It was personal, not city-issued, but not cheap either. A Ruger American Pistol.

Sherman squinted through the morning light and held up the gun he'd taken from the deceased passenger. "Same as the shooter."

"Can't be a coincidence."

"They must buy in bulk or Costco started carrying Rugers."

"About six hundred a pop," noted Gournsey. "Nice Glock alternative."

"All the more reason to order in bulk," joked Sherman, but realized there was a kernel of possibility to his idea.

Darrel moaned and spluttered into consciousness. His eyes sprang open and squinted at the two unfamiliar faces. Pain contorted his expression, and it took him a few moments to see the full weight of his troubles.

He tried to stand up and scramble away, but only fell to one side crying out in pain.

"What... who..." he stuttered.

Gournsey propped him back against the pine like a parent righting a toppled toddler.

"Where am I?"

"Mr. Bradford," said Sherman who met the man's gaze eye-to-eye. "Or should I say, Detective Bradford? You are, what'd we call, miles from nowhere."

Darrel looked down at his lap. "I can't feel my hands."

"Yeah, sorry about that," said Sherman. "It's hard to tell how tight to bind someone when they're not squirming."

The detective's pupils expanded faster than eggs cracked into a frying pan. His expression flattened into a dark understanding reflecting the precarious moment.

"I see we're on the same page now," said Sherman.

"What do you want?" asked Bradford, his voice a hoarse whisper.

"We have questions, and you have answers."

"And then?"

"Ah, if the tables were turned, metaphorically speaking, of course, how would you answer?"

Darrel's gaze bounced between the soldiers, searching for something, be it reason or leverage. He said, "I'd say you could go home."

"If you answered truthfully," Sherman added.

"Yeah," agreed the detective.

"And if our hypothetical person answered untruthfully?"

Darrel hesitated and then answered, "I'd throw them in lockup for a night."

"Well, that's where we differ, you see. We don't have badges or a cell to put you in. But we have shovels and a lot of open ground to pick from."

The detective sniffed back some blood and looked

around as if expecting a friend to jump out saying it was all a joke.

He puffed out his chest and said, "You're making a big-ass mistake. Do you know who I am?"

Sherman turned to Gournsey. "Why do they always say that?"

Gournsey shrugged. "Denial is a powerful drug."

"Yes, of course, we know who you are," said Sherman as he held up a driver's license. "Detective Darrel Bradford. You live at 117 Welthan Court, Denver, Colorado. Age forty-eight. Height six-foot-one. Weight two hundred and five. Although, I think you lied on that last part. A little bit of rounding up on the height and quite a bit of rounding down on the weight."

"More like two hundred and thirty," said Gournsey.

Sherman nodded and said, "We don't really give a shit who you are, Mr. Bradford. We care about who you work for and why you drove that SUV this morning."

"You were the one in front of the apartment," replied the detective.

"Top-notch observation skills," said Sherman.

"A real Sherlock Holmes," added Gournsey.

"This is the part where we start breaking bones, Mr. Bradford. My friend is very fond of doing it to people like you."

Gournsey flashed an effortlessly cruel smile.

Bradford's face paled even more than his already chalky color.

"But I think we can avoid all that messiness if you answer and stop stalling. What do you think, Detective?"

"It was a contract gig," said Bradford, hurrying to get the words out. "Five hundred to drive this guy around and make sure he didn't get into trouble with the LEOs."

"Did you know your passenger?"

"Never met him before this morning."

"Who hired you?"

"This local fixer. A few of us do odd jobs now and then for extra cash. They always pay better than the nightclubs or supermarkets."

"Name?"

"Chartreuse Plumbing."

Gournsey laughed and Sherman tried to keep a straight face.

"Where do we find them?"

"I don't know. These aren't face-to-face kinds of jobs. I call and they give me the details."

"Where did you get the SUV?" asked Sherman.

"A warehouse off I-70. The keys were on top of the back wheel. The cash and a gun were inside the console."

"And the passenger?"

"He just appeared a few minutes later."

"Appeared?"

"Yeah, like he was waiting nearby or something."

"This warehouse. Was it next to a truck stop?"

"Uh, yeah. Oh, what was it called… Pluto's? No. Something outer-spacey."

"Comet's?" asked Sherman.

"Yeah. That's it."

"Tell us about this guy that just appeared."

"Like I said, I'd never met the man. He didn't give a name or anything. Just told me where to drive. We were gonna pull over and park when he saw you and told me to gun it."

"And then he started shooting at me," added Sherman.

"I swear, I didn't know he'd do that."

"But you had a gun," Sherman reminded him.

"Okay, okay. Sometimes things get a bit messy, but it's always been gang shit in the past. I figured this morning was some kind of turf war."

"Please don't lie again, Mr. Bradford. I'd hate to see you lose a toe or finger."

"Okay, okay, okay."

"After the shooting, when your passenger got hurt, were you headed to a hospital?"

"No, there were strict instructions not to use hospitals. Too many questions about gunshots. They'd log the incident, and once that happened, I couldn't help them anymore. The guy gave me an address of a local doctor that operated in a gray area."

"I'm going to need your plumber's phone number."

Bradford relayed the digits and Sherman typed them into his phone.

"Now what? I've told you everything I know. I'm sorry about earlier. It wasn't my fault, you know that, right?"

Sherman wasn't above burying the detective in a shallow grace. He detested men like Bradford. Men who played both sides. Their duplicity bothered him to no end, but he was a bit of a romantic when it came to allegiances. An all or nothing kind of guy.

"It's almost eight now. I imagine you might find your way out of here before nightfall," answered Sherman.

"Wha... what?" stammered Bradford.

"He said enjoy the hike," replied Gournsey.

The two soldiers left Detective Bradford bound and hobbled against the pine. A small magnanimity from men would never receive such a gesture from the Taliban or ISIS.

As they piled into the Jeep, Gournsey paused and said, "Seems risky to leave a loose end like him."

"You think he'll talk?"

"To the authorities? No. But maybe word gets back to the truck stop boys. The detective knows what we look like."

"They already know what I look like. Probably why the passenger started shooting."

"But not me," said Gournsey. "I could go into the diner."

Sherman laughed at the suggestion. "You're a walking billboard for trouble."

Gournsey shrugged. "I'm sure they get all types."

"I think we make a run at someone else."

"The middleman or the doctor?"

"The middleman. They might have information on what else the Comet boys have been doing. Going back to the truck stop isn't worth the risk. I already messed that up once."

"Three-to-one? I've seen you make it past those odds."

Once upon a time, thought Sherman, but if he'd done something so foolish in Afghanistan, they'd all be dead. The only other time he'd misjudged so badly, it nearly cost him everything. Only Colonel Khada's selfless bravery had saved him.

"I'd like to keep my pretty face intact," he joked and Gournsey laughed.

"I know they're wolves."

"Then you understand my hesitation," said Sherman.

"Even wolves bleed."

Sherman nodded. "Weakest link first."

The sergeant gave a big grin. He never missed a fight.

The first call Sherman made went to Landers. She and the Khada women were in the middle of breakfast burritos and the sounds of a television blared in the background.

"Where are you?" asked Sherman.

"My place," she replied.

"Are you sure about that?" he asked.

Helping a friend was one thing, but taking in potential persons of interest in a federal investigation carried serious repercussions. Sherman didn't want Landers to jeopardize her career. She'd done enough already in his eyes.

"I'm not leaving them out to dry," she said firmly. "I told Asal they're staying with me until this gets sorted out."

"Thanks. Your support means more than you know."

"Good, now you owe me one."

"I don't know if you want me in your debt."

"Oh, don't worry about that. I know what I'm getting into. Speaking of which, what did your passenger say?"

"He's still breathing, if that's what you're wondering."

"I tried not to think too hard on the subject," she said.

"Turns out he was a detective moonlighting as a getaway driver. A nice side gig to pad his retirement or gambling habit. We didn't get into specifics."

"That doesn't surprise me."

"I suppose not," said Sherman. "Anyway, we're on our way to find his contact, but I think we should burn the wick from both ends."

"What did you have in mind?" she asked hesitantly.

"We need to know more about who's running the truck stop. Zarak pissed them off. I'm not sure how, but we need actionable intel."

"I can't just go poking around a case of this magnitude."

"You'll think of something."

"Now you're really gonna owe me."

"Be careful what you wish for," said Sherman.

Landers waited a moment before replying, "Just be careful. These aren't some street-level thugs you're up against."

"I'm aware," he said and hung up.

"You're aware of what?" asked Gournsey.

"Wolves, not bears."

Gournsey nodded. "Are the girls safe?"

"They're at Landers' apartment."

The answer apparently mollified the sergeant. He switched gears and merged onto the freeway heading east.

Sherman made his second call to the number Bradford provided. Hoping the middleman might answer an untraceable call because they dealt with criminals, and criminals didn't like leaving trails of breadcrumbs the cops could follow. It stood to reason a person like that might pick up when others would not.

He dialed and waited.

A woman's voice answered.

"Chartreuse Plumbing. How can I help you?"

Middle woman, thought Sherman.

"The plumber you sent let us down with his driving."

"Who is this?"

"You know who," answered Sherman, not knowing what else to say. Either she knew or he'd misjudged Detective Bradford.

"I'm sorry to hear that. He's usually very reliable."

"We'll need a replacement."

"We can send someone else. Tell me when and where."

"No, we need to discuss the repercussions in person. We don't want any more inadequacies."

The woman paused. Sherman could hear her breathing.

"City Park. By the boathouse. 3:00 PM."

Sherman pressed his luck. His gut said he had leverage. "No. Two hours from now. Don't keep us waiting."

Another pause followed—the silence of fear and calculation. The broker needed the business.

"Two hours," she repeated with no discernable accent or age in her voice.

Sherman hung up and turned to Gournsey. "Do you know where the City Park boathouse is?"

"Not a fucking clue. You know I hate boats."

Google knew, and according to his phone, they were only sixty minutes away.

"You want to stop for coffee, don't you?" asked Gournsey.

"Don't tell me you want breakfast too?"

"What? I haven't eaten all day."

"Fine, but we get it to go."

Chapter Fifteen

Fat geese squawked in protest as Sherman and Gournsey made their way toward the City Park boathouse. Fowl blocked most of the walking paths, leaving a smelly trail of cylindrical poop in their wake.

The two men headed toward the lake in the middle of the park, approaching from the far side. The sun was warm for an autumn morning and people flocked to the wide-open green spaces in droves. Dozens of joggers ran around the perimeter. Even more people traversed across on bikes, stopping in sunny patches to spread out picnic blankets or set up lawn games Sherman could not name.

An active crowd for an active city. Sherman and Gournsey didn't look out of place. Except for the sergeant, whose size drew attention everywhere but the most hard-core of gyms.

Sherman's watch said they were forty minutes early. More would have been better, but they worked with what they had, not phantom desires.

The boathouse was more pavilion than house. Large

stone columns rose like some mini-Parthenon next to the lake. Except, this one had a roof.

A small pier jutted into the water nearby. Blue paddle-boats bobbed against the wooden structure, shaded by the neoclassical architecture. Some families were already on the water, dodging geese and the occasional geyser of water that erupted from a fountain in the lake's center.

From a surveillance perspective, the open layout and long sightlines provided ample opportunity for snooping. Unfortunately for Sherman, that also meant the broker could easily spot his approach—assuming she knew what to look for.

An unsettling thought occurred to him as he watched the swelling Sunday crowds. He didn't know what the broker looked like or if the woman on the phone was anyone important. His gut said she ran the operation. The way she mulled over his demands had an aura of manage-ment. A person capable of accepting risk. But that didn't help him pick her out of the crowd.

Conversely, if this woman was the broker and she already had an established relationship with the truck stop group, Sherman might have trapped himself. They could wait nearby behind a high-magnification scope for him to show up. One trigger pull and it'd all be over.

The thought didn't particularly bother Sherman. He'd seen enough death to know his own would likely arrive suddenly and violently. But even that was no real comfort. Just a fact.

"Where do you want me?" asked Gournsey.

Sherman looked across the lake, toward the pavilion. There were tables and chairs and a snack shop—the kind that sold nachos in a plastic container with cheese that squirted out of a pump from a giant bottle.

"Get yourself a snack and keep your phone on. I'll stay out of sight until it's time."

"Any idea who we're looking for?"

"No, not really. Maybe the woman from the call. Maybe someone else."

"Maybe trouble," added Gournsey.

He took an earbud out of his pocket. One of those Bluetooth ones that everyone wears. He put it in one ear and gave it a tap.

"Call me when it's time. Keep it on speaker, that way, I can hear what's going on."

Sherman nodded and slipped between two groups of passing revelers out enjoying the unseasonably warm morning.

Two laps around the lake revealed nothing. No sign of other parties. No obvious surveillance or counter-surveillance.

By the end, it was time to meet. Sherman called Gournsey, put the phone on speaker, and slipped it into his pocket.

Not knowing the broker meant he needed to look the part so they would find him. Sherman leaned against a prominent pillar. Not the most obvious spot, but in the top five. He crossed his arms, cranked out a frown, and waited.

The space filled up and he kept on waiting, but Sherman had the distinct sensation of being watched. His skin could feel the hidden gaze like rays of summer sun.

Footsteps scuffed behind him on the other side of the column. He turned slightly to see who and found a petite woman in her mid-forties looking back. She wore a thin windbreaker and kept her hands in her pockets. Umber hair framed a freckled face and pale skin. She was innocuous. No one looked twice, which meant no one saw her coming.

"You're late," said Sherman.

"I take precautions for a meeting like this. Precautions take time."

"What are you scared of?" asked Sherman.

"You," she answered.

"Why me?" he asked.

"Because you lied to me."

Sherman said nothing.

"You're not one of them."

"That's a colossal risk you're taking with that assumption. Maybe I'm not, but if I am, then you're in trouble."

The woman didn't blink or bite at his remarks.

"You don't have the same tattoos."

"Not everyone likes tattoos."

"They do and you don't."

"We're leaving," she said, and Sherman heard the distinctive click of a pistol hammer being cocked. She didn't need to do it. But the warning was clear.

"From the sound of that sub-compact in your pocket, I'm guessing 'no' is not an option."

"Head south," she ordered. "I'm guessing you know your cardinal directions."

He did, and the fact she guessed so told Sherman a bit more about the woman who was holding the gun.

"What if I'm a cop?" asked Sherman.

"You're not."

"How do you know?"

"Cops don't ask stupid questions like that. They try to talk you out of things. Keep the rapport going. Be your friend. There's a whole textbook on it."

"What does it say about kidnapping at gunpoint?"

"This is a conversation," said the woman. "It stays that way as long as I get answers."

Sherman walked south out of the pavilion and across several paths. Warm air tousled the leaves and great batches of them fluttered to the ground.

"For someone who wants answers, you haven't asked questions," said Sherman.

The woman pointed to an ancient American Elm towering gracefully over the park's edge.

"Sit down. Hands on knees, legs straight."

Sherman complied. The position made it difficult to do much of anything. The woman knew her tradecraft.

She kept standing with her finger on the trigger and her hand in her pocket.

"How did you get my number?"

Sherman smiled. She'd started the game. A tit-for-tat compilation of questions that revealed as much about the questioner as those forced to answer.

"A mutual acquaintance."

"Who?" she asked.

"He'd rather not say."

She scoffed. "Detective Bradford. I should have known. He was bait. And you don't look like one of Jordie's boys. Too pale. And Cinch wouldn't cross me like this. Not a cop because the SWAT would tackle me right now. Which leaves me wondering… who do you work for?"

"He goes by Sam," said Sherman, watching how the woman pivoted to scan the area without moving the pistol from his direction.

"I've never heard of him. Which means you're new or out-of-town."

"A bit of both," said Sherman.

"Sam… Sam…" she muttered with wandering eyes, then asked, "Why did you call me?"

"I want to know about a job on Friday night or early

Saturday morning. Two men in an SUV drove another somewhere."

"I don't get you," she said. "Are you trying to poach my roster? Because they ain't working with you. Even if you walk away from here in one piece, those boys don't like strangers. They only work for folks they know."

"Which is you," said Sherman.

"Precisely."

"Good, then you know who took that job. I need names and addresses."

"What? Who the fuck are you? You're sounding like a cop, and I don't like cops anymore."

"You said I wasn't, remember? I just merely asked the rhetorical what-if question. You answered for yourself."

"I have a fucking 9mm pointed at your chest," she growled.

"And he has one aimed at your back," replied Sherman, pointing to Gournsey who had snuck within twenty feet of their conversation.

The woman swiveled in pure reflex to look at Gournsey. He waved and took the pistol out of his own jacket, which dangled over his arm like a proper gentleman.

"Not a step closer or I'll ruin your friend's facetious smile."

Her eyes twitched back towards Sherman but only found a tree. Sherman was already up and behind her.

The gun and her hand remained hidden in the pocket, which prevented lateral movement. Good for concealment, but a newspaper or bag would have worked better.

Sherman grabbed her elbow and clamped down on the pressure points like a vice. Pain radiated up her arm. Her brain's reaction to such pain was immediate.

The pistol tumbled out of her pocket and thumped onto

the green grass. Sherman stepped on top of it for safe-keeping.

Without letting up pressure on her elbow, he checked the rest of her pockets. Sherman found car keys and a flip phone. The most basic of models. No internet or data. Most importantly, no GPS.

"Have a seat." Sherman pointed to his recently vacated spot against the elm.

The woman begrudgingly obliged, and Sherman took a seat next to the pistol. He slipped it between his legs and quickly checked the chamber and magazine. Everything about it was pristine. Well-oiled and often cleaned. The gun of someone who'd spent a lot of time around them. A cop, perhaps.

"What should I call you?" he asked.

"Does it matter?"

"I suppose not, but humor me."

"K."

"As in Kelly or Karen?"

"Killer Kangaroo," retorted the woman.

"Alright, KK it is."

She said nothing.

"Look, KK, I'd like to ignore this misunderstanding. I'm just after a name or two."

"I can't do that. Discretion is the only thing keeping me alive."

"No. Your willingness to break that discretion is the only thing keeping you alive."

KK gave him a penetrating stare, sizing him up, and then called his bluff.

"You're not gonna shoot me here, in this park, with all these witnesses."

"Why not? You were."

The broker said nothing.

"Besides," he continued. "I don't need a gun to kill you."

KK sniffed the air. It smelled of sap and decay and cotton candy. She looked resolute in her decision to say nothing. Stuck between rocks, she didn't have much choice. Death loomed in either direction. Seeing this, Sherman tried to thread the needle.

"Did you ever play twenty questions when you were a kid?" he asked.

KK frowned, but it slowly receded. "Sure."

"Let's play, for old times' sake."

She nodded.

"Animal?" he said cordially.

Nod.

"City Police?"

KK shook her head.

"Sheriff?"

Shake.

"State Patrol?"

Nod.

"Lives in Denver?"

Shake.

"Denver metro?"

Nod.

Sherman didn't know enough about Denver geography to hazard a guess of city names, but the airport was south, so he guessed that direction.

"South metro?"

Nod.

The traffic camera quality wasn't great, but the two men in the front seat were visible. One old and white. One young and not.

"White guy?"

Nod.

"Over fifty?"

Nod.

Sherman paused. Narrowing the search further required something identifiable. Something unique.

"Low ranking?"

Nod.

Which made sense. An older guy, nearing retirement, but not promoted up through the ranks. Someone like that might harbor a resentment against the badge. Maybe he needed the money to cover a divorce or gambling habit.

"Married?"

Shake.

"Tall?"

Nod.

"Did he call in sick that day?"

Nod.

Sherman got to his feet. "You've stumped me."

In the grass lay the broker's pistol, completely disassembled.

"I think it's best we forget about this conversation," he said.

KK said nothing, but her eyes said yes.

"Oh, last question. Who do you think I work for?"

"Rivals, I suppose, moving in on their operations. You're too polite for the cartel." She paused. "Sam... as in Uncle Sam."

Sherman nodded.

Her eyes flitted around, trying to grab meaning out of the air. "Not FBI or ATF. Hmm... that leaves the internationals, which means you're playing against one of your own. But judging from your question, you didn't know that."

"The world is full of surprises," said Sherman.

"And you?" asked KK.

"I'm the one you don't want to meet again. Am I clear?"

"Crystal."

"Goodbye," he replied and tossed her back the phone and keys.

Before KK could gather herself, they were gone. Disappeared into a thicket of pedestrians drawn out by the pleasant fall weather.

Chapter Sixteen

Asal tried to make sense of her new surroundings. The walls had nothing on them. The bare floors had no rugs. Lots of room but nowhere to sit. A gleaming kitchen but nothing to cook with. No food in the fridge. Lots of booze but no tea.

Her girls were on the couch watching a cartoon. They looked content, but she knew this latest spasm of violence cut deep. They'd left all that behind. She and Zarak told them so. That was their exodus story. Escaping the violence.

Now the story had changed, and they were running again. Fatherless. Rudderless.

"I'm sorry I don't have much to offer you," said Landers. She stood by the kitchen island with a polite smile and remorseful eyes.

A decent woman, thought Asal.

"It's okay. I am the one that should be apologizing. We've upended your life and intruded into your space."

Landers took a seat on a stool.

"I wouldn't have it any other way. Now, I was going to

order some groceries. Would you mind helping me pick out things the girls will eat?"

Asal sat at the adjacent stool and they scrolled through a seemingly endless selection of goods. Supermarkets had overwhelmed her when they first arrived in Colorado. Not just the size but the selection and the crowds. She didn't understand why so many versions of the same product existed.

As a child, crackers came from the baker. Either plain or with sesame seeds. Now entire aisles carried hundreds of versions. Small ones. Big ones. Fish-shaped ones. She could only wonder why.

After completing the order, Landers stood and snapped her fingers excitedly. She began furiously opening and closing cabinets until she emerged holding a battered tin of peppermint tea.

"I'm sure this is old and terrible, but would you like a cup?"

Asal nodded. She appreciated the gesture and the support.

Landers heated the water and poured two cups. The girls kept watching the cartoon and Asal didn't have the energy to stop them.

"How long have you known Frank?" asked Landers.

Asal held her mug with both hands, absorbing the warmth and comfort.

"Oh, many years," she said. "He and Zarak fought together in the war."

"Yes, Frank mentioned that. He said something about a debt he owed your husband."

"Zarak helped him in a time of great need."

"How?"

Asal smiled. It wasn't her story to tell, and she didn't feel comfortable relaying it to a relative stranger, even a kind and protective one.

"You'll have to ask them for the details." She choked back a fearful tear. "But I'll tell you what I know."

"Only share what you're comfortable with."

"Thank you. What I know is that Captain Sherman's team needed help, and none was coming. Zarak was flying in the area when he overheard the rapid calls. Being the foolishly kind man he is, Zarak landed his helicopter and picked them up."

"Under enemy fire?"

Asal nodded. She hated that part of his work but loved Zarak's conviction for doing it.

"He still has the jacket he wore that day. He won't let me sew up the hole in the sleeve. He says it's a reminder of things. Terrible but important things."

"Was he hurt?"

"No, Zarak has always been a lucky man. The bullet went through the jacket but missed his arm."

"Amazing," replied Landers.

"I worry his luck has run out."

"Don't be so sure about that. If anyone can find him, it's Frank Sherman."

"How did you meet Frank? You were both in the Army. Did you know him then?"

"No, not directly. I was an MP back then."

"An MP?" asked Asal. The acronym meant nothing.

"A military cop," said Landers. "Trying to keep order and such, but I never ran into Sherman. Those guys operated on another level."

"How so?" For all her time near Sherman, Asal didn't know that much about his past.

"Special Forces had their own world over there. Waged their own war."

"If you didn't meet then, when?"

"Ah," said Landers with a nervous laugh. "That is one of those stories best told without many details."

Asal nodded. She understood the need for secrets.

"We bumped into each other in California a couple of years ago. He was looking for someone I was investigating. Things got complicated after that. To be honest, I hadn't seen him since... until two nights ago."

"Really?"

"He came out of nowhere and took a seat at the bar next to me."

"What a small world," said Asal. The connectedness of everything still amazed her.

The phone on the counter buzzed and Asal's heart leaped and then plummeted. It was Landers' phone, not her own.

"Speak of the devil," said Landers, looking at the unknown Caller ID on her screen.

Sherman spoke quickly and precisely. He didn't mince words or add unnecessary details. Everything flowed in plain, logical English like the thousands of after-action reports he'd made.

Landers listened well. She always had. It made her a good cop. Details about the state patrolman flowed by. She wrote them down on a sticky note. Everything Sherman deemed important enough to tell her.

"Did you get it all?" he asked.

"Yes, call me back in twenty."

"We're on our way to you now."

"Even better," she said and hung up.

"Did they find Zarak?" asked Asal.

Landers opened her work laptop and set it on the counter.

"No, but they found someone that might know."

"Who?"

"That's what I need to find out."

Landers began searching through law enforcement employee records. Whittling down the list with each data point Sherman described. State Patrol records were easier to get, so it didn't take that long to create a suspect list.

Three men. All lived in the south Denver metro area. Late forties and early fifties. Over six feet tall.

Landers called the State Patrol office. A woman answered. She sounded tired.

"This is Special Agent Landers with the FBI. I'd like to speak with the watch commander."

The woman didn't hesitate at her request. "What is this regarding, Agent Landers?"

"Just checking on a possible suspect sighting."

"One moment please."

The moment turned into a minute, then two. Local agencies never enjoyed federal interference, despite their claims to the contrary.

"This is Captain Fox speaking. How can I help you, Agent Landers?"

"I'm running down some details, nothing serious," she said.

"I'm listening."

"This is a little embarrassing," she began, hoping to ease the tension. "One of our junior agents took down some notes about a suspect sighting but missed the Trooper's name. I have a list of three it might be. Can you tell me if they were on duty yesterday morning?"

"What time?"

"Two in the morning."

"The names?"

She read the names in quick succession and apologized again for her imaginary colleague's error.

"O'Conner and Bryant were on duty then. Where did this sighting occur?"

"East on I-70 near Limon," she said, mentioning a name she'd seen on a map.

"Sorry, Agent Landers, your colleague really messed this up. Neither of those Troopers were that far east."

Landers let out a loud sigh. "Well, I'm sorry for wasting your time, Captain Fox. Thanks for humoring me."

"Any time," said Fox and she imagined him railing against federal disorganization. He'd probably have a good laugh with his buddies about it over a beer.

Such trivialities mattered not. She had a name.

Trevor McNair.

Trooper Trevor McNair.

Resident of greater Denver.

Part-time criminal.

Sherman and Gournsey arrived a few minutes later. The sergeant had a giant pizza box in one hand and a bottle of unsweetened iced tea in the other.

The girls squealed with delight as the two men entered. They dashed for the pizza.

"Sorry for not asking," said Sherman at Asal's furrowed brow.

"It's not that," she replied. "I just don't think I'll ever be able to return your kindness."

"If I get to share another one of your dinners, it will be worth it."

"With Zarak," she whispered.

Sherman nodded. "Of course."

Gournsey bounded off to eat on the couch with the girls, leaving the adults alone on the other side of the apartment.

Sherman took a slice and looked at Landers. "Did you find him?"

"I did," she answered and swiveled her laptop so he could see.

"Trooper Trevor McNair," he repeated and memorized the address. "He wasn't working yesterday?"

"Not according to the watch commander."

"Do you know if he's on duty now?"

She shook her head. "Didn't want to pry."

"I appreciate the name and your help."

"Not more than I," added Asal.

They all took a deep breath together. A trio of concerns and fears mingling over a freshly baked pizza.

"When are you leaving?" asked Landers. There was no hesitation in her voice over the decision to go after McNair, just over the timing.

Sherman glanced down at the cheap Casio watch on his wrist. It told time and nothing else, which was all he needed or wanted.

"An hour. Gournsey called in a favor, and we need to pick up a few things."

"Are you gearing up?" asked Landers.

"Yeah. Between our near miss at the apartment and what the broker told me, something doesn't feel right."

"What did she say?"

"She thought we were NSA or CIA and joked about going up against one of our own."

"You don't think they're actually involved?"

The possibility occurred to both Sherman and Gournsey on the drive over, but neither man could see a reason the agencies would get involved in petty local squabbles. No, that didn't make sense with what they knew. Unless the girls on the plane were terrorists, but they looked more terrorized than anything else.

"I think she meant a single person or maybe a small group. Not the intelligence community. But the broker said it as if such a fact was common knowledge."

"Why would she think you are a spook?" asked Landers.

"Apparently, I'm too nice for the cartel," he said.

Landers laughed. Asal followed. Both knew what lengths Sherman would go. There were few boundaries he wouldn't cross. 'Nice' did not stand in his way.

"I'm going to make sure they don't eat the whole pizza," said Asal as she wandered towards the girls, who were laughing at Gournsey's attempt at some game on his phone.

"Be careful," said Landers in a conspiratorial whisper. "You don't know who else is on their payroll."

"I don't know who 'they' are," he replied.

"Exactly, but they've seen you. Hell, they probably have photos of you in circulation."

"Can you keep digging on your side?" he asked. "No one can tell me who Zarak got involved with. Just rumors and gossip."

"I'll try but I doubt they'll give up any details of the investigation without a fight."

"What if you brought them something?"

"Like some intel?" she asked.

"Something they don't have."

"They'd wonder where I got the information."

"Tell them an anonymous source or a snitch."

"I work white-collar crime. I don't have any snitches."

"Fine, what about a reporter?" asked Sherman.

"Would he mind?"

"He owes me."

She paused again. "I'll keep it vague, maybe I won't have to use his name."

"Your call."

"Remember, they're wolves," she said.

"Oh, I know. We're going hunting," Sherman said and took another slice of pizza.

Chapter Seventeen

From Landers' apartment, they headed south through a tangle of one-way streets. Past modern high-rises, brick warehouses, and the giant blue bear gazing longingly through a glass façade.

Gournsey drove.

Sherman pondered.

Somewhere, sandwiched between the river and a freeway, they stopped. The street was empty. There were no homes nearby. Only businesses. Mostly construction or fabrication-related. Not the Sunday type of crowd.

Gournsey parked in a vacant lot. Long shadows criss-crossed the asphalt. They kept their windows down, enjoying the lingering warmth. Between the buildings, Sherman saw the not-so-distant Rockies, rising like tiny teeth toward the sky above.

A few minutes passed in comfortable silence before Sherman heard an approaching vehicle.

"It's them," said Gournsey and stepped out.

A black Ford pickup pulled up next to them. Sherman

recognized the two occupants. Brothers from a distant war. Members of the same tribe.

Both held the same rank as Gournsey. Non-commissioned officers. The backbone of the Army.

Gournsey gave them back popping bear hugs. Brief pleasantries came and went. Then they turned to the business at hand. The two long duffle bags in the back of the truck.

"We brought you everything we could find on short notice," said the driver, who Sherman only knew as Parker.

"I appreciate the assistance," said Gournsey. He loaded both bags into the Jeep like he was putting groceries away.

"Care to tell us what's so urgent?" said the other sergeant who went by Thumbs.

Sherman didn't know his backstory, just the nickname.

Gournsey looked at Sherman for permission.

"A friend ran into a spate of trouble," said Sherman.

"With all due respect, Captain, that's a lot of trouble you just loaded."

Sherman nodded. "He's missing. Got involved with a nasty group."

"The human trafficking sort," added Gournsey.

"Fuckers," said Parker.

"Burn 'em down," added Thumbs.

"We plan on nothing less," said Gournsey.

"Good," said Parker. "Call if you need an extra set of hands to go with that hardware."

"We appreciate the offer," said Sherman.

The men nodded in some unspoken understanding. The truck left abruptly, just as it arrived. There and gone in minutes. Gournsey opened the bag. The sergeants had not disappointed.

Four rifles. Semi-auto. Military-grade attachments.

One suppressed MP5. The origins of which were unclear.

Two pistols. One 9mm and one .45 caliber with suppressors.

Night vision.

Helmets, the FAST type used by JSOC.

Ballistic vests. Level IV. Strong enough to stop a .30-06 round.

Ammo. Lots of ammo.

"Where'd they get all this?" asked Sherman.

"I didn't ask."

"Will it trace back to them?"

"They wouldn't have given it to us if it did."

"Then I'll shut up and be grateful."

Gournsey laughed and started loading magazines.

"Just to be clear," Sherman began but Gournsey cut him off.

"I know you're not about to give me the 'things are about to get messy' speech you've been practicing. I ain't no minor leaguer."

Sherman smiled. "I was going to say, just to be clear, if they hurt any kids, I'm not taking prisoners. They're all going in the ground."

Gournsey nodded back. "It goes without saying."

"Good. Let's gear up and go find this bent cop."

―――――――

Staying south, they drove along the river, keeping the mountains to their right. Apartments and bars and trendy restaurants faded into warehouses. Then the industrial strip faded with distance, gradually petering out into leafy streets and green lawns. The houses got bigger. The lawns widened. Old money style, but new money construction. Twenty years old, maybe less. Not quite the outer edges of expansion and suburban sprawl. More like a small town swallowed by the larger metropolis.

Gournsey turned east on a nominal thoroughfare that transected the area. Golf courses and cemeteries came and went. Gradually, the wide lawns shrank along with the homes. Post-post-war development. Split-level homes from the seventies. The heyday of the style.

From the thoroughfare, they turned south into a neighborhood called Bellweather. No street ran straight. They all looped back onto themselves, twisting like a skein of yarn.

"His house is up ahead on the left," said Sherman.

He'd memorized the address and location within the neighborhood, which served him well because all the homes were shades of white with one large tree in the front yard for shade or swings.

Only the doors differed. The one unique characteristic that people felt confident changing. Bold yellows and reds. The cop's door was, unsurprisingly, blue.

Gournsey passed at a normal speed. Just another Jeep driving back from errands or church. A slow weekend out. An elderly woman out walking her Pomeranian even waved at them. Sherman returned the gesture.

At the end of the long curving block, Gournsey parked in front of a house up for sale. Maybe they could pass as an interested couple for curious onlookers. Maybe not.

"His car is in the driveway," said Gournsey.

Sherman nodded. A 2020 Chevy Camaro, just like the DMV record.

"Getting in might be problematic," added the sergeant.

Sherman nodded again. Walking up in full tactical gear might invite calls to the police or an armed response from the trooper. A poor choice. They needed another, less obtrusive option.

"Thoughts?" asked Sherman.

"Wait 'til dark or kick down the door."

Sherman glanced around the Jeep looking for an idea. He found one in the back—sandwiched between the two large duffle bags was a small box. It still had the shipping label. A tiny part of the larger e-commerce economy. No one questioned a man carrying a box. Even without a uniform, delivery workers remained ubiquitous. An army of underpaid hourly workers crisscrossing the neighborhoods of America.

He grabbed the box, a piece of paper from the glovebox, and a baseball cap.

"This is your plan?" asked Gournsey.

"Unmarried guy in his early fifties. I bet he orders shit all the time."

"Fair point."

"If I'm wrong, you can kick down the door."

Gournsey smiled. "Damn right."

"Drop me off a few houses down."

"And then?"

"Follow me in if he opens the door."

"And if he doesn't?" asked Gournsey.

Sherman said nothing.

"Right. Kick the door down."

Gournsey didn't wait for an order. He pulled back onto the sinuous street and made a lazy U-turn.

Four houses down, Sherman hopped out and tried to look like a lost delivery driver. He checked the paper, which was nothing more than an oil-change receipt. Up and down went his head until he reached McNair's house with the blue door.

The Camaro hadn't moved. The garage door remained closed. Behind him, Sherman heard the Jeep idling one house over.

He walked up to the blue front door and rang the bell. The box remained in his left hand about chest height. Tall enough for McNair to see if he looked through the peephole.

Faint footsteps sounded from the other side. Sherman kept on smiling his shit-eating grin like it was his dream to deliver packages to crooked cops who abused the power given to them.

The door swung open with a quick jerk. Trooper McNair stood in the gap. A thick, hulking man accustomed to intimidating those unlucky enough to cross his professional path. He stood an inch taller than Sherman's six-foot frame but carried an extra mini-fridge worth of weight. Once brown hair had streaked gray at the edges and the faint edge of a second chin hung under the original. He wore paint-stained jeans and a Margaritaville T-shirt.

"You could have left it on the porch," he growled.

"Sorry," said Sherman, having already sized the man up. "This one needs a signature."

"Since when do they need signatures?"

Sherman shrugged and held out the package with the paper on top.

McNair reached out to grab it,

As he leaned forward, Sherman twisted in and let his fist fly. He aimed for the newly forming double chin and connected with the mandible full force. A perfect cross. His old man, who fancied himself a scrapper, would have been proud of the punch.

McNair's knees gave out and he sagged against the door, clinging to consciousness.

Sherman was on him in a flash. He followed up one punch with another, knocking the cop on his ass and splashing blood across the beige entryway carpet.

The guy was big and dazed, but not out of the fight. He tried to roll and toss Sherman off, using that extra mini-fridge worth of mass. Had it been someone else, McNair might have created some space. Maybe he would have gotten to his feet and fought on.

None of that happened.

Sherman caught McNair's arm like a hard throw to first base and twisted it around his body. The cop ended up face-down in a half-nelson with Sherman's knee pinning him to the ground.

Gournsey arrived moments later. In one quick but violent motion, the sergeant wrenched the trooper's wrists together and securely bound them with a zip-tie. Not the cheap crafting ones, but also not the two-loop ones used by the police. It was thick and white and cut off McNair's circulation almost immediately.

To the left was a living room of sorts. A TV the size of a dumpster hung on one wall and a leather couch sat against the other with a cheap coffee table in between. Gournsey pulled the cop across the room face-down with the ease of a parent dragging a reluctant toddler attached to their leg. He dumped McNair on the couch and Sherman took a seat on the particleboard coffee table facing the bloodied trooper.

"Mr. McNair… can you hear me?"

The cop's head lolled from one side to the other in a great elliptical path. Finally, it came to rest.

"I did what you asked," he said. "I dropped him off and left."

The sudden confession confused Sherman, who glanced at Gournsey.

"Where did you drop him off?"

"The airport, as instructed. Please, I didn't know."

"Explain how you didn't know," said Sherman.

"We didn't talk on the ride. I can't read minds. How was I supposed to know?"

"Know what?" asked Sherman.

McNair stopped speaking and looked first at Sherman, then at Gournsey.

"You're not them," he said.

Sherman shook his head slowly. "No, we're worse."

McNair moaned and hung his head.

"You're going to tell us what happened and why you apologized. I want specifics. Who you picked up... when you did it... where you took them... and why you think I'm someone else."

"No," replied McNair with an aura of defiance.

Without hesitation, Gournsey stepped over and kicked the trooper's shin so hard, it bent in two, angling inward unnaturally. McNair screamed out in pain. His body spasmed with shock.

"Stall again and he breaks the other leg," said Sherman.

"But... but..." whimpered McNair.

"None of this 'but they'll kill me bullshit'. If you want to make it through the hour, you need to talk with me. Prioritize the here and now."

McNair nodded. Blood dripped from his nose onto the couch.

"Who did you pick up?" asked Sherman.

"Some guy. We didn't exchange names."

"Describe this guy."

"Indian dude, I guess. Not sure about that part of the world. They all look the same."

"Where did you pick up this Indian dude?"

"Comet's truck stop."

"When?"

"Yesterday, early morning. Around two, I guess."

"Where did you drop him off?"

"The airport. Always the airport."

Sherman frowned. "This wasn't the first time?"

"No… no. A few times before."

"Same guy? Are you sure? Even though they all look the same."

McNair nodded. "Same."

"And what happened that made you apologize to us?"

"He took the girls."

Sherman tried to shrug off his confession, but it hung like a wet towel over his perfect image of Zarak.

"Where did he take the girls?"

"I don't know. No one knows. That's the problem. They're property. And they don't like lost property."

"This Indian guy flew off with some girls and then disappeared?"

"Haven't you been listening?" howled McNair. "That's exactly what I fucking said."

"And who are they? The people who don't like to lose things."

"Them."

"Trooper McNair, be more specific or I can let my friend break your collarbone. An easy bone to break. Hurts like hell. Not much the doctors can do either."

The cop stared at his broken leg and groaned.

"They call themselves The Company or something like that. I don't know why or who. I get paid through a broker. No direct contact. It's part of the rules."

"But you know what they're called."

"People talk. Gossip. Watercooler nonsense. I didn't think it was real. Then suddenly it was."

"And this guy you picked up. Do you know what happened afterward? It seems you're more knowledgeable than you think."

"I overheard a call afterward," said McNair, breathing fast from the pain and fear.

"When? Be specific."

"Uh, I... I didn't look at my watch. It was later. The sun was up."

"What did this call pertain to?"

"The guy we dropped off, the Indian fellow, he was picking up a bunch of girls from somewhere... I don't know where, I swear. Anyway, he never dropped them off. They just disappeared."

Sherman started shaking his head in comic disbelief. He'd never truly doubted the colonel's moral compass, but here was proof that Zarak didn't stray or bend. He'd hidden the girls to keep them safe. Sherman was sure of it.

"What else did you hear?"

"Yelling and cursing. Those girls cost a lot."

"You said the call came after sunrise. What were you doing for four hours after dropping him off?" asked Gournsey.

McNair looked down at his broken leg, gingerly running his fingers over the unnatural bend, wincing as he went.

"Answer me," Gournsey bellowed. His eyes widened into large orbs of anger.

"We dropped off some girls downtown and then picked up some more from a trashy motel off Colfax."

"Where did you take them?" asked Gournsey. His voice was dangerously low.

"A warehouse near the river," answered McNair in an equally quiet tone.

"And then what happened?"

McNair silently sobbed.

"I don't know. I stayed in the car."

"Bullshit," said Gournsey. "You know. What happened to those women?"

"I heard shots and screaming."

"You heard shots and screams," repeated Gournsey. "Well, you're a cop. Tell me what happened."

"Retirement. The guy I drove around with from The Company said they were having a retirement party. The girls had paid off their debt."

"And you said nothing!" roared Gournsey.

He was standing over McNair in an all-consuming rage.

"No," muttered McNair. "I couldn't. They would have killed me on the spot."

Under more pleasant circumstances, Sherman would have talked down Gournsey's sodden anger to a level of intense dislike, but he didn't care for McNair or his ilk, so he kept quiet and said nothing.

The sergeant's wrath ballooned until he burst and smashed the trooper's face clean through the particleboard coffee table.

After that, only silence remained. No whimpering or lies or truths. Just the muted drip of blood onto the carpet.

Gournsey sat down on the couch and took a deep breath. Abuse of young women always boiled his blood. Sherman was aware of it, but he couldn't do anything about it. The sergeant never confided why it caused such ire, but Sherman knew it involved a sister from back home in Kentucky. Judging by the damage to McNair's skull, whatever happened all those years ago must have been truly terrible to still haunt the man.

"I may have gotten carried away," Gournsey said.

"It happens. I'm not losing any sleep over this."

"At least the colonel is still doing the right thing."

Sherman nodded. "That he is."

"We need to find him before the wolves do."

"Or kill the wolves," said Sherman.

"That's even better."

Chapter Eighteen

Behind the relative privacy of her bedroom door, Megan Landers was hard at work writing an email. No one at the bureau called anyone unless they were in trouble. It reminded her of childhood. Whenever her mother used her middle name, she knew the proverbial rock was rolling downhill... like the time she found a love note in Megan's pocket. Nothing more than seventh-grade infatuation, but her mother called out 'Megan Tiffany Landers'. That night didn't end well.

Typing up the email involved considering every word. Turning them over like precious stones. Seeing how they sparkled from every angle. Landers hated doing such laborious work to make sure so-and-so didn't get hurt by clear and concise language. They always took it personally. The Army taught her brevity, but no one in the government seemed to use it.

She hit send on her well-considered request for more information about the task force. The reference to an anonymous source was bullshit, but the rest was true.

Landers had a personal interest in the case and her request did not jeopardize any ongoing investigation—at least she didn't think it did.

The only threat she knew of was Frank Sherman, but he only threatened someone's glory, not the act of justice. Thinking that made Landers worry about her own career. Sherman operated with no guardrails. Best to get what he wanted to know before he burned the place down in search of answers.

A few minutes later, while considering how crazy things were, her phone rang—a work number. The phone knew as much. She almost didn't answer. It was Sunday and she didn't want the headache. The labyrinths of government bureaucracy. It hurt her soul. The paperwork and red tape. The list went on.

She gave in and tapped the green button.

"Agent Landers speaking."

"What kind of flaming horse shit just landed in my inbox? You better have a good fucking rationale to ask for such a brazen request. There's a reason you're not on the case, Agent Landers. Need I spell that out to you? Or have you completely forgotten about your mess in California?"

Landers took a silent breath. She recognized the voice despite the lack of introduction. Special Agent in Charge Harrington. The asshole without decency of decorum.

"Sir, I meant no disrespect. I've had several reporters reach out regarding a story about human trafficking in Colorado. They mentioned Comet's Truck Stop by name. I'm just looking for some cursory notes to make sure they're dealt with properly."

"These reporters shouldn't be calling you in the first place," said Harrington.

Ego reared its evil head and Landers choked down a biting retort.

Instead, she said, "I think it's for the best if they don't know you're in charge. Such a senior official only shows the seriousness of the investigation. If a reporter found out, so would the criminals."

The Special Agent in Charge remained silent.

"I'm happy to deflect on the matter, sir. God knows why they're calling me. Probably just a name in the directory."

"The weak link," said Harrington.

Landers bit her lip. She wanted to break his jaw and see who was weak. Worse, she wanted him to feel the full weight of his own inconsiderate bullshit, but she kept it to herself.

"The reporters mentioned dirty cops," she added, poking her own proverbial bear.

Silence followed.

"Sir?" she asked.

"It's a small team and a large case, Landers. I can only give you the vaguest of outlines."

"Just enough to hold my own if they ask again," she said.

"Fine, but if any of this shit lands on the front page, it's your ass on the line."

"Understood, sir."

He cleared his throat and began, "We believe an international criminal organization is operating in Colorado, primarily smuggling women into the country. They then forced these women into various forms of sexual slavery. I imagine you know the process."

She did and tried not to take his tone personally. She knew because she was a good cop, not because she was a woman.

"One of their hubs appears to be Comet's Truck Stop. Ease of access and good infrastructure makes it ideal for moving people and goods."

"Do you have any suspects?"

"None that I can say out loud, but the group calls themselves The Company. That's all I can divulge."

Landers thought back to what Sherman had said about the man in the parking lot. The one with the same boots. She took a stab in the dark.

"Sir, one more thing. The reporter suggested a link to former military personnel."

"We'll be leaving that out of any future press release."

"It's true?"

"Only if it leaks. Right now, we have everything sealed up tight."

"Understood."

"Good, now fucking delete that email and don't say shit to any reporters about this case. Are we clear?"

"Crystal," she replied.

Harrington hung up without another word.

Something about the whole mess chafed like an ill-fitting boot. They were missing something that Harrington wouldn't pencil in. Something significant. She knew it in her bones, like the smell of lavender from her mother's garden or the crinkle of her father's newspaper. The way he folded and re-folded it throughout the morning.

She was on the verge of feeling sentimental when her phone rang for the second time.

An unknown number.

Which meant Frank Sherman. Almost unknowable in his own right, but also familiar. The well-worn scratch on the dining room table. Her table.

"Yes," she answered, hedging against a scammer.

"Everything okay?" asked Sherman.

"We're fine," she said. "Did you find him?"

"We chatted. He shared some new information."

"What?"

"He dropped the colonel off at the airport but doesn't know where he went from there."

"Unsurprising. It all seems very compartmentalized."

"Agreed, but the interesting bit is what he overhead later."

"As in, he was still working after the airport drop-off?"

"Correct," he answered. "I'll get to that later. He overhead why they are so upset. Apparently, the colonel picked up a load of freshly trafficked women but didn't bring them back."

"Shit," said Landers.

Lost women meant lost revenue. Missing money created many angry people. Mad enough to send thugs out to the Khada apartment.

"He's certainly created a mess of it," said Sherman. "But I think the colonel is trying to protect them."

"That's better than the alternative," said Landers, which was Zarak taking the women for himself. As if they were property to be passed back and forth like poker chips.

"We also got a name for the outfit at Comet's. They call themselves—"

"The Company," interjected Landers.

"Ah, you reached out internally," replied Sherman, not missing a beat. "The reporter trick worked?"

"It got their attention, which I suppose is what you wanted."

"You've got to poke the bear occasionally."

"Well, the bear is almighty angry, but he gave me the outline on the case, which included their name."

"Anything we didn't know?"

"Smugglers and human trafficking. Nothing new on that front. But I threw out a curveball and asked if the suspects were former military. He swung hard. Full deflection on the question, which means yes."

"The guy with the boots."

"And others."

"The broker mentioned something about playing against one of my own. She thought I was CIA or NSA."

"That doesn't bode well for us or Zarak," said Landers.

"No, it doesn't."

"Are you going to look for him?"

"No, he could be anywhere in a four-hundred-mile radius. Maybe more if he refueled. If the colonel doesn't want to be found, he'll keep it that way."

Landers saw the writing on the wall. There were two options to save Zarak. One involved finding him, which didn't seem likely based on Sherman's assessment. That left option two. Removing the threat.

"That leaves the wolves," she said.

"Correct."

"I don't think head-on is a good idea. You're likely to wind up dead or in cuffs if Special Agent Harrington finds you."

"Agreed."

"Does that mean you have a plan?" she asked.

"I have a sketch."

"Am I going to like it?"

"I'm afraid not."

Sherman's plan was straightforward. Nothing murky or deceptive. No feints or fake armies like the Allies created for

D-Day. He wasn't that kind of person. Not at his core. Speed and violence ruled the day. Not in that order but in unison.

They left McNair in his house. Exsanguinated was the technical term but the blunt force trauma also hurt his survival odds. Neither did meeting Gournsey. Sherman didn't dwell on the cop's fate. All people died. The essence of humanity was impermanence. By the time they left, he'd forgotten all about McNair but not his car. That they took.

Gournsey drove the Jeep and Sherman followed in the Camaro. It was nice as cars went. Leather seats. A fancy computer screen in the console. Most cars had those, but for Sherman, they remained fancy. He didn't own a car at all, so on some level, all cars were a novelty. And it was loud. Loud engine. Loud stereo. Loud color. Red, of course. All Camaros were red in his mind. The quintessential American color. The one cops liked to pull over. But if the driver was a cop, maybe that didn't matter. Sherman didn't care. He barely remembered the owner.

They finally stopped off at some industrial street near the river. The brick buildings were old and leaned to one side. Few had complete roofs. Most had plywood over the windows. No trespassing signs festooned the walls like beer posters and a dive bar. Graffiti covered the area.

Not the nicest part of town, which suited them just fine. They weren't after a fancy meal or a twenty-dollar cocktail.

Gournsey got and transferred all the gear into the Camaro. The two bags barely fit in the back seat. He didn't bother looking in the tiny trunk.

With all the guns and gear inside, Gournsey opened the gas cap on the Jeep and stuffed a rag down it.

He lit the rag and walked away.

Chemistry and physics took care of the rest.

"Shame," said Gournsey as he tried to fit himself into the Camaro. "That was a decent Jeep."

"A decent amount of bullet holes," added Sherman.

"Still."

"We'll pay your friends back."

"They don't care about the money. It's the principle."

"The principle here is don't get caught," Sherman replied. "A Jeep full of holes draws attention."

"Still."

Sherman laughed. "Come on. Let's go and find the runt."

The truck stop parking lot seemed fuller than normal. It was rush hour but also Sunday, with the latter contradicting the former. Maybe people stopped for pie after church or got supplies for a football game. Sherman didn't know the rhythms of a normal American city because he hadn't lived in one for any meaningful amount of time. He knew Kabul and Baghdad like he knew an M4A1 rifle. He knew Denver like the back of his hand, which always had a surprising number of new lines and cuts and never quite looked the same.

Parking front and center was out of the question. Too many cameras. Too many eyes. Gournsey offered to go in and look, but his size telephoned trouble. A walking billboard of potential violence.

No, thought Sherman. *Better to wait it out. Don't charge into the den. Observe the pack first. Pick the weakest link. The runt of the litter. There is always one.*

They settled for a warehouse away from the colonel's car, which was still there. Maybe they hadn't got around to crushing it yet. Maybe they were waiting to catch Zarak before disposing of it. Or maybe they didn't care.

Gournsey found a pair of binoculars in a duffle bag next

to some previous-generation night vision monocles. All military grade, but none of it from Uncle Sam. Civilian gear, but only just.

Sherman wanted to move into the back seat to stay out of view, but it wasn't big enough for toddlers and the bags took up all the room. So, he stayed put and tilted the seat back, hoping the tinted windows worked.

From their oblique angle across the street, they could see the back parking lot of Comet's. Like the front, it had lots of vehicles, but they didn't move often. Most businesses didn't want their employees taking up prime parking spots. Sherman guessed it was a similar situation.

Whoever worked in that back room at the diner would park out back. It stood to reason a fire door exited that direction. City code required one. From there, it was a straight shot to the quietest part of the parking lot.

"Tell me again, how many did you see inside?" asked Gournsey. The binoculars he held against his face looked comically small, even though they weren't.

"At least six on both occasions, but judging by the size of the room, I'd say eight reasonably. Round up to ten for safety's sake."

"Ten on two. Not great odds."

Sherman said nothing.

"Any personnel rotation?" asked Gournsey.

"Not that I saw," said Sherman. "But they spotted me pretty quick."

"Loose lips sink ships," Gournsey added.

"A calculated risk. I needed to poke the bear."

"Sounds like they almost poked you back in the parking lot."

Sherman nodded at his recent failure. "It might have gotten messy."

"Three on one. Not bad odds."

"For you," Sherman replied.

Gournsey laughed so hard, he dropped the binoculars. "Your false modesty always amazes me."

"I'm getting old," Sherman admitted.

"Not that old."

Neither man said anything else for a long stretch. They watched and waited like patient hunters from a long genetic line of patient hunters.

The sun set. Dusk fell and shadows deepened into dark pools. No one exited out the back. The front turned over at a steady clip. Some people filled up with gas. Others went straight into the convenience store. Those that stayed longer came back out with to-go boxes from the diner or taco place.

Sherman picked up his phone and called Landers. A sit-rep of sorts. Courtesy and habit rolled into one action.

She answered on the third ring. Laughter filled the background. The girls and Asal. He was thankful for that.

"Not making it back for dinner?" she asked.

"What's Asal cooking?"

"Who said she's cooking? Huh?"

"You don't even have condiments in your fridge," countered Sherman. "Everyone has at least some expired condiments."

"Do you?" she asked.

"I don't have a fridge."

"Well then," she exclaimed in muted triumph.

"We're watching Comet's now."

"From far away, I assume."

"Across the street."

"Anything interesting?"

"Besides Gournsey's stomach rumbling? No. The place

is packed though. I can see how so much stuff gets moved through here, figuratively speaking. We haven't seen anything untoward yet. Have we?"

Gournsey shook his head.

"The sergeant agrees. Lots of traffic but nothing suspicious."

"Maybe they have twelve-hour shifts," said Landers.

"Wouldn't that be overtime?"

"Do you think these guys pay hourly?" asked Landers.

"No clue. Do they?"

"Usually a flat rate, plus bonuses if the job requires it."

"What jobs?"

"Like burying two outsiders who stuck their noses in too far."

"Got it," said Sherman.

"I only say that as a friendly warning. If the FBI hasn't brought a case by now, it means this group is very good at staying under the radar."

"By any means necessary," added Sherman, thinking of the attack that morning.

"Exactly."

"We'll be safe. One target at a time."

"Just don't lead them out back again. That didn't end well."

"It would end fine. I have Gournsey now."

Landers sighed. "Call back soon."

"Will do."

———

The hours wore one. Pangs of hunger rumbled through Sherman's stomach, but he ignored them. He could block out most sensations like heat, thirst, hunger, and even boredom. *No such thing as boredom,* his father once said. *Just a lack of imagination.* Sherman wasn't much for flights of fancy, but he had a keen eye for detail.

In his brief college career, he'd taken an art history course. The professor's first assignment made them sit in front of the same painting for three hours. A herculean task for a horny teenager just escaped from the confines of parental supervision. After the first ninety minutes passed and all the normal distractions failed, he noticed patterns. Unseen bits of symmetry and geometry that had previously eluded his eyes. Time forced his concentration and distilled his observations.

Having watched Comet's for an equal amount of time, Sherman began noticing the unseen rhythms and patterns.

One truck driver caught his attention. A barrel-chested man wearing a Hawaiian shirt. He parked next to a dozen other rigs and, like most, went inside. Thirty minutes he exited, looking wider and carrying a plastic bag filled with Styrofoam to-go containers from the diner. *Not unusual for a hungry guy,* Sherman thought. Until he got in an unfamiliar truck and drove away.

Gournsey, ever a student of minutia, leaned forward to get a better look.

"Did you see that?" he asked.

"Not the truck he drove in," said Sherman.

"Similar but not the same."

"Maybe that's part of the system. They're moving goods around, coordinating, but not unloading."

"The nexus," said Gournsey.

"That's a nice ten-dollar word."

"Used to be the name of my brother's band in high school."

"I never knew," said Sherman. He'd not heard that fact

before, but he knew Gournsey's brother died of a drug over-dose years before.

Kentucky. Not just full of bourbon.

"Check out the food service truck," said the sergeant.

A small cargo truck parked behind the diner. One of the national brands. Bread or pastries. Probably both. Sherman didn't go to the grocery store often enough to know.

"Two deliveries in one night," Sherman observed.

"Different driver," said Gournsey.

"I'm not a restaurant manager, but I assume you order in bulk. This isn't a just-in-time kind of business model."

"They order for the week. Maybe longer."

"Maybe they forgot something. Easy to miss a pack of buns in a truck that size."

"He's pushing a whole dolly worth of stuff inside," said Gournsey.

Which was true. The driver was gingerly navigating a dolly down the truck ramp and into the diner's back door.

"Which is the real delivery? This one or the earlier one?" asked Sherman.

"Maybe neither," answered Gournsey.

Another truck driver parked and headed inside. He carried a gym bag over his shoulder. A towel hung out. Comet's had showers. It was a full-service establishment. It even said so on the wall.

Not unusual, thought Sherman.

Twenty minutes later, the driver exited with wet hair and different clothes. A routine stop for a well-deserved hot shower.

Yet the bag he carried hung awkwardly to one side. It wasn't over his shoulder but held low and at full exertion. He leaned a little to that side while walking. Not much but noticeable. The way people do when carrying something too heavy.

"And look at this guy," said Sherman. "He's holding that bag like it's full of cement."

"Looks like a grunt carrying two cans of fifty cal."

"Came in with only a towel and clothes."

"Leaving with a keg," added Gournsey.

"Shit, I didn't see it before. The guy that drove off in a different truck. He came out with a plastic bag filled with leftovers. A guy like that doesn't leave with that many leftovers."

Gournsey nodded. "The nexus."

"Agreed, but of what?" asked Sherman.

Gournsey had no answer. Neither did Sherman, but an opportunity to answer emerged a few minutes after the freshly showered truck driver left in something other than what he arrived.

The bakery truck rolled up its back door and disappeared into the still busy street. Not more than a minute later, a group of men streamed out of the diner's back door.

In the dim parking lot lights, Sherman thought he recognized some from the day before. He couldn't tell if the man with the matching boots was among them.

Three of the men got in an old Crown Vic bought straight from the police auction. The fourth seemed like he wanted to go but then changed his mind. Maybe he got left out.

The runt of the litter.

There's always one.

He watched the Crown Vic pull away before ambling over a boxy-looking car that Sherman couldn't name. The reverse lights came on. He was leaving.

"Him?" asked Gournsey.

"Him," answered Sherman.

The sergeant pressed the ignition and the Camaro's V8 growled to life. Sherman slid his vest on and jammed a pistol next to his seat.

The boxy car pulled out and turned right. Gournsey followed, passing by a plumber's van with tinted windows. Both men looked the other way. Prying eyes were everywhere.

182

Chapter Nineteen

For a professional, the guy in the boxy car drove a plodding, unambiguous path. He didn't switch lanes or circle back. No sudden turns. He drove like a man set in his routine without the need of excitement. A man abhorring change.

Gournsey called the car a cube. Sherman wasn't sure if that was capitalized or not. The sergeant stayed back as they exited the freeway and entered a modest neighborhood of single-family homes—a late 1950s or early 1960s suburb. The streets still ran straight, and the houses looked alike. Door on the left. Two windows on the right. Garage out back. A standard affair. Not fancy, but not lacking either.

Most of the houses had security doors, but no bars on the windows. *Against fire code*, Sherman guessed.

The cube slowed in front of a blue house with a plain white door. Vinyl siding with broken bits covered the exterior. In the dark, it came off a silvery gray, but the headlights said periwinkle.

Gournsey kept driving another block before parking. In the distance, Sherman saw the guy sit in his car.

Waiting or wasting time. Maybe he didn't want to go inside. Maybe his girlfriend gave him grief for coming home so late. Those things happened, or so Sherman had heard.

They waited and watched.

Satisfied with the wait, the guy went inside.

The lights came on. A TV flickered to life.

Gournsey took a shotgun in case things got messy or they needed to take apart a door. He also grabbed an industrial-looking crowbar and bolt cutters.

Sherman favored a suppressed MP5. A workhouse of the special forces around the world. How the Delta boys got one was a question he didn't want answered, but he felt more confident with it in his hands.

His watch read 1:00 AM.

Most of the neighborhood was asleep, save for the cube guy and his television. A long streetlight cast a yellow pall across the asphalt. Otherwise, it was dark for a suburb. Maybe the HOA didn't like porch lights. Stranger things happened.

They hurried down the street, staying in the deep shadows. Pockets of warmth lingered, but a chilly wind tossed leaves down the street with a hollow scratching.

Sherman turned left as they reached the edge of the man's property. Like everywhere else in the area, a privacy fence connected to the side of the house. Behind it was the mystical backyard oasis of the American dream.

Or it could have been.

What they found was a bare and neglected patch of sunburned turf and a few plastic chairs. A ubiquitous charcoal BBQ stood next to the back door. One wheel at the base had broken off and the whole thing tilted precariously to one side. Dilapidated but functional.

The back door looked like the front. A plain white exterior door. Wooden and cheap.

A small window overlooked the yard. In the flickering of late-night television, Sherman saw a faucet and refrigerator. The kitchen and dining room. Beyond that was the living room, inhabited by the cube man and his TV binge.

Gournsey tried the handle but shook his head.

He took three steps back and looked at Sherman.

Sherman flipped the MP5's selector switch to full-auto and nodded.

One, two, three—crack.

The door splintered apart as Gournsey smashed his size fourteen boot just below the handle.

Sherman slid through as broken chunks of wood clattered across the floor. He cleared left in a brief swing of the gun, then headed toward the living room at a fast walk—a speed he'd perfected over the years. Quick enough to catch the target by surprise but not so fast that he couldn't shoot accurately.

He reached the living room in five quick steps and turned the corner, gun at the ready.

And that's when things got weird.

Sitting on the couch, the cube guy held a gun to his own temple. The gun didn't surprise Sherman, he'd expected resistance. But this was something unexpected. A game-breaking change.

"Not a step closer," said the man.

Up close, he looked older than Sherman imagined. Mid-forties. Still fit but worn and scarred by time. Tattoos crawled out of his shirt sleeve and down one arm. The one holding the gun. A Ruger. Part of the bulk order.

Sherman paused.

He'd no qualms about shooting the guy but something

else was at play and it didn't feel right. The warning bells tolled loudly in that over-developed caveman kernel of his mind.

"Sweep and clear," he told Gournsey.

"I'm alone," said the man.

His expression remained calm and his arm steady.

"Clear," shouted Gournsey.

"See," said the man.

"Pardon me for not taking your word for it," replied Sherman. "Why don't you lower the Ruger, and we can chat."

"Did you have a chat with Mike before putting a bullet through his forehead?"

The SUV passenger. Mike. Sherman hadn't bothered asking for names that morning.

"He shot first," Sherman answered.

"As was his job."

"He should have found alternative employment," said Gournsey as he moved out of the man's sightline and into the kitchen.

Sherman didn't take his eye off the Ruger, still angled against the man's temple, making an impression in the flesh.

"Secure our exfil," he said.

Gournsey moved toward the back door. The man didn't flinch.

"That's quite the ink you've got," said Sherman.

"I like to keep my past close. Don't you?" asked the man, still as a statue.

"I'm more of *c'est la vie* kinda guy."

"*Un vie trop tranquille est une mer morte.*"

"Did you learn that in the legion?" asked Sherman. He recognized the tattoo on the man's arm. That and the French quote about a life too quiet was a dead sea.

"You're good. I thought he was paranoid but now I see you're cut from a different cloth."

"Who was paranoid?" asked Sherman.

"The guy who said you'd show up."

The warning bells thundered in Sherman's mind. "And why am I here?"

"You're hunting. Same as they are."

Not the runt, thought Sherman. The decoy. One went home, three went off somewhere else.

"And what are they hunting?"

The man smiled. "Not the conversation you envisioned."

"No. You were bleeding on the floor in my version."

"Ah, I imagine that's still a likely outcome."

"No. You'll bleed out on the couch."

The man shrugged with indifference. "Another likely outcome."

"Who are your friends after?"

No answer. Just a smile in the silence.

Sherman didn't quite know what to make of the situation. He'd come to inflict harm in a quest for answers. Instead, they found a man willing to self-harm to avoid them. Was he bluffing? Or was it something else?

No fear equated to no leverage. The guy showed none of the usual motivations to live. He sat calmly, facing down his potential last moments like a patient in the doctor's waiting room.

"I'm getting one of those feelings," said Gournsey.

"Me too," said Sherman. "Last chance to say something redeeming."

"You're a genuine believer, aren't you?"

"No," replied Sherman and intentionally fired just over the man's arm. The one holding the Ruger.

The man didn't flinch. Not one muscle. No finger spasm or fatal error.

"You're lying to yourself," he said.

Sherman had seen crazy in his time, from suicide bombers to World War I-style infantry charges, but this ex-soldier turned mercenary won the most bizarre award.

After a moment's hesitation, Sherman backed away. He could have shot the guy. Maybe even should have, but something told him not to. Not morality or brotherly code. Something deeper. A shared sense of camaraderie in the face of pure madness or maybe just the madness itself.

Bathed in shadows, they moved down the street and into the stolen Camaro. Gournsey wasted no time in leaving.

"What the fuck was that?" he asked once they were heading towards downtown.

"I'm not sure but we need to get to Landers."

"Why?"

"Because we're not the only ones hunting wolves tonight."

Chapter Twenty

Asal and the girls were asleep in Landers' bed. Megan had insisted and made a spot on the couch. Hospitality ran deep in Afghan culture. So deep that some outsiders mistook it for weakness. But Asal knew better. She understood everyone needed a helping hand and that the intricate web of life would unwind without kindness. Therefore, she accepted the bed with the included comforts and consequences.

Soft and even breathing told her the girls were asleep. She was not. Could not. Her mind kept drifting back to Zarak.

Questions filled her mind. Questions with no answers.

Racked with anxiety, she watched the ceiling dance with the city's reflection. Energy buzzed around them, humming and vibrating through the walls.

No, she thought. *Not the walls. My phone.*

She leaped out of bed and dashed into the kitchen, hoping she didn't wake the girls.

"Zarak," she answered, wishing so forcefully it hurt her heart.

"Mrs. Khada," replied a plain American male with no hint of accent or region. "I'm glad we get to speak in person."

Asal gasped and Landers padded over from the couch.

"Who is this?" she asked and held up the phone between them.

"Names," said the man with a long sigh. "Names are just constructs, Mrs. Khada. They come and go. Bend and twist. Do you understand me, Mrs. Khada? Or should I call you Asal? Although that is awfully presumptuous of me. We're not even acquaintances yet... here I am calling you by your first name. What really matters is actions. Specifically, the actions of your husband."

Landers held up her finger and Asal bit her lip, stifling her desire to ask about Zarak.

"Zarak Khada," continued the man, "put us in an uncomfortable position. Without resolution, I will respond in kind. A homage to the Old Testament God. Eye for an Eye and all that rather messy retribution."

"What do you want?" asked Asal.

"How considerate of you to ask. I want what your husband took returned to me. I want what is mine. Nothing less. Nothing more. A rather simple request, if you ask me."

"Tell him that."

"Ah, but we can't find him. However, we can find you."

Landers grabbed the phone out of her hand and dropped it in a nearby glass of water.

She said, "Wake the girls. We don't have much time."

Asal ran into the room to wake her children, but they needed no cajoling. They stood ready with bags in hand.

Landers grabbed her gun, badge, keys, and jacket. She'd slept in her clothes—a trick picked up in the Army and continued out of stubbornness.

She called Sherman next, having convinced him it was wise for her to have his number. He answered immediately. The man was reliable.

"I need you back here, now!"

"We're already on our way. What happened?"

"Asal just received a call from The Company. They threatened her. Said they could find her."

Sherman paused on the other end and switched to the speakerphone.

"What kind of phone does she have?" asked Gournsey.

Landers glanced at the cup of water. "Not sure. An older Android by the looks of it."

"Okay, that's good and bad," said the sergeant.

"How bad?" she asked.

"Easier to hack but less reliable for location data."

"Do you think they're coming here?"

"Yes," said Sherman. "Everything about these guys says they're serious and capable. We're ten minutes out."

"How much time do I have?" she asked.

"Assume less," said Sherman.

Landers turned off the light and edged to the door. Her view through the peephole went from one end of the hall to the other. Both ends had stairs. The elevator was in the middle.

She thought fast.

The elevator was the easiest but tactically terrible. All the targets crammed into one space that told your opponents where it was going. Not good.

The stairs to the left were closer. Less time exposed in the hall.

Nine flights of stairs lay beyond the door. The height made for magnificent views but a lousy escape route. A fact she hadn't considered when signing the lease. A fact, she assumed, Sherman already knew.

"Alright, girls, we are heading left toward the stairs. Stay right behind me. Don't say a word. Frank and Raylan are on their way."

"I'm scared, Mama," said Esin.

Asal pulled her youngest closer. "I know, my love. I know. Listen to Ms. Landers. She'll keep us safe."

I hope, thought Landers as her leg quivered with an old pain.

"Okay," she said. "Here we go."

Gently, she opened the front door and slipped into the hallway. Asal closed it behind them just as quietly.

Nothing sounded but the swishing of fabric and the faint buzz of the building's HVAC system.

Nothing until the mechanical revving of the elevator whirred to life.

"Hurry," hissed Landers and jogged towards the stairwell.

The fire door was closed. She opened it a few inches and listened. Somewhere seven flights below, a door closed. The faint echo carried upward.

Options raced through her mind. Few ended well. Down ended in bloodshed. The roof had no place to hide. Neither did the hallways. Pulling the fire alarm would create enough chaos for them to blend in, but there was still someone in the stairwell they'd have to get past.

Keys jingled in her pocket.

Keys, she thought.

"Of course," she muttered.

Asal looked confused and scared.

"We're going two flights down."

Two down was quicker than five up, she hoped.

Down they went. The slap of feet on concrete filled the air despite their attempts to be quiet. There was no avoiding it.

Above them came the chime of an arriving elevator. Landers urged them on. One more floor remained.

She practically shoved the girls through the fire door.

"This way. Follow me."

The four of them made a mad dash down the length of the hall to the other side.

At apartment number 756, Landers stopped and flipped madly through her keys. Adrenaline made her hands shake. She took a breath, focused, and grasped the correct key.

The door opened. They jumped inside into the dark, silent interior like a concrete void.

As she closed the door, Landers heard the heavy sounds of someone running up the stairwell.

Asal clutched her daughters. They were breathing so hard.

"Whose apartment is this?" she asked.

Landers kept her eye to the peephole. "A friend. I water his plants when he's out of town."

"Is he out of town?"

"On a cruise in Alaska," she answered, hoping he hadn't come back early. "We can stay here until Sherman shows up."

Landers fumbled through the dark, closing all the blinds she so assiduously left open so the plants would get the 'good' light her friend wanted.

Only once the blinds were closed did she turn on a

lamp. The apartment mirrored her own, but it had furniture, artwork, and charm. Everything she lacked.

"Make yourself comfortable."

Asal put the girls on a corduroy couch and covered them with blankets. She returned and whispered, "Those men were coming for us?"

"I believe so," answered Landers.

"Why us?"

"You're leverage. Zarak took something they want, and it appears they can't find him, so they came for you. Again."

"It's my fault," said Asal. "I thought, hoped, Zarak was calling."

"It's fine, neither of us assumed they'd get your number. These things happen. Things go sideways."

"We can't go back to your apartment, can we?"

"No," said Landers. "Not any time soon."

"I'm sorry," said Asal.

"Me too," added Landers. "Me too."

Chapter Twenty-One

For ten tense minutes, Sherman sat helpless in the Camaro's passenger seat. He hated the feeling. Knowing someone you cared for was in danger but not being able to help. Memories of sitting in the JSOC command center surfaced. They'd watch drone footage of comrades on missions. Little white dots on the infrared camera. Sometimes there were other dots too. Tracers zipped across the monitors in detached blurry lines. But Sherman knew the full force of those lines. The hissing snap of close calls.

A few blocks out, Sherman called Landers back.

"Are you here?" she asked, her voice barely a whisper.

"Two blocks out. I need the garage code."

She told him the number. He repeated it out loud for Gournsey to hear.

"Are you safe?" he asked.

"They're here," she replied. "We heard them in the stairwell."

"But you're not in the apartment, right?"

"No, we're in—"

"Don't say," interrupted Sherman. "I'll call when it's safe."

"Okay."

He hung up as Gournsey pulled up to a keypad and punched in the string of numbers Landers gave them.

The door opened with a cranky groan and the steady hum of an electric motor. They drove to the nearest stairwell and parked.

A Crown Vic sat empty three spaces over—the same car they'd seen leave Comet's.

No one milled about the concrete cavern. Only three guys got in earlier, which meant one in either stairwell with one more on the elevator. The greatest coverage level given their unit size. Common sense.

Sherman left the MP5 and grabbed a pistol built from mail-to-order parts. A ghost gun. Untraceable. Most important to him was the suppressor. He exited the Camaro and promptly stabbed gaping holes in all the sedans' tires. An angry hiss swirled about with a tinny echo.

Gournsey met him by the closest stairwell, just outside of the security camera's gaze.

"What's the plan?" asked the sergeant.

"Speed and violence."

"Survivors?"

"No. I want to send a message."

"Breaking some eggs."

Sherman nodded. "Keep your hat on and your head down. There aren't many cameras, but we don't want to make the nightly news or an FBI most-wanted list."

Gournsey nodded back and they kept looking at the concrete floor until they slipped inside the vast stairwell shaft that rose the entire height of the building.

Nine flights of stairs.

Three minutes at a jog, thought Sherman. But jogging was loud, echoing against the concrete walls.

They started off fast. The speed part of speed and violence. Move quick. Act fast.

Around the seventh floor, Sherman slowed and pretended to open the door. A decoy of sorts. Maybe some drunk tenants came home late after the bars closed. Stranger things happened.

They took the next two floors patiently. Plodding steps, almost silent from years of practice.

The building's structural engineer had decided against visibility in favor of safety. One couldn't gaze up or down the stairs. Each flight was self-contained. Two walls and the steps in between. Then a landing and a turn, followed by more of the same. Every other landing had a door leading to a floor.

Surprise, by very design, cut both ways. Sherman didn't know who was above him, but neither could someone at the top tell who approached from below.

They reached the landing between eight and nine. Sherman listened. He heard nothing but the hum of the HVAC system.

He shook his head and Gournsey squeezed his shoulder. Confirmation the sergeant was still with him and ready to move.

Maybe they were wrong, thought Sherman. Maybe he was wrong. Nothing more than an overactive imagination.

The ninth-floor landing was empty. Gournsey checked ten just in case but came back shaking his head.

Sherman pointed to the door handle. The sergeant stood aside and, on Sherman's signal, opened the door.

Instead of a gaggle of goons, they found an empty hallway. Sherman motioned forward.

They moved in unison. A well-rehearsed dance between two vintage professionals. Gournsey watched behind, Sherman covered the front. A slow but easy rhythm of approach.

The two were so in sync that Gournsey didn't need a cue for when to swivel around. He felt it in Sherman's movements.

Such it was that both men were facing Landers' door when a man stepped out. About the size of an NFL linebacker, he practically bulged out of his black long-sleeved shirt. On his head was a Yankee's cap, but what caught Sherman's attention was the Ruger pistol casually held in the man's right hand. Part of the bulk order.

To his credit, the linebacker reacted fast. His mind pulled together the facts, assessed the risk, and acted.

He raised the Ruger about three inches before Sherman shot. Move quick. Act faster.

Sherman was faster. He always had been. His survival depended on it. That night, he put a subsonic 9mm from the Frankenstein pistol right into the linebacker's forehead.

There was a clack, a wet splat, and a thud in quick succession. Sherman stepped over the corpse and into Landers' apartment.

The entry was small, maybe a yard long, leading into the popular open floor plan. Between the kitchen and the living room, in a sort of Feng Shui no-man's land, stood another guy.

Same shirt and pants. Same Ruger held casually at his side. Different hat. A Met's fan.

Sherman didn't let him draw three inches. He hit the second goon center mass with five shots. A quick burst of clacks. Shell casing tinkled off the walls and onto the vinyl floor, followed by another thud, slick and squelchy.

Two down and one to go.

Expect there wasn't anyone else in the apartment. Not in the bedroom or bathroom. Not on the balcony or hiding in the closet.

"We're missing one," said Sherman.

Gournsey was busy searching the former Met's fan. "Could be on another floor or running."

"He won't get far in that sedan."

Sherman was nearing the front door as the elevator door dinged and opened.

From down the hall, Sherman watched and waited. At first, all he saw was a hand and a phone. Thumbs hard at work tapping out a message or searching for something.

He held the angle. Hoping it wasn't a resident about to walk into a bloody mess or a bullet.

Then a foot stepped out. A foot comfortably ensconced in a combat boot. It didn't go far. Just enough to see the outline.

Sherman leveled the pistol and lined up the shot. Less than a hundred feet. No wind or impediments. An open opportunity.

Except the boot didn't move. The legs and torso didn't follow. The phone came down. The thumbs stopped tapping. But no one stepped out.

Against the elevator's stainless-steel doorframe, Sherman saw a reflection. Nothing concrete, but he knew decisions were in the works. Risk assessments and ballistics and geometry all done in milliseconds. The wonder of the human brain.

Without warning, the boot slipped back inside the elevator. Doors closed and the occupant disappeared into the bowels of the building.

Gournsey ran to check where the numbers stopped.

"He got out in the basement. We might catch him."

"No, let's get Landers and the girls. We need to exfil quickly before everyone wakes up and sees this mess."

Sherman called Landers.

"Did you find them?" she asked.

"Yes, but we need to move. Where are you?"

"Two floors down. Room 756."

Sherman pointed to the stairs. "Room 756. Take Asal and the girls somewhere safe."

Gournsey nodded and left without a word.

"The sergeant is on his way down. Give him your car keys and meet me up here. You'll need to pack quickly."

Landers paused but didn't ask why.

Three minutes later, she arrived from the opposite stairwell. She still wore running clothes, but her hair fell loosely around her shoulders. Sherman's watch read 2:30 AM.

She stopped at the door, looked down at the Yankee fan and then at Sherman.

"You sent a message."

He nodded.

"In my apartment."

He nodded again.

She glanced around. "Can I claim self-defense?"

"Not unless your service weapon is a suppressed 9mm."

"A .40 caliber, but you knew that."

He nodded.

"How will I explain this without involving you or the Khada family?"

Covering things up was not something Sherman did with regularity, but he was flexible. He handed her the ghost gun and picked up a Ruger from next to the door.

"You took it off him. Say you went out for a run and they were here when you got back."

She squinted for a moment and then nodded. "Fine. Give me a few minutes to pack. Try to stay out of sight."

Sherman took a picture of the Ruger's serial number while he waited. Bulk orders came with paper trails. He sent it to Major Sanders just in case.

Landers reappeared with a small gym bag over her shoulder and a bottle of bourbon in her hand.

"Take these with you to your car, then check-in down the street. There are a few options. Use that company card, you owe me that much. I'll call when this shit is sorted out. It's gonna be a long night."

Sherman nodded and disappeared down the stairwell. The keys were on the dashboard of the Camaro, no doubt where Gournsey left them. He pulled out of the garage and drove aimlessly for 30 minutes in order to confuse anyone watching. Then he circled back.

Red and blue lights flashed down the street, reflecting off the glass facades like some distorted hallway of misery.

Parking at a hotel brought scrutiny, cameras, and maybe even a valet. Sherman opted for a surface lot that took cash. He stuffed enough in the slot to cover three days. He didn't want anyone looking too closely.

Grabbing the bags and Landers' bottle of bourbon, he walked to the nearest hotel. It was a national chain. One with a fancy letter or name. Brand loyalty meant nothing to Sherman.

The young woman at the front desk only looked mildly surprised to see a guy checking in at such a late or now early hour.

"Do you have a reservation, sir?"

"No, I had one at your competitor but then bungled it."

"Oh, which one?" she asked curiously.

"I bet you can guess."

She smiled conspiratorially. "I sure can. Now, how can I help you?"

"I need a room for a few nights."

"A few is rather vague. Is that three or four?"

"Four, just to be safe. Business…" he said and trailed off as if it was an answer and excuse.

"I understand completely. One bed or two?"

"Just me."

The woman smiled again and typed away for a moment. They agreed on a rate and Sherman handed over the company card he kept for such unusual circumstances. The clerk countered with a plastic keycard and Sherman followed the signs up to the fourth floor.

He sent Landers a text, put a Glock under his pillow, and passed out.

Chapter Twenty-Two

Sherman awoke hours later to a soft knock at the door. Red and orange rays of light danced through the hotel's heavy curtains. He was too tired for it to be sunset.

Padding over with the pistol in hand, he stood to one side of the door and asked, "Who is it?"

"Jesus Christ, Frank! How many women did you text your room number to?"

Sherman unlocked the door and let Landers inside. She looked haggard. Twenty-four hours straight did that to a person.

She glanced at the gun in his hand and asked, "Expecting someone else?"

He shrugged, but the truth was, he always expected someone else. Paranoia was the term an Army psychologist used, but that guy wouldn't have made it a country mile in Sherman's boots.

"How did it go with the cops?"

"You mean Denver PD, the ATF, and the FBI?"

Sherman handed her the bottle of bourbon and watched her take a long swig.

"I'm on paid administrative leave until they sort this out," she added.

"And what did you spin it as?"

"Self-defense," she said and took another drink. "I'm not sure if the Special Agent in Charge bought it, but the locals seemed impressed with your shooting."

"Did they read you in on any of the investigation?"

"No, Frank, they didn't. In fact, they were quite curious to know how these guys found me. I admitted to driving by the truck stop after I got the reporter's call. Which, if you can believe it, fucking pissed off the SAC. He read me the riot act. Fingers got pointed."

"You came off incompetent," he said, reading her disdain.

"Worse. I appeared like a liability. They wanted to assign a couple of rookies to protect me. There was talk of a safe house and witness protection until I reminded them that I didn't witness shit."

"Good," said Sherman.

Landers laughed. "Good? How does your twisted brain translate this as good?"

"The FBI will be all over the truck stop now, correct?"

"Yes."

"Which makes it harder for them to look for Zarak or come after us, correct?"

"I suppose," admitted Landers.

"I'd say that's message received."

Landers threw up her hands. "I thought you were sending a message to The Company, not my fucking boss."

"It works both ways," he replied. "Same message, two different meanings. Whoever is calling the shots witnessed what we're capable of, which should inspire some modicum of restraint. And your boss is now forced to speed up his case against said shot caller."

"Win-win?" asked Landers, clearly not seeing any silver lining.

"Not exactly. You're out of an apartment and Gournsey is out of pocket until he finds a safe spot for Asal and the girls."

"I'm sorry about that."

"Not your fault. I never thought they'd make the connection."

"They must have done their homework," said Landers.

"Of course, they did," added Sherman. "Shit, I should have seen it earlier."

"Seen what?"

"Have you ever read an asset intelligence file?"

"Above my pay grade," she replied.

"Whenever we worked with a local in Afghanistan, the spooks would write up this report detailing everything we knew. Family was always top-line information. We wanted to know how the enemy might compromise them. Their weak spots and pain points."

"Makes sense."

"That's what these guys did. They wrote up a file on Zarak. On how to pressure him if things didn't work out. A contingency plan of sorts."

"Not all crooks are dumb," admitted Landers.

"Because not all crooks used to work for the CIA. The broker in the park practically told me as much. She assumed I was from the Agency and then joked about going up against one of my own."

"That would explain why the bureau is taking so long with the case. Something like this would be an epic pissing contest. Careers burn over these things. Depending on the guy's service record, it could tarnish entire clandestine operations."

Sherman nodded in agreement. "How much time do you think we have before the FBI act?"

Landers lay down on the bed with a sigh. "Weeks, maybe longer, but those two bodies will certainly speed up their timeline. Why does it matter?"

"I see two resolutions. One, these guys are behind bars and Zarak comes out of whatever hole he's in. Or two—"

"Do I want to hear number two?"

Sherman lay down next to her. "I think you already know what that plan entails."

She pointed down at the small arsenal. "I imagine it relates to what's in those duffle bags next to the bed."

"You got the gist."

Landers closed her eyes. "I need to sleep on it."

Sherman nodded and rolled onto one side, but she was already asleep.

The colorful morning hues were long gone when Sherman woke up again. His watch said noon. His mind said coffee. Landers still slept where she'd crashed.

Sherman got up and called room service. He ordered coffee and breakfast. The place was fancy enough that they didn't argue over whether breakfast should still be served.

Killing time and evidence, Sherman took a hot shower. Then he changed into what few clean items remained and bagged his old clothes for a future dumpster.

As the food arrived, Sherman stepped outside to sign.

When he came back in, Landers lay propped up on one elbow.

"What meal are we on?" she asked.

"Technically lunch, but I opted for breakfast as we skipped that part of the day."

"And coffee?" she asked, hopefully.

"Two pots."

"You're a good man, Frank Sherman."

"I try," he replied.

Then, as if suddenly remembering she'd left the stove on, Landers bolted upright. "Are Asal and the girls alright?"

"Yeah. Gournsey texted to say they are staying with some colleagues south of here."

"Is it safe?"

"It's a bunch of operators living in the mountains. I'd rank it just above Fort Knox."

She sank back down in relief and said, "About that coffee."

After licking the plates and consuming all the caffeine possible, Landers took a long shower. Sherman used the time to plan his next move.

He'd thinned the pack, but that barely scratched the surface. Based on the numbers he'd seen at the diner, The Company had upwards of thirty shooters. Eight guys on a rotation. Three rotations a day. Plus a few extra for sick days or exigent circumstances. Throw in some more for surge capacity and you got thirty.

The two from last light wouldn't mean much for daily operations—it wasn't the number that counted. Splattering some gray matter on a wall conveyed several things he wanted the guy in the boots to know. First, actions carried consequences. Second, Sherman knew his craft well. Third, he had no intention of stopping.

Sherman guessed he'd gotten across points one and two. The third, however, needed underlining. Something bold. Something painful.

Gazing out the window, an idea struck him or, more precisely, a familiar sight struck him. A fancy building with a glass façade and a bar across the street.

"What are you looking at?" asked Landers, who'd just come out of the shower.

She'd changed into jeans and something resembling a cowboy shirt but alluring.

"A piece of the puzzle."

"You Army guys and your riddles. I never got it."

"Do you recognize the building down the street?"

Landers looked. "I haven't forgotten about those women."

"You've heard the term degradation before, right?"

"I went to law school, remember."

"I do, but do you know how the Army uses it?"

"Body counts," she replied.

"Part of it, yes. But killing soldiers only goes so far. There are always more people to fire the guns and fill up body bags. In order to win, you must degrade their ability to acquire the guns and soldiers."

"The money."

"Exactly. We need to cut off their cash. Something that will disrupt their normal operations. Sow some panic."

"And you want to do that a few blocks from your hotel room? They say don't shit in your own backyard, right?"

"I'll risk it," Sherman replied.

"They've probably increased security at the building."

"I'm counting on it."

"And what about the FBI agents watching the place? I don't want to lose any more colleagues."

Sherman knew she'd already buried one partner and two other agents in their recent past. Not his doing, but he didn't stop it either.

"I'll steer clear," he assured her.

"How?"

"Hopefully, with your help, but I can manage without it."

"And what happens if you get caught? Are you going to surrender peacefully to the police?"

Sherman gave his charming smile. The one that got him into or out of trouble. He hoped it was the latter.

"Charming your way out won't work," she chided.

"Then let's hope it doesn't come to that."

Landers folded her arms across her chest. "What are you saying?"

"They didn't teach me to surrender," he answered.

She took a deep breath in and held it while she thought. "No, I imagine not. What do you need from me?"

"I need to know if the bureau has any other eyes on the place besides the obvious guy out front."

Landers bent down to tie her shoes. "I'll ask around, but I'm on leave and if I push too hard, the SAC will get suspicious. I'm on thin ice. His words, not mine."

"Do what you can."

"It's Monday, aren't you supposed to be teaching a class? Wait. Are you AWOL?"

Sherman laughed. "We have sick days too."

"No, you don't."

"Fine, the major is covering for me this week. He came up with some false emergency. I'm sure no one is missing my lectures."

Landers spoke but Sherman put his hand up to stop her.

"What?" she demanded. "I wasn't going to say a thing about your monotone diatribes."

"And there it is."

She winked. "I'm off to track down your surveillance. Where will I find you?"

"At the bar."

Landers waved goodbye. "Save me a stool."

The door closed behind her, and Sherman searched through the duffle bags. He'd given away one suppressed weapon and the doorman would call the cops if he walked out with an MP5. Digging deeper, he found a small Glock 21 with a threaded barrel. It worked with the remaining suppressor supplied by the Delta boys.

Slipping both items into his coat, Sherman placed the Do Not Disturb sign on the handle and stuck a toothpick from breakfast in the door. He placed it shin height with only the tip sticking out. If someone opened the door, the toothpick would fall, and he would know to run or shoot his way out.

Chapter Twenty-Three

Landers took the stairs up to work that afternoon. The front security guards were unavoidable, but the elevator opened into the center of her floor. Everyone noticed who arrived and departed. A bit of voyeurism left over the J. Edgar Hoover days, like a stranded gene in a long sequence of DNA. The stairs, however, stood at either end. Twin pillars of escape should the worst occur.

That afternoon, the worst came as Special Agent in Charge Harrington. After reading her a rather profane riot act, he'd told her to stay out of sight. She'd initially assumed he cared about her safety, but such naivete disappeared as the reprimand continued. Harrington clarified that she was a *persona non grata* at the office. His words, although Landers didn't need a translation.

She kept to the outside edges of the office, which consumed an entire floor. At the heart was a mass of cubicles. Not the shoulder-height kind favored by stodgy corporations. No. These were waist-high affairs that removed all forms of privacy.

Endless work hadn't bothered Landers. Work-life balance never entered her vocabulary. Life and job were so intertwined that she often showed up well past midnight to get in some last-minute paperwork.

An array of offices and conference rooms ringed around the cubicle heart. The sleekest suits sat in them. The glass windows looked towards the elevators and across the vast inner farm of agents. Narcissism at its finest. Nothing like the gaze of a hundred subordinates to polish one's ego.

Landers headed for the furthest breakroom—the one reserved for rookies and outcasts like her. Those agents falling down the corporate ladder and hitting every rung on the way.

She grabbed a cup of tasteless coffee and angled herself away from the opening, which once had a door but now only had open space with the remorse of lost privacy. Her idea was to wait for someone new. Engage in a little flattery followed up by some watercooler talk. Nothing intense, just casual conversation. Then work her way towards any hint of building surveillance.

The first person to walk in worked with her on white-collar cases. Not her target audience. Landers smiled and exchanged brief pleasantries. The type most people did, even though the answers didn't matter.

The woman moved on with her day.

"What are you doing in today?" said a voice.

Landers turned to find her second potential source leaning against the doorless doorframe. His name was Todd or Tim, she couldn't recall. A tall man of limited intellect but excessive charm. Tim or Todd grated against her sensibilities.

"It's Monday," she replied.

Todd, as she now remembered, smiled wide and gleaming. "I heard the SAC placed you on leave after that mess in your apartment."

Landers nodded. "I'm just getting a few things."

He looked over his shoulder in a conspiratorial gesture and stepped closer. "Is it true you shot two perps at your place?"

Landers nodded again at the scraps of truth.

"Holy shit, that's… crazy. You're a badass."

"I'm homeless for the time being. Nothing badass about that."

"Right," said Todd, and Landers could see the little testosterone-fueled wheels turning in his mind.

Wanting to cut off any awkward roommate offers, Landers asked, "Do you know anything about that fancy apartment building down the street from the convention center? I'm thinking about subletting a place there while they sort this mess out."

Todd still looked like he wanted to offer his bedroom as a place to stay but answered her question.

"Uh, yeah. I'd avoid that one unless you want to be on Bureau footage."

Landers tried to act surprised. "No shit. Video and audio?"

"Only video on the fourth floor, so I guess you might avoid the frame if you went high enough."

"I never liked all that glass anyway."

"Not the voyeuristic type?" asked Todd.

Landers gave a false smile and put her mug in the sink. She wanted to kick Todd in the balls and then see who was voyeuristic, but she didn't. *Maybe later*, she thought.

"I'm late for a showing," she said and excused herself.

Todd's stare followed as she left, lingering on her all the way to the stairs.

After a circuitous route out of the hotel, Sherman found the bar across from the glass-clad apartment building. He claimed a stool with a good view of the street. The interior of the building had an upscale industrial look that seemed to be everywhere downtown. His stool had a live-edged walnut surface. The bar top appeared concrete with inlaid chunks of colored glass.

The place was almost empty.

His watch said afternoon, so Sherman ordered a bourbon from the woman behind the fancy bar. An early-twenties-something with silver hair and a nose ring. He understood why Gournsey liked the place. The sergeant certainly had a type.

Sherman drank slowly and watched the day unfold. Down the street, he spotted the FBI car *du jour*. A green Chevy Malibu. The occupant looked young and too hyper-vigilant for a veteran agent. A rookie fresh from Quantico happy to be sitting in a forest of take-out containers, watching hard for nothing at all.

Only a few differences separated him and Sherman. Notable among them was Sherman sat inside sipping a drink, not in a car eating Cheetos. Second was the FBI agent watched people coming and going to establish patterns while Sherman only cared about getting inside. After that, he'd make it up as he went.

The front door had an RFID keypad and there weren't any retail spaces inside that might allow customers to enter the building. Tailgating someone seemed like the ideal option from what he'd seen. People wanted to help others.

Beyond the front door was a security desk. Sherman observed at least one rotation of guards. He guessed at least five in total. Maybe more. Which made tailgating through the front door risky. They'd spot him for sure.

Or maybe not.

As Sherman watched, a thin and bald middle-aged man approached the building. He wore a suit and didn't look out of place among the professional crowd. Yet his actions said otherwise. He appeared nervous as if trying to sneak into a second matinee after only paying for one. Not the crime of the century, but obvious in its own way.

He timidly approached the front door, looking over his shoulder. Satisfied with his anonymity, the suit typed in a code on a small keypad that Sherman hadn't even noticed. The door opened and the man shuffled inside, all left feet and anxious.

The security guard at the front desk didn't question or stop him. Instead, he nodded toward the right most elevator. It opened and the suit stepped inside.

Sherman watched the interaction with increasing interest. He needed that code. Breaking a bone or two was a small price to pay.

"Can I get you another?" asked the bartender.

"Sure," said Sherman, figuring he had another wait in his future.

"You're the second guy to sit there staring across the street in as many days."

Sherman smiled.

Bartenders were an attentive lot by nature, but that usually developed over time. The woman wasn't old enough to have such a disposition.

"Big guy?" he asked.

"Like a mountain," she replied. "Friend of yours?"

He nodded.

She poured another finger of bourbon.

"Are you still in the service?" she asked.

Sherman said nothing. He'd underestimated the woman and suddenly felt on the back foot. Was she FBI? Or worse?

"My brother served in Afghanistan," she continued, filling in his silence. "He left wearing the same boots you got on right now."

"And when he came home?"

She sniffed. "Couldn't say. He came home in a metal box."

"I'm sorry to hear that. Truly. I lost a lot of friends over there. They all came back in boxes."

She nodded and remained quiet. Tears welled in her eyes but defied gravity and remained suspended.

"What are you and your friend looking for over there?" she asked in a shaky voice.

Sherman sipped on his bourbon and pondered how to proceed.

"You seem observant… what would a guy like me want in a building like that?"

The woman paused and planted her elbows on the counter, cupping her hands under her chin.

"You don't live there. No one stares so attentively at their own home. Which means you want to get inside, but you don't look the type for the average visitor."

"Why not?"

"You're wearing jeans and a T-shirt. Most guys I see wear a suit."

"Why are they wearing suits?"

She shrugged. "Beats me, but they're wearing less of it when they come out. No tie. Jacket in hand. Maybe an untucked shirt. It doesn't take a genius to figure out what they were doing."

"Humor me," said Sherman.

"The world's oldest profession or whatever bullshit name they call it now. I'd say politician is an older profession, but I suppose a guy came up with the phrase to begin with."

"I agree with both parts of your argument."

"Does that mean you want to get inside?" she asked, her eyes narrowing.

"Yes, but not for that reason."

"What then?"

"They harassed a friend of mine. I want to voice my objections over their behavior."

"No offence, but they don't seem the type to embrace constructive criticism."

"You've seen them before?" asked Sherman.

"Just once. A few weeks ago. This stunningly gorgeous lady walked out dressed to kill but it was barely afternoon. No clubs were open then. She stood there looking confused for a minute. Then this big bald guy charged out after her like a fucking bull. He grabbed her by the hair and pulled her back inside."

"That sounds familiar," said Sherman. "What did you do?"

"Called the cops but no one ever showed up."

Sherman gave a sympathetic smile but said nothing.

"Sometimes the guys come over here for a celebratory drink afterward. Maybe that skinny creep will too."

"You saw him?" asked Sherman, impressed with the bartender's skills.

"Not for the first time either."

Sherman slid the finger of bourbon across the bar. "I better switch to water while we wait."

"I'm Julia, by the way," she said, extending her hand.

Sherman took it. "Nice to meet you, Julia. I'm Frank."

"Likewise, Frank."

The bar remained mostly empty while they waited. Sherman turned down Julia's offer of a free dinner from the kitchen. He didn't want a full stomach for the things he planned on doing.

They kept chatting and Julia's sad tale slowly unfurled. Sherman recognized the plot immediately. Her brother, Ben, joined the Marines straight out of high school, over her parent's loud objections. They wanted him to go to college. Ben had other ideas. He shipped out a few months before the war ended, excited for the opportunity. Next thing she knew, two guys knocked at her parent's door and told them a truck bomb had blown Ben to bits.

The story hit Sherman with an unexpected weight. Ben wasn't even alive when the 'Forever' wars started. He'd only know the Twin Towers as a distant idea, almost mythical in the greater American ethos. Sherman wondered if he would have joined under the same circumstances.

Suddenly, the thin man with big ears disgorged through the front doors of the apartment building. A half-twisted smile of satisfaction stole across his face.

Sherman stood up to follow.

He needn't have bothered. The thin man looked left and right, then straight. He stood there in contemplation as if assessing his options for what remained of the day. Deciding, he sprung forward and crossed the street, heading for the bar.

Sherman sat back down.

"Told you so," said Julia.

"I need that door code," Sherman replied.

She nodded as the suit barreled inside and took a seat on the far side of the horseshoe-shaped bar.

Up close, Sherman liked the guy even less, but he didn't

rush to judgement. *To each their own*, he thought but then remembered the women trapped across the street. Did the man know of their ordeal? Did he care or was their suffering part of the attraction? Maybe the answer was yes. Maybe no. Either way, a broken arm would teach him a lesson.

Julia chatted him up while Sherman drank water and tried not to look interested in their conversation.

The guy ordered a bottle of domestic beer and gulped it down like a college drinking contest. Julia brought him another, which he drank slower, tempered in his thirst. The glow of whatever happened dulled, but he remained content with his situation. Sherman wondered how long the high lasted or if remorse settled in later.

Beer two turned to three and Julia kept the conversation alive. Small talk mostly, but she weaved her way through the guy's life without giving away her own story.

The suit refused Julia's offer of a fourth beer. Fumbling through his wallet, the guy tossed some cash on the bar and headed towards the bathroom. Sherman stood to follow but Julia held up her hand and walked over to his side.

"Is this what you're looking for?"

She held up a sticky note. Scribbled across the yellow paper in shaky writing was a six-digit number. Below that read, 'Ends at 10 PM'.

"It fell out of his wallet when he paid," she said.

Sherman took the note and smiled.

"Out of curiosity," she continued. "How were you going to get that? Ask nicely?"

He shrugged. "Not nicely."

She nodded towards the restroom. "You've still got a chance."

"It's tempting, but I'll give him a pass."

"And the people across the street… do they get a pass?" she asked.

"Not likely."

Julia bobbed her head along with his answer.

"Thanks for the help," said Sherman as he put a hundred dollars on the counter. "I hope that covers my tab."

"I comped your drinks."

"Then consider it compensation for dealing with him."

She smiled. "Tell your friend to stop by again."

Sherman nodded and waved on his way out into the reddening evening sky.

Chapter Twenty-Four

For a Monday evening, the city still thrummed with life. Summer still dazzled in recent memory and the first awkward early snow had not arrived. People enjoyed themselves in the warm air. Sherman eyed the steady stream of pedestrians from his hotel window.

He'd headed straight back from the bar with the sticky note in tow. Landers was still at her office. He took a shower and napped. Sleep mattered, so he took it.

Around seven, he heard a knock and got up. Landers had a key, but he appreciated the warning, and she appreciated not having a gun in her face when she walked in. A genuine win-win situation.

"Are you napping?"

"Past tense. I was napping. No longer."

She didn't apologize and poured herself a small, neat glass of bourbon. They sat together on the bed in silence with neither one quite ready to speak.

Landers broke first. "I'm not sure this is a good idea."

"I take it the guy out front is not alone."

"No. Apparently, they have the fourth floor under video surveillance."

"Audio too?"

"No, but if you go up there…" she trailed off.

"They're watching the apartment from across the street, right?"

Landers nodded.

Something clicked in Sherman's mind. "I don't think they're dumb enough to have the operation in plain sight. The FBI might watch the women, but not the action."

"They'll see you coming out of the elevator."

"The Johns don't take the normal elevator. I watched a guy enter this afternoon. The security guard pointed to his left. The normal elevators are behind him. They must be using a freight elevator. Something that keeps their clientele hidden."

"Assuming that's true, how are you going to get on the freight elevator?"

He held up the note. "I have the entry code for today."

"You didn't pay for—"

"Of course not. I took it from a satisfied customer."

Landers cocked her head to one side.

"He's unharmed and still breathing," countered Sherman. "The note fell out of his pocket."

She looked unconvinced. "After you dangled him over a roof?"

"I was planning on breaking his tibia, but the note fell out before I did."

"Lucky guy."

"Twice over."

Landers frowned. "Fine. You can get inside, but I'm sure they have cameras too. The cops could use it against you. Assuming you're going to do your thing up there."

"No way they keep the footage. It would compromise their entire client list. I bet it's for internal use only."

"Which means they'll see you coming. Frank, I don't care how good you are, waltzing in like that is suicide. I'm sure they all have your photo by now. Be on the lookout for a crazy bearded guy. Armed and dangerous."

Sherman hoped they had his picture. That meant they were scared. Fear makes people do dumb things. Mistakes they wouldn't make under normal circumstances. He wanted them to be afraid. It made any additional collateral damage more meaningful.

"Leave that part to me," said Sherman.

"Can Gournsey help?"

"No."

"Maybe I could—"

"Not a chance," he interjected. "If your colleagues catch you inside… well, you know the consequences. I imagine wherever they send you will make Denver look like paradise."

"You're not wrong."

"Then grab a seat at the bar across the street. If Julia is still working, tell her I sent you. Trust me, you'll offer her a job afterward."

"Why?"

"She needs to work for the acronyms, otherwise, her talents are going to waste."

"What makes you think she isn't already?" asked Landers.

Sherman paused. He hadn't fully answered that question for himself. "If there's a SWAT team waiting for me, then I got played. If not, offer her a job."

"It doesn't work like that."

"Fine. Give her a referral."

"Okay," agreed Landers. "I'll go to the bar. Then what, call you when the SWAT team shows up?"

"I'm thinking if anyone shows up, it will be guys in a black SUV. Not law enforcement."

"Understood," replied Landers. "I'll be your spotter."

The body armor in the duffle bag wasn't designed with fashion in mind. Sherman struggled to keep it concealed under his jacket. The extra bulk added thirty pounds to his appearance. Not that Sherman cared for appearances, except if it prevented him from getting past the security guards.

Landers insisted he ditch the boots in favor of tennis shoes. Reluctantly, he agreed. The baseball cap he wore was non-negotiable. Both knew he'd need it to keep his face off camera and the news.

"Remember to change your gait," she said. "They have programs—"

"That can track you by how you walk. I know."

"Of course, you know," she replied.

"You should go first. I'll follow in a few minutes," said Sherman.

She squinted at him like there was something left unsaid but exited the room anyway.

Sherman listened to her footsteps in the hall and the familiar ding of the elevator. Only then did he load magazines for the pistol. The simplicity of bullet on top of bullet centered his mind. Simple steps for simple actions. No matter how complex the war was, each battle unfolded in discrete steps. At the heart of it all was a plain equation of brutality. He understood that equation. He was the sum.

He slipped the loaded magazines into their appropriate holders on his vest. The suppressor went into a jacket pocket, the pistol in another. He would assemble them in the elevator. With one last look at the street below, he left the room and took the stairs.

Sherman kept to the shadows and edges. He took alleys and avoided crowded crosswalks. Anything to stay out of sight and mind. A man not seen was a man unconsidered. Anonymous. Faceless. He liked those things.

Emerging between blocks, Sherman crossed the street behind the FBI car *de jour*. He slowed while approaching the apartment. Bending his back, he slumped forward, losing two inches of height. His left leg dragged ever so slightly. He kept his eyes down, glancing furtively like a man uneasy with his surroundings.

Sherman stopped at the apartment's front door, looking left and right. He fumbled for the sticky note, feigning nervousness. Mimicking all the mannerisms of the thin man with big ears.

The code still worked. The door beeped and clicked.

Sherman stepped inside.

The security guard on duty looked up. He eyed Sherman carefully, thoughtfully, like a carpenter sizing the length of lumber. The man had the shoulders of a linebacker but with gray streaked through his beard. An ex-linebacker. A college player that never turned pro or a professional with a brief career.

"Take the freight elevator up to four," said the guard. He motioned toward his left.

Sherman followed the instructions. The door opened. Gray moving blankets covered the wall. Protection for the furniture. People who moved into a glass building had fancy furniture, he reasoned.

He pushed the buttons for three and four.

The door closed. Sherman attached the suppressor behind his back without looking up. Elevators usually had cameras. He assumed this one did as well.

The door opened with a ding on the third floor. Sherman glanced down the empty hallway and made for the nearest stairwell. He didn't know what reception awaited him one floor up but didn't intend on experiencing it from the inside of a metal box.

Only the whirring sound of air met him in the stairwell. Sherman moved fast up the next flight of stairs, arriving at the metal fire door as the elevator dinged.

He cracked the door, revealing a small alcove. The elevator was around the corner to his right.

"What the fuck!" said a voice with a deep, commanding edge. "Call down and make sure those pricks sent him to the right floor."

"Amateurs," said another voice.

One guard was polite security. Two were an unwelcome party. Three spelled trouble. Four or more meant they'd fully reacted to his presence.

Remember to make a mess, he thought to himself. *They tried to kill Asal and the girls. They showed up at Landers' apartment. Zarak's life was at stake. Stoke their fears.*

He slid out from the alcove, pistol at the ready. Two gruff men stood by the elevator. They wore suits. Cheap suits, but they still dressed the part. Big burly guys like bouncers. A show of force for the clientele. A reminder to behave.

One watched the elevator while the other talked on the phone. Neither saw him approach.

Sherman made a mess out of them.

Blood splattered across the walls. Bright red rivulets slid

down the slick stainless-steel doors. It pooled on the fancy carpet. Chunks of skull stuck to the light fixtures.

Satisfied with part one, Sherman stepped back into the alcove and waited for a moment. No one came running.

It occurred to Sherman that he didn't know which apartment to enter. The guards knew but that knowledge now dripped down the walls. He turned north, per Landers' warning about surveillance.

The hall stretched left and right. All the doors looked the same, minus the numbers. Lots of options for lots of girls. Too many.

Only then did he notice the QR codes attached next to the numbers. They linked to images of women, often nude or compromised. All were young, some more than young. The codes went all the way down to his left. At least five doors.

To his right were four more. The fifth had nothing but a small metal sign that read 'Private'. Sherman knocked on the door and stepped to the side.

Scuffling sounds came from inside, followed by an obscenity in a foreign language.

The door swung open.

The bald guy they'd seen escorting the women from the airport SUV stood in the doorframe. He was half-dressed and redder than an angry bull.

"Can't you fucking read?" he bellowed.

Sherman shot him an inch above the right eye. No warning. No hesitation. Pull. Clack. Gone. All in the blink of an eye.

The bald guy fell back into the apartment with a slippery thump. Screams followed immediately. A woman rightfully yelling bloody murder. People stirred. The floor thumped with activity. Doors cracked open and curious young eyes gazed out.

Sherman retreated toward the stairwell. Before he rounded the corner, the furthest door banged open and the guy with the shiny shirt ran out into the hallway like he was a movie hero coming to save the maiden in distress.

He saw Sherman, stopped, and tried to say something. His lips moved but no sound came out.

Sherman made a mess of him too.

Three to the chest and one in the face for good measure. Tight groupings too, just in case anyone at The Company mistook his actions for a jilted customer exacting revenge.

Make a mess. Send a message.

He'd checked all the boxes. It was time to leave.

One flight down the stairs, his phone rang. Landers was calling.

"You'd better take a rear exit. The FBI are coming in the front."

"Thanks," he said and hung up.

Sherman stepped out onto the second floor and casually strolled to the furthest stairwell. He took that down to an emergency exit on the east side. It led to an alleyway that connected with another and so on. Downtown was filled with them.

He barreled through the door and, minutes later, disappeared into a crowd of pedestrians enjoying the waning nights of warmth.

Chapter Twenty-Five

Megan Landers hadn't waited at the bar for over thirty minutes before her work phone rang. Red and blue lights reflected down the street in front of the bar. A gruesome carnival of sorts. One she'd seen many times. But this time, she knew the perpetrator. She'd even helped him.

"This is Special Agent Landers," she said, answering the call.

"Agent Landers," came the reply. She knew the voice. Even despised it.

"Special Agent in Charge, what can I do for you?"

"There's been a development in your case."

Landers said nothing.

"We need all hands on deck to help with the investigation."

"Of course, sir. How can I help?"

He rattled off the address she could see out the bar window. "Meet me there in fifteen minutes."

"Yes, sir, fifteen minutes."

He didn't bother with a reply.

Landers threw a twenty onto the counter along with her business card. Sherman was right about Julia. The woman possessed undeniable talents wasted behind the counter of a bar.

Slipping out the back door, Landers ran flat out for the hotel a few blocks away. The sprint ate up a third of her fifteen minutes. She changed into work clothes, left Sherman a cursory note, and sprinted back.

Fourteen minutes after the call, Landers arrived back at the scene of the crime. SAC Harrington glared at her like she was already late.

"You look flushed," he said with a disapproving glance.

"I was out running when you called, sir."

He sniffed in apparent disbelief or disdain. "We've got four bodies upstairs, Agent Landers, and a potential turf war on our hands. I need all available agents, including you."

"I'm here, sir. How can I help?"

"Start with some answers. Then you can get on with your job."

Landers didn't like the sound of his demand. The SAC may have been an asshole, but the FBI was still a meritocracy for those coloring inside the lines. She knew Harrington deserved intellectual respect.

"Answers, sir?" she asked.

"To my questions," he retorted.

"I'll do my best," she replied with a fake compliant smile.

"CCTV footage from your apartment captured five men entering the basement. Two of them you shot in self-defense upon re-entering your apartment."

"Correct," she replied, but something made her feel concerned with agreeing to the statement.

"And the other three assailants? You omitted them in your statement."

"I didn't encounter anyone else, sir."

The SAC raised an eyebrow and continued, "Our review of footage tonight suggests a man of similar build was at both locations."

"Are you suggesting a connection?" she asked.

"I'm merely stating that the same shooter was at your apartment and this one. Perhaps you'd like to offer a theory explaining such a coincidence."

Now Landers really didn't like the SAC's tone. It skewed in a direction ending with her incarceration.

"Sounds like he's our primary shooter," she said, realizing her remark made Sherman suspect number one in multiple homicides.

"And yet, you didn't see him?"

She shook her head. "No, sir. Maybe he's the boss."

The SAC didn't blink. "Care to guess how many suspects carried out this brazen act of violence?"

Landers didn't need to guess. She knew.

"Three to five," she offered.

"Precisely one," replied the SAC.

"I'm not the only one they're after."

"It depends how you look at the situation, Agent Landers. The four bodies upstairs all worked for The Company. Along with the two corpses in your apartment. The question I keep asking myself is, why would the same person be at both crime scenes? Unless, of course, you didn't do the shooting. But that couldn't be, Agent Landers, right? I don't need to remind you of the penalties for lying to a federal officer."

Landers recognized the monumental amount of shit

that could rain down on her. The SAC was smarter than his smug, Ivy League smile betrayed.

"That would be problematic, sir, but I have no reason to change my statement. Maybe I beat this man you speak of to the punch. Do you know anything about him?"

The SAC gave her a severe look. "Nothing, other than his remarkable skill-set. I can only assume military experience, but lacking proof, it is only an assumption. Inferring from our two crime scenes, I also assume he works for a third party."

"Hence your potential turf war," said Landers.

"Unless you'd like to proffer another theory linking the man to both locations."

"No, sir," she said.

"I thought as much," said Harrington, studying her carefully. "You can start by taking witness statements from across the street. I'd like to know what they saw or what video they might have. The bar is a logical choice to start."

"Of course," she replied, feeling incredibly insecure in her position.

Several Denver police officers were already inside talking with the patrons. A young officer with close-cropped blonde hair and a bright smile spotted her walking over. She held up her badge before he said a word. Landers hated explaining who she was to those that should already know but were too blinded to see.

"I already knew," said the young man. He had a pleasant demeanor and a kind face.

"I'm Special Agent Landers," she said and read his nametag. "Have you questioned everyone, Officer Keller?"

"Everyone but the bartender."

"Good, I'd like a recap after I talk to…" Landers trailed

off and looked to confirm Julia was still working. "After I talk with her."

"Of course," said Keller, who followed diligently behind her."

"I can handle this," she said.

"If it's all the same, Agent Landers, I'd like to have my own record. I don't want to blow something this big because of missing notes."

She forced her mouth into a smile, wondering if the SAC was watching from across the street. "Of course, Officer Keller. Why don't you take the lead?"

"Thanks," he replied with satisfaction.

Earnest and naïve, she thought.

Julia stood behind the bar watching their approach.

"Hello, I'm Officer Keller and this is Agent Landers of the FBI. We'd like to ask you a few questions about tonight."

Julia smiled and nodded toward a quieter side of the bar. She winked at Landers as Keller glanced away.

The officer was thorough if conventional and by the book. He was not a bad interviewer. For her part, Julia acted smoother than velvet. She said all the things Landers wanted and nothing extra.

"Are you sure you don't remember anyone out of the ordinary?" he asked.

"It's a bar," said Julia. "I have enough trouble remembering who ordered what."

Keller started to counter her remark but stopped himself. Landers sensed his uneasiness, like Julia intimidated the officer.

"I think that's enough," said Landers. "Thanks for your help." She smiled at Julia and made for the front door.

"Agent Landers," said Keller, chasing her down. "I hope I did alright back there."

"You did fine," she replied.

"Thanks, I've got one more witness to interview if you want to supervise."

Landers didn't. She wanted a hot shower, a glass of bourbon, and a soft bed. But she was curious.

"Okay. Who else?"

"A homeless guy in the alley out back. Said he saw someone else."

Landers gave a faceless grimace. The shit was piling up. "Lead the way."

Officer Keller walked toward the back door she'd run out of not more than an hour before. Landers didn't remember seeing anyone loitering in the alley, but she'd been distracted by the SAC's call. She wasn't looking for people camped out in the shadows. She hoped they hadn't gotten a good look.

Landers stepped through the back door followed by Keller. The alley was dark, lit only by faintly pulsing emergency lights. Not a chance they'd recognized her. Too dark.

"Where is the witness?" she asked, turning toward Keller.

Peripherally, she saw something yellowish in his hand.

Then came a pop, clicking, and body-shaking pain.

Fuck, she thought.

The last thing Landers remembered was a long shadow in the alley, a trick of the light, and the world went black.

Chapter Twenty-Six

The next thirty minutes of Landers' life existed as a terrifying blur. There was motion. A car, she guessed. But no sound or light. Her hands were bound behind her back. Hard, thick lines cut into her wrists and ankles. Zip ties. The kind cops keep for crowd control.

This is it, she thought.

The end of ends. Tricked by a kind smile and badge. How foolish she'd been. The anger and shame ate her up, clawing great gashes in her ego.

Vibration from the floor meant they were still moving. Landers kicked her cramped legs but only hit metal. Tasered and dumped in a trunk. How undignified.

As the minutes ticked by absent of any sense but smell, her foreboding grew. Death was one outcome—an inevitability she'd come to accept in her line of work. She'd nearly met that fate in California, and if it wasn't for Sherman, she would have. Afterwards, the great unknown wasn't such a grand mystery. She understood death in some small way.

What she didn't know was the immediate mystery. What awaited her once the car stopped? Dying didn't particularly perturb her, but pain did. Landers understood no one went to such lengths without demanding answers. Since she had no intention of giving anyone up, that entailed pain. Lots of it. The Company didn't take half-measures.

Memories of the night tumbled upon each other in great waves as she reconstructed her mistakes and impending doom. No matter how she broke it down, one question kept coming up. How did they know about her?

Her answer, the only one that made sense, was a mole. The Company had other cops on the payroll, Officer Keller included. Having an FBI agent in their pocket wasn't a far stretch. In fact, it was an inevitability and Landers hated herself for not seeing the obvious elephant in the room.

Only one person could have kept an indictment at bay. Only one person called her in and sent her across the street.

Special Agent in Charge Harrington was the mole. The traitor. She knew it in her bones. In her rattled, tired, aching, terrified bones.

The car stopped moving and ceased vibrating. Engine off. Nowhere to go.

Here they come, she thought.

Even with the advanced warning, Landers still flinched when two pairs of hands reached down and jerked her roughly out of the trunk. She fell on the ground, which was hard and cold like concrete. A sharp pain zipped up her arm after she hit the ground.

The world was still dark and soundless, but Landers smelled oil and gasoline. A mechanic's workshop of sorts. Judging by the travel time, they weren't anywhere close to Sherman and downtown Denver.

The hands returned and scooped her up under her

arms. They pulled Landers across the floor and deposited her on a hard metal chair. A folding chair, judging by the way her hands hung in the open space behind her back.

With a sudden swiftness, sound returned to her world. Landers heard everything all at once like a firehose of noise. The hum of machines. The soft whisper of voices. Footsteps slapping on concrete. The distant howl of a train horn.

She waited, trembling with anticipation of the pain.

"Agent Landers," said a voice she didn't recognize.

The man had none of Keller's youthful exuberance nor any discernible accent. West Coast adjacent was all she could guess.

"I'd apologize for all this rather elaborate to do, but I don't think you'd believe me and, to be candid, I'd be lying. Having said that, I'd like to skip the formalities and strike at the matter's core."

She said nothing, as nothing she said would change this preamble.

"I appreciate your brevity, so let me return the favor. We have questions about your friend. The one you saved in the parking lot. The one who is currently wreaking his own brand of useless havoc. I want his name and location. If you can answer truthfully, we'll return you to your apartment alive, assuming the crime scene tape is gone."

"Is that all?" she asked. Her voice sounded stronger than she felt.

"I'd also like to know the location of Asal Khada and her daughters. They are collateral against a deal with Zarak and we need them back for the sake of fairness."

"That one's easy," she said. "I have no fucking idea where they are."

"Ah, I knew you had a warrior's spirit. No matter. I leave

you in capable hands. Grouch here did this professionally in a former life. Well, I suppose he still does."

"That's right," said a deep, resonant voice that made Landers flinch.

"With that settled, I must depart. It was a pleasure to meet you, Agent Landers. Although, I dare say I would have enjoyed seeing what's coming."

Textbook psychopath, she realized. No other way to describe a man like that. He sounded in charge. The boss. Landers still couldn't see, but she bet he wore combat boots.

"Megan Landers," said the deep voice. It was smooth like a movie trailer, and she was the star. "Did they teach you advanced interrogation techniques at Quantico?"

She said nothing.

"Silence only buys you pain."

A thick, calloused hand grabbed her elbow and dug deeply into the joint. Electric tendrils of pain burned upward from her fingers to her shoulder. Landers yelped, trying to catch the sound, not wanting to let them win.

"I've broken all manner of people," continued the interrogator. "I've seen batshit crazy terrorists piss themselves. Watched a Chechen go so mad, he ate his own finger to get out. You… well, you ain't gonna last ten minutes. Best to tell me names and locations. Then you can go back to that lovely bourbon collection."

They know everything, she realized. Everything. They probably got her personnel file straight from that crooked asshole, SAC Harrington.

"I don't know where Asal or the girls are hiding. I haven't seen them since your two shithead friends broke into my building and tried to kill us. Why don't you ask them? Oh, wait, I splattered their fucking brains on my walls. Thanks for the free redecoration."

The hand came back and caught her wrist on the inside edge. Pain rolled through her arm. She squealed but kept most of the hurt hidden.

Grouch scoffed. "We haven't even started yet. Wait 'til I break apart those joints with a fillet knife. Then we'll see what you're really made of."

Landers considered giving Sherman up. He was a big boy who could handle himself. Why not stop her own mutilation? But she knew that slippery slope would end with her in an oil drum full of acid. These guys didn't hesitate to kill. The only reason she was still alive enough to be tortured was that Sherman scared them. Landers would cease to have value once they knew his name.

She constructed a lie. Reaching back in time, she remembered the names of men she'd locked up in Iraq. Soldiers that didn't care about the flag on their shoulders.

"Don't bother lying," said Grouch as if reading her mind. "I always know when people lie. Call it a gift. Silence gets you pain. Lies cost you a finger. Understand?"

Landers nodded.

"Good. Now tell me who shot the men in your apartment and our operation?"

Landers scrambled to come up with a name, but her memory sagged and leaked like an old roof. Why couldn't she remember?

Shit, she thought.

The hand grabbed her elbow again.

"Wait," she yelled and tried to think of someone. Anyone but Sherman. Nothing came. "Oh, go fuck yourself."

Excruciating pain once more raced through her nerves. The tendons in her elbow popped. White streaks covered the inside of her eyelids. Her breath came short and fast.

Somewhere during that overwhelming wave of pain, Landers heard a distinctive clack-whoosh sound, but her brain struggled to place the noise.

Then it came again in quick succession.

Clack-clack-clack-whoosh.

The pain stopped.

Landers heard a heavy, squishy thump like a wet sandbag hitting the ground. Silence followed. No talking or snickering. No threats or questions. Just the tiniest hint of movement. Almost imperceivable. Had she not been blind-folded and her hearing heightened, she would have missed it.

"I'm here," said a voice. A voice she knew. A voice she craved to hear.

"Frank?" she warbled.

"I'm going to cut the zip ties. Try not to flinch."

Even with his warning, Landers jumped a little when the blade brushed against her skin.

Once free, Landers gingerly removed her blindfold and blinked into a bright overhead light.

She was in a mechanic's garage. Tools lined the wall and several nearby workbenches overflowed with car parts. Her nose got that part right.

Directly to her left lay the wet sandbag she heard hit the ground. Grouch had two holes in his tan forehead and barely any brains left. Two more bodies lay just behind Sherman, next to a door with a tin exit sign nailed into it.

"Are you whole?" asked Sherman.

Landers appreciated he didn't ask if she was okay because she certainly was not. Her arm hurt like hell but still bent in all the right places.

"My arm fucking hurts… and my ego, if I'm honest."

"Arms heal," he said.

Landers smiled at the joke before realizing he was there, in the flesh.

"How are you here?" she exclaimed.

"I saw the cop toss you in the trunk."

"You were the shadow in the alley."

"I was going to sneak in through the back door when I saw you with the badge."

"And from there to here? How'd that happen?"

"Julia drove me."

"She gave you a ride here. Why?"

"I'm a trustworthy guy."

Landers said nothing.

"She was already onto the cop," he said and pointed to the smug face on the floor, now missing vital bits.

Landers sensed something was missing. She looked around at the three bodies. None of them wore boots like Sherman, even if she never saw them.

"Did you see the man talking with me?" she asked.

Sherman pointed at the floor.

"No," she replied. "The man talking with me called him Grouch. There was someone else. I think he was the guy from the parking lot. The one who has the same boots."

"Did he speak strangely? Not an accent, but speech pattern?"

Landers nodded.

"The spook," said Sherman.

"Oh, shit," she said.

Sherman, who was busy searching through dead people's pockets, turned. "What is it?"

"If your spook was here, that means he's working directly with the SAC."

"The Special Agent in Charge?"

"He called me in. He sent me across the street to interview people in the bar. The Company has other cops on the payroll, why not him too?"

"Only one thing to do," said Sherman.

"Am I going to like it?"

"Depends on if you enjoy going in to work."

"Show up and see how he reacts?" she asked.

The plan was not far off her own, but in her version, the SAC ended up taking a long elevator ride to the basement with no brakes.

"We play this close to the vest. See who acts surprised. In the meantime, you'll have access to the case files. Find out who the spook is and where I can find him."

"Funny thing," said Landers. "That's exactly what he wanted to know about you."

Chapter Twenty-Seven

The next morning rose like a cruel reminder of her precarious situation. Even the alarm clock's beep came out unusually harsh. Landers slipped out of the hotel bed and straight into the shower. Sherman didn't budge.

She let the hot water run over her body. Digesting the previous night threw off unpleasant thoughts. Betrayal, treason, conspiracy, and murder were but a few in a long list. Dueling images of Harrington and Officer Keller swirled through her mind. An entitled smugness lurked beneath their thin facades. Two sides of the same traitorous knife stuck in her back.

The nagging fear instilled by them burrowed under her skin. A sense of powerlessness sapped her confidence, unraveling it bit by bit. The aftermath was almost worse than the actual attempts on her life. Dark second-guesses lingered and simmered.

Toweled dry and dressed, Landers emerged to find coffee and croissants on the little table. A note nearby read, 'I'll be close'.

A tad condescending perhaps but reassuring after her previous encounter. Landers sat and ate while the morning unfolded. She headed out just before her first meeting of the day.

Eight in the morning meetings were not new in the pantheon of government agencies, but Landers knew SAC Harrington relished the time with a torturous exuberance. She'd seen him gesticulate and cajole from her pint-sized cubicle but had not endured his scrutiny.

She walked into the conference room at 7:55 AM and everyone looked at her like she was late.

Harrington eyed her disdainfully but not with surprise. At least not that she saw.

Good actors, she thought. *Never miss a beat.*

"Glad you can join us, Agent Landers. I hope I didn't inconvenience you with such an early briefing."

"Apologies, sir. It won't happen again," she replied, knowing any attempt at reason would only erode her standing.

"It surely won't," he replied and went on talking.

"All his briefings start fifteen minutes early," whispered a woman next to Landers.

"Noted," she replied.

Landers glanced around the table of fellow agents searching for a clue. An unguarded look. A gaze held too long. Anything suspicious.

Most of her fellow agents didn't acknowledge her existence, which made sense after the SAC's reaction. They were merely modeling his disdain for her.

The only person to look in her direction was Todd, the one who'd told her about the surveillance. Landers hoped he wouldn't connect the dots. He wasn't the sharpest crayon, but long shots happened every day.

The meeting unfolded with little progress to show for their late-night efforts. The deceased men were Lithuanian by birth. They'd overstayed their visas by years. No one questioned why they were not deported except for Landers, but she kept the thought to herself. The trafficked women didn't want to talk or testify against their traffickers, so they were being deported back home. To this, Landers objected verbally, but the SAC waved her comment away.

"Our hands are tied," he said.

As for the overall case against The Company, Landers saw no reason for hope. The apartment was rented by a shell company buried under so many other shells, it made the forensic accountants dizzy.

Landers said nothing as the long list of investigative failures rattled on. She didn't want to draw attention to herself but bided her time to access the files.

As the meeting adjourned, she caught one of Todd's looks, which felt more licentious than anything else. He struck her as the type of guy to hit on a co-worker at a company party.

"I didn't realize you were on this case," he said as they walked out.

"I think the SAC is just trying to keep tabs on me so I don't muck it up."

Todd smiled and his eyes flicked further down than necessary. "You almost got shot the other night. Do you know why those guys followed you?"

"Wrong place, wrong time, I guess."

Todd nodded. "Well, if you need a place to crash, I have room."

"Thanks, I'll manage."

Todd smiled again and walked away.

Landers practically ran for her computer and the

recently unlocked case files. She grabbed a legal pad and pen, settling in for a long note-taking session.

Time rumbled by for Sherman in a blur of traffic and customers. Having resumed his surveillance of Comet's truck stop that morning, he'd found nothing different. Same grouping of vehicles out back. Same group of guys inside. A steady stream of people coming and going. The usual suspicious switching of semi-trucks and excess to-go containers. The FBI surveillance van hadn't moved. Even Zarak's car remained parked behind the warehouse.

For all the previous night's activity, he'd expected some change in the normal operating procedures. As a generalization, if one base got attacked in the region, the Army heightened security on the rest. Yet he didn't see any outward difference. Eight to ten guys inside, nothing extra. Sherman gave space for the possibility of extra security cameras, but cameras don't prevent crime. They only provide evidence after the fact.

As for an explanation, the only thing that made sense to Sherman was The Company felt protected by the FBI's presence. In some bizarre twist of fate, law enforcement protected the crooks from Sherman.

A strange new world, he thought.

Lunch came and went before his phone range.

"Are you there?" asked Landers.

"That leaves a lot to interpretation."

"You know what I meant."

"I'm watching American capitalism in action. Did you confirm your suspicion?"

"Nothing definitive yet but I have some information you'll find interesting."

"I'm all ears," said Sherman.

"Not now," she said and sounded off.

"Pillow talk then," he suggested.

"Of a sort."

"When?" he asked,

"An hour."

"Eyes up. Head down."

Landers grunted something and hung up.

She'd sounded overly cautious, bordering on paranoid, which didn't fit her personality at all. Sherman turned on the Camaro and eased into traffic. With thirty minutes to spare, he grabbed a burrito before heading to the hotel. He parked in another low-tech lot and stuffed a small box full of cash he'd borrowed from the guys at the garage. With luck, the car would last one more day before the cops figured out it was missing. Eventually, they would find their colleague and start looking for his missing car and whoever took it.

Sherman had just finished a thigh-sized serving of *carne asada* when Landers walked into the hotel room. She tossed her jacket on the bed and poured herself two fingers of bourbon from a rapidly disappearing bottle. It was three in the afternoon.

"That bad," said Sherman.

"It ain't good."

He sat until she finished.

"We have three main issues," she continued. "First, they don't know the name of the guy with your boots. They ran a few photos through facial recognition and got bupkis."

"Makes sense if he worked for the CIA."

"No I.D. and no name, but there are rumors."

"What kind of rumors?" asked Sherman.

"That he still works for the government."

"As in the CIA is active on US soil?"

Landers nodded. "Officially, that is a big no-no. Unofficially, that is the rumor."

"Is that why they're not pursuing a case?" he asked.

"If he's acting on behalf of Uncle Sam, arresting him would cause an almighty avalanche of shit."

"Heads would roll," said Sherman.

Landers nodded and poured another finger of bourbon.

"And the third problem?" asked Sherman.

"Actually, four. I misspoke."

Sherman sighed.

"Third is the goods moving in and out of Comet's are tied to the cartels. In case you were wondering about going after the merchandise. Don't."

"Noted. Don't blow up the cartel's drugs."

"Which leads me to the fourth problem."

"The wind-up makes it sound worse," said Sherman.

She nodded. "Zarak is on the FBI's list of known associates. They have a file on him. Everything immigration knows, plus some."

"Like his wife's phone number?" asked Sherman.

Landers nodded.

"Any way to see who accessed that file? It might point the finger at your mole."

"I already checked," replied Landers. "Everyone from the SAC on down looked at the file."

"Any recent ones?" asked Sherman.

"No, but you're avoiding the bigger issue."

He nodded. "Why is Zarak a known associate? And was I wrong about him?"

"People change," said Landers. "I don't know him, but

maybe the stress of starting over and living in that shitty apartment got to him. There are thousands of stories with the same ending. Zarak wouldn't be the first or the last."

Sherman didn't take offense at her words because they carried the truth. Circumstances morphed all the time, and with them, came the shifting sands of human desire. He couldn't fault Zarak for wanting more. The man deserved more.

"Let me tell you a story about the man Zarak was and, I think, still is."

Landers sat down next to him without a word, looking like she'd expected to hear something.

"This was a good six years into the war. The Taliban's strength had not diminished like the generals imagined but it wasn't as bad as Iraq. My team rotated between the two so that we knew how to fight both wars."

"Keeping your feet wet," added Landers.

"In vastly different rivers, but yeah. We'd just rotated back into northeastern Afghanistan when shit started rolling downhill. The snow had melted, and the mud dried up. The Taliban moved back in, and the fighting season was in full bloom. We had this grand plan to helicopter in behind them when they went to attack the next outpost. Pure hubris. We thought of it as dropping behind enemy lines, but the entire area was behind enemy lines. Our outposts included."

"The graveyard of empires," added Landers.

"More of a potter's field of grand plans, ours included. We inserted late at night near some British garrison long forgotten and reduced to rubble."

"Ironic."

"Yeah, but I didn't find that out until later. We set out in the dark and made shitty time. When dawn broke, we'd barely got to where we expected the Taliban to retreat from.

Except they weren't retreating. They were attacking. And not some Army outpost, but us. Someone's cousin's brother's uncle heard us land and word spread like wildfire. I had eleven men under my command and the Taliban commander had fifty."

"Fuck," exclaimed Landers.

"I did what I'd always done and called in close air support. Which would have been fine, but it was exceptionally stormy that day. Great swathes of gray clung to the mountains. The fast movers couldn't see, leaving the Apaches, who got grounded because of poor visibility."

"Shit," interjected Landers, who had edged closer.

"We fought a running battle all the way back to the British rubble. By the time we got there, I had five walking wounded and one critical. I called in for evac and a couple of crazy bastards spun up and headed our way, but things deteriorated fast. They pinned us in on three sides with effective fire and we nearly spent all our ammunition. I remember watching my friend, Tillerman, dig an impromptu hole in the rubble only to discover a bunch of spent cartridges. They were ancient .577 shells from the Martini Henry rifle. Some poor British bastards died shooting them."

Landers' jaw dropped progressively as he continued.

"In the midst of nearly getting overrun, we get this call from some Afghan pilot who happened to be in the area ferrying supplies. He asked if we needed help, as if it was the most normal thing in the world. Tillerman gave our coordinates and he responded that he knew the place. 'The British graveyard', he called it. We were down to pistols and knives when he broke through the clouds. To be honest, I still don't know how he did it. I asked some Blackhawk pilots if they would have landed in those conditions. They all nodded that they would have tried, but none saw it resulting in anything but a crash landing."

"Asal said he was stupidly brave, but that sounds suicidal," said Landers.

"All twelve of us made it out alive that day because of Zarak," said Sherman.

"Don't sell yourself short, Frank. You got your men back."

Sherman looked away. Even after all those years, the emotional scar still hurt. "Yes, but I planned the mission to begin with. It was my hubris that nearly got everyone killed."

Landers didn't skip a beat before countering, "And you learned and grew and got better. That's being human, Frank. You fuck up and come out wiser. Don't fault yourself for a shortcoming inherent in humanity."

Her words of affirmation fell softly across his tense shoulders. "Thanks, but a mistake like that should not be forgiven. Because there are no second chances."

"But you got one."

"And Zarak deserves his. He might have worked for them, but I don't believe he did so knowingly."

Landers said nothing. He could see the doubts she still harbored swirling around. She was entitled to them the same way Sherman was with his convictions.

"You said they looked in the shell companies, right?" he asked.

"And found no concrete ownership links."

"But did they find any other assets or leases?"

Landers paused with her glass halfway to her lips. "I don't know. They found the SUVs, but I think they stopped there."

She raced over to her bag and aggressively turned the

pages of her legal pad. "They found the SUV and lease for the apartments under the Lithuanians but nothing else. I imagine they would have gone deep there. The next shell company had nothing but an address in the Cayman Islands. After that, it gets really murky."

"What was the name of the Cayman company?"

"Uh, hold on," replied Landers as she flipped pages back and forth. "Cobalt Ventures."

"Did you know the CIA base in Kabul was codenamed Cobalt?"

"Shit," said Landers.

"Who signed off on that?"

"Todd did the research or lack thereof. The SAC signed off on it." She turned to grab her coat. "I have some home-work to do tonight."

Sherman stood to follow.

"I'm fine," she said.

"No is not an option."

"We can't be seen together."

"You won't see me, and neither will anyone watching," assured Sherman.

"I'm not some asset that needs protecting."

"No, you're a friend, and I've already buried too many friends."

"Ah, Frank. That almost sounded sweet. Don't let it happen again."

Chapter Twenty-Eight

Despite her best efforts, Landers didn't spot Sherman once they left the hotel. The fact unnerved her. She was a capable agent, notwithstanding her mistake in trusting Officer Keller. Not seeing the obvious grated at her sense of competence. She had half a mind to double back and mess with Sherman, but toying with her protector didn't feel like a great idea. Fun, yes. But not safe.

Once inside her office, Landers moved past the guards who did not look twice at her nighttime arrival. She often worked late. So did her colleagues. Exiting the elevators, she made straight for her desk. Landers slouched in her chair, trying to minimize her silhouette above the half-height cubicle. Only a dozen co-workers remained, but the space still hummed with conversation and keyboards clacking.

Landers logged into the system.

She opened the case folder and scrolled through the files looking for Cobalt Ventures.

Reaching the last file, she stopped. She'd missed the

name. The file was somewhere with the other shell company investigations.

Landers tried again. Slower this time. She still came up empty. The file wasn't there. She checked the other folders. Nothing.

A normal person might have questioned their sanity or chalked up the discrepancy to a brain fart. Things like that happened all the time, but Landers was not a normal person. She had written the file name and read the meager contents.

The file had existed, but not anymore.

That traitorous weasel Harrington must have deleted the file. Even the case log carried no record and that supposedly kept all actions.

Undeterred, Landers grabbed a cup of coffee and settled down for a long, boring night of financial records and legal disclosures. Tedious, but necessary work. Not all FBI work involved knocking down doors and chasing suspects.

Hours passed. Outside sank into an inky darkness. Landers barely noticed.

"Burning the midnight oil," said a voice from behind.

Landers almost jumped out of her desk chair. She whirled around.

"Sorry, I didn't mean to startle you," said Todd, who leaned over the edge of her cubicle.

"It's fine, I was too deep into research to hear you."

Todd smiled his 'I want to get in your pants' smile. "What brings you in at this hour? I hope the SAC didn't assign you some financial crap."

His smile stayed wide open, but his eyes darted around her desk and piles of notes.

"Just trying to catch up on the case," she replied and

merged her notes into one pile. "Don't want to make a fool of myself in the morning briefing."

Todd nodded. "Just between us, the SAC threw you under the bus."

"Hopefully, I miss the wheels," she replied, feeling increasingly awkward with the conversation.

As Todd walked away, Landers logged out and gathered up her notes. While benign, the conversation left her feeling uneasy—a nagging sensation in the recesses of her mind.

She took the stairs down and hurried the last few flights, spurred on by a deeply buried paranoia of being followed. Landers had no rational reason to believe so, but her flight response exploded into panic.

Past the relative safety of the security guards, she waded out into the night. The street in front of the federal building had plenty of streetlights and few pedestrians.

Landers resisted the urge to call Sherman.

Paranoia, she thought. *Nothing more.*

One street led to another and she left behind the psychological safety of a well-lit place. Still, no one stood out as suspicious among the smattering of people walking their dogs and stumbling between bars. Even the homeless guys on the corner didn't look twice as she crossed the street.

"Get a grip," she muttered to herself.

Not letting Sherman know she'd left struck her as a mistake. She looked around but couldn't spot him, not that she had earlier and that was in the light of day.

Further down the block, she crossed over the light rail tracks and another street. Only four blocks remained to the hotel, but the sidewalk was closed off by orange cones and yellow tape.

Landers hesitated and turned right, meaning to skirt around the construction by moving one block over.

She scanned the area.

No one in front or behind. Nice and empty.

A train bell dinged in the distance. The late-night light rail. Probably the last one of the day. It was coming toward her, clanging away.

She glanced over her shoulder.

Someone was walking parallel to her on the other side of the street. A man. Average all around.

She glanced again.

Like Sherman, but not him. His movements were too jerky and hasty. But not drunk. He wasn't stumbling.

Landers quickened her pace and unsnapped the catch on her holster. She shifted her bag to her left shoulder, not wanting it to impede drawing her weapon.

The train rumbled toward them. The man walked faster. Landers tried to calm her growing fears.

Keep going, she silently urged. Otherwise, she'd be liable to shoot him for looking sketchy.

The man did not keep going. He made to cross the street toward her but hesitated. The oncoming train ran down the middle of the road, bells clanging loudly.

Landers saw him hop back up onto the curb. Through the passing cars, she watched him wait, hands crossed in front, with one hidden under his jacket.

She took a step behind a parked car and drew her service pistol. Her brain screamed with danger.

The train was short. Five cars, no more, but it moved along slowly. In the blur of movement, she lost sight of her pursuer. His sudden disappearance raised the hairs on her arms.

She tried to spot him through the train.

Nothing.

As the train passed, Landers crouched low, bracing for what came next.

Instead of a man charging across the street, she saw a body laying prostrate on the opposite sidewalk. Face-down on the concrete. Around his head, something viscous glinted in the faint white streetlights. In his hand was the black outline of a suppressed pistol.

Landers didn't say a word. She moved on. Gratified that her gut was right, and that Sherman kept his promises.

Sherman watched from the shadows as the man crashed to the concrete—an inert pile of flesh and bone. He unscrewed the suppressor from the pistol and placed them back into his jacket pockets. He watched Landers turn toward the hotel. She hurried, but with more confidence in her step.

Despite her unease, Sherman knew Landers would have dealt with the man similarly. But that would have brought more questions and scrutiny. They couldn't afford a spotlight on Landers' situation. Better to leave it with the local police. Maybe they'd chalk it up to a gang shooting or forward the case onto the FBI. Either way, Landers would remain anonymous.

To the Denver police, at least. Once they found out about their man's death, The Company would keep Landers firmly in their sights. But that was nothing new. They'd tried to kill her three times and failed. He relished that part most. Somewhere, the man in the boots was livid, pacing about, trying to uncover the thorn in his side and failing. In an ironic twist of fate, Sherman was the insurgent, waging a three-person war against a much larger adversary.

As insurgencies went, he was running an efficient campaign. The bodies kept piling up and the damage multiplying. Eventually, one of two things would unfold. Either The Company would cut their losses and move on, or they would go on a counter-offensive. A surge of sorts like the ones in Iraq and Afghanistan. Using overwhelming force to pacify.

That they hadn't been hunting him on the streets told Sherman his adversary's power was not absolute. Risks still existed, which meant they had weaknesses. Chinks in the armor that he could exploit.

He smiled at the thought and continued back to the hotel.

Across the street, a small crowd gathered around the prostrate man and his slowly spreading pool of blood.

Landers was already one glass deep when Sherman entered their room. She lay on the bed, tumbler in hand, staring up at the ceiling, swimming in her own thoughts.

"That's three I owe you," she said without getting up.

"You had him pegged," said Sherman. "I saw you clear leather."

"Barely, if he'd crossed earlier, we'd be having a different conversation. Maybe even a one-sided chat."

Sherman took a seat on a small couch upholstered with oddly shaped triangles.

"When did you spot him?" she asked.

"A block after you left. He came out of an alley across from your office."

"Which means he was waiting for me."

Sherman nodded.

"Shit," she groaned and sat up with a jolt. "I had it wrong."

"What?" he asked.

"No, who. I had the who wrong. I thought SAC Harrington was the mole. Even convinced myself he was to blame. But he wasn't in the office tonight."

"Who then?" asked Sherman.

"The same fucker who looked surprised to see me at my first briefing. I assumed it was workplace gossip, but he thought I'd be dead."

"Name?"

"Todd."

"Why does that sound familiar?" asked Sherman.

"He's the agent who researched the Cobalt Ventures shell company and came up empty-handed."

She began sorting through case files and notes.

Holding up one page, she said, "And he wrote up Zarak's file with all their contact information."

Anger rose inside Sherman, but he focused it on the task at hand.

"Okay, if he fudged the research, what did you find?"

"Nothing at first. The file was gone. I mean, no trace at all. There are logs to prevent this, but it disappeared completely. Todd must have deleted it to slow me down or cover his tracks, but I took notes."

"That sounds pretty technical to bypass all the security," said Sherman. Computer systems were not a technology he cherished by any means. If the world devolved back to muskets and cannonballs, nothing much would change for him.

"I'm sure he had help. If The Company hacked Asal's

phone, they have the technical capacity to bypass security and delete a file."

"What are they hiding?"

Landers handed him the legal pad.

"Two things that I know and one I don't," she added.

"Start with the known," said Sherman.

Chapter Twenty-Nine

Landers took a deep breath before continuing. "Lease records. Normally, no one records this stuff in a government database, but when it involves aircraft, the FAA is a stickler."

"They leased a plane?"

"Technically, a Learjet and a Eurocopter."

"If Zarak flew the helicopter from South Denver, where's the jet?"

"Aspen," she answered.

"The ski town?"

"The billionaire playboy's ski town with upwards of seventy private jets parked on the tarmac at any given time."

"East to get lost in all the shuffle," said Sherman.

"They're not checking anything or anyone coming into the country. The jet could fly in from Mexico and they could shuttle the cargo around by helicopter. No one would bat an eye. People assume it's just some rich asshole."

"Did the jet land recently?" he asked.

"I've got a call out. We should know tomorrow."

"Good work. Maybe we can figure out Zarak's route or narrow down his hiding spot."

"Fingers crossed," she said.

"What about the unknown?"

"That's where things get interesting." She handed him the legal pad. "To be honest, I'm not sure. I only found one real estate transaction registered to Cobalt Ventures and no definitive owners. It doesn't even give a location. I searched for the name listed on the document but came up empty. I thought it was a parcel name. Nothing came up on the county assessor's website. All they have is a name and price."

Sherman scanned through her notes, impressed by Landers' attention to detail. Combined with her own self-styled moral compass, he could see why she'd gotten into trouble with the Washington D.C. power players.

Midway down the page, he came across two words that struck a chord of memory: *ATLAS XIV. Next was a sum of $100,000.*

"Atlas 14," he repeated aloud.

"Do you know what that means or are you just trying on the words for size?"

Sherman grabbed his phone from the nearby table and dialed the major's number.

"Captain," answered Sanders. "Have you secured Colonel Khada?"

"Still unraveling that puzzle, but I've got another one in the meantime. What does Atlas 14 mean to you?"

Silence filled the call as Sanders considered the question. Awkward pauses did not bother the major and he relished long stretches of quiet.

Sherman waited.

"That was even before my time and, before you make some snide remark, I'm not much older than you."

"I wouldn't dream of it, sir," lied Sherman.

"The Atlas program was a group of early ICBM sites scattered across the country. I might be mistaken on the decade, but I think the program ended in the mid-sixties and the missiles got decommissioned."

"Do you know what happened to the sites?"

"Like I said, before my time. But I imagine the same fate for all government property past its prime. Either cut up for scrap or sold to the highest bidder."

"Say for $100,000?" asked Sherman.

Landers snorted. "Pennies on the dollar against the original cost, but sure, that might buy some land."

"Thanks, sir."

"Do I want to know more?" asked Sanders.

"No, I don't think you do."

"Very well, Captain. Good hunting."

Sherman put down the phone and looked at Landers. "How much of that did you get?"

"The Company bought a decommissioned ICBM site. Just fucking perfect," she replied and grabbed her laptop. Within a few keystrokes, she had old government maps overlapping her screen.

"Start near Denver and we can circle out from there," said Sherman.

Landers zoomed and panned. "Why did he say good hunting?"

"You heard that?"

She nodded.

"The major and I have known each other for a long time. He knows who I am and what I'm capable of doing.

Hell, he puts those skills to use all the time. But he doesn't question my motives and I don't involve him in the details when situations like this arise. 'Good hunting' is a *fait accompli* for my misdeeds."

"Saving a friend isn't a misdeed," replied Landers.

"I'm glad you and I see it that way, but your boss might think otherwise."

Landers shooed away the comment with a wave of her hand. "For all I know, he's still a suspect."

"Guilty until proven innocent?" asked Sherman, fully in agreement but unable to resist the jab.

"Sometimes it works better that way," she said in a serious tone that Sherman knew concealed a much larger story.

He added the comment to the growing pile of mysteries that surrounded Megan Landers.

Sherman pointed at the map. "There's Atlas 10 and 11."

Landers zoomed in on the eastern side of Denver. Two innocuous circles marked the site of former weapons of mass destruction. No larger than the square designating the Army PX. Under the names, in even smaller print, was the word 'Decommissioned'.

"These things are almost seventy years old," she said.

"Built to last and outlast."

"Here's number 8 and 9," she said, jabbing her finger at the map.

"Up there," added Sherman. Another circle had caught his eye.

Near the border with Wyoming was number 13.

"All alone," said Landers.

"Odd. Did we miss it?"

Landers shrugged.

"Scroll down to the east," instructed Sherman.

Landers did. Their eyes watered from staring at the screen so closely.

"Wait," said Sherman. "What's that dotted circle?"

She zoomed in but they both had to lean closer to the screen.

In faint letters under a dotted circle were the words '*Atlas 14*'. Beyond that, in even smaller print, read, '*Unfinished and abandoned*'.

"Shit," exclaimed Landers. "There's not much out there."

Pulling up a modern map, they compared the two locations.

"What's that?" asked Sherman. A rectangular smudge midway down a road at the pavement's end had caught his eye.

She zoomed in. "I'll give you one guess."

"A truck stop," he said.

"Ding-ding. We have a winner. Oh, shit… look at the name."

"Cupid's Truck Stop," he read.

Landers broke out in laughter. "I thought they were space-related. It's Santa's reindeer. "On Dasher and Dancer, Prancer and Vixen, Comet and Cupid…"

"I take it the FBI doesn't know about this."

"Nope. Thanks to Todd's fine subterfuge, the bureau is flying blind."

With all the tangents swirling about, Sherman ruthlessly prioritized three questions.

"We need to answer three things. Where did the jet come from? Which way did the helicopter go? And where can I find Todd?"

"I'll ask the Aspen air traffic controller when we talk in

the morning. As for Todd, I don't know, but he wants to get in my pants. He offered his place to stay if I needed it. I don't think he mentioned anything about a spare bedroom or trying to have me killed."

"Text him. Say your hotel is shit and ask if he has a room."

Landers shook her head. "If he's working for The Company, you'll be walking into a trap."

"If it's a trap, then we know he's a mole. Either way, I'd like to know about the deleted file and Cupid's Truck Stop."

Landers scowled and steadied herself for a fight but relented.

"I'd like the record to show my objection," she said.

"Noted," said Sherman. "Make sure you use your work phone. Harder for them to hack."

"You think it's a trap," she retorted.

"I think everything is a trap," he replied.

"That explains a lot."

Sherman shrugged and handed her the phone. It didn't take more than a few texts and some suggestive language for Todd to supply an address.

Unsurprisingly, Todd didn't live far from his office. A young guy like that would want to be near the nightlife and work.

Unlike Landers, he didn't live in an apartment but a house. A newly built row home in a gentrifying neighborhood, according to a cursory Google search. An expensive purchase. Beyond the average government salary, or maybe it was family money.

Sherman tossed a few essentials into a backpack before zipping up the duffle bags. Landers watched him with a weary look.

"We're moving hotels, aren't we?"

He nodded. "It was time anyway. We've been in one spot too long."

"But it's late."

"Come on," said Sherman, picking up the bags. "I'll let you pick."

Chapter Thirty

Deep folds of night covered Todd's neighborhood when Sherman arrived. The last vestiges of activity had vanished, and the winds blew cold. Even the city itself slumped down for a few hours of rest before the roar of rush hour and the shrill slice of horns.

Todd's home was a few doors down in a group of twelve new luxury buildings. All were skinny and tall, taking up what used to be four single-family lots. Density was the word used to describe it, but Sherman still found the row home spacious. Five to a room on a sweltering day in Kabul was dense. Two thousand square feet next to downtown was no hardship.

The dichotomy of have and have nots was never stronger than across the street. Sherman stood on the other side, hidden in the shadows of a shabby brick building that even the homeless population found unsuitable to camp under. The faded remains of a post-war collapse. A gutted city, hollowed by poverty and crime. On Todd's side were fancy homes built on top of a long-lost American dream.

Sliding down the street, Sherman cloaked himself in the darkness. He dodged the paltry glow of an occasional streetlight. Nothing obvious stirred on his side. The poor side. No cars parked in alleyways. No SUVs full of armed thugs.

On the other side was a different story. Under the glow of copious streetlights, Sherman saw at least four men waiting in their own limited shadows. Two under trees, clinging to the trunks for camouflage. Two more were in a parked car. Their bulky silhouettes were visible through the back window.

An unfriendly welcome. That put Todd near the top of Sherman's shithead list—a list that had grown substantially longer in the preceding days.

He moved further up the block to get a sightline down the alley running behind Todd's house. Only the occasional security light penetrated the veil of darkness. Someone was out there. He knew it to be true as the sun rising in the morning.

Sherman turned to hide the light of his phone and sent a text to Landers.

Tell Todd you're running late and you'll be there in a few minutes.

Turning back, Sherman waited for the invisible but undeniable transfer of data. Not more than a minute later, the faint white glow of a screen illuminated the alley. It shone next to the stubbly face of a young man standing guard.

Sherman crossed the street, threading the narrow needle of darkness between streetlights.

He held the young man's position and distance in his mind. Locked in and memorized like his home phone number from eighth grade.

The gap between them diminished until Sherman heard

the bored shuffling of feet of someone waiting for something to happen.

Something happened and it happened quickly, but it had nothing to do with the murder of an unsuspecting federal agent.

Instead, Sherman poked a half-dozen holes in the guy's kidneys and liver. Quick, practiced strikes. No wasted movement or energy. They landed just below the bottom edge of the man's body armor. The brutal encounter ended quickly with a gurgled moan lost in the din of city life.

Sherman pressed deeper down the alleyway.

Todd's house had no back yard. The garage opened onto the alley. Above the garage was a deck. Strings of fancy industrial lights crisscrossed the area.

There was no obvious way up. The garage was tall and connected to the other houses. Good for security, bad for burglars.

Sherman, however, did not let himself be deterred. He pulled over a trash cart and climbed on top. With the help of some decorative molding, he reached the railing around the deck.

Slipping over the top, Sherman crouched behind an assortment of expensive patio furniture and adjusted to his new environment. A set of French doors opened into the house. Beyond, bathed in yellow light, was a kitchen and dining area. A set of stairs on the left most wall led down to the front door. Another, unseen, led to the third floor.

A man paced around a wooden dining table. He was in his early thirties with boyish features and wore comfy clothes. Not a hired gun. Todd the turncoat. The phone in his hand never left his face as if he was waiting for important news. Every so often, he'd peek out the front window before pacing again.

Sherman texted Landers.

Stall. I need fifteen minutes.

A moment later, Todd's screen lit up. He threw up his hands and placed a call. Sherman couldn't hear the conversation but it stressed Todd. Their plan had not completely fallen apart but was leaking serious water.

Sherman slid closer until he leaned against the wall next to the French doors. A muffled yell came from inside. The frustration boiling over into anger made Sherman smile. Angry people make mistakes. Mistakes created opportunity. Simple math.

All he had to do was wait. Todd's alpha ego did the rest.

The porch light popped on. A deadbolt clicked over, and the door opened. Todd charged out like an angry bull with its balls in a vice. He spluttered expletives then sighed loudly.

Todd was an athletic guy with lots of lean muscles. *Maybe water polo or lacrosse*, thought Sherman. Not that it mattered.

The crooked agent had too many frustrations on his mind to sense Sherman's approach, and too much anger in his system to react.

Sherman wrapped his arm around Todd's neck and choked away his consciousness. He squeezed until the agent flopped to the floor like an overcooked noodle.

Sherman pulled Todd inside by the ankles, over the polished hardwood floors ripped from some Brazilian rainforest. After a quick peek through the blinds, Sherman kept dragging the inert form downstairs. Todd's head thumped softly on the carpet down fifteen steps.

The stairs connected to the garage. It smelled of fresh paint and plastic. Todd drove a BMW sedan. Had Sherman cared to guess the make and model, he would have been correct. A typical striver's car.

The keys hung on a hook. Sherman grabbed them and pulled Todd into the backseat. Unrestrained, he remained a threat, so Sherman unplugged the nearest lamp and cut the cord. The length was long enough to tie Todd's hands behind his back.

Two minutes later, they were speeding out of the alley and onto a main road. Sherman left the garage door open in case some have-not wanted a hot shower or an expensive sweater from Todd's closet.

Todd awoke a few blocks east of downtown. He reacted like a privileged person facing consequences for the first time. He yelled obscenities and acted poorly. Sherman let him have a moment before holding up the Glock in his right hand. The gesture silenced Todd's vociferous tendencies toward the dramatic.

They stayed east, past the fancy City Park homes and the old-money neighborhoods. Further out, the yards collapsed in size and the homes shrank. Soon enough, the white picket fences turned to chain-link and metal security doors protected entryways.

Sherman turned onto a commercial strip and found a disused strip-mall ideal for the next phase in his plan. Most of the stores had long ago closed. Plywood covered the windows and doors. The only surviving stores were of the liquor and adult variety. Staples of a once vibrant neighborhood now in decline.

Todd's BMW stuck out like a luxury car in an area of twenty-year-old Honda Civics. Sherman guessed they had ten or fifteen minutes before the boldest of the unsavory characters came to check them out.

When they parked, there was just enough light to see Todd's expression, which split between unbridled fear and stout indignation.

Sherman swiveled to face the man.

Todd swallowed, breathing hard. "What do you want?" he asked.

"Presumptuous of you to start with that question," said Sherman. "What if I don't want anything?"

Todd struggled to sit upright. Despite the circumstances, his eyes projected coherence. "Everyone wants something."

"And what do I want?" asked Sherman.

"Answers."

"You play the dumb jock stereotype pretty well, but I see your wheels turn just fine."

"What are my answers worth?" asked Todd.

"You haven't heard my questions," replied Sherman, relishing the inequality of the exchange. "You might not like them."

"Doesn't matter."

Sherman nodded. "If you answer truthfully and completely, you'll be sitting up here and I'll be walking away."

Todd frowned.

"Like I said, you haven't heard my questions," said Sherman.

"Fine, I answer and then you leave me be."

"You answer, I leave. That is the agreement," said Sherman.

A moment of internal struggle crossed Todd's face, but he had no other option. Talk or die. Simple math.

"Ask away."

"Do you know who I am?" Sherman began.

"A ghost. I couldn't find anything about you. Not even a name."

Sherman guessed it was the truth, but the agent had a good poker face.

"And what do you know about The Company?"

Todd didn't look away. No hesitation. "Head guy goes by Grimes. Ex-military or military adjacent. I'm not sure which. He runs the thing like an operation. All codenames and acronyms."

"And what is their operation?"

"Don't you know?" asked Todd incredulously. "I assumed you worked for the competition."

"Assume I don't," said Sherman.

"Uh, okay. I'm not privy to all the details but consider them a fulfillment company. Last mile delivery or the like. They move and store goods."

"What goods?" asked Sherman.

Todd snorted. "Anything worth money. Guns, drugs, women. You name it and they dabble in it."

"Tell me about the girls."

Todd raised an eyebrow. "Don't tell me this is about your sister or cousin or ex-wife. They ain't worth the trouble you're stirring up."

Sherman tapped the pistol's barrel on the seat.

"Okay. Okay. No judgement here. The girls come through a broker from all over the world. I don't know names. They stayed at an apartment downtown until recently."

"I'm aware," said Sherman.

"Oh, shit. Of course. It was you who blasted through the place."

"Details."

"Right," said Todd. "They get flown in and then moved around the state. Big ticket clients usually."

"Where were they last?" asked Sherman.

"I don't know the details. Not my area."

"You just keep the FBI from making a case against them."

Todd shrugged. "The SAC is an idiot. I doubt he'd connect the dots anyway, but, yeah, I keep Grimes out of the spotlight."

"Last questions and then you can get on with your life. You said they move the women around. How?"

"Plane and helicopter."

"Who pilots the helicopter?"

Todd looked confused but carried on. "Some Afghani. He and Grimes go way back. I heard them talking about some operation they ran during the war."

The bottom of Sherman's world flung open like bomb doors and all the certainties he held threatened to fly away.

He got out of the front seat and untied Todd's hands. The agent tentatively sat down behind the steering wheel while Sherman stood nearby holding open the door.

"Are we done?" asked Todd.

"Last question. Why are they trying to kill Agent Landers?"

"Who?" asked Todd uncertainly.

"The four guys in front of your apartment and the one I let bleed out in your alley. They were waiting for her to show up because you told them she was coming. What I can't wrap my mind around is why. Why try to kill a colleague like that? How is she a threat?"

Todd's eyes widened. He fidgeted in his seat.

"That... that wasn't my call. Grimes spotted her and said she was a threat. She was wrapped up in something else and it all got out of control. Tit-for-tat. She killed some of his men. I couldn't stop him from retaliating."

"Easier to lead her to the slaughter."

"No, that's not what I meant."

"Well, I have a message from her."

Todd looked around like he expected Landers to walk out of the shadows. "What message?"

"This."

Sherman raised the Glock and shot Todd in the temple. Point blank. No hesitation. No remorse. Simple math.

He tossed the keys on the blood-splattered seat and walked toward the nearest bus stop. He needed some time to clear his head. If Todd was right, then Zarak really did work for the enemy.

Chapter Thirty-One

When Sherman slipped back into their new hotel room, Landers didn't ask questions. Not about Todd or what happened. After he showered, she pulled him into bed and that's where they stayed until her phone rang around noon.

"This is Agent Landers," she answered.

Sherman couldn't hear the conversation, but she bolted out of bed stark naked and made straight for her laptop. Of all the morning views possible in a hotel room, he liked that one best.

"Repeat what you said. Okay, yeah. I got it. No, that won't be an issue. Okay. Thanks for your help."

"That sounded promising," said Sherman. "Who was it?"

"An air traffic controller from Aspen. He recalled the private jet landing and the helicopter Zarak piloted. He also remembered it changing course a few minutes after departing and the rather angry guests it left behind."

"That could narrow down the search area."

"That's not all," said Landers.

Sherman sighed. Good news never traveled alone. "You're not the first person he told."

"No."

"Did he give a name?"

"No, but he said the bureau should sort out their communication issues."

"When?" he asked.

"Yesterday."

"Assuming it was Todd, then The Company knows."

She nodded. "Only logical. Did, uh, Todd say anything useful?"

The way she danced around the question assured Sherman she still cared about the bureau and that line in the sand he'd long ago crossed.

"A lot of talk. Little substance. Save for one bombshell. He said the leader of The Company, a guy he called Grimes, and Zarak knew each other in Afghanistan."

"You knew Zarak in Afghanistan. Does that mean you know Grimes?"

Sherman had replayed their brief encounter in the truck stop parking lot many times and he was sure they'd never met before. No spark of recognition flashed between them in those moments.

"Not socially, but Todd called him military adjacent, which is a nice way of saying a mercenary or spy."

"Or both," said Landers.

Sherman nodded. "Or both."

"Do you believe the part about Zarak?"

Belief was a flighty thing, coming and going in its own time and inclination. It didn't drop anchor for Sherman.

"Todd had no reason to invent that but I didn't even call Zarak by name, so he had less incentive to leverage a lie."

"Still, you don't look sure."

"I'm not. Nothing about this feels straightforward."

"Like a bent nail," she said.

"You should get back to the office. Todd confirmed the SAC is clean. Impotent but clean."

"Alright, what about you?"

"I'm going for a drive out east to the other truck stop."

"Be careful."

"Always," he replied. "But maybe you should get dressed before you head into the office."

Landers looked down at her birthday suit and laughed.

Eastern Colorado shared many of the same qualities as western Kansas or eastern Nebraska. Land came cheap and flat. The roads ran wide and straight. People were scarce. All ideal qualities for a government that needed to build ICBM sites at the infancy of a long Cold War.

The Rocky Mountains had all but disappeared over the endless grasslands when Sherman spotted his exit. It was hard to miss.

A giant pink sign proclaimed the last gas station for fifty miles. Above the bold font teetered a giant heart with an arrow shot through it.

Cupid's Truck Stop and Emporium, it read.

Sherman eased the Camaro off the freeway and down a freshly paved road. There was no town to pass through. No Main Street to traverse. Unlike most interstate commerce, Cupid's existed alone. Not a house in sight. Only a few concrete structures stood out behind the truck stop. Innocuous, old, and overgrown. The eye slipped right by without a second thought.

Except for Sherman, whose gaze lingered on the leftover military installation and its many buried secrets.

The truck stop, like Comet's in Denver, was massive. Twenty-plus pumps out front for gasoline-powered vehicles. An equal number of diesel pumps stood in great rows behind the main building. Closest, Sherman noted, to the old concrete bunkers so craftily hidden.

An obnoxiously colored building stood in the middle like a fresh pimple. The walls were pink. The trim was red. Even the windows looked tinted in some shade in between. Gaudy was the word that came to Sherman's mind, but it made an impression. Judging by the packed parking lot and lines at the pumps, any publicity was good publicity.

Sherman didn't bother to go inside.

He knew the interesting bits were underground. Going inside only created risk. He kept his hat low and refueled quickly.

There were cameras everywhere. Underneath the great awnings covering the pumps. Scattered along the pink walls of the main building. Perched atop poles in the parking lot. Surveillance covered every inch of the place.

Well, almost every inch.

Sherman found an empty spot at the very edge of the parking lot below a camera and out of sight. He parked the Camaro, rolled down the windows and waited. For what, Sherman couldn't say. His gut said wait, so he did. He waited and watched and listened.

Cupid's, like Comet's, was a hub of commercial activity. Most of which was legal. All the normal pieces of commerce still existed. The gas and snacks, supplemented with beer and cigarettes. Food too. Another diner with lots of stainless steel that glimmered through the windows. Maybe a retro design. Maybe not.

Lots of people came and went with to-go bags stuffed with containers. Too many containers. The same racket on repeat.

If the playbook works, he thought. *Don't change it.*

Beyond the revolving door of Styrofoam boxes, Sherman noticed another pattern. Women kept coming and going. The same women. Young women.

They went inside alone and emerged with a man in tow. Often, they went to a truck cab. Other times, a car.

Then back again to the truck stop.

The women looked familiar. Maybe girls from the apartment. Maybe not. Sherman couldn't put his finger on the familiarity, not for the first few hours. Not until two of the women snuck out for a smoke break. They stopped under the tilted camera by the Camaro.

At first, they said nothing. They inhaled and paused and sighed.

Then they spoke. Sherman's eyes widened and he recognized them as sure as sand. They spoke Pashto and looked like Asal.

They were Afghani.

As a percentage of those unfortunate souls forced into sexual slavery, Afghan women formed a small slice. A minuscule statistical sum for most, yet everything for those taken.

Sherman clenched his fists as the women talked.

Mostly, they complained about the clientele and working conditions. The shitty food. Their asshole boss who snuck in for unannounced visits late at night.

Finally, they came to a touchy subject. Their voices lowered to hoarse whispers.

Missing girls, they said.

Disappeared.

Gone.

Dead in a cornfield.

A lesson from the boss.

They spat out the name 'Zarak' as if unholy.

As the women stomped out their cigarettes and returned inside, Sherman's mind abounded with questions.

About Zarak's past.

About his connection with Grimes.

About his job with The Company.

Was finding him even worth it?

The more Sherman learned, the less sure he became. Doubts surfaced at every turn. The latest information unsettled him most. After everything that happened to Asal's family, how could Zarak get involved with such people? The same type of men that abducted his sister-in-law from the streets of Kabul. Monsters, not men.

Sherman left soon after.

He didn't need to see any more. A call was all he needed. Words from the source, from Zarak, but he was missing, so his wife would do.

The place in the mountains where Gournsey stashed them didn't get cell reception. Part of the charm and security. He called a landline instead.

A man answered. He didn't offer a name. Just a question: "What?"

"It's Frank. Tell Raylan to call."

The man hung up without giving a response and Sherman drove west. A great angular horizon, like tiny shark teeth, appeared in the distance.

His phone rang.

"You okay?" asked Gournsey.

"I'm whole."

"But you ain't right."

"Something came up," said Sherman.

"Let's hear it."

"Colonel Khada worked for the CIA in Afghanistan."

"Tell me something I don't know," said Gournsey.

Sherman was astounded. "You knew he flew for the spooks?"

"Suspected is a more accurate term. Rumors and such, nothing concrete, but all those guys ran side missions. Hell, we paid a lot more for one afternoon than their monthly salary. Plus, it wasn't treason or anything. Same side and such."

"How did I not know this?" asked Sherman.

"You only see what you want with friends. And you owe him your life, so add some extra blinders for that whopper."

"Do you know what he did?"

"Black book stuff. Probably smuggling dope for the CIA."

"Well, it didn't stop back there."

Gournsey said nothing.

"We found another truck stop east of Denver. There are more girls. Young ones. And guess what. They speak Pashto. Dead ringers for Asal. Some are almost Dara's age."

"Shit."

"Damn right. I need to pick Asal's brain about this. She's been through a lot, I get that, but there's no way Zarak hid all this without her knowing."

"We'll call back in fifteen," said Gournsey. "Don't be too accusatory. They're practically family."

"Scout's honor," said Sherman, then he hung up before Gournsey could ask if he ever was a Boy Scout.

The mountains rose ever higher yet remained impossibly distant. A great chain of unyielding angles and stubborn geology. The prickly thought of Zarak's past snagged and tore through his mind while he waited. Sherman couldn't shake the duplicitous nature of his friend. Zarak saved his life, many lives, yet Sherman didn't know if he could forgive him for everything else.

The hardness of taking such a line, so moral and arbitrary, also gave him pause. A self-dose of the pot calling the kettle black. He'd done terrible things that polite society would lock him up for, yet there he was judging a man for something he didn't fully understand. Sherman hoped Asal wouldn't hate him for what he had to say.

The call came within view of the distant Denver skyline. Gournsey put Asal on.

"Are the girls nearby?" asked Sherman.

"No, why do you ask?" she asked, sounding tired and confused. "Oh, God…"

"It's not that call, Asal," added Sherman. He was upset with himself for not being more forthright and adding to her stress level. "I need to ask you some questions about Zarak when you lived in Afghanistan. I need you to tell me everything you know, no matter how small the detail. Understood?"

"Yes, I understand."

"Okay. Back when he was on active duty, do you know if Zarak ever took side jobs?"

"Like what?" said Asal. Her tone was sharp.

"Any extra missions in the helicopter. Moving stuff for an NGO or shuttling gear for the Americans."

"Yes, he did."

"Do you know for who?"

"No. Occasionally, he'd come home with extra money. I asked where he got it and he answered, 'The Americans'."

"Did you ever question him on what he did?"

Asal sighed. "No, Frank, I didn't. It was a war. He did

those things because he had to. And we needed the money to put the girls through school. To buy a house in a safer neighborhood. To eat. So, no, I didn't."

"I'm not judging, believe me, but Zarak slid back into that side business here. Whoever he worked for back then is the person after you now. Can you remember anything?"

"He'd fly out of a different base. I remember that. It took him longer to get home and he missed a lot of bedtimes."

"A name? Or even a direction?"

"I… I don't think he ever called it by a name, but it was south of the city."

"How far south?"

"A couple of hours."

"Great, that's perfect. Did you have an inkling what he did?"

"Move supplies, I guess. Ignorance is a shield, Frank, do you understand?"

"I do," said Sherman.

"I never asked. So many terrible things happened back then. I just knew he wasn't working for the Taliban and that was enough for me."

"Look, I discovered he is working for the same people. They are trafficking women into the United States."

Asal said nothing, but Sherman heard her breathing short and ragged.

He continued, "I think he flew out the other night to pick up a fresh group of women. Something happened after that. I don't know what, but he never delivered them. He disappeared with the helicopter and the women. I choose to believe he did this with good intentions. The disappearing part, at least."

Asal, who had remained silent, let out a long string of

curses in Pashto. She took a breath and continued, "I... I didn't know. I swear, I didn't know. After everything that happened to my sister. How could he?"

Sherman said nothing.

"He wouldn't—couldn't—do that. Please, Frank, tell me he didn't do this."

"I wish I could, Asal, I really do. We've all done some terrible things. Made unforgivable choices."

"Not like this. Not this choice."

"I know."

"We don't need money that bad. We've seen worse."

"Don't play the 'what-if' game. You'll circle down the drain doing that," said Sherman.

"Then what? He's missing. Our daughters are in danger. We can't keep hiding in the mountains. That's no life. And where's Zarak? Where is the man I married? The one that vowed to stand with me. To be there for me."

"I can't speak for him, but I can try to find him. I just need your help."

"I thought you said he could be anywhere."

"We got a direction of travel from the airport, but he wouldn't land somewhere he didn't know. Too risky. Did he ever take trips up to the mountains? Even a family road trip."

"No. He worked almost every day and we still scraped to get by. I don't think he's ever been to downtown Denver, outside of the immigration office. Wait... Zarak took a day off to go with Dara's class. It was a big deal then. They took a field trip to some science camp up in the mountains. I'll ask Dara the details and tell Raylan."

"Good. Listen, I'm sorry you had to hear this from me."

"Me too, Frank. I'm sorry we dragged you into this mess. Truly, I'm sorry. You've already done so much."

"You all matter to me. Despite his shortcomings, Zarak is still a friend. I don't have many of those left."

They ended the call as a great red wall of snarling traffic appeared before Sherman. Too early for rush hour, or maybe not. Maybe the congestion never ceased. Maybe it was construction. Different names, same result.

Gournsey called back as Sherman came to a standstill.

"Petrified trees," said the sergeant as a greeting. "They went to some monument to look at petrified trees for Dara's science class."

Finding such a location didn't take more than a few taps on his phone. "That jives with his last recorded heading," said Sherman.

"I'm close," said Gournsey. "I could start searching."

"Are they safe to stay?"

"You wouldn't believe the security they have if I told you. They're safe."

"Start drawing up the search grid. I need to grab the gear, but I'll be there by sundown."

"Copy that."

Traffic lurched forward, swerving between haphazardly placed orange cones. Sherman drummed his fingers anxiously on the steering wheel. It wasn't quite hope that bloomed in his mind, but it was something close.

Landers was sitting on the hotel couch behind her laptop. A pale white glow highlighted her growing fatigue. She stopped typing when Sherman walked into the room.

"I almost got worried about you. Almost."

"Traffic," said Sherman.

"What did you find?"

"A truck stop full of trafficked women."

"Shit."

"It gets worse," he added.

"Lovely."

Sherman sat down next to her. "Not any women either. Afghani women. I overheard them talking. They know about the missing women. The Company spun it as a warning to the other girls."

"Christ, that's clever," she said.

"The women mentioned him by name."

"Who?"

"Zarak. They called him some real nasty names. Terrible names."

Landers took a deep breath and closed her laptop. "I'm sorry, Frank."

"I called Asal. She took it... well, she took it. But she had some facts."

"What sort of facts? Good facts?"

"I'm on my way to find out. Want to come?"

"I'd slow you down," she said.

"Is that a no?" asked Sherman.

"No."

"Good, start packing."

"I can't just leave work."

"Call in sick," said Sherman.

"One day?"

"Two—it's an extensive area."

Landers frowned, then relented. "Okay, let's check it out."

Chapter Thirty-Two

The sky shifted from fuchsia to creamsicle as Sherman turned into the parking lot of the Rustic Motel. First impressions, which can mean anything or nothing, said it was an apt name. No funny signs or sales gimmicks. Only a neon red sign flashing 'Vacancy' and the promise of free HBO. The latter hadn't been a selling point for at least a decade, so Sherman assumed they were in the right place.

Where that place was on a map was two miles from the fossil monument Zarak visited. Beyond that, it was miles from nowhere of interest. South of any helicopter route from Aspen to Denver. Geographically isolated. Devoid of cell reception.

An ideal hiding spot.

The motel wore the worry lines of a structure well past its prime but with no intention of crumbling. A post-war alpine building with two stories and an impressively steep roof. The only question in Sherman's mind was, what war? There were enough coats of paint on the siding to be his great-grandfather's war. Not that he knew much about that one. He'd never met the man and the stories passed down always seemed sun-bleached and shallow as if no one ever really wanted to hear the truth.

"Looks quaint," said Landers.

"Looks open," replied Sherman.

"Glad you're setting the bar so high," she added.

"Harder to be disappointed that way."

Inside the office, they found an elderly woman named Barb who smelled of pine and lavender. Her short gray hair swayed as she welcomed them with a wide smile. Sherman draped an arm around Landers, who squeezed back and played her part. She explained to Barb that they were passing through on a long overdue road trip.

They got a room on the second floor—Sherman's choice. Barb happily accepted cash with a little extra deposit to cover incidentals or damage.

Getting to the second floor led them around the side of the building and up a creaking set of wooden stairs weakened by continuous exposure to the elements.

Contrary to expectations, the room was well-maintained and clean. Polished wood floors gleamed under a pleasant pale-yellow light. The walls carried a fresh coat of paint, and the king-sized bed didn't squeak when Sherman sat down.

"This is better than I expected," said Landers.

"Only the best," added Sherman.

"Only one choice," she replied with a smile. "But it beats a trailer in Baghdad with lukewarm AC that smells of mildew."

Sherman laughed. "We always got the one that smelled of cat piss, which boggled my mind as I never saw a damn cat."

"Taxpayer dollars at work," added Landers.

"Someone has to spend it."

Landers parted the thick green curtains with a finger and glanced outside. She stayed for a second before taking a seat on the live-edged pine chair.

"Do you miss it?" she asked.

"My war? Yeah, I miss parts of it. Not losing my friends or blowing up fathers and sons. But other parts."

"Like the cat piss trailer?"

Sherman laughed again. "No. That I'm happy to have in my rearview."

"The people then?"

"Oddly enough, yeah. Half wanted us dead, but I never held that against them. They have a dedication that speaks volumes."

Landers added, "They certainly ground everyone else to a nub. The Brits. The Soviets. Us."

"And we thought twenty years was a long game. The mujahideen could do two hundred years and still come out on top. Their wars are generational. Handed down from father to son and so on. No Congressional budget. No political meddling."

"You almost sound jealous," said Landers.

Sherman shrugged. "Admiration, I suppose."

She peeked out of the window again but didn't return to the conversation. Sherman instinctively reached for his pistol.

"Who is it?" he asked.

"A black SUV pulled through and checked your plates."

"Are they still here?" he asked.

"No."

"Good thing I switched the plates," he said.

She swiveled in surprise. "When?"

"At the last hotel. We'd had the car too long."

"Is that standard operating procedure?" she asked with a smile.

"The standard operating procedure is staying alive. Everything else is allowed."

Her smile faded. "Everything?"

He shrugged. "Yes. Same as it's always been and will remain."

Ever the lawyer, Landers looked like she wanted to argue the finer points of the laws of war but said nothing.

"Did you see their plates?" asked Sherman.

"Generic Colorado. Didn't catch specifics. It was a newer model GMC."

"Law enforcement?"

She shook her head.

"I guess we're not alone in our search. The Company got the same bearing from the air traffic controller. Only a matter of time before they started looking."

"Shouldn't we start now?"

"Not until morning. Searching in the dark is useless without a trail and we've got no starting point. Better to wait."

"What about Gournsey? Should we warn him?"

"The sergeant can take care of himself. Of that I have no doubt."

Landers sat back down. "We wait?"

"I saw a sign for pie down the road," offered Sherman.

"Pie is good," she said.

"Yes, it is," he agreed.

Morning arrived with dappled rays of orange light and a racket of blue jays perched on the motel roof. Given the weight of the preceding days, Sherman almost felt light. A younger version of himself. As if one could reach back and reclaim such faded vigor. Maybe it was the mountain air or the pie or the lithe creature curling across his chest. Maybe it was all of the above. Either way, Sherman liked the feeling.

Peeling himself out from under Landers, Sherman showered under a tepid tap. Even his scars seemed duller, less red, angry, and ringing with the trauma that had imprinted them in flesh.

They packed quickly, stopping only for coffee at the pie ship on the way out. Sherman functioned fine without caffeine if there was adrenaline, but bereft of both was not optimum. Junkies need their fix. Weeks of teaching green lieutenants had taught him as much. Chemistry was a cruel mistress.

They arrived a few minutes after the monument opened. The guy at the entrance—a garrulous retired teacher named Greg—appeared chuffed at their early arrival.

"Wow," he exclaimed. "Quite the busy morning. Barely opened the gates and already got three visitors. Enjoy the araucarioxylon."

Sherman paid and smiled. He had no clue what Greg said, but it was Latin and long, therefore, scientific.

"Fossilized trees," said Landers. "He said enjoy the fossilized trees."

Sherman said nothing.

"I took Latin in college," Landers explained.

"Latin?" he asked, not surprised.

"I liked classical history. It made sense then."

"And now?"

She shrugged. "I'm very good at crosswords."

"Worth every penny then," he said with a smile.

Beyond the bend, numerous brown signs told the geological story beneath them. Gournsey was there, perched next to a tiny car.

He stood as they parked and exited the dead trooper's Camaro.

"You're late," chided the sergeant.

"Frank refused to leave without coffee," Landers replied.

They were alone in the parking lot. A fact that did not escape Sherman.

"Did the others get called in?" he asked.

Gournsey nodded and Sherman didn't ask where or why. It didn't matter. The call came. They deployed. End of story.

Landers twirled around in a slow circle. "That's a lot of space for three people to search. What's the plan?"

"We take a walk," answered Sherman. "See what Zarak saw and then we'll know."

"Know what?"

Gournsey laughed. "When we see it."

Landers frowned. "So, it's porn. You'll know it when you see it."

"More or less," added Gournsey.

"Come on," said Sherman, pointing toward a finely detailed map of the area. A red line snaked around in a large loop. The legend in the corner described it as the guided tour route. Like the kind used for schools and retirement homes. "Let's follow in the colonel's steps."

The finely packed gravel path wound through a variety of rocks that had once been trees of various sizes and shapes. Only bits and pieces remained. Signs filled in where pure imagination could not. Sherman kept his eyes on the horizon while Gournsey couldn't help but read the snippets of history posted along the trail.

In the stubby shadow of an ancient redwood, Sherman stopped. His eyes snagged on a blot in the distance. A small brown structure on the side of a distant mountain, except they were in the mountains, so it looked more like a hill.

Gournsey stood next to Sherman and they both gazed off into the distance. They calculated distance and elevation and a host of other variables. Experience had proven them important for hiding from a superior force.

"Did you find your porn?" asked Landers, squinting in the same direction.

"Maybe," said Sherman. "Do you see that cabin on the furthest ridgeline?"

"I see a brown dot."

"That brown dot is above a canyon, and canyons are good for hiding large objects," Sherman explained.

"You think Zarak is over there?"

"He ain't here," said Gournsey. "And if we saw it, so did he."

"Okay, I'm sold," replied Landers.

As they left, Greg, the geological enthusiast, gave them a searching look that clearly intoned they had not stayed long enough to fully experience the wonders on display.

Another day, thought Sherman, and meant it. Colorado was growing on him. Maybe it was the mountains. Maybe it was Landers.

Going from Point A (the parking lot) to Point B (the cabin) proved navigationally difficult. They went south to another road before traversing northwest. Whatever they saw did not exist on a map and was certainly not next to any meaningful road. Satellite images confirmed a single-track trail of sorts left by animals or humans. That part remained unclear.

Veering north took them off the asphalt and onto a dirt road. The dusty scar curved over rolling hills and between vast swathes of pine trees. Rocky ridges protruded on either side and Sherman knew they were close.

They parked off the dirt road, near to where it swung back east and towards parts unknown. A morning chill still clung to the air, but the sun cast a pleasant warmth, hinting at a glorious autumn day.

Sherman got out and began the methodical process of preparation. He slipped on a tactical vest and double-checked his magazines. Next came his rifle and sling. Finally, he slipped on a backpack and adjusted the straps. Satisfied with his own kit, he turned to Gournsey and inspected everything. Despite an indignant look from Landers, he checked her gear as well.

It was a ritual he never skipped.

Landers glanced between the surrounding pines and the GPS on her phone, orienting herself.

"It's this way," said Sherman as he set out at a brisk pace.

"Does he always know where he's going?" she asked Gournsey.

"I've never seen him lost."

"There's a difference," she insisted.

"Is there?" asked the sergeant.

Landers didn't reply and the three settled into a pattern of stop-and-go with Sherman on point.

They passed under scraggly pines, thickly carpeted with brown needles and between boulders cast down from distant mountainsides. The air had warmed and smelled of dirt and sap and the luxury of nature. The scent invigorated

Sherman, reminding him of a youth spent far away from civilization and the watchful gaze of adults. His father, when around, never minded Sherman's long excursions. In fact, he probably preferred solitude, away from the nascent father-son conflicts and the inherent struggle of parenting a teenager.

"Aren't we getting close?" asked Landers after a brief stop.

Sherman broke away from his reverence for the forest and pointed uphill. "About a quarter-mile along that ridge."

Landers nodded.

The pines remained unbroken until two hundred yards away from the cabin. An ideal rifle range for just about any caliber. Sherman paused low next to a rangy shrub and watched.

Before them was a small log cabin. No larger than a suburban master bedroom. Maybe 200 square feet in total. It sat low against the hill, built up from stone to pine logs to shingles on the roof. A throwback to an earlier age when wagons crisscrossed the continent and electricity was but a fantasy.

The helicopter, if it still existed in one piece, was nowhere to be seen. No smoke rose from the stone chimney, yet something told Sherman people were inside. An intuition that came from the recesses of his mind. The part that warned cavemen about caves and deep shadows.

The longer he looked, the surer he became that someone was looking back. Gournsey shifted uncomfortably in the undergrowth. Evidence he too felt the unnatural pull of observation.

"It ain't empty," said the sergeant.

"No, it's not," agreed Sherman. "Best to have a look."

He unslung his rifle and stepped into the wide clearing

surrounding the cabin with hands held toward the sun. The distance wasn't great, but it felt gargantuan. A great gulf of possibilities fit into the space. Some good, most not. Sherman got within fifty feet before the front door opened and he heard a familiar voice.

"Captain Sherman?"

"Zarak."

The door cracked open, revealing the colonel's face.

"Thank God," he said. "I wasn't sure if you'd show up or not."

"Colonel," replied Sherman in a measured tone. "I wasn't sure we'd find you here."

Zarak glanced inside and then back again. "Come in. I have some explaining to do."

"And them?" Sherman asked, jerking his thumb toward Gournsey and Landers, who stood up to reveal themselves.

"Them too," said Zarak, holding open the door.

What exactly Sherman expected to see on the other side of the door, he wasn't sure, but what he found astounded him. The cabin wasn't crowded with trafficked women. There were only two. One heartbreakingly young. Five or six by her outward appearance, but her eyes felt ancient. A soul worn down by trauma. The second woman carried the ferocity of a mother tiger in her light blue eyes.

In that moment, everything made complete sense to Sherman. He knew many versions of those two women, albeit removed by years of war and unfathomable grief.

"Let me introduce my sister-in-law, Damsa, and my niece, Nahal," said Zarak, motioning toward the two diminutive figures huddled in the corner.

Sherman nodded.

Gournsey bowed.

Landers gasped.

"I owe you an apology," continued Zarak. "I took advantage of your sense of honor and duty. For that, I am truly repentant, but I could not think of another way to keep them safe."

Still shocked, Sherman sat down on a hand-hewn bench. "They were on the plane in Aspen?" he asked.

The colonel smiled. "I see you figured it out. Yes, they came from Afghanistan via Mexico."

"Did you know beforehand?"

Zarak shook his head. "I have not seen Damsa since Kabul. The surprise overwhelmed me."

"And you couldn't go through with delivering them?"

Shame overtook the colonel and he lowered his head. "No, I couldn't."

"It's true, then. You work for them," said Gournsey.

"Unfortunately, my friend, that is the case. I feel ashamed to confess to such poor judgement and actions, but I can't find any excuse. I've done much harm in my life, yet coming here was one positive thing I could do. Delivering Damsa and Nahal was never an option."

Damsa looked cautiously in Sherman's direction as if to speak but said nothing.

"You were delivering them to The Company," said Sherman.

"You never disappoint, Captain. I take it you met them?"

"You didn't leave me any choice, Zarak."

"I know... I'm sorry. Things happened so quickly... I couldn't think of anything else to do. I tried to warn Asal... oh, God, are my girls safe?"

"Physically, they are fine. Mentally, things got twisted."

"Were they targeted?" asked Zarak.

"Did you expect anything less?" asked Sherman.

A deep sigh rattled Zarak's chest. "No, I knew the risks, and I'm sorry to say, I passed them on to you. But I couldn't have made such a choice if you and the sergeant weren't around. And I couldn't have lived with myself if I didn't act."

"I understand," began Sherman. "Leaving you and your family behind in Afghanistan was never an option either."

"All or nothing," said the colonel.

"No half measures," said Sherman.

"Now, where are my manners," added Zarak, taking on a honeyed tone. "Damsa, Nahal, this is Captain Frank Sherman. A loyal friend. He rescued us from the… Taliban." He said the last word much quieter, almost in a whisper.

Damsa kept a wary gaze on the newcomers while her daughter sheltered behind her thin frame.

"This is a friend too," said Sherman. "Megan Landers."

Zarak bowed. "A pleasure."

"Can we see my sister now?" asked Damsa, urgency running through her voice.

Zarak looked to Sherman, who nodded.

"Yes, we can."

They left the spartan cabin without another word. Five adults and one child, who'd probably experienced more trauma and deprivation than most Westerners saw in a lifetime.

Sherman took point again. The sun shimmered high in the autumn sky. His head swam with questions for the colonel, but he pushed them aside and concentrated on the task at hand. Guiding everyone back was all that mattered. Nothing more. Nothing less. No half measures.

He kept a languid pace for the sake of Nahal. She

300

looked tired and hungry, although Gournsey had already plied her with snacks.

Halfway back to the cars, below the ridge but not yet exposed between the sporadic clumps of trees, Sherman stopped. He hadn't heard something so much as he felt something. Everyone followed as he sank to a low crouch— one knee digging into the blanket of brown pine needles.

They waited in silence. Six bodies rippling with tension. An act as old as time. Waiting and listening.

Silence followed. An empty void of time and space.

Then it broke.

A bullet hissed cruelly over their heads, snapping with menace as it went. The distant crack followed like muted thunder.

They were not alone.

Chapter Thirty-Three

Collective tension rippled over them as the gunshot faded. They endured in silence. Not a word or sound. Pressed against the ground, the odd group hid. Landers and Zarak looked about, confused about the direction of the threat.

Sherman did not.

His ears recognized everything about the shot as easily as a civilian knows the screeching of a tea kettle or a toaster popping. Gunfire was commonplace.

The shooter missed high and left of their position. A reflexive shot at a perceived target. Not direct or sustained fire. Maybe they'd been spotted. Maybe not.

Sherman caught Gournsey's eye and motioned uphill toward an outcropping of boulders mixed with trees. Solid cover for Damsa, Nahal, and Zarak. Good sightlines for Landers and the sergeant.

Gournsey nodded and shepherded the new arrivals along a line of trees and up to the rocks.

"Where do you want me?" whispered Landers.

"Have you ever shot a long gun?" he asked.

Landers almost looked hurt, as if he'd insulted her driving skills. "Second highest score in my class at Quantico."

"Good enough. Grab the case from Gournsey and then head another thirty yards uphill. Remember to compensate for the downhill angle."

She frowned.

"Right, top two in your class," he replied.

Landers left at a low run, grabbing the Remington 700 off Gournsey's back. The sergeant insisted on bringing the rifle, which Sherman agreed to because Gournsey could carry a howitzer on his back and still move like a cat.

While everyone else pulled back, Sherman pushed forward. Had it been Iraq or Afghanistan, Sherman would have pushed right down the enemy's throat. Speed and violence. The two keys he kept trying to teach those West Point noodles. Sometimes it worked to meet enemy contact with overwhelming force and aggression.

This was not one of those times.

Sherman slipped between tree trunks until his feet treaded on level ground. The pines spluttered out into an open field. Across the wide meadow, he made out several figures weaving through another stand of trees.

Three men dressed in fatigues. Rifles on slings. Body armor and helmets. Certainly not hunters, despite the open season.

Two of them moved with confident ease. Their eyes stayed up and scanned for threats. The third walked haltingly, tripping over rocks and making a racket.

Which one took the premature shot was painfully obvious. The runt of the litter. Manpower shortages for The Company after Sherman thinned the herd.

The two competent operators kept a wide berth from

the third—a survival instinct, no doubt. Keep away from the weak link. They went right around the clearing.

The foundling went left.

Sherman followed, stalking in the bushes like an apex predator waiting for its next meal.

The inexperienced hire fumbled forward like he wore boots three sizes too big. He had no awareness of space or sound. A podgy twenty-year-old with a fancy rifle and few survival skills.

Sherman, hidden amongst an overgrowth of sage, wondered if he was bait. A lure of sorts strung out on a long line waiting to be yanked back in.

He took the chance.

Speed and violence, he thought.

The knife in his hand was a wicked six inches of German steel. As the kid walked by, Sherman was ready.

In mere heartbeats, Sherman put a half-dozen holes into the man's kidneys and spleen. The pain overwhelmed his brain, and he couldn't call out for help. A trick Sherman learned from a family friend who was a frogman in Vietnam. While most teenagers learned about sports or cars at backyard barbeques, Sherman received other life lessons.

The guy slumped to the ground, slick and lifeless.

Sherman pulled the body into the blood-splattered bushes and out of view. Then he circled toward the other two threats.

They were filtering through the pines, making all the right moves, but short a man. The realization of which dawned on them in that moment.

The soft static of a radio sounded in the distance. A voice grew louder and more insistent. Indignation gave way to concern and then panic.

Sherman slipped behind a fallen tree and waited. The

two ex-soldiers were fast approaching a decision point. Would they continue with their tactical sweep-and-clear approach or search for their missing partner?

The answer came quickly.

Human nature prevailed. It almost always did. Worry and compassion overwhelmed logic. The search began.

The two men moved nearer to Sherman with methodical steps that grew looser with each passing minute. Radios hissed. Voices strained with stress.

Sherman waited. Patient, hidden, and focused. All concentration. Urging the men forward and into the unobstructed clearing.

They stopped just before exiting the relative protection of the trees.

Sherman held his breath as the radios chattered to life.

Reinforcements, he thought.

The dead guy had not risen like Lazarus and tipped them off. Sherman slipped lower into the grass surrounding the fallen tree. Two-on-one was fine with the element of surprise. Any more might end with him in a body bag.

Two quickly became six.

The panic in their voices subsided with numbers.

Sherman's stomach twisted. A six-to-one ratio never ended well. Be it in combat or mixed drinks.

Five hundred yards uphill, Landers watched the gathering storm of trouble muster around Sherman, who minutes earlier had butchered a man in less time than it took her to reload. She'd winced at the initial attack but couldn't help admiring the pure violent power of the man. Sherman did the work. Nothing less. No complaints. No shying away from the unpleasantries.

Now things were turning against him. She saw as much through the convenient distance afforded by the 8x scope. Six mercenaries. One Frank Sherman.

She glanced toward Gournsey waiting down the hill. He pointed toward the group and held up his finger, miming the pull of a trigger.

Take the shot, she thought.

Many moons had passed since she last lay behind the stock of a bolt-action rifle. Doubts crept into her movements.

Landers took a deep breath to clear the cobwebs and voices of uncertainty. She focused on the magnified images and let everything else drop away.

Gone were the doubts and the fear for Sherman.

Gone was the nervousness for Damsa and Nahal.

Gone was her self-doubt over work and the shame of being demoted.

Gone was the pain in her leg and the terror of that day.

She flipped the safety and adjusted for a slight left-to-right breeze.

The range, she thought. *What is the range? Five hundred yards, maybe less.*

Landers twisted a knob on the scope and centered the reticle mid-chest over one man. Even a little high or low would still put him down.

She took a deep breath, channeled all her attention to the gun, and gently pulled the trigger on her exhalation.

The rifle roared to life.

In the diminutively claustrophobic world of her scope, she saw the aftermath. One mercenary was on his back, clutching at his profusely bleeding stomach. Worse, it wasn't even the one she'd centered on. Just an unlucky bystander standing to his left.

"Shit," she muttered and adjusted the windage.

Landers racked in another round and that's when her small world shrank even further. The men below reacted with experienced speed. Soon enough, her portion of the hill zipped and hissed with incoming bullets.

"Shit, shit," she muttered again, and picked out another target.

Hidden behind his fallen tree, Sherman smiled as the first guy took one to the gut. The man's suffering brought him no pleasure, but the distraction saved him from meeting six angry men.

The woods rippled with gunfire as the five remaining mercenaries tried to suppress Landers. Carefully, Sherman raised himself to the edge of the log. The remaining men were twenty yards in front of him and tunneled into the uphill threat. They didn't even glance in his direction.

Sherman watched and waited for the second shot. There had to be a second shot.

He didn't wait long.

Even amid the chaotic shouts and crackling gunfire, his mind picked out the Remmington's report. The larger caliber carried a certain thumping energy.

Despite the heavy suppressive fire raking the hillside, Landers hit a clean shot. A man in the middle of the pack caught a round mid-shoulder. The impact spun him to the ground in a painful pirouette. He landed face-down in a pile of pine needles already splattered red.

Fatal or not, it didn't matter. Snipers struck fear in

soldiers. The four uninjured men panicked. Their shouts grew frantic. Their movements were unsure.

At this chaotic zenith, Sherman opened fire.

The target closest to him took the first five rounds from his magazine. The man never stood a chance. At twenty yards, Sherman couldn't miss. Five bullets left him in a bloody heap on the ground. Head askew. Arms folded underneath.

Ten yards further, the second mercenary saw his friend die. Hearing the shots, he tried to react. But turning ninety degrees and finding an unknown assailant took time. Time that he did not have.

Sherman fired ten bullets in his direction. More than necessary, but he had lots of ammunition and not that many targets.

Further out, the two survivors understood their predicament and retreated. Sprinting headlong through the forest, they ran between the trees, hoping the cover would soak up the incoming rounds.

Sherman burned through one magazine and then another in quick succession. By the end of the third, there was no one left running. Let alone moving.

The only surviving member of the original seven mercenaries was the one Landers shot in the shoulder. He was face-down and moaning when Sherman found him.

Having seen too many booby-trapped corpses, Sherman kept his distance. No need to end up as a statistic after the fact.

The vest hadn't stopped much of anything. A gruesome exit wound told the story. The guy had twenty minutes left. Probably less.

Landers arrived as Sherman searched through pockets.

"He's still breathing," she said and pointed.

"I know."

"Are you going to help him?"

"No."

She looked conflicted over his response. "Why not?"

"He needed a Level One trauma center five minutes ago. Nothing I do will change that."

"Oh," she replied.

Sherman kept searching and Landers kept watching the man ebb away.

"What's your pill of the moment?" he asked. "Remorse? Shame? Anger?"

"All of the above," answered Landers.

Sherman stopped searching and put some cash into an empty magazine pouch on his vest.

"Sounds about right," he said.

"And you?" she asked, surveying the carnage. "How do you feel about all this?"

"Pissed at the waste. Seven dead and for what? A vendetta? The principle of it?"

"The cartels lop off heads for less."

"True, but these guys aren't narcos. They may work with them, but—"

Landers interjected. "They still tried to kill me three times. After saying that out loud, I don't feel much of anything for them."

"It's all context," said Sherman, who whistled for Gournsey to move out.

Landers followed behind him and said, "Either way, Zarak owes you a much longer story on how all this started."

"That he does," agreed Sherman.

Chapter Thirty-Four

The ride back smelled of gunpowder and sweat. Sherman drove the Camaro with Zarak in the passenger seat. Unwilling to leave his flock, Gournsey rode with Damsa, Nahal, and Landers in the cramped car. Despite his protests, she wouldn't let him drive.

Zarak sank into the leather seat like he might melt on the spot. Stress had deflated him. Speckles of gray dotted his otherwise black hair. He carried the look of a man who had stood at the edge and stepped off, only to survive the fall. Sherman knew the look all too well.

They said nothing. Not for the first few miles as the adrenaline faded. Not even the next few miles as syrupy tiredness set in.

Only when Sherman merged onto pavement did Zarak speak.

"Thank you again, my friend. I worried they might find us first."

"You could have told me where to find you."

"They might have listened in on my call. I couldn't take the chance."

"Time to come clean. Start at the beginning and don't bullshit me, Zarak. These guys tried to kill my friend on three, no, four different occasions. Not to mention they came after your family, twice."

Zarak took a long breath in like he'd need all the oxygen in the car. "I suppose it started right after the liberation. With the Taliban gone, life changed. Suddenly, we had music and movies and Western clothes. Our own little American dream. At first, we reveled in the change. We couldn't imagine it would last. Then it did and things normalized. Suddenly, the old TV wasn't good enough. We had to get a bigger place for the family Asal and I dreamed of. I couldn't do that on my salary."

"American credit card debt says you're not alone in those desires."

"Except, we didn't have credit. Only what you could stuff in an envelope and deliver in person. A side gig was my only option. I started looking and that's when I met him."

"Who?" asked Sherman.

"Jimmy Grimes, or that's what he went by back then. Real name or not, I don't know. He worked for the CIA but never said so. I figured he was one of the good guys."

Sherman sighed. "If it were so simple, what was the job?"

"No different than my normal duties. Fly cargo from here to there. Extra money from the Americans seemed like the best of both worlds."

"I don't blame you."

"You should," said Zarak. "I never asked what was in the boxes. Never cared. If Jimmy Grimes wanted to move heroin or guns, then it must be for the greater good. At least, that is what I told myself."

"Afghanistan wasn't the CIA's first dirty war nor their last," added Sherman. He'd almost said more. Told of all those doors they'd knocked down and the mangled casualties. All because of information passed down from CIA sources.

"The day we met, I was flying for Grimes," said Zarak.

"What a small, strange world," said Sherman after a moment of awe. "I always wondered what you were doing out there, but never asked. My father always told me that gratitude shouldn't come with a question mark. Unless the gift came from the North Vietnamese, but I think that was his own personal demon and not a general rule."

Zarak rumbled with laughter. "My father told a similar story that involved a diseased donkey and wicked Pakistanis. The moral always escaped me as a child but I imagine the sentiment was the same."

"And here we are trying to unlearn those lessons."

"I should have told you sooner," said Zarak. "I was too ashamed."

"That past is long buried. Tell me about the here and now."

Zarak hung his head low. "I'm afraid the plot didn't change much. Working at the airport was fine until it wasn't. I could only watch others fly for so long before it felt like a personal insult. As if I wasn't good enough after all those years of service. I wanted more. A taste of my old self."

Sherman nodded. He understood that yearning for past glory all too well.

"One day," Zarak continued. "I stop at this diner for pie after work. A co-worker told me it was good. I'm sitting there enjoying a slice when a familiar voice calls out. I turn around and it's Jimmy Grimes in the flesh. Like that magic trick where the magician pulls a rabbit from a hat. Suddenly, he was there looking not a day older than the last time I saw him in Kabul."

"Small fucking world."

"Serendipity. I wasn't proud of my work with him before, but it paid well, and we were on the same side. We chatted that night. I still wore my dirty work uniform, so he guessed at my fall from grace quickly. Said it was a shame my skills were going to waste."

"Preying on your weakness," said Sherman.

"It worked. I was weak. Weak enough to agree to help him even though I knew he was no longer in the CIA. I helped, knowing he broke the law."

Sherman shrugged. He wasn't much for black and white lines.

"They started me slow at first," said Zarak. "A glorified flying chauffeur. Then came some cargo. Again, I didn't ask what was in the boxes. I didn't want to know. Ignorance is bliss, I told myself. Then came the women. I flew them around to fancy corporate retreats. Entertainment, I told myself. Nothing wrong with that."

"Everything is wrong with that," countered Sherman.

"I know. I figured it out quickly, but the money… I couldn't let it go. It paid for orthodontists and doctors. I almost had enough stashed for a down payment on a house."

"Asal would see the blood on that money in one glance," said Sherman.

"I know, but I'd deluded myself. I kept flying and lying until the other night. When I saw Damsa and Nahal, my heart broke. I knew what Jimmy Grimes did with those women—the broken life they led. I couldn't let that happen to my family. In a moment of pure madness, I left without the others. I had no plan or destination. The only place that popped into my mind was a cabin I'd seen on Dara's field trip. And so, I disabled the GPS and ditched the helicopter in a little box canyon. I figured we'd hide out until you found us. I wanted to tell Asal, but I worried Grimes might find her."

"He did," said Sherman. "Twice."

Tears streamed down Zarak's face when he spoke. "Never have I been more ashamed or in your debt. I knew you'd keep them safe. I had to believe."

"That's a gigantic leap of faith, even for you."

Zarak shook his head. "No, it wasn't. I watched you drag a wounded man through an open field of machine gun fire. Years later, you appeared from nowhere and saved us from summary execution in that dusty apartment. I watched the gunfight from the helicopter until you were but distant victorious specks. I had every reason to put my faith in you."

"I wish you would have asked first," said Sherman.

"Me too, but would you have acted differently?"

Sherman thought about the question. Knowing all the facts would have changed absolutely nothing. He had no regrets for his actions.

"I suppose I would have shot Jimmy Grimes at the start. That would have solved our troubles."

"Hindsight…" said Zarak.

"Ain't good for nothing," added Sherman.

The two men shared a fleeting laugh.

"Tell me about Mr. Grimes," Sherman said.

"Where to start? Uh, he's smart. Very smart. Ran all sorts of operations in northern Afghanistan for at least a decade. Used to be a Ranger, I think. Can you imagine the stories he's got?"

"I can," muttered Sherman.

"What?"

"Nothing," said Sherman. "What makes him tick? What motivates him?"

"I don't know. The man is like a house with no windows. You never know what is going on inside."

Sherman rubbed his chin. "He didn't strike me as crazy or a zealot, which leaves money or power. Or both."

"Respect," said Zarak. "Power and respect, if I had to guess. He liked that the Taliban knew his name. They respected him because he played their game. Almost better than they did."

"Sounds like he's doing the same thing here."

Zarak nodded. "Only among thieves, though. He operates at the edges and in the shadows."

"Maybe respect and fear then."

"Probably," said Zarak.

"Any proclivities? Does he visit his girls or sample his products?"

The colonel shrugged. "He didn't back in Afghanistan. Very business-like. Cold and efficient."

Sherman pivoted and grabbed his phone. Major Sanders answered after a few beeps.

"Status?" asked Sanders with his usually gruff demeanor.

"He's sitting next to me, but before you talk, I need you to run down an ex-CIA officer named Jimmy Grimes."

"Jimmy Grimes," repeated Sanders before continuing. "Any casualties?"

"Just on their side."

"Damn fine work, Captain."

"I'll let you two chat," said Sherman as he handed the phone over.

The men gabbed like schoolchildren for the next twenty minutes as Sherman drove. From the one-sided snippets, the topics ranged from apartment decorations to recent events. Their banter rolled on without pause—delightful and verbose.

When Zarak finally handed back the phone, they were minutes away from Asal and the girls.

"How did you and Major Sanders meet?" asked Sherman, curious about the closeness of their relationship.

"Our fathers knew each other before the Taliban took over in 1996. The major's father once taught at Kabul University. Our families stayed in touch over the years. Once the war started, we finally met in person."

"Small fucking world," Sherman repeated.

"Serendipity," said Zarak.

A large metal gate loomed off to their right, surrounded by long strands of razor wire. The level of effort reminded Sherman of the DMZ in Korea.

"We're here," he said.

Zarak stuck his head out the window to get a better look. "And where is here?"

"A friend's house."

"I see."

Chapter Thirty-Five

Asal stood in the dirt driveway and held her daughters close. Despite heroic efforts to stay positive, her faith had wavered. Perhaps it even cracked as the days wore on with no word from Zarak. Yet the impossibility of another chance was nearly upon them. In the distance, a dusty plume rose in the air. The girls giggled with excitement.

As the cars pulled up and Zarak got out, Asal burst into tears. All the pent-up fear and anxiety flooded out of her body in great emotional torrents. Zarak ran to them, pulling all three into a wonderful embrace.

She cried.

He cried.

The girls cried.

Words failed her. Asal just smiled and cried until her eyes stung and her cheeks hurt. Zarak hugged her tightly and whispered a hundred apologies. Their love, though tested, remained intact.

"There's one more thing you need to see," said Zarak. "Actually, two." He motioned toward the second car.

Asal focused on the figures in the back seat. A familiar ache burned in her chest. That lovely face. A lost face.

"No," she whispered. "Can it be?"

As her sister stepped out of the car, it was Asal's turn to run. She ran like they used to as little girls, racing each other home from school.

Asal squeezed Damsa with all her might, hoping to make up for all the years of missed hugs. Yet, knowing nothing could repair the harm her sister had endured.

"Dearest Damsa, I can't believe you're here. Oh, I'm so sorry for… everything."

Damsa smiled wide. Tears streaked down her face. "Dearest Asal, I want you to meet someone."

Asal lowered her head to look in the backseat.

"This is my daughter, Nahal. Nahal, this is your Auntie Asal."

Asal waved at the shy little girl curled up in the back. Her heart burst with love and gratitude and happiness.

"Welcome, my loves. Please come inside, I've been cooking all day. You two must be hungry."

"Mother's recipes?" asked Damsa.

Asal nodded. "Please join us."

Damsa guided Nahal out of the car and held her close like Asal did with her daughters. An almost unconscious urge to protect them from further harm.

Everyone feasted until not one cranny of hunger remained. Asal could barely contain herself. She'd witnessed not one, but two miracles. A husband and sister returned to her. Even a niece to rejoice over.

Despite the smiles and laughter and joy, Asal saw a darkness in Damsa's eyes. The lingering unease of horrific trauma. Her pain resonated in the air like a tuning fork, vibrating from a million unseen scars.

Asal leaned over to her sister. "Let us talk elsewhere."

Her sister glanced at Nahal, unwilling to leave her alone.

"She's safe here. I promise you that," Asal said.

Damsa nodded, and as they stood to leave, Esin and Dara played with Nahal as if reading their mother's unspoken wish.

In the warm autumn light, the two sisters found a bench outside. They sat and held hands, thankful for the companionable silence.

"I have something you need to know," said Damsa.

"There's no rush," replied Asal. "You can say as much or as little as you want."

"Dearest sister, there are many things you deserve to know and many more I can't bear to tell. But there is one thing you must know. It's about Nahal's father."

Sherman hadn't noticed the dried blood speckled across his thighs. Dara had and quietly told him as much. He was on his way to change pants when Asal stepped inside.

"Frank," she began, a little out of breath. "We need to talk. Now."

"What's wrong?" he asked, sensing her alarm.

"It's not my story to tell. Come with me."

Asal led him around the house to Damsa sitting on the bench. He sat down next to her.

"Okay," said Sherman in a quiet tone. "I'm listening."

Damsa sighed and gazed up at the pines as if gathering up her words.

"Mr. Sherman, I'd like to tell you of my escape from

Afghanistan. Please be patient with me, it is a burdensome story to tell."

Sherman nodded for her to continue. He didn't understand the urgency, but he knew to shut up and listen.

"For my sake, I'm going to skip the parts I'd rather forget."

"Of course," said Sherman with an inkling of how bad things got.

"After the Taliban took me from Kabul, I ended up in the northern mountains. I wasn't alone. There were lots of girls. They turned us into wives."

Sherman glanced back at the building, instinctively thinking of Nahal.

Damsa shook her head as if reading his thoughts. "No. They didn't want children."

"Understood," said Sherman, knowing he only understood a fraction of her ordeal.

"I stayed there for years. Terrible years. Then, one day, it all changed. An American showed up. Not a soldier. He didn't want to kill the Taliban but work with them. He said 'the great currents of history' were changing and so must the Taliban. I'm not sure he believed it and I know the Taliban didn't, but things changed. Negotiations in Doha. They made promises. Promises they had no intention of keeping, but lying to infidels didn't count. White lies such as those carry no weight with Allah."

Sherman nodded in agreement.

"My husband went to Doha often as part of the negotiations. The American kept coming to visit. We saw each other often in passing. At the market or on the street. I liked him and his strange way of speaking. He found my story compelling and enjoyed speaking in English. What followed wasn't inevitable, but it was my best way out of the country.

We kept the affair quiet at first, but my husband was no fool. Time was not on our side."

Sherman didn't like the story's direction. "What was the American's name?"

"Jimmy Grimes," said Damsa with a sigh. "He convinced my husband to sell me off before I started showing. For what price, I'm uncertain. But he freed me from that prison and pain. He set me free. Got me an apartment in Kabul. New clothes. Prenatal care. For a while, he even cared about us. We talked about a future together. Then the US withdrew, and he left with them. We were alone."

Asal squeezed her sister's arm in support.

"When the Taliban took over, I knew it was only a matter of time until they came for me and Nahal. A single mom, divorced, adulteress. I had no place in their Afghanistan. They would've stoned me to death. I called everyone I knew until I finally got in touch with Jimmy."

"Was he in the United States?" asked Sherman.

"Yes. He promised to get us out. We just had to wait. So, we waited. I pretended to be a widow and scraped by with the kindness of neighbors. Then a car showed up one day to take us to the airport. We didn't even have time to pack."

"When was this?"

"About a week ago," said Damsa. "We flew to Dubai, then France, then Mexico. Our last stop was Colorado."

"Where Zarak picked you up."

"Yes, I didn't recognize him at first." She looked at Asal and smiled. "Too many home-cooked meals. But he remembered me. And he knew Jimmy."

Sherman ran his hands through his hair and massaged his scalp. The simple story he'd told himself about Grimes and his motives was wrong. The impetus for all the violence was muddier than a swollen river. Whether benign or malignant, Jimmy's reasons for wanting to get his child back were powerful. Zarak impeded that reunion. An insult not easily forgotten.

"What did Zarak say about Jimmy Grimes?"

"Nothing I didn't know," said Damsa.

Which was something Sherman didn't. He'd assumed she'd been conned. An innocent bystander on the darker side of life. He should have known better. No one left Afghanistan cleanly. Everyone carried scars from their choices. Be it lost limbs or PTSD, or children born from human traffickers.

"Can you elaborate?" asked Sherman.

"Jimmy was always doing the work no one else wanted to do. He smuggled dope for the CIA so they could pay off warlords. He played both sides by flying guns to the tribes fighting the Taliban and then accompanying the Taliban to Doha for the peace negotiations. Everything they asked, he did. At least the things he admitted to me. You don't end up buying a Talib's wife without knowing how to play their game."

"He didn't stop playing that game when he came back to the United States," said Sherman.

"I don't care. He got us out." Damsa's words were hard and short.

"Why didn't you leave Zarak and go to find him?" asked Asal.

"Go where? I don't know this place. Zarak told us we were in danger. I didn't know from who."

"I don't think you and Nahal were in danger," said Sherman. "They were after Zarak, not you. Those men in the woods were coming to kill him. I can only assume they would've spared you two. But that is conjecture."

"I didn't know," said Damsa.

"Nor could you have," said Sherman. "You were looking out for your daughter. No one blames you for that."

"And Zarak was looking out for his sister-in-law," said Asal. "He didn't know your story. He saw my beloved Damsa and did what he thought best to keep you safe."

No one spoke and the forest around them sang on without their words.

Finally, Sherman broke the silence. "The only question I have is, do you want to go back to Jimmy Grimes?"

Damsa sighed and lowered her head, trapped between impossible choices.

"He got me out. The last one of us to get out. I owe him for that."

"You owe him nothing," said Asal in a steady voice. "Not for getting you out or buying your freedom. Those were his choices, not yours. Take control. Do what your heart commands, not what some imagined debt dictates."

Sherman smiled at the forcefulness and depth of Asal's words, but he didn't see that fire in Damsa.

"I don't have such luxury, Asal. Maybe if we go back, he'll stop. You'll be safe. The girls will be safe."

"Let us worry about that," replied Asal. "It is our burden, not yours."

Damsa raised her hand to stop her sister. "No, I learned long ago that things are never so simple. Burdens are shared by all. Hardships are shared by all. Death is shared by all. That is the nature of community. And I won't let you take more risks."

"Don't you see—" began Asal, but Damsa cut her off.

"I still have Jimmy's phone number. Let me talk to him first. Maybe there is a way out of this mess."

Sherman calculated the risk while Damsa looked at him unintimidated.

"Not here," he said. "They might trace the call and find this place. I can't allow that, but we can drive somewhere else to make the call."

Damsa nodded and stood up. "Now?" she asked.

"I suppose so," Sherman answered.

Chapter Thirty-Six

Leaving Nahal behind took some convincing but Damsa finally relented and left her daughter in Asal's care. Sherman thought two passengers were safer than three. He wasn't sure how Grimes would react, but positively didn't seem a likely outcome. The body count almost guaranteed a negative response. Maybe lukewarm.

They drove southwest for an hour, heading away from anything Sherman had yet visited. Small towns with Old West names came and went. Sherman didn't stop. He wanted something smaller.

Damsa didn't say anything. She kept staring out the window with a glazed contemplation in her eyes. The blank look of someone tangled within a great web of emotions and choices.

Or maybe, he thought. *It was the look of resignation.*

Two sides of life's shitty coin.

Sherman finally stopped in a three-building town near a junction of smaller byways. There were two houses and a store. The latter advertised Beer-Deli-Gas on a faded sign.

The first letter of Deli hung askew, and the paint lacked color as if it no longer figured in the trifecta of options.

Sherman parked out of the view of the lone camera hanging above the door.

"I need you to stay in the car," he told Damsa.

She nodded, not looking eager to get out and speed up the process.

An old man with missing teeth stood behind the counter. He gave Sherman a polite but wary nod. Sherman gave a perfunctory wave and grabbed some snacks for the drive back. As expected, the deli counter was closed and covered with clear plastic sheeting.

Sherman deposited two iced-teas and a bag of chips on the counter and eyed the wall behind the old man. Next to the rows of cigarettes, he saw a few pay-as-you-go phones collecting dust on their cases.

The cashier squinted when he asked for one but said nothing. Money spoke volumes and the dust on the case said inventory had not turned over recently. Sherman paid in cash and left.

He handed the phone over to Damsa as they drove away in search of service and a parking spot.

"Do you know what you want to say?" he asked.

Damsa shook her head.

"Can I suggest what not to say?"

She nodded.

"It's best if you don't mention anything about where we are now or where we are staying. Skip the location part altogether. He'll figure it out on his own. Don't mention me or the sergeant by name. They don't know and I want to keep it that way."

"You think this is a bad idea, don't you?"

"What I think is less important than what you can achieve. If this call stops the craziness, then it's golden."

"And if nothing stops?" she asked.

"I'm going to burn his world down," said Sherman.

Damsa sighed. "I just wanted a better life for Nahal. All this… I had no idea."

"Focus on what you can control. Let go of the rest. This is still your choice."

"I owe him a call," she said.

"But not your life."

Damsa smiled. "Isn't that what you did for Zarak?"

Sherman sighed. She had a valid point.

"You're right. I shouldn't have said anything."

"Americans have a saying about this, right?" she asked.

"The pot calling the kettle black," he answered.

"Because both are tarnished from the fire?"

"Correct."

She nodded in understanding. "I hope you don't get burned."

"I hope no one else gets hurt," added Sherman.

"You don't seem certain."

"Grimes lost many men in the process of finding you and Zarak. I don't think he'll let our actions go unanswered."

"But it's worth trying," she said.

"It's worth trying," Sherman replied.

"Okay, I have signal."

Sherman pulled off to the side of the two-lane road.

"Can you put the call on speaker? I don't want to intrude, but I need to know."

Damsa agreed and dialed the number written on a faded scrap of paper.

The phone rang several times before connecting. No one spoke, but they heard breathing on the other end.

"It's Damsa. We're here. Nahal and I."

Silence.

"Jimmy. Thank you for getting us out. We couldn't have made it without your help."

"I placed my trust in you, Damsa." The voice was flat and emotionless. "Trust is a contract. A two-way street of mutual respect and accountability. You broke that trust. You ran away."

"I didn't," she protested. "Zarak is my brother-in-law. He didn't know. He was trying to protect me."

"From me," said Grimes. "He was protecting you from me. The father of your child. The man who arranged for your escape from that wretched country."

"Zarak didn't know about us. When I told him everything, he let me go."

A long moment of silence elapsed, and Sherman practically heard Grimes think.

"Who else is there?" he asked.

Damsa looked at Sherman. "No one."

"And Zarak just gave you a burner phone out of goodwill after you told him our story?"

"Would that be so surprising?" she asked.

"What's surprising is the ghost no doubt listening next to you hasn't said anything. Your assumption of my foolishness, Damsa, insults me."

"Please, Jimmy. I didn't mean for any of this. Nahal and I were coming to be with you. That doesn't have to change."

"Oh, my sweet, naïve, Damsa. The wheels of change budged forward the moment you asked for my help. I've changed. You've changed. Our situation has changed. My men are dead. My business is at risk."

"Can't you stop?"

Grimes sighed loudly. "If only life was so simple. Actions lead to consequences. I know that from personal experience. And not all outcomes merit regret. But—"

"But what? You're risking your daughter's life for revenge."

Grimes didn't answer.

"Jimmy," pleaded Damsa.

"I wish you would have called earlier. Don't do it again."

"Please," she pleaded again. "I don't want anyone else to get hurt."

Grimes laughed angrily. "You know what they've done. He's sitting right next to you, isn't he?"

Damsa glanced at Sherman, who nodded for her to continue. Best to give peace a chance, however remote the possibility.

"They were protecting Zarak and Asal. My family."

"Who are they?"

Sherman shook his head as a reminder. "Zarak's friends. That's all I know."

"What do you want me to do? Forgive and forget. Turn the other cheek against those who trespass against me?"

"We could make a life together," she offered.

"I've been accused of many things, but foolish is not one of them. Ours was never a star-crossed romance. You used me to get out of a forced marriage and I enjoyed you. It was transactional. Same as when I paid off your husband and smuggled you two out of the country. I gave and, therefore, expected to receive in kind, but no. I only experienced loss. Why would I want peace without recompense?"

"You could have a life with me and your daughter. Isn't that payment?"

"No, that's purgatory. I got you out of Kabul from a twisted sense of responsibility. But that ember of guilt is long since cooled. My advice to you is get out of my way. I'm coming for my pound of flesh and I will take it from whoever remains. Do you understand?"

A look of cold calculation crossed Damsa's face. Any chance of averting violence had faded. Like a true survivor, she pivoted.

"He's going to burn your world down," she said.

"Let him try," said Grimes, then he ended the call.

Damsa sat stony-faced for a few moments.

"You gave that a valiant effort," said Sherman.

"I knew trying to stop him would fail."

"Why did you try?" asked Sherman.

"What if it had worked?" she replied.

"Good point," said Sherman. He believed there were always solutions to unsolvable problems. The answer just hadn't been conceived of yet.

"What happens now?" asked Damsa.

Sherman took the phone and tossed it out the window.

"That, for starters. Then I'll drop you off with Nahal and Asal."

"He's coming for you," she reminded.

"Grimes doesn't know who I am. The only person he knows is Agent Landers."

"He'll come for her then."

Sherman nodded. "I'm counting on it."

Chapter Thirty-Seven

Landers threw up her arms in disgust. They were sitting inside on a dented corduroy couch discussing the call with Grimes.

"Absolutely not," she replied after Sherman described his plan. "I'm not bait. You can't dangle me in front of Grimes and wait for him to bite."

Sherman thought otherwise. Releasing her back into the world would surely get attention. Convincing her of the merits was the problem.

"You're the connection," said Sherman. "He doesn't know us. Only you."

"And he tried to kill me three times already. Now you want to give him a fourth attempt. No one ever gave Mike Tyson a free shot. They'd end up on the floor or missing an ear."

"We could go straight at them," offered Gournsey. "Take out the truck stop."

Landers glanced uneasily in his direction.

"If they're in that back room, we could rig some C4 on the wall and blow it down. Then it's just a matter of putting down the survivors."

Tactically, the plan worked. Speed and violence all wrapped up with an explosive bow. The downside was that they'd all end up in jail or a shootout with the FBI. Landers, seeing the flaw, shook her head.

"That's suicide," she said.

Gournsey shrugged. "But it would work."

"Don't you have anything else?" asked Landers.

"Yes," said Sherman. "Find out where Grimes lives."

"I'm not a magician. That's not his real name. The task force doesn't know either."

"I'm sure Todd had something to do with that. Keep digging through the case files and I'll see if Major Sanders found anything."

Sherman stood up from the couch. He stretched his arms high above his head. Joints jarred by years of stress cracked and loosened. He stepped outside and dialed the major.

"Captain," said the gruff voice.

"Sir. Did you find anything on this Grimes character?"

"Not enough to fill a sticky note. Langley buried him so deep, I can't even access the server. A real ghost, if I've ever seen one. At least you boys have service records. There's nothing but redacted reports and an unreachable server."

"Asal's sister mentioned Grimes went to Doha with the Taliban. Can you find a security list?"

"I can try, but I'm not a bloodhound."

"Good point," said Sherman, considering an alternative. "Never mind, I already know one. Thanks for your help, sir."

"Wrap this up soon, Captain. I can't cover for your class much longer."

"Understood," said Sherman, then he hung up.

The next call went straight to Danny Bashir, the reporter.

"Captain Sherman, are you calling to coerce me some more? I thought we were even."

"Do you have access to the security check-in lists from the Doha peace talks with the Taliban?" asked Sherman, heading straight to the point.

"Uh, no…" replied Danny, processing the request. "But I know who does."

"I need those lists."

"There were a lot of meetings. Care to give me the name and I can run it down?"

Angling for the story, thought Sherman.

"Can you get the lists or not?"

Danny sighed. "Yes, I can get the lists."

"Jimmy Grimes is the name he used back then. I'm looking for anything similar."

"Jimmy Grimes," repeated Danny.

"You can't publish a word of this story—which I'm sure you're writing—until I say so."

"I can't guarantee that."

"I know where you live, Danny. Please don't make me visit," said Sherman. He wasn't above naked threats if they furthered his goal.

Danny paused again. Sherman knew the reporter was carefully weighing the facts at hand. A good story for a delay in publishing or a broken bone for rushing. Simple math.

"Two weeks," said Danny. "I can get you the security lists and a two-week warning before we go to print."

"And no names," added Sherman.

"Naturally."

"Deal. I need those lists yesterday."

"Yeah, yeah. I got the urgency—"

Sherman hung up before Danny could finish his lament.

Dusk approached as Sherman stepped inside the house and returned to the dented couch.

"Well?" asked Landers.

"The major didn't know anything substantive."

"I'm sensing a 'but' here," she said.

"But Danny Bashir does. He's tracking down a lead."

"Frank, you're playing with fire," Landers said. "You know he's already writing up a story. You might be a main character."

"I know. We agreed to a two-week heads-up and no names."

"And if he breaks that agreement?" she asked.

"The captain breaks him," said Gournsey, who already understood where naked threats thrive.

"Correct," said Sherman.

"You threatened a reporter," said Landers, not so much with surprise, but grim acceptance.

"Correct."

She rubbed her face against her palms. "How long until Danny has something?"

"By morning."

"Good, I could use a shower and a strong drink."

"They've got a decent single malt collection if you know where to look," said Gournsey.

Landers sighed with satisfaction. "Lead on, good sir."

They disappeared, leaving Sherman alone with his thoughts. Over the preceding days, his focus never wavered from finding Zarak and protecting the Khada family. With the colonel found, he'd hoped for quiet. A pause. After the call with Grimes, he knew there would be no such break. A man like that thrived on the gray slivers of life. The cracks of humanity. No one co-opted the Taliban without a sharp wit and bloody hands. Sherman knew that after one glance across the truck stop parking lot.

About the time Sherman decided to join Landers and Gournsey on their whiskey raid, Zarak entered the room. The colonel walked on the edge of exhaustion with dark crescents under his eyes. The gray streaks in his hair had thickened. He sat down next to Sherman with a thud.

"Asal told me about the call with Grimes. I didn't know Damsa knew him, let alone he was Nahal's father."

"Would that have changed your desire to keep her safe from Grimes?" asked Sherman.

"I suppose not," said Zarak. "I knew he was trouble back then and he hasn't changed. I suppose I wanted to change Damsa's story. Twice the victim of horrible men. It was too much for me to handle. But I guess it was never my story to change. She was doing right by her daughter, and I mucked it up."

"I get it," said Sherman. "We're doers. We see a nail and hit it. You saw a problem and acted to the best of your ability. Given the circumstances, you acted with integrity."

Zarak shook his head. "No, you acted with integrity. This was never your fight, but you took up arms without hesitation. I am the one who sold my integrity on the cheap for a few thousand dollars."

"I don't believe in coincidences," said Sherman. "If you hadn't intervened, how long would it have been before Grimes put Damsa to work at the apartment? What would have become of Nahal then?"

A great sigh tumbled from Zarak's chest. "Those are questions for God, not a mere mortal like me."

"Then stop kicking yourself. Leave it to your higher power."

Zarak patted Sherman's shoulder. "Thank you, old friend. For everything."

"I wouldn't have it any other way."

Chapter Thirty-Eight

Sherman arose early the next morning and took his coffee to-go. He drove down the long dirt driveway as the sun peeked over the Rockies and filtered through the pines. Crisp air swirled through the open windows. Under other circumstances, Sherman would have stopped to enjoy the glorious sunrise. But he was expecting a call and the red horizon portended a different warning.

True to expectations, Danny called before Sherman finished his first cup.

"Did you get the lists?" asked Sherman.

"Good morning to you too, Captain. I stayed up half the night sorting through this stuff."

"Results get my gratitude, not effort," said Sherman.

"How long are you going to hold a grudge over the article?"

"You wrote a hit-piece on Special Forces in Afghanistan."

"That was my editor, I wrote about what I saw. He inserted the accusations of impropriety, not me."

"It was your name on the by-line."

Danny sighed. "Fine. I accept the blame. Do you want the info or not?"

"What did you find?"

"No one named Jimmy Grimes appears in the security logs, which is not surprising given what you said. However, I found a person of interest with the same initials. A James Grimmali signed in twice during the negotiations. The list states his occupation as consultant."

"Did you dig into James Grimmali?"

"Don't insult my professionalism. Of course, I dug into his past, but there wasn't much to find."

"Born in Oregon to divorced parents, he bounced around the juvenile court system for minor crimes until he turned eighteen. After that, he drops off the grid."

Sherman scratched his chin. He knew a lot of guys who dropped off the grid when they joined the Army.

"Any service records?"

"I didn't even ask. Shit like that comes back to haunt me."

"Fair enough," said Sherman. "I appreciate the help, you did good."

"Our deal still stands?"

"Yes. Two weeks' notice and no names. But keep your editor out of the details."

"They fired him already."

Sherman laughed. "Good."

"Can I ask you a few questions off the record?"

"No."

"Worth a try. Have good a day, Captain."

"You too, Danny," replied Sherman before ending the call.

He didn't set the phone down but dialed Major Sanders a moment later.

"Did your bloodhound sniff something out?" asked Sanders, skipping the morning pleasantries.

"A name. James Grimmali."

A keyboard clacked in the background as Sanders pecked away. A few moments of silence passed.

"Sergeant James Grimmali served with the 21st Infantry in Iraq. One commendation for service. General discharge a decade ago."

"Not exactly a stand-out," said Sherman.

"No. Not much here."

"Any notes on further recruitment or applications?"

"Let's see... one application to transfer to the 25th Infantry in Afghanistan, which he then withdrew a few days later."

"I guess he found another way to get there," said Sherman.

"This file is almost too tidy. Limited officer notes on performance. Generic psych evaluation. Nothing specific about his actions."

"Do you think someone cleaned it up?"

"Or he is the most average soldier to have ever served. Wait... there is one interesting fact. The sergeant taught himself Pashto."

"That's worth recruiting," Sherman said.

"It certainly is."

"Does it list a forwarding address with his discharge?"

"A P.O. Box in Pine Creek, Colorado."

Sherman smiled at the new piece of information. "Now, that is something."

"Good hunting, Captain," replied Sanders and hung up.

A quick search turned up an insignificant municipality in the mountains east of Denver. Calling it a town was generous. Pine Creek had no main street or central business district. There was a coffee shop and a diner. One gas station and no supermarket. The houses in town were scattered among the trees. Dirt roads spread across the land like spiderwebs, connecting and looping back on one another. Sherman turned the car around.

When he returned to the compound, Gournsey was dressed and waiting on the front steps with a fresh cup of coffee. The sergeant's vest and rifle leaned against the wall. A flashback to past missions.

"Judging by your expression, I assume you have good news," said Gournsey as Sherman walked toward the front door.

"Danny pulled a name from the security lists in Doha. Major Sanders matched that name to a service record. Sergeant James Grimmali of the 21st Infantry. Does the name ring a bell?"

Gournsey shook his head.

"Me neither. He was discharged a decade ago and never heard from again. Except, the forwarding address is a two-bit town northwest of here."

"That can't be a coincidence. Maybe a family connection?"

Sherman took the cup of coffee and shrugged. "Not a clue, but we're going to have a look."

"Just us?"

"And where am I?" asked Landers, appearing around the corner.

"You're going back to the office," said Sherman. "We've got a name and the bureau has the data."

Her hands went to her hips. The idea clearly did not land. "And then you'll let the FBI deal with him?"

"It may come to that," said Sherman. "Right now, we need an address for Mr. James Grimmali. All I have is a decade-old forwarding P.O. Box."

Her eyes narrowed. "An address."

"Yes."

"Fine," she said and walked back inside.

"She doesn't believe a word you just said about the FBI arresting this guy," said Gournsey.

"No, but I like that she keeps trying. Means she hasn't lost hope in the system," said Sherman.

"What does that say about us?" asked the sergeant.

"Nothing good."

"If that's the case, I'm ready to go."

Sherman finished the last of his coffee and set the mug on the front porch railing.

"Me too."

Chapter Thirty-Nine

The Pine Creek coffee shop impressed Sherman in surprising ways. Unlike the sleek, modern look favored by young businesses, the coffee shop embraced the one-hundred-year-old floors and tin ceiling. It didn't shy away from worn brick or faded paint. *Quirky and dirty and delicious*, thought Sherman. Not bad for a town that was anything but a town.

They'd found a table in the front window and were sipping extra-large cups that might have served as soup bowls in another establishment. The day unfurled. Locals came and went. Some stopped for coffee. Their orders needed no names. Others grabbed groceries from a small store advertising Beer, Gas & Goods. What the goods included remained a mystery, but judging by some patrons, cat food and milk made the list.

Two buildings further down the street, just visible from their seats, stood the post office. A drab brick building, it no doubt replaced something much grander and easier on the eyes, all in the name of progress.

Lots of locals had come and gone by the time Sherman finished his scone and coffee. The post office was a hub of activity. A dozen people stopped to converse during that brief period. Not just about the weather, but long, meaningful conversations that stretched beyond the casual. A genuine community spirit.

Sherman and Gournsey were in danger of overstaying their welcome in the coffee shop when a trio of black SUVs sped past. Suburbans or Tahoes. Sherman still couldn't tell.

The tip was already on the table, and they left without another word.

The sergeant broke a half-dozen laws catching up to the SUVs, but they finally spotted the group north of town, exiting off the main pavement. Gournsey slowed as they passed a dirt road marked 'Private Drive', under which warned against trespassing. Two giant timbers framed the entrance. A third spanned the gap, creating an imposing threshold over the driveway. There was nothing cheap about the entrance. Even the fencing on either side cost a small fortune. Not to mention the horses grazing in the fields.

"Looks too ostentatious for a spook," said Gournsey as they drove past.

"We haven't seen the house yet," replied Sherman, but he understood the point. The wood gateway spoke loudly enough.

"Maybe it's not him," Gournsey suggested.

"Maybe a politician or a billionaire," agreed Sherman.

"Certainly not a criminal mastermind keeping a low profile."

"Certainly not," said Sherman.

They kept to the main road, chasing it over a hill and

into a wide swathe of pines that crowded down to the asphalt shoulder.

"Park here," ordered Sherman.

Gournsey pulled over into a small clearing across the road and reached for his gear. Sherman did the same.

They slipped on vests in silence—neither man in the mood for conversation. Nothing needed saying. Either this was the place, or it wasn't. No gray about it. If they were wrong, they'd have another scone. If they were correct... well, things would escalate.

Waiting for the sound of oncoming traffic and hearing none, the two men set off. They appeared as a menacing duo in full combat gear.

Swallowed by the pines, they kept to the ridgeline, taking it back toward the house Sherman knew existed. Not in a factual, printed on paper knowledge, but a gut-level understanding. No one built a gateway so grand without an even grander abode. What he didn't know, and couldn't guess, was just how far back the property went.

They were a good two miles in when the ridge narrowed toward a point and the trees thinned. Below them was a true Western gem. A vast green valley richer than anything advertised on a bottle of ranch. Cutting through the middle like a shimmering silver line was a lazy stream. A fly fisherman's dream.

At a crook in the stream's path, on a small rise, stood a log cabin—if log cabins could be so big. This structure shared none of those humble traits associated with Lincoln's boyhood home.

"Now can I call it ostentatious?" asked Gournsey.

Sherman nodded. The house was three times bigger than anyone could ever need, but the location took his breath away.

Parked next to a barn or garage were the three SUVs. Beyond that, closer to the water, was a smaller house. Older and modest by comparison. The original dwelling. Built long before the fancy gates and displays of wealth.

From within his backpack, Gournsey produced a spotting scope.

"What do we have?" asked Sherman.

"Two guards on the porch, which looks inviting. Two more patrolling the grounds. Hard to tell from here, but I'd say they have the same hardware as the crew we met earlier."

"Same or similar?" asked Sherman.

"Can't be certain."

"Eyes on anyone else?"

"Negative. Can't see into the house."

"Maybe it's some rich asshole," Sherman suggested.

"A paranoid rich asshole," added Gournsey. "That's a lot of security."

"Could be a senator."

"Maybe," muttered Gournsey. "Look... I think we found the hen house."

Sherman took the spotting scope and held it to his eye. Deep in the distance, he saw men patrolling their perimeter and two more watching from the porch. The men moved purposefully, yet hurried, covering the open spaces with extra-long strides. They didn't want to be caught without cover.

"They're spooked," he said.

"I would be too," said Gournsey.

"How many seats in an SUV like that? Eight?"

"They have third rows now," said Gournsey. "Up to eleven if they squeezed in like third-graders."

"Not with all that gear. Say eight per car, but Grimes

345

wouldn't want to be packed in like a sardine. Four max in his vehicle. Twenty guys at most. Six at least."

"Two on twenty ain't gonna end well for us," said Gournsey.

"Agreed, but there's no telling how long they'll be up here."

"I'm game for a fight," added Gournsey, but Sherman knew he was only joking. The sergeant liked a fight but wasn't suicidal, despite his bravado.

"We need more shooters," said Sherman.

"Put your girlfriend on the long gun again. She did alright."

Sherman frowned at both ideas. Certainly not his girlfriend. And a mile of open space separated them from the house.

"Too far," Sherman replied.

"My comment or the range?"

"Both."

Gournsey chuckled to himself.

"Any word on the Delta boys?" asked Sherman.

"Still out of pocket. No ETA on their return. What about Zarak?"

Sherman drummed his fingers lightly on the scope. "Doesn't feel right to pull him in."

"It's his fight as much as ours," Gournsey retorted. "Add in Agent Landers and we've got a chance."

"Not a good chance."

"No," admitted Gournsey, then chuckled again.

Sherman kept watching in silence.

"Are you gonna call him or me?" asked Gournsey, as if he could no longer bear the wait.

"Major Sanders won't approve. All three of us in one

spot is too risky. Losing us is one thing, but Corporal Lopez is another."

As one of the best shots on this side of any ocean, Sherman reckoned Lopez was worth ten men. Sanders would not approve of such an unsanctioned risk.

"Good thing I already called him," said Gournsey.

"You what?"

"Just to see where he was at."

Sherman frowned but took the bait. "Well?"

"He is hunting up in Wyoming as we speak. Not more than a six-hour drive away."

Sherman looked at his watch. It read 11:00 AM. Lopez could be there by dark if they called soon.

"You should have run that by me first," he said.

"And you would have said yes because it makes tactical sense, so I saved us an unnecessary conversation."

Which was true, but Sherman felt salty.

"Fine," he relented. "Make the call."

Gournsey disappeared deeper into the pines while Sherman kept watching through the spotting scope. The two-story log mansion dominated the area. Despite not being able to see the interior, Sherman imagined trophy heads mounted on the walls.

There were a few leafy trees nearby, but the second floor had nearly unobstructed views of the surrounding wilderness. Sneaking up on such a spot was near impossible against a skilled opposing force.

Even the old cabin appeared updated with a new roof and windows. A place for extra guards to shelter during rotations.

The shadows stirred behind him and Gournsey emerged with a smug smile.

"He was already on his way and pissed you didn't call earlier."

"Did you tell him to meet us here?" asked Sherman.

"Yes, with dinner. I assumed you weren't leaving."

Sherman nodded. The sergeant knew him well.

"Good work, I have one more task for you."

Gournsey leaned in and listened as Sherman explained his plan.

Chapter Forty

A scene of pandemonium met Megan Landers as she stepped off the elevator. The office's cubicle heart bustled with agents rushing across the great expanse. Ensconced in the largest conference room, Special Agent in Charge Harrington gesticulated towards a whiteboard covered with wild writing and photos.

What in the world, thought Landers.

A passing team member caught her confused expression and sagging jaw.

"Where have you been?" asked the woman. "The SAC called everyone in hours ago."

Landers hadn't bothered to check her phone on the way into the office. A mistake, she now realized, that put her on the back foot.

"My phone is on the fritz," she said before the woman, whose name started with a vowel, asked more questions. "What's going on?"

"Todd's dead and they found six corpses up in the mountains. The SAC thinks it's a gang war."

They got the war part right, she thought and thanked her teammate.

Of all the angles to take, internecine violence among criminals provided the most cover for Sherman's actions. No one would suspect someone like him, and Landers wanted to keep it that way for his sake. For her sake too, even if she didn't admit to such a self-centered notion.

Caught in the sea of people, Landers tried to squeeze toward her cubicle. She'd made it halfway before the SAC caught her in a searchlight-like gaze. Even across the room, his anger glowed bright and clear.

He pointed at her and then jerked his thumb towards the office adjoining the conference room. His office. Landers marched forward like condemned sailors on the plank, waiting to fall into the abyss below.

SAC Harrington ushered her inside and closed the door. His face flushed red with anger.

"Where have you been?" he snarled.

Shooting men in the woods, she thought, but career suicide didn't sit well. Neither did a lifetime behind bars.

"Chasing down a lead," she finally said.

"What lead? I don't recall you running any leads by me."

"It seemed too trivial to waste your time, but I was wrong. I found something critical to the case."

The SAC narrowed his eyes, but they were more exhausted than exasperated. As if one more thing might sink his barely floating sanity.

"Well, spit it out. What else could go wrong with this shitstorm?"

"I found another truck stop belonging to The Company east of Denver."

Harrington looked confused. "Todd vetted that avenue of inquiry and came up empty-handed. We moved on."

Landers nodded. She wanted him to make the next logical leap. Spelling out Todd's treason wouldn't have the same effect.

The SAC said nothing, but his eyes danced with concentration.

"Maybe Todd missed something," offered Landers. "Mistakes happen. I can ask him after this and clear things up."

Harrington tilted his head towards the ground and shook it slowly. "You really need to check your email. Todd died two nights ago. Murdered."

"No!" exclaimed Landers in her best attempt at shock. "What happened?"

"I assumed it was drug-related based in the location," said Harrington, running his hands through his hair. "But now I'm not so sure."

"Do you think Todd was mixed up in all this?"

"I can't rule out the possibility. Fuck, this keeps getting worse. Any other whoppers up your sleeve, Agent Landers?"

"No, sir," she said, lying through her teeth.

"Good, because we have a half-dozen corpses coming down the mountain, and D.C. is breathing down my neck to put a lid on this mess before it spills across state lines."

"What corpses?"

"A bunch of 'Company' thugs were killed west of here in a clear ambush. A real bloodbath. I think we're witnessing a power play by a rival organization."

Landers nodded in agreement. "Any theories on who is behind the attack?"

"Speculation only. The DEA suggested the cartels, but I

don't buy it. My guess is someone local. A competitor making a move for the top rung."

"I don't recall any competition listed in the case file," said Landers.

"You're right. They killed the competition last year. What goes around, comes around, I suppose."

"Karma," she added.

"We need to stop this ASAP. Get your ass back to work, but don't think I've forgotten about your tardiness."

"Yes, sir."

"Oh, and one more thing, Agent Landers."

"Sir?"

"Good work on the truck stop. I expect a full report on my desk by tomorrow morning."

Landers smiled and walked out. The smile was genuine, but it had nothing to do with Harrington's half-compliment. She might just keep Sherman's name out of this mess after all.

Twenty minutes later, Landers still had a smug smile when Sherman called. She answered in an official tone, using her full title, hoping no one around would notice she was using her personal phone.

"You're at the office," said Sherman.

"Yes, how can I help you?" she asked and tried not to look paranoid. Personal phones and work did not mix.

"Here are the cliff notes. James Grimmali is his name. Find everything you can. I'm texting an address. Confirm he owns it. I'm also sending you coordinates. Meet me there at midnight."

A hundred questions flooded her brain, but Landers ignored them.

She said, "Thanks for the tip, we'll look into it," and hung up. No one around her noticed. They were all too busy running down a potential turf war to care about her conversation.

Two texts arrived in succession.

The first showed an address, which she quickly pulled up on a map. A ranch of sorts in the front range, west of Denver.

The second text listed map coordinates. These, she searched on her personal phone for fear of being tracked on a bureau device. The screen showed a clump of trees close to a small country road. She zoomed out. A small road west of Denver. She panned left and the connection clicked. Sherman had found the home of Grimes and was already there.

Her fingers flew across the keyboard searching for property records. The ranch deed went back centuries, before Colorado was a state. From there, it exchanged hands a few times. The latest transaction occurred three years prior. Landers pulled up the county records to look for names.

Spanish names to Scottish names to English names. The trail ended with a company name that Landers recognized: Cobalt Ventures.

She flipped through her notebook until she found a list of shell companies associated with Grimes. The name on the property deed matched one company investigated and cleared by Todd. Another sleight of hand that Grimes paid handsomely for.

Satisfied with the connection between Grimes and the property, she texted Sherman.

Connection confirmed.

He replied: *See you tonight. Bring your badge.*

Landers took a steadying breath and began writing a report for the SAC. It took a good deal of time for the many details sprawled across pages. When she finished, she composed a brief email and attached the file. She set it to send the following morning.

Then she left to take a nap, knowing it would be a long night.

Sherman kept watch over the ranch for hours. He studied the guard's movements and rotations. Not once did he see Grimes in the shimmery distance, but more SUVs came and went. Some carried more men. Others had supplies. A few newcomers stopped and surveyed the valley with keen eyes. They stared up towards Sherman's ridge as if measuring the distance and judging the ballistics. Slowly, yet assuredly, they all turned away and went inside.

Something's afoot, thought Sherman.

Hours passed and the sun arced across a near cloudless sky. Somewhere between high noon and sunset, Sherman sensed movement in the pines behind him. He stepped into a shadowed shrub and waited.

The sounds continued unabated. Soft but consistent steps. Neither fast nor slow. Deliberate movements.

Soon enough, he saw a single silhouette snaking between the brown and gray trunks. Not large like Gournsey, nor slim like Landers, but familiar.

"How long are you gonna wait over there?" asked the figure.

Sherman smiled in the shadows. "Just seeing how long it took you to spot me."

Corporal Lopez emerged into a sliver of afternoon light. "I spotted you thirty yards back."

Sherman's ego sighed ever so slightly. He'd only seen the corporal emerge fifty yards ago. Not much of a difference.

"I brought tamales," said Lopez.

"Home cooked?" asked Sherman.

"Is there any other kind?"

The two men embraced and sat down to eat. Tender bits of pork melted with the soft masa heightening Sherman's momentary bliss. Over the years and many continents, Lopez grew his skills as a chef and they'd deepened into a great well of knowledge. Whereas Gournsey happily ate anything, Lopez keenly absorbed the techniques and ingredients. Sherman became a taste tester of sorts, along for the culinary ride.

Satiated, Sherman edged back towards his concealed viewing spot overlooking the valley. Lopez followed.

"Sarge didn't give many details," said Lopez.

"Down there is a man who'd like to see us and Colonel Khada's family in the ground. I aim to put him there first."

Lopez nodded thoughtfully. He needed no further explanation or justification. A threat to one was a threat to all. He'd grown up in a large close-knit family. Mutual protection was a matter of survival.

"A shade over eighteen hundred yards to the *hacienda*. A little less to the *casita*."

The corporal's nearly perfect estimate made Sherman smile in wonder.

"About a thousand feet of elevation drop," Lopez continued. "The .338 Lapua will work."

The lanky man slinked back and returned with a rifle case, which he reverently opened.

"Do you want me up here or closer?" he asked.

"Here," answered Sherman.

"I can be closer," Lopez assured him.

Sherman knew but didn't need or want the risk. A mile was close enough.

"Here's fine."

"How's the weather been?" asked Lopez, squinting down at the trees near the house.

"Intermittent breeze. Otherwise, still and cool."

Lopez nodded as if absorbing all the potential data points in one giant inhalation of knowledge. Sherman could shoot better than most—a byproduct of his father's preternatural ability and insistence. Despite that genetic advantage, he paled compared to Corporal Lopez. Some soldiers learned their craft, Lopez was born with it.

"Do you want to go in tonight?" asked Lopez.

"I'm considering it. Any issue?"

"I've got a thermal scope, but I won't be able to positively identify anyone. In case you wanted to end it with one shot."

"If we get a shot. I haven't seen him step outside."

"Do you know this guy's in there?"

Sherman shook his head. "No, I can't say for sure."

"And what does that gut of yours say?" asked Lopez.

"No reason for him not to be in there."

"I'll take that as a yes," said Lopez.

Despite the corporal's trust in his judgement, the task ahead weighed on Sherman's mind. Incongruencies grew in his mental image of Grimes. The man didn't seem the type to turtle-up when things got rough. If he wasn't the hiding type, then why was he up here surrounded by a dozen men and two top lieutenants? Were they planning something?

"What do you make of the house's defensibility?" he asked Lopez.

"Good sightlines all around. Logs soak up bullets. The road is only wide enough for one vehicle. Easy to block. Natural chock points on the way in. Not much foliage on the surrounding hills. Hard to sneak up on."

"Not bad, but not the best," Sherman summarized.

"Yeah, why?"

"I'm getting a sense they're not hiding up here."

Lopez chuckled gently. "Are you saying this guy is using himself as bait?"

"They cut this guy from a different cloth. I'm thinking such a move would be right up his sleeve of tricks."

"Okay, say it's a trap. What now?" asked Lopez, amused at the idea.

Sherman rubbed his beard and considered the question. "We play along. Make him think his plan is working. They're going to draw us into the perimeter and use their numbers to overwhelm us. We need to disarm that advantage."

"Speed and violence," said Lopez.

"My thoughts exactly," added Sherman.

Chapter Forty-One

At 8:00 PM, in the gloaming of almost night, Sherman slipped out of the pines. He moved discreetly down the hill, passing through knee-high sage and orange sprays of globe mallow. The day's residue left just enough light to navigate. Too soon for night vision, yet dark enough to conceal his movements.

When Sherman reached the bottom, the first stars sparkled into view. His legs burned from the crouched movement and a twinge of pain crept up his lower back.

You're getting old, he thought.

From behind a clump of lichen-covered rocks, Sherman could just see the buildings silhouetted against the surrounding hills. He flipped on the night vision goggles so generously donated by the Delta boys. The world sprang to grainy-green life.

A hundred yards in front of him was the barn. Beyond that was the old cabin. Furthest out stood the log mansion. Unsurprisingly, the place had more lights than Times

Square on New Year's Eve. Porch lights, flood lights, and motion-sensitive lights blanketed the landscape.

The radio earpiece hissed to life with Lopez's voice.

"Their electric bill must be astronomical."

"Eyes on the prize," whispered Sherman.

"You're clear to the back left corner of the barn."

Sherman flipped up the night vision to gauge how much light there was around the barn. The right side glowed brightly but the left stayed dark.

"Moving," he said.

Slipping through the grass with every sense on full alert, Sherman knew this was where he belonged. Not behind a desk. Not teaching green lieutenants. But at the tip of the spear. Even if it killed him.

Cold air wafted through the valley, settling in pools. A thick layer of nature's perfume hovered and sang. Sherman's entire being came alive. He noticed everything. The distant crunch of gravel under boots. A finch's call of alarm. The scurry of chipmunks. Distant voices chatting amicably.

He absorbed it all.

Weaving forward, Sherman reached the barn undiscovered. Three SUVs sat out front in a neat row on the gravel driveway. They faced away from the house, not ready for a tactical escape. The work of city drivers who spent too much time fitting being white lines.

Two of the three cars glistened under a floodlight protruding from the barn's front façade. Thick shadows fell across the third vehicle, obscuring the front hood.

Sherman touched the transmit button, "Anyone watching?"

"All clear," replied Lopez.

Sherman scooted through the shadows and wriggled

under the third SUV. Lying below the behemoth, he went to work. Anything that didn't leak got cut. All the fancy electronic controls and quality of life features ended up worthless at the edge of his blade.

Satisfied the SUV wouldn't start, Sherman rolled to the next vehicle. He repeated the process twice more. Turning expensive machines into overpriced yard ornaments.

Lopez spoke on his roll back to the shadows.

"Movement at the hacienda."

Sherman mushed his face against the ground and saw a slender man heading towards the SUVs. He held up something in his hand and waved it about with increasing frustration.

He's got the key, thought Sherman.

"I've got the shot," said Lopez.

"Hold."

The footsteps grew louder and angrier. Cursing followed.

"Stupid piece of shit," said a youthful voice, full of vinegar and rage.

The driver stopped next to the middle vehicle and mashed the remote buttons. Nothing happened. He tried the handle, but the door was locked.

He circled around the vehicle once, kicking it along the way. On his second traversal, Sherman slipped out from underneath.

The man didn't see or hear him. Didn't sense the shadow swelling behind him. Only when Sherman's hand clamped down over his mouth, and the knife struck flesh, did panic ripple through the man's body. By then, it was too late. Too late to scream. Too late to survive.

Sherman pulled the limp form off into the grass. The sweet scents of descending night mingled with the metallic tang of blood and sweat and piss. He wiped the knife on the man's fancy pants and circled deeper into the shadows behind the barn.

"A patrol is circling back your way," said Lopez with a soft hiss of static.

Two guards made their way from the small cabin towards the barn. They took a well-traveled path. Matted grass and broken twigs marked the route like any highway sign. Their radios hissed in the quiet night.

Questions about a team member floated by, although Sherman couldn't hear the details. The two guards answered monosyllabically and kept on coming down the trail.

Sherman waited behind a squat pine that smelled of urine. A pit-stop on the perimeter tour.

The guards sped up as they entered a wide swath of inky darkness. They had no night vision, and the crevices hastened their steps.

"Hold," whispered Sherman.

Killing the driver prevented any knowledge of the sabotage from escaping. Taking out the two guards patrolling the perimeter would raise alarms. The question in Sherman's mind was, how many men would Grimes commit to such a counterattack? Would he release the floodgates and drown him out with numbers? Sherman doubted that. Too risky. Too many unknowns.

The answer left the two guards as collateral damage. Nameless facts on a ledger. As disposable as a picnic plate.

Sherman recognized the primal unease plastered on their faces. They were young and fit and in the prime of their lives. A fear lingering in their furtive glances said they knew mortality hung on a sharp edge and they'd suffer a greater loss than most.

Twenty feet out. Sherman waited.

Ten feet away. Sherman waited.

They passed his pine tree.

Sherman slipped into view and fired two quick shots from his MP5. A hiss of gas and the click of a bolt cycling escaped into the cool air. No screams. No echoes. Just the soft thuds of bodies collapsing onto the ground in a garbled heap of extremities.

Done and dusted and dead.

What a waste, he thought, but moved on before the idea could sprout into doubt.

He pushed the thought into his mental box along with all the others too heavy to hold and focused on the tasks at hand. Pulling the bodies out of view. Covering them with grass and twigs. Snagging a radio and turning it down low. The list wasn't extensive.

Having checked everything off, Sherman swung wide towards the old cabin and closer to the stream. He guessed that more guards would emerge soon enough, and he assumed they would stay in the rustic comforts of the smallest building.

"Any movement?" he asked.

"Negative. No one outside."

"Moving up," said Sherman as he slipped between two halves of a much larger boulder, born from some distant mountain.

"I'm getting one of those feelings," said Lopez.

Sherman felt it too. A nagging sense of dread in the back of his mind, just out of reach. Unexplainable but unignorable. The feeling fluttered around, swooping in and out like moths around a porch light.

"Focus," Sherman instructed, although he'd never seen Lopez lose focus, so the comment was self-directed.

The cabin came into his faintly green focus. It was old and small and squat. A tin pipe stuck out of the shingled roof and Sherman smelled the faint whiff of food cooking. Something savory with cheese.

Thick curtains covered the closest window and Sherman couldn't see inside. He moved against the back wall and listened. Muffled voices seeped out of the cracks. A conversation. Nothing tangible, but two voices stood out in their uniqueness.

"At least two more inside," he whispered into the radio. "Moving to clear."

"Copy. No movement at the hacienda."

The solid wood front door faced the creek, burbling away in the darkness. Off to the right was a window with a faint stream of light pouring out. A lone porch light cast a yellow pall over worn timbers.

Sherman watched the shadows flicker inside and sized up his next move. He turned the stolen radio over in his hand. The ploy had worked in the forest.

Fool me twice, he thought and mashed the transmit button.

Inside the cabin, the shadows gathered speed, sliding across the room. More muffled voices, a faint clack, and then the door opened inward. A man stood half in and half out as if his legs did not want to follow his head.

"Don't do that," said a voice from inside.

"Shut up," said the uncommitted man, who was thick and wore a bushy mustache. He raised the radio to his mouth to say something.

The words never came out. Sherman's MP5 made sure of that. The two shots were so closely spaced, they overlapped. On paper, they would have formed the outline of an eight, but they didn't hit paper. They found flesh and bone and brain, making an awful mess.

Sherman came crashing through the door before his first target slumped to the floor. Speed and violence and urgency propelled him inside.

He cleared his corners and found a lone figure standing at a small stove in the corner. He did not wear the same surplus store outfit as the others, but faded fatigues and worn-out boots. Sherman recognized the face. He'd seen it before. Although, the last time they'd met, the man held a gun to his own head.

"You," said Sherman.

"You," replied the ex-soldier with deep exasperation bordering on sadness.

Sherman reached back and flipped off the porch light.

"Clear," he said into his radio.

"Copy. I'm seeing some movement inside the hacienda. No visual yet."

"Who is inside?" asked Sherman, his words sharp.

The ex-soldier sighed and turned back to cooking an omelet. "Nothing worse than burned eggs," he replied.

Sherman thought of many things worse than over-cooked eggs, including the aftermath congealing on the doorframe, but he was not a narrow-minded man. In the former legionnaire, Sherman saw not a willful disregard for survival but a dedication to the task at hand. Having long ago surrendered his hope for a long life, the ex-soldier lived for the moment.

"What's in it?" asked Sherman.

The legionnaire smiled. "Sauteed mushrooms, onions, and Gruyère. Would you like some?"

"No, I don't, but if you tell me who is inside, I'll leave you to eat."

Carefully, the man slid the omelet onto a plate and retrieved a fork from his front pocket.

"Grimes and others," he said.

"How many others?"

"How many have you killed?"

"Four," said Sherman, looking at the man. Then he added, "Maybe five."

"That makes nine left inside, but it's not what you think."

Sherman didn't get to ask what he meant because Lopez's voice screeched in his ear.

"Contact! Get out!"

Urgency rippled through the corporal's words and Sherman turned enough to see a half-dozen men streaming out of the main house.

He didn't think. His legs ran hard towards the back window with the heavy curtain hanging over it.

Gunfire roared outside.

The cabin erupted.

Logs splintered, bullets hissed and snapped.

The world shrank.

Time slowed.

The legionnaire chewed a bite of his omelet with a smile on his face. A moment of bliss but fleeting. Bullets smashed into his plate, his food, and his jaw.

Sherman kept running.

He felt heat and pressure and pain.

Then he jumped, crashing through the window and into the chilly night air.

Chapter Forty-Two

For a moment, looking up at the undulating river of stars, Sherman wondered if this was his moment. When everything turned black, and all the assumptions of a lifetime were put to the test. He certainly felt close.

Breathing hurt.

His back throbbed.

A stabbing pain sent hot irons up his arm.

The sky looked cool and inviting, like a swimming hole on a hot summer's night.

"Get up!" yelled Lopez.

Sherman blinked back into the present.

Gunfire still bellowed from the main house. The old cabin shattered into bits from the lead maelstrom. Yet above the crackle of rifles, the surging energy of Lopez's caliber clearly resonated.

Standing hurt, but Sherman managed. His back felt like a mule kicked it, but there was no blood, which meant the vest stopped whatever hit him.

His arm was another story.

A splinter the size of a chopstick stuck out of his right forearm.

Fearing a nicked artery, he snapped off the excess wood and shuffled towards the split boulders he'd passed earlier. Even as he moved out of the kill zone, bullets sizzled by, lopping off chunks of sagebrush.

Another rumbling crack arrived as Lopez fired again. In his peripheral vision, Sherman saw a doublewide man catch the round just under his armpit. The force knocked him over faster than a bowling pin on league night.

Lopez fired again, this time, hitting his target just above the pelvis. A crunching sound followed that made Sherman's skin crawl like fingernails on the chalkboard. The man didn't get up.

Was that three or four? Sherman wondered.

One more shot spun a man to the ground screaming in agony.

The shooting stopped and a strange ringing silence descended upon the valley.

"Four down," said Lopez. "The rest pulled back inside."

Sherman took out his phone and called Gournsey. "You're up," he said.

"Understood," said the sergeant, then he hung up.

"Nice shooting," radioed Sherman. The minor action made him wince.

"You whole?" asked Lopez.

"Not exactly."

"Can you walk, or do I need to carry you?"

"I'm shot," huffed Sherman. "Not dead."

"Better hurry then."

Sherman looked up at the hill begrudgingly and climbed, one painful step after another.

The GPS directions took Landers off the familiar freeways of central Denver. She headed west. The city's brightness thinned, then faded. By the time she turned onto some numbered byway, only the stars twinkled any light.

At a quarter-mile out, she slowed down. Thick rows of pines hugged the shoulder, and she didn't want to miss it.

What it was, she didn't know. Only the coordinates.

Landers eased off the accelerator.

Even then, she almost missed the gap in the trees. Only the faintest reflection caught her attention. She pulled into the gap and parked next to two vehicles. One she knew and one she didn't.

Chilly air and the resinous scent of evergreens greeted her exit. Without headlights, the forest was impossibly dark. Landers slipped on a vest and grabbed a flashlight from her trunk.

She took a deep breath and stepped into the forest. The stars flowed like rivers of light between the towering trunks. Such vastness almost made her dizzy.

Using the red spectrum on her flashlight, she headed towards Sherman's second set of coordinates. The hike took hours in her mind. Time seemed to bend under that celestial sea.

Eventually, Landers felt the contours sharpen and the trees thin at the edges as if narrowing to a point. She took slower, more deliberate steps, uncertain of what came next.

"Over here," hissed a voice.

Landers caught a scream in her throat and stifled it back into her lungs. She realized her hands were shaking and so was the pistol she didn't remember un-holstering.

"Frank?" she asked the darkness.

One dim red light flashed for a moment to her left. Landers followed and found Sherman sitting against a tree trunk. A med kit splayed across his lap and his right arm rested on his leg. The red light made it difficult to say for certain, but Landers guessed his arm was covered in blood.

"Shit. Frank, are you okay?"

Sherman momentarily set down the needle he used to stitch up the wound and held out something resembling a golf tee.

"Shrapnel," he said.

"That was in your arm?"

He nodded and struggled to finish the last stitches.

"Here, let me finish. You're making a mess of it."

She bent down and completed the last two—a skill she'd learned the hard way as an MP. She wrapped the wound with gauze and gave him a hard look.

"What happened?"

Sherman rose gingerly to his feet in obvious pain.

"Everything went according to plan," he said.

"You planned on getting a hole in your arm?"

"Maybe not that part," he replied.

"Did he mention the getting shot part?" said a voice in the darkness.

Another yelp almost slipped out and Landers bit her lip. She hadn't noticed the prone figure laying stiller than a log.

"Anyone else hiding up here?" she asked.

"No one good," said Sherman, pointing towards the voice. "Agent Landers, meet Corporal Lopez."

"Nice to meet you, ma'am," said Lopez.

"Don't ma'am me," she huffed.

"Yes, sir," he replied.

"The corporal here is monitoring for movement," Sherman explained.

Beyond the man and the rifle was a distant house bathed in yellow light. An extra-large house that a greedy toddler would have made from all the Lincoln logs they could steal.

"You're avoiding the getting shot story," Landers said.

"The vest stopped it," said Sherman nonchalantly.

"And that all happened down there?"

"Correct."

"Care to fill in the details?" she asked, knowing Sherman never cared to paint with broad strokes.

"Eight confirmed," said Lopez in answer to the question.

"What the hell, Frank!"

"Nine, technically, but he died to friendly fire," interjected Sherman.

"Grimes?" asked Landers, hoping she was there to identify the body and nothing more.

"No, he's hiding inside," Sherman answered.

The idea of getting him out of that log monstrosity did not appeal to Landers. Too much risk.

"Are we going in?" she asked.

"Not a chance," said Sherman. "Too risky."

"Then why am I here?"

"The next part of the plan," he replied without further explanation.

"Frank, what does—" she said when a distant explosion echoed across the valley.

Gournsey's voice came from Sherman's phone. "Lead car down. Engaging security."

Another explosion rumbled through the night. Sherman turned up the radio he'd taken from the guards. Desperate shouts and pleas came out. Chaos and fear seeped from the voices. Then silence.

"On the move," came Gournsey's drawl from the phone.

Sherman picked up the radio. He took a breath and then spoke in a panicked voice.

"This is car two, under fire at the entrance. Multiple targets down. Heading to your position now, be ready for immediate evac."

He let go of the button and waited.

"Good job, two. Pull up front, we'll be ready."

"Did you get that?" Sherman asked, holding up the phone.

"Copy that," said Gournsey.

Headlights bounced down a distant dirt road, casting great arcs of light across the green valley.

"You baited him," said Landers, trying not to sound impressed.

"It was this or burn the house down," said Sherman.

"The sergeant and I voted for the gas can," Lopez added.

Landers suddenly understood her role in Sherman's plan. "You're bringing Grimes in, aren't you?"

"Assuming he gets in the car," said Sherman.

"He'll get in the car," said Lopez.

Landers squinted. "You sound sure."

"If he doesn't, the corporal will put him in the ground," Sherman explained.

"Does Grimes know those are his options?" she asked.

"He'll figure them out really quick."

The headlights grew closer. Sherman picked up the radio again and spoke in a slightly less panicky voice. Nervous, but not witless. "Thirty seconds out."

"We're ready," came the reply.

Sherman bent down and squeezed Lopez's shoulder. "You're up. Let them know we're still here."

Even in the darkness, Landers sensed the corporal's quiet concentration. She stepped back and accepted the earplugs Sherman offered.

When the vehicle was thirty yards out, Lopez fired. The bullet sheared through a wall next to the front door of the house. The door opened and Lopez fired again. Thousands of pounds of force struck the guard in the chest. All that kinetic energy knocked them back into the doorframe.

Lopez racked and fired one more into the open space. There was no one there when he pulled the trigger, but the bullet found flesh as a second person tried to drag the first to safety.

"Go, go, go," yelled Sherman over the radio.

Five figures darted over the two dead guards and ran erratically towards the open SUV door. Even from a mile away, Landers knew something wasn't right. Her brain didn't register what, only the essence of an issue with Sherman's plan.

Three people made it inside. The doors closed and Gournsey sped off.

"Captain," said Lopez. "We have a problem."

Chapter Forty-Three

Sherman stood, gazing into the SUV's open door and muttered, "This complicates things."

In the first row, Grimes lay bound with zip ties. Blood trickled down his broken nose. A gift from Gournsey, who wanted to establish the rules for their brief car ride. Behind him, huddled in the back row was a young woman and her child. A boy, no older than two. Red-faced from crying. The mother bounced him on her knee. She too had puffy eyes and cheeks streaked with tears. They looked terrified.

"Shit," said Landers.

Zarak milled about uneasily.

Sherman pointed to Grimes. "Get him out."

Grabbing a leg, Gournsey yanked the man clean out of the vehicle and onto the dirt. Grimes hit with a thud and groaned in pain.

Sherman motioned to Landers and asked, "Can you get their story?" Something told him it wasn't straightforward.

She nodded and slipped into the SUV.

Gournsey pulled Grimes across the dirt and propped

him up against a nearby tree. Rage simmered in his eyes, but Grimes said nothing. He watched as the three men grouped around him in a brutish huddle.

"Hi, James," said Sherman, who gingerly took a knee. His back still throbbed.

Grimes spat out a wad of bloody snot.

"Who's in the backseat?" asked Sherman.

"Did you break his jaw?" asked Lopez.

Gournsey shook his giant head. "Not yet."

"Look," said Sherman. "I'm trying to do the right thing here, but I'm thinking you're not worth the energy."

"He's my son," said Grimes in a low growl. His eyes sparked with accusations.

"Don't look at us like that," said Sherman. "We don't hurt kids."

Grimes scoffed. "You reek of death. Don't bother taking the moral high ground."

"Ironic, coming from a man who tried to kill Zarak's family."

"We weren't going to hurt them. They were leverage. Zarak understands, don't you?"

The colonel hovered in the background, head low, almost embarrassed.

"He forgot the terms of our agreement," Grimes continued. "He still owes me."

"For what?" asked Sherman.

"The colonel's misguided humanity cost me a shipment of opium during the war and now this. His compulsion to help those in need is maddening. You should have let those soldiers die. Such is war."

Sherman glanced back at his friend, but Zarak couldn't meet his gaze.

Grimes snorted out a laugh. "Of course, just my luck. He saved you that day."

"He did," said Sherman. "I'm repaying that humanity you scorned."

"By killing all my men."

"You do what you know," said Sherman with a shrug.

"I guess we're next," said Grimes in a low hiss.

"No, I'm turning you over to Agent Landers of the FBI. You remember her, right? You tried to kill her... shit, I lost track of how many times."

Grimes said nothing.

Sherman smiled at his outrage and said, "I imagine they'll make an example out of you. Federal charges. Life in prison. All that good stuff."

"Assets like me don't go to prison. I know all the skeletons and all the closets."

Sherman didn't disagree. In his experience, the CIA cut deals to prevent anyone like Grimes from entering the system. But he wanted to give the FBI a chance to prove him wrong.

"Here she comes now," he said. "Let's ask her. Agent Landers, James here doesn't think he'll get any jail time."

Landers strolled up with a look on her face that Sherman read as unmitigated rage. Before he could stop her, Landers grabbed his pistol and shot Grimes between the eyes. No warning. No justification. The gunshot echoed off the pines and into the stars above. Smoke curled slowly up from the barrel.

No one spoke for a moment.

"Well, that's done," said Gournsey.

Done and dead, thought Sherman.

He held out his hand and she returned the pistol.

"I would have given it to you," said Sherman.

Landers pointed down at Grimes. "He raped that poor woman, and when she got pregnant, he locked her in an apartment until she gave birth."

Sherman understood her rage. He raised the pistol and put another bullet into Grimes. A gruesome act of solidarity. Lopez and Gournsey followed without hesitation. Three more gunshots echoed after the first.

As the ringing in their ears dimmed, Sherman reached down and took Grimes' wallet. He pulled out the cash and cards, handing them to Landers.

"Give those to her. Tell her to take the SUV and get as far from here as she can."

"Thanks," replied Landers as she walked back to the vehicle.

"You tried," said Gournsey.

"I'm glad we didn't burn the house down," said Lopez.

"What a fucking waste," added Sherman before turning to find Zarak.

The colonel stood away from the rest, gazing up at the stars.

"It's strange how life drifts away from you over time," he said as Sherman approached. "I remember such lust for all life offered, and now… well, look at what I've caused. All for what? A few extra dollars."

"I could give you an 'it's not your fault' speech, but I don't think it will do much to ease your guilt."

"No, old friend, it would not."

"Then take solace in knowing you get to try again," said Sherman.

Zarak smiled and tears rolled down his cheeks.

"Thank you, with all my heart."

"Come on, let's get you home to your family."

They turned away from the trees and joined the others.

Gournsey and Lopez had already started stowing gear in their vehicles. Landers stood off to the side with her phone ready.

"Go ahead," said Sherman. "Make the call."

"I'd rather not."

"I'm sensing a big promotion opportunity," he said.

Landers shrugged her slender shoulders. "I'm starting to like Colorado."

"Me too," replied Sherman. "And don't be a stranger. You still owe me a drink."

"I think we're even, but who's counting."

"See you around, Agent Landers."

"See you around, Captain Sherman."

Chapter Forty-Four

The last days of Sherman's teaching career ticked by like a slowly dripping faucet. Each class wore on with excruciating glances of contempt and boredom. On the next to final day, Sherman offered the lieutenants a glimmer of retribution—field exercises instead of a written exam.

"The aim is simple. If you capture the primary building, you pass."

"And if we don't?" asked one of the least annoying of the alpha males. The one with at least an ounce of hubris.

"You'll be re-enrolled with a different instructor."

A general sigh of relief rippled through the group.

"Who's the opposition?" asked a blonde-haired man with no lack of ego.

"Myself and two others."

"Against the twelve of us?" asked the blonde.

"Correct," said Sherman.

Another sigh of relief made its way around, although a fair amount of snickering went too. Twelve against three. The West Pointers liked those odds.

Their final exam began just after dawn the next morning. Cold mountain winds pummeled the training facility—a conglomeration of buildings built to hone close-quarter combat skills.

Sherman let Lopez pick his hide, knowing they'd come to the same decision in the end. He'd hiked off to cover the likely approach, leaving Gournsey and Sherman to finalize their plan.

"They'll take those buildings first," said Gournsey, pointing to a set of small structures on the outer perimeter.

"The tactically sound choice," said Sherman.

"What's our plan?" asked Gournsey.

"I think you know."

"Speed and violence."

"The two things they need to learn," said Sherman.

"Looking forward to it," Gournsey replied with a grin.

Sherman glanced at his watch. A minute remained before the test began.

As expected, the lieutenants took the outer buildings with stodgy precision. From there, they set overwatch and plowed forward. It all went according to their plan, the one taught in textbooks.

Until Lopez fired and the laser tag system beeped loudly, informing one woman she'd died. She played the part dutifully and flopped to the ground. Chaos ensued.

The overwatch group panicked and fired in the sniper's direction, thus missing Sherman as he snuck into an adjacent building.

When the order came to move, he caught four soldiers in the open. They all went down with anger and resentment etched on their faces.

Sherman moved before they assaulted his position. The grenades popped into empty rooms, but Lopez caught a straggler at the rear. As two teammates attempted to drag the wounded man into cover, Gournsey stepped out and ended their day.

Absolute panic and confusion sounded on the radio. The four survivors regrouped for one final push. A suicide mission, but they didn't want to fail the class.

Pushing the tempo, they moved faster and more aggressively. One house to another. Breach and clear.

One block from their objective, they breached but didn't clear. Lopez once again hit the last soldier. Gournsey caught the helpers. Only the blonde lieutenant remained.

He stood in the center of the living room panting. The beeping of dead comrades echoed off the walls. The man was so intent on winning that he didn't hear Sherman slip down the stairs or sense movement in the darkened room. Only when Sherman placed the barrel of his pistol against the man's neck did he understand.

"I'm dead," he said with a sigh.

"That you are. Along with all of them," said Sherman.

"Can we run it again, sir?"

Sherman lowered his weapon. He hadn't expected the ask. Complaining? Yes. Excuses? Probably. He had a few more hours left. Why not?

"Sure, Lieutenant. We can run it again."

They played the scenario back three more times. With each attempt, the students gained invaluable experience. None of them survived, but they got closer and lived longer.

On the fourth attempt, something clicked. Most of the team still died, but they took the objective, which counted as a win in the Army's eyes. War has always been a numbers game.

"What changed this time?" asked Sherman.

The blonde lieutenant smiled. "Speed and violence, sir."

"Good, my job is done," said Sherman and turned to leave as a Blackhawk roared overhead.

"Where are you off to, sir?"

"My next war," said Sherman as he walked out the door.

Next in the Frank Sherman Thrillers Series

vinci-books.com/regime-change

**Betrayal, danger and intrigue: Frank Sherman navigates
a maze of deception in Equatorial Guinea.**

In the sweltering heart of West Africa, Frank Sherman navigates a
deadly labyrinth of deception, political intrigue, and shifting
alliances. As a sinister conspiracy threatens to engulf Equatorial
Guinea, Frank races against time to unravel the clues and prevent
the region from descending into chaos. With mercenaries, murder,
and great power rivalries at play, Frank must confront dangerous
adversaries and uncover the truth before it's too late.

Turn the page for a free preview…

Regime Change: Chapter One

EQUATORIAL GUINEA, WEST AFRICA

The room jittered into focus like a kaleidoscopic with each piece slowly fitting into the next. First came the ceiling, dirty and stained. Then came the fan, squeaking and vibrating with each languid rotation. Sergeant Raylan Gournsey's eyes slid painfully across the spackled surface. His head hurt —no, throbbed—with the blows of thousands of tiny hammers. A hangover of epic proportions. Not since high school had he felt so terribly useless the next day… assuming it was morning. Sunlight streamed through the blinds, which meant daytime, although he did not know the exact time. The thin plastic slats also showed a more salient fact. This was not his hotel room. His had curtains and no fan, nor a water-stained ceiling.

Not my room, he thought.

The strangeness did not bother Gournsey. He'd woken up in many mysterious places over the years. During his junior year of high school, it was a coal mine in his home state of Kentucky after too much bourbon. Then a jail cell in Lexington right before he enlisted. He'd even woken up in a flattened kiddie pool two houses down from the Base Commander's house in Japan.

Despite his checkered history, Gournsey had not blacked out in years. This meant one of two things—he had a great night and would suffer the consequences, or he had already suffered some indignities, and more were coming.

Gournsey searched his memory for any sliver of the previous night but came up empty. Nothing. A dark hole of hours. But how many? He raised his arm, took a painful glance at his watch, and couldn't recall anything in the last… twelve hours.

Not great, he thought.

Despite the piercing pain in his skull, he chanced a glance around the room.

The walls were off-white in color and smudged with dirt, but not disgusting. A lone picture hung on a wall above a plain pine dresser. The image looked stock, like it came with the frame and no one bothered to change it.

Tilting his head further, Gournsey discovered a wooden chair in the corner and a nightstand next to the bed. On top of which was an alarm clock and a set of keys.

Keys to what?

Attached to the keyring was a tag. A big green plastic diamond like dozens of cheap motels used. The realization brought him some comfort. He'd had the foresight to sleep off his bender away from his unit and the other Americans.

Assuming he was still in Africa. Still in Equatorial Guinea. Still on the main island.

A lot can happen in twelve hours, he thought.

The sounds of movement outside the door gave Gournsey reason to sit up. He didn't want to, nor did the hammering pain make it easy, but he'd realized there wasn't a stitch of clothing on his body. Anyone coming into the room would be in for an awkward sight.

Elevating his torso took a good deal of effort and two waves of nausea, but he managed. His mind ached. His body shook.

Worse hangover ever, he thought.

The scuffling outside grew louder, then came a knock at the door. Gournsey rolled to his right and looked for his pants. Finding none, he rolled to the left.

What he found on the floor was not any form of clothing, but a naked young woman face-down on the brown tile floor. Gournsey knew death intimately, and it didn't take him more than a glance to know the woman was dead.

Shit, he thought.

The knocking grew louder but Gournsey couldn't take his eyes off the woman. She was painfully young and exquisite. A local to the country if not the region. Her beauty and youth only made the tragedy even more powerful. Life snuffed out before it could shine brightest.

The knocking stopped and Gournsey looked up in time to see the door frame splinter apart as four men charged into the room.

"*Policía!*" they shouted.

Their dark blue uniforms were a blur of movement in Gournsey's eyes. He pointed down toward the woman as if to say 'get help' but the words caught in the dryness of his mouth.

He raised his arms in the face of the armed officers as they encircled him. A fifth man stepped inside the cramped motel room. He was thicker than an oil drum, wore a shiny polo shirt, and smelled of aftershave.

"*Estas bajo arresto,*" said the shiny man.

Gournsey's Spanish was rusty, but he didn't need a translation. Those twelve missing hours loomed large in his mind. He looked at his hands and then down at the woman on the floor.

I didn't, did I? he wondered.

Regime Change: Chapter Two

On the other side of Malabo, in a much nicer hotel, Captain Frank Sherman enjoyed a cup of coffee under the shade of a banana tree. The coffee contained plenty of cream and Sherman contented himself with watching the hotel guests.

At the closest table, a Spanish couple on holiday bickered passionately over a plate of cured meats. Beyond them, a businesswoman read a German newspaper, no doubt several days old. She ignored the loud couple and took notes in a small journal. Further out, with his back to the wall, sat a wiry man in athletic clothes. Sherman guessed he was a shade over fifty, but fit and deeply tan. Not the kind you got in a store, but the sort burned into your very soul by sheer toil under its rays. The man's eyes skittered around and he spoke accented English the way only Afrikaans speakers could.

None of the guests surprised Sherman or seemed out of place. West Africa drew all sorts. Equatorial Guinea was no exception. The capital, Malabo, had a quiet majesty that

Sherman couldn't shake. Something about the air or the light made the world sing.

A Saturday morning with no agenda only buoyed his contentment. Sherman's team had landed a week before at the behest of some Equatoguinean general who'd gone to school with a senior leader at the State Department. They called it a *Joint Combined Exchange Training*. Sherman called it a vacation.

State put them up in the fancy hotel around the corner from the embassy and, in return, they trained a small Equatoguinean army unit in counterterrorism. The soldiers were motivated but not exactly skilled, and Sherman had spent most of the last week covering the basics.

Behind the scenes, in private rooms and dark booths, people in suits gushed about economic ties and negotiated mineral rights. Sherman tried not to listen, lest their sleaze spoil the beauty of Bioko Island. A vacation was a vacation, and he was intent on enjoying it.

The waiter, a man named Diego, approached and smiled. He and Sherman liked to play a game of linguistic 'guess who' each morning. Diego spoke at least a dozen languages and enjoyed Sherman's unusual background.

"*Bonjour Monsieur*," said Diego with a low bow.

"*Bonjour. Comment allez-vous?*" asked Sherman, whose French remained sharper than his Spanish.

Diego smiled and didn't miss a beat while switching to German. "*Sehr gut. Wie geht es dir?*"

The businesswoman glanced in their direction upon hearing her native tongue, but quickly returned to notetaking.

"*Gut. Mehr Kaffee, bitte,*" replied Sherman. The exchange exhausted his German skills, save for swapping coffee for beer or schnitzel.

Diego nodded and left to retrieve a fresh pot of coffee.

The morning smelled of hibiscus and jasmine with just the faintest hint of unregulated car exhaust and raw sewage. Even in the early hour, Sherman's shirt clung to him like plastic wrap and clouds loomed heavy in the distance.

When the waiter returned, he had the pot of coffee and a visitor. One of the embassy staff trailed behind Diego. The American looked flushed and out of breath as if he'd ran the quarter-mile to the hotel. Sherman recognized the thin, pale face, but couldn't recall the name.

Something British sounding, he thought.

"You have a visitor," Diego announced. The switch to English only highlighted the urgency.

"Captain Sherman, my name is Edward Rake. I'm the political officer at the embassy." Edward raised his badge as if to prove his validity.

"Good morning, Edward. Do you want some coffee?" asked Sherman, curious why the embassy would intrude upon his Saturday off.

"Uh, um… no, thanks. I'm afraid this is an official visit."

"I hope you don't run around in a collared shirt for fun," said Sherman.

Edward glanced down at his sweat-stained shirt and rail-thin frame. A moment of embarrassment cast across his face before he plowed on.

"I'm afraid there's been an incident, Captain."

Sherman didn't like the tone of their developing conversation. "Care to elaborate?" he asked.

Edward looked around at the other guests suspiciously before leaning in closer. He whispered, "One of your team is in police custody."

Sherman suppressed a laugh. "Who drank too much?"

"Sergeant Raylan Gournsey."

The answer did not surprise Sherman. The sergeant had a penchant for mischief and the bulk for serious violence.

"Can you bail him out?"

"No," said Edward. "They're charging him with murder."

The news caught Sherman off-guard. Drunk and disorderly made sense if that was even a crime in Equatorial Guinea. Judging from the average Friday night, it was not. Murder... well, that was something else entirely.

"Bar fight?" asked Sherman, naming the most logical of scenarios in which Gournsey might inadvertently kill someone. He was a mountain of a man.

Edward leaned ever closer with his voice barely audible. "They aren't saying much, but a source said he killed a woman. A sex worker. The police found him in bed next to the body."

Sherman finished his cup of coffee and stood up. He didn't need a fancy degree to know the optics were terrible. *Crazy American kills local.* The newspapers would be all over the story, which would make serious waves in the international community. Any goodwill they'd built would burn up quicker than a cheap barroom matchstick.

"Lead the way," said Sherman.

"Uh, where?" asked Edward, suddenly taken aback.

"Wherever they're holding my man."

"Right, he's downtown, but the police will not turn him over."

"Look, he didn't do this. We need to poke enough holes in their case, apply enough pressure, and they'll let him out."

"Sorry to be blunt, Captain, but what if he's guilty?"

Sherman motioned toward the exit and explained, "Two things you should know about Raylan Gournsey. First, he abhors violence against women. Saying he killed a sex worker is like saying Santa ran over the Easter Bunny. Second, the man is the size of a couch, he can drink a gallon of beer and walk straighter than a nun's ruler."

They exited the hotel and hurried along the recently paved road towards the embassy. The dense morning air swirled with a mix of charcoal cooking fires and flowers.

"Captain," said Edward, a little breathless from Sherman's pace. "I don't think you understand the situation."

"And you do?"

Edward gestured towards the embassy, just visible above the hedges. "I'm the Chief Political Officer."

"Okay, then politic my man out of this mess."

"I'm afraid the situation is not so simple, Captain. Factions within the Equatoguinean government view America rather poorly, and the Chinese—not to mention Russians—are gaining favor in this part of the world. These ministers don't approve of our joint training exercise, and they certainly won't let this opportunity pass by."

Sherman frowned. He didn't like politics. "You're saying Gournsey is the scapegoat."

"Simplistically, yes."

They stopped near the front gate and Sherman locked Edward in his gaze.

"I'm a simplistic sort of man. Three plus three is six. Six thousand pounds of force to break a man's femur. Thirty rounds in my rifle magazine. Simple math, I think you get my point. So, why don't you tell me how I'm going to get my guy out of a Malabo jail before we're all kicked out of the country."

Edwards's eyes remained narrowed, as if lost in concentration. "Does it really take six thousand pounds of force to break a femur?"

"Yes! But that's not the point. Focus, Edward."

"Right, getting the sergeant out is tricky. Innocence doesn't usually matter in cases like this. A big enough bribe will make many crimes disappear."

"Great, tell State to fork over some shoe money."

"Well… things are proportional here. You can't extort a poor merchant the way you would a business mogul. The police take an equitable share and Uncle Sam won't pay what they'll ask."

Sherman ushered them through the ramshackle embassy security as they spoke with a look of utter indignation.

"This faction that doesn't like us… what do they want?" he asked.

"Well—" Edward began.

"Never mind, I don't care. How do I get Gournsey out?"

Edward stopped as they crossed the manicured lawn. "That's what I've been trying to say, Captain. I don't think you can."

Dead ends did not sit well with Sherman. His mind didn't work that way. It whittled and twisted and turned until an option appeared. Often, those options weren't palatable to the civilized bureaucrat, but the army didn't train him to act like one. They taught him to survive at all costs.

"Bullshit," Sherman retorted. "We just need to apply enough pressure on the right person."

"Captain! We can't just go around beating people up."

Sherman took a deep breath before speaking. "Edward, you look like a smart guy. Nice college, good internship, impressive track record. All that shit. But you misunderstand me and my methods. I don't beat people up. My unit is surgical. We disappear terrorists from their homes in the night. We are the boogeymen. What I need you to do is point me in the right direction. You're the political officer, think politically. I need to know who wants America out of the country. Where do I start?"

Edward sat down on a nearby bench looking out of his element. Events such as this were not in the State Department handbook and the Chief Political Officer wanted time to think it over.

"No," commanded Sherman. "You can think in the car. Come on. We're burning daylight."

Regime Change: Chapter Three

The tea kettle expelled a harsh lament into the stuffy apartment air. Miguel Ondo reached across the table and switched off the small electric burner. It was the only appliance he owned and the only one he needed.

Miguel was on his third cup of Nescafe. The morning chaos of his crowded building still echoed as people left for their jobs—if they were lucky—while others sat outside on plastic chairs facing the street and talked. For some, there was nothing else to do. Lots of people in Malabo wanted to work, but jobs were scarce.

Others, like Mrs. Obiang, were too old for anything but the gossip afforded to those who paid attention. She sat in a white plastic chair outside of Miguel's apartment.

"*How are you?*" she asked in Spanish, through the open slatted window. Mrs. Obiang insisted on speaking the colonial tongue.

Miguel finished making his coffee and sighed.

"*Good. And you?*"

"*Mr. Edu lost another chicken,*" she replied as if that summed up the entire existential crisis of the country. Forget about poverty or inequality. Mr. Edu's chicken made up all the conveyable news.

"*Is that two or three for the week?*" asked Miguel.

"*Three,*" answered Mrs. Obiang enthusiastically.

Miguel rubbed his forehead. He wanted a bigger place, not because he needed more space, but because privacy didn't exist in his building. Everyone knew intimate details about their neighbors they never wished to know, save for the gossipers.

"*Shouldn't you be at work?*" added Mrs. Obiang.

"*The police don't work normal hours,*" he replied.

"*Join the Gendarme,*" she offered.

Miguel didn't care for the militarized police. They were new and flashy and full of themselves. Besides, it went against his family tradition. He was the third generation of police in his family, stretching back to his grandfather. Trading that in for a new uniform and a fancy gun didn't sit well with his sense of convention.

"*You've said that already, Mrs. Obiang.*"

"*What, can't I tell you again? Don't hold age against an old woman.*"

Miguel sighed again. "*Yes, Mrs. Obiang.*"

"*Are you going to work or not?*" asked the woman.

Had Miguel not been up late watching smugglers by the dock, he would have gone in already, but the three cups of instant coffee weren't doing much good, and he was tired. "*I'm going,*" he replied and grabbed his gun and badge.

From his door to a paved road took only a few minutes' walk, but Miguel trudged slowly. He waited outside the petrol station with a dozen other commuters until a minibus arrived with enough room for everyone to fit inside. Miguel handed the boy manning the sliding door a few francs for the ride downtown.

Lost in thought, Miguel almost missed the shout for his stop. The boy slid open the door, releasing him into the subdued chaos of a Malabo morning. Horns honked. Vendors called out to pedestrians. People yelled at each other across the street. None of this bothered Miguel… he found the activity comforting, like a familiar dish or a favorite drink.

The woman who made omelets in a small stand on the corner called out. "*Hey, skinny!*"

Miguel waved. "*Good morning.*"

"*When you gonna get a wife to fatten you up?*"

"*No need,*" he retorted. "*I've got you.*"

She waved him off with a good-natured flick of her wrist and Miguel continued inside the police headquarters. The building was old—a remnant of colonial rule masquerading as history. Chunks of faded blue paint littered the dirt outside. The windows were more wood than glass. Nothing like the new Gendarme building down the street.

"Good morning, Lieutenant," said the officer at the front desk. His voice rose with each word.

The strangeness of his greeting did not escape Miguel. "What am I walking into?"

"They arrested an American. The chief is asking for you."

Practically speaking, Americans didn't get arrested often. Miguel recalled a handful of drunken tourists over the years, but someone from the embassy staff usually came by to pick them up in the morning. Americans meant paperwork and lost revenue. Tug at the purse strings and even the stodgiest bureaucracies budged.

Walking into the chief's office, Miguel hoped it wouldn't be his paperwork mess.

"Close the door," said the chief no sooner than Miguel had opened it. He obliged and the chief motioned toward a battered wooden chair that once belonged to the Spanish colonists. The chief took a perverse pleasure in knowing dozens of Equatoguineans suffered terrible fates in that very chair.

Miguel sat.

"We have a situation. A delicate situation that needs our upmost discretion."

"The American?" asked Miguel.

"Shhh," hissed the chief as if the walls had ears. "Where did you hear that?"

"The sergeant at the front desk."

"Eesh, if he knows, the damn building will know. What did he say?"

"Nothing… other than you arrested an American."

"Shhh," repeated the chief, waving his hands about to dispel the words.

Baffled, Miguel leaned closer. "Care to tell me what happened?"

"I need your eyes on this, Lieutenant. Be careful, be thorough. We can't afford to mishandle the case. Do you understand me?"

Miguel didn't. The chief made no sense. Drunk Americans were tiresome, but not dangerous. "What happened?" he asked.

"Go here and then report back to me. No one else. No stops. Straight back here," said the chief.

Miguel glanced at the paper his boss had slid across the desk. He knew the spot. A middle-tier hotel that mostly catered to Indian or Chinese workers. Not the typical place for an American, at least not one traveling on the government's dime. Those stayed near the embassy. The oil company suits stayed downtown in an opulent place dripping with luxury.

Maybe a backpacker, thought Miguel. *Someone out from an adventure. Or worse… a sex tourist.*

From the police station, Miguel took an unmarked police sedan and headed east then south. It didn't take over ten minutes with traffic. He parked his car across the street from the hotel. The modest three-story building looked like most others in the area. A brown concrete brick façade with glass walls on the first floor. A thick metal fence and gate protected the facility.

Miguel crossed the street and held up his badge to another officer on the other side. The woman nodded and creaked open the gate.

"Second floor," she said solemnly, and Miguel realized he wasn't getting any more details.

Not great, he thought and ascended the stairs to the second floor. The desk manager hadn't said a word either, which only gave Miguel worse vibes.

He opened the door to the second-floor hallway and quickly spotted an officer guarding a door halfway down. Bright fluorescent lights flickered across the brown tile floor reminding Miguel of a dingy hospital in which he'd spent a long week recovering from malaria.

The guard stepped aside without a word and Miguel entered the musty hotel room that smelled faintly of mildew and… death.

On the floor, draped over with a white sheet, was a body. Bare feet with painted nails protruded. Miguel leaned down and gingerly peeled back the covering. Bile rose ever so slightly in his throat. Even after fifteen years as a police-man, death did not sit well with him.

Anger closely followed. The woman looked a year or two younger than his niece, which made her seventeen or eighteen.

Too young, thought Miguel.

A thin bruise wrapped around her neck. Ligature marks from a wire or cord. Strangulation.

There was no blood on the tile floor. No sign of a strug-gle. The room appeared orderly but sparse. Not much to break.

Miguel turned, poked his head out the door, and spoke to the officer in the hall.

"Do we know who she is?"

"No, Lieutenant."

"Any ID or purse?" he asked. She seemed like the type to have a purse.

"No."

"A phone?"

"Nothing else, sir."

Miguel turned back. The woman was naked. "Where are her clothes?"

The officer shrugged. "We didn't find any."

Miguel scanned the room. He went to the dresser and searched but found nothing. The nightstand contained a bible, but no clothes. Nothing under the bed either.

Odd, he thought.

"Did you make the arrest?" Miguel asked the officer.

"No, we came after."

"Who did?"

"The Gendarme."

Miguel whipped around the drawer he'd been searching through. "What did you say?"

The officer looked quite nervous. "Well, technically, we made the arrest, but the Gendarme did the initial questioning."

"Who?"

"I don't... know."

Miguel didn't like the meddling of another group in his investigation—assuming it was still his investigation. If the case ballooned in size and turned against the American, the Gendarme could take the credit. If it went badly, like such cases often did, then the blame would fall solely on the underfunded police. Park the blame and steal the credit. A classic solution.

"Did you question the manager?"

"Yes," replied the officer. "He saw the American and the woman come in together."

"Video surveillance?"

The officer swallowed hard. "We didn't ask."

Miguel furrowed his brow but said nothing. He headed down the two flights of stairs and up to the front desk. The manager, who was not keen to have the hotel closed for any reason, smiled as Miguel approached.

"Are you done, Lieutenant?"

Miguel ignored the question. "Do you have surveillance cameras?"

"Yes. The front gate and front desk."

"Good, I'd like to see them."

The manager didn't move. "We have very discerning customers that won't appreciate my sharing."

"I'm sure you do, but I imagine a police blockade of your front gate would not help them or your bottom line."

The manager sniffed and cracked a patently false smile. "This way," he replied and ushered Miguel into a small office that smelled of sweat and curry. A desktop computer sat on a metal table and the manager clicked through a few screens until finally pulling up the footage.

"When did the couple in question arrive?" asked Miguel.

"Around one this morning."

"Show me."

The video sped backward in a flurry of frames until it arrived at the allotted time. At first, there was nothing, only the stillness of night. The exterior camera caught their arrival on foot from the north. Miguel took note. The woman rang the buzzer. They appeared a bit intoxicated, but not stumbling. Drunk and happy.

"The inside video too," said Miguel.

The manager obliged and a second video appeared, which showed two people entering through the front door. Maybe it was the high angle of the first camera, but Miguel had missed the sheer size of the American. The man was a mountain, both in width and height.

"That's a big guy," he mused out loud.

The manager nodded. "Got a little worried when he walked in. Although he seemed nice enough."

"You talked?"

"Briefly. He apologized for his bad Spanish and asked for a room."

"And why did you call us?" asked Miguel.

"One of the guests heard something like a scream."

"Which guest?"

"Uh, I don't recall. A woman called into the desk phone and said something terrible was going on in their room."

"But you don't know who called."

The man looked embarrassed, as if details were his business and he'd missed an important fact.

"I'm afraid not."

404

"Can you tell which room called?" asked Miguel.

"Not for certain. We had several calls around that time."

"About the screaming?"

"No, sir. Mostly breakfast."

Miguel glanced around. "You serve breakfast?"

"No, sir, but it's mentioned in one of the old brochures."

"That no one bothered to update?"

The manager shrugged innocently.

"Can you write the room numbers that called in around that time?"

The man did and slid across a piece of paper with five numbers.

"And do you have names?"

Based on the snide look, Miguel knew the answer was a resounding 'no'.

"Okay," said Miguel. "Thanks for your help."

Begrudgingly, he walked back up the stairs and knocked on the doors listed. Three rooms were recently vacated. The fourth held a rather angry Cantonese businessman who shooed Miguel away. The fifth room was empty and not recently occupied or cleaned. Miguel made another note.

He returned to the crime scene and the tragically young woman with the thin bruise around her neck, took one last look, then returned to his car.

For a murder case, this one was straightforward. Guy meets girl. Things get heated. Guy kills girl. A crime of passion or premeditation, it didn't matter. He got caught red-handed. An open and shut case, if the legal system worked, which was not always true. It tilted toward the highest bidder and America had deep pockets.

Still, Miguel couldn't complete his report without questioning the accused, so he drove back towards the police headquarters.

Traffic clogged the streets. Throngs of people milled about. Several vendors hawked red, white, and blue striped flags.

Not French, thought Miguel. *The other one.*

An electric charge rippled through the crowd as if they were all watching the World Cup. People jostled and jumped. They sang and chanted, but Miguel couldn't quite hear what.

Circling the roundabout that led to the police station, Miguel had to weave between groups spilling onto the street. He exited at the top of the circle and stopped in front of the flimsy metal gate protecting the police parking lot. The officer in charge pulled it open by hand as rusty hinges squeaked in protest.

"What's all this about?" asked Miguel.

The young officer looked toward the growing crowd and shrugged. "Unemployment?" he offered.

Miguel parked and headed toward a side door but observed the growing crowd.

Not unemployment, he thought. *Wrong building.*

The government buildings were one roundabout up the road. His block held the police station and courthouse. Nothing directly related to job creation or economic policy.

Miguel shrugged at this incongruence and headed inside. He didn't have the luxury of time to ponder such questions.

He went straight to the chief's office, who acknowledged his return by leading Miguel to a small holding cell removed from the others. This VIP section was reserved for the rich and famous, who occasionally got caught doing something a bribe cleared up, but only after they sweated in the cell for an hour. It was discreet and the chief wanted discretion.

"What did you learn?" asked the chief in a low whisper.

"The killer strangled her, probably with a thin rope or wire."

"The American?"

"The perpetrator."

The chief frowned at Miguel's indirect assertion of innocence until proven guilty. "Witnesses?"

"A guest called to report screams, but I couldn't find them to ask what they heard."

The chief nodded. "How strong is the case?"

"They found him in the room with a dead woman. The video shows them checking in together, likely drunk or drinking. I'd say it's an easy prosecution."

"I'm sensing a 'but'," added the chief.

"There are some incongruencies in that narrative."

"For instance?"

Miguel pointed toward the American, whose size up close baffled the policeman. He didn't think men came that big.

"Look at him. Does he seem the type to use anything but his bare hands? Also, the purported call reporting screams came from an unoccupied room."

"Circumstantial," said the chief, but he seemed interested in Miguel's line of reasoning.

"Did you know the Gendarme questioned him already?"

The chief said nothing but rubbed his wide bald head with both hands.

"What's going on here?" asked Miguel. Secrets practically dripped from the walls but he didn't understand their meaning.

"Something feels off," said the chief.

"The entire city feels off. People are running around

outside with Russian flags like they're supporting Manchester United or Chelsea."

The chief grunted something Miguel didn't hear and then said, "Go and question your suspect. I don't want this case to linger any longer than necessary."

Grab your copy...
vinci-books.com/regime-change